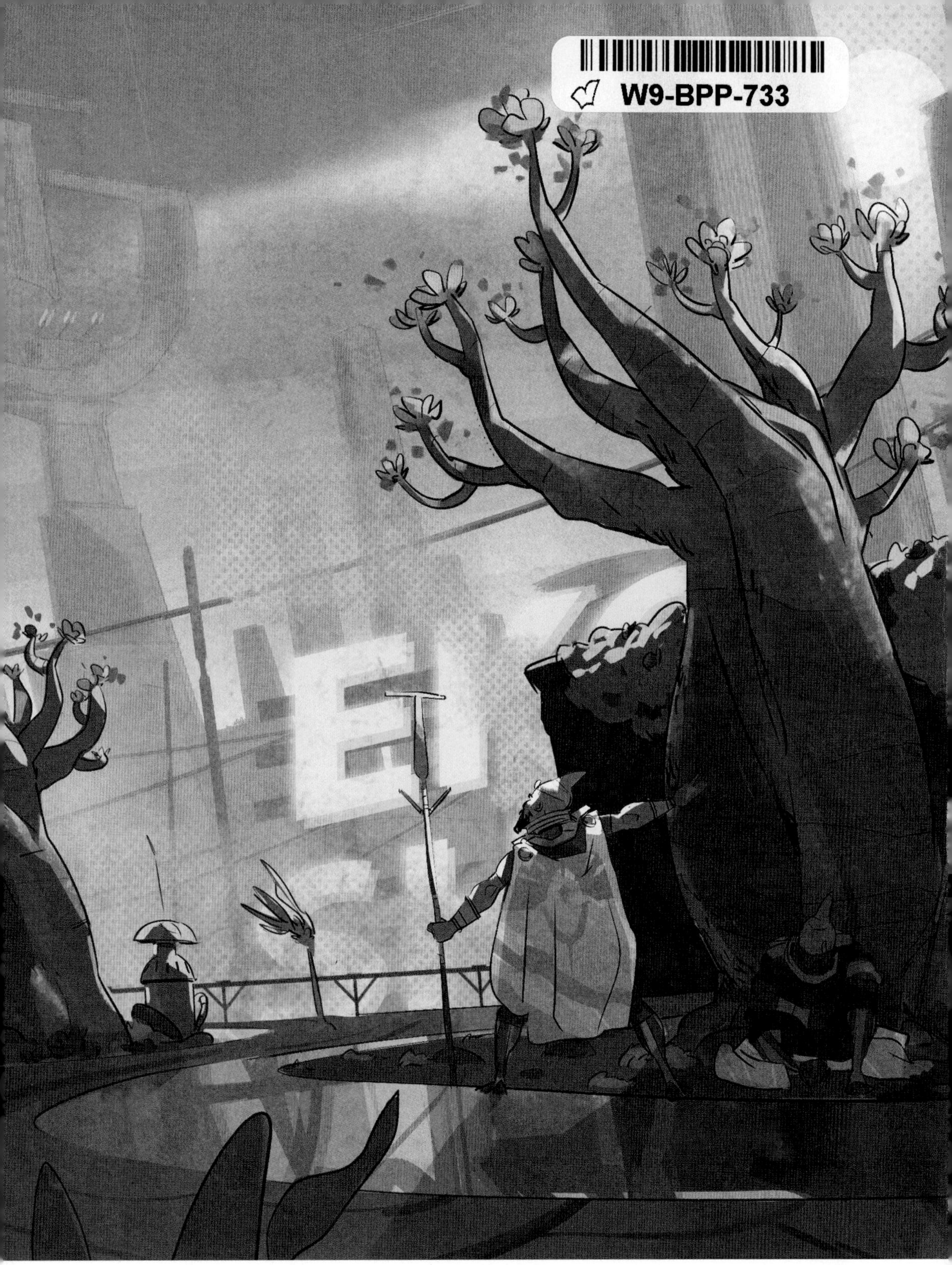

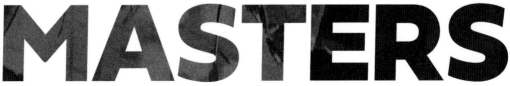

MASTERS

NEW MASTERS

Created By
Shobo Coker & Shof Coker

SHOBO
writer

SHOF
artist

FRANCESCO SEGALA
COLORS (pg 67–119)

HARRISON YINFAOWEI
COLORS (pg 120–173)

HYE MARDIKIAN
BOOK DESIGN

JULMAE KRISTOFFER
COLOR ASSISTANT

IMAGE COMICS, INC.

Robert Kirkman – Chief Operating Officer
Erik Larsen – Chief Financial Officer
Todd McFarlane – President
Marc Silvestri – Chief Executive Officer
Jim Valentino – Vice President

Eric Stephenson – Publisher / Chief Creative Officer
Nicole Lapalme – Vice President of Finance
Leanna Caunter – Accounting Analyst
Sue Korpela – Accounting & HR Manager

Matt Parkinson – Vice President of Sales & Publishing Planning
Lorelei Bunjes – Vice President of Digital Strategy
Dirk Wood – Vice President of International Sales & Licensing
Ryan Brewer – International Sales & Licensing Manager
Alex Cox – Director of Direct Market Sales
Chloe Ramos – Book Market & Library Sales Manager
Emilio Bautista – Digital Sales Coordinator
Jon Schlaffman – Specialty Sales Coordinator
Kat Salazar – Vice President of PR & Marketing
Deanna Phelps – Marketing Design Manager
Drew Fitzgerald – Marketing Content Associate

Heather Doornink – Vice President of Production
Drew Gill – Art Director
Hilary DiLoreto – Print Manager
Tricia Ramos – Traffic Manager
Melissa Gifford – Content Manager
Erika Schnatz – Senior Production Artist
Wesley Griffith – Production Artist
Rich Fowlks – Production Artist

IMAGECOMICS.COM

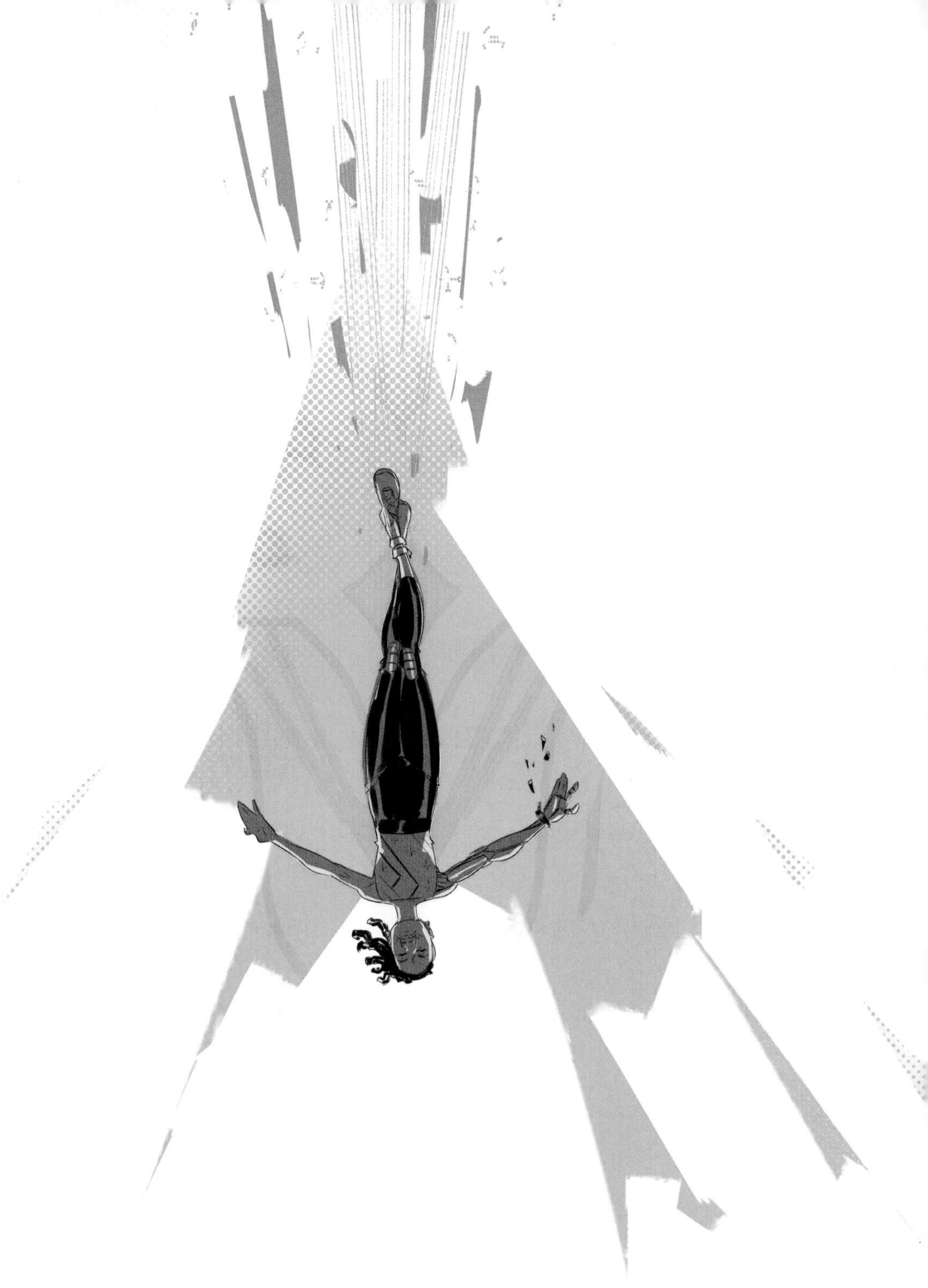

For our family— across continents.
Always one.

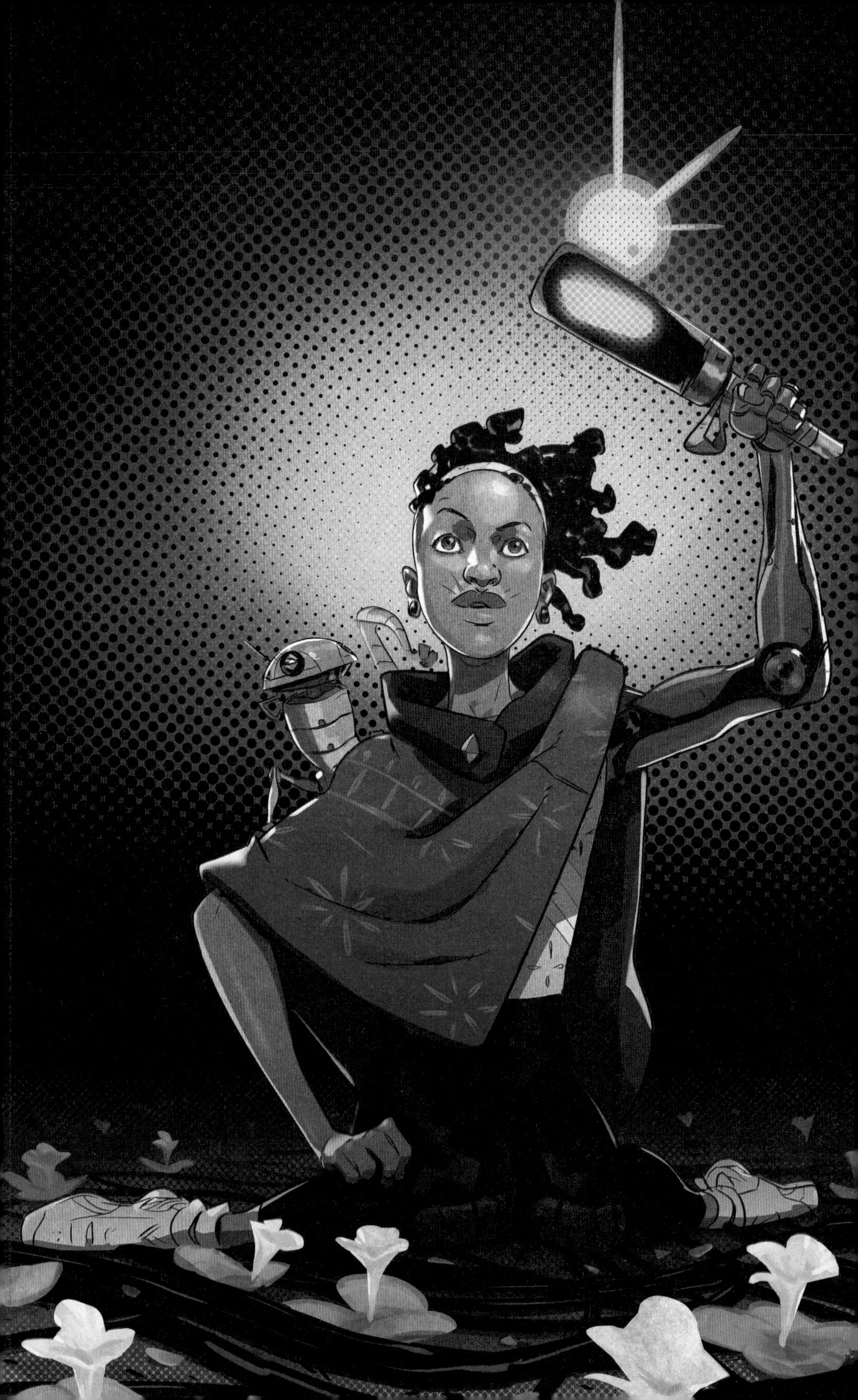

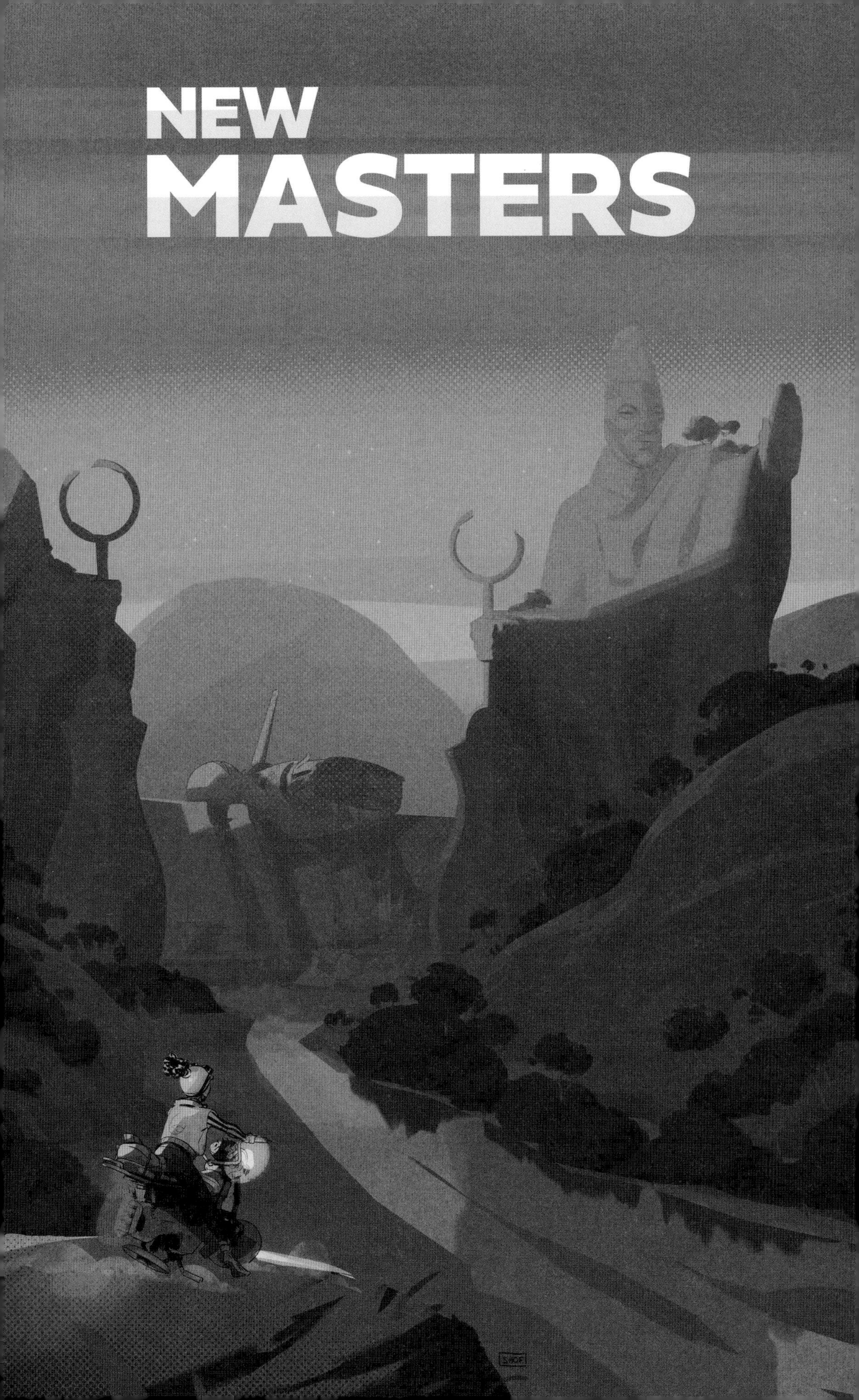
NEW
MASTERS

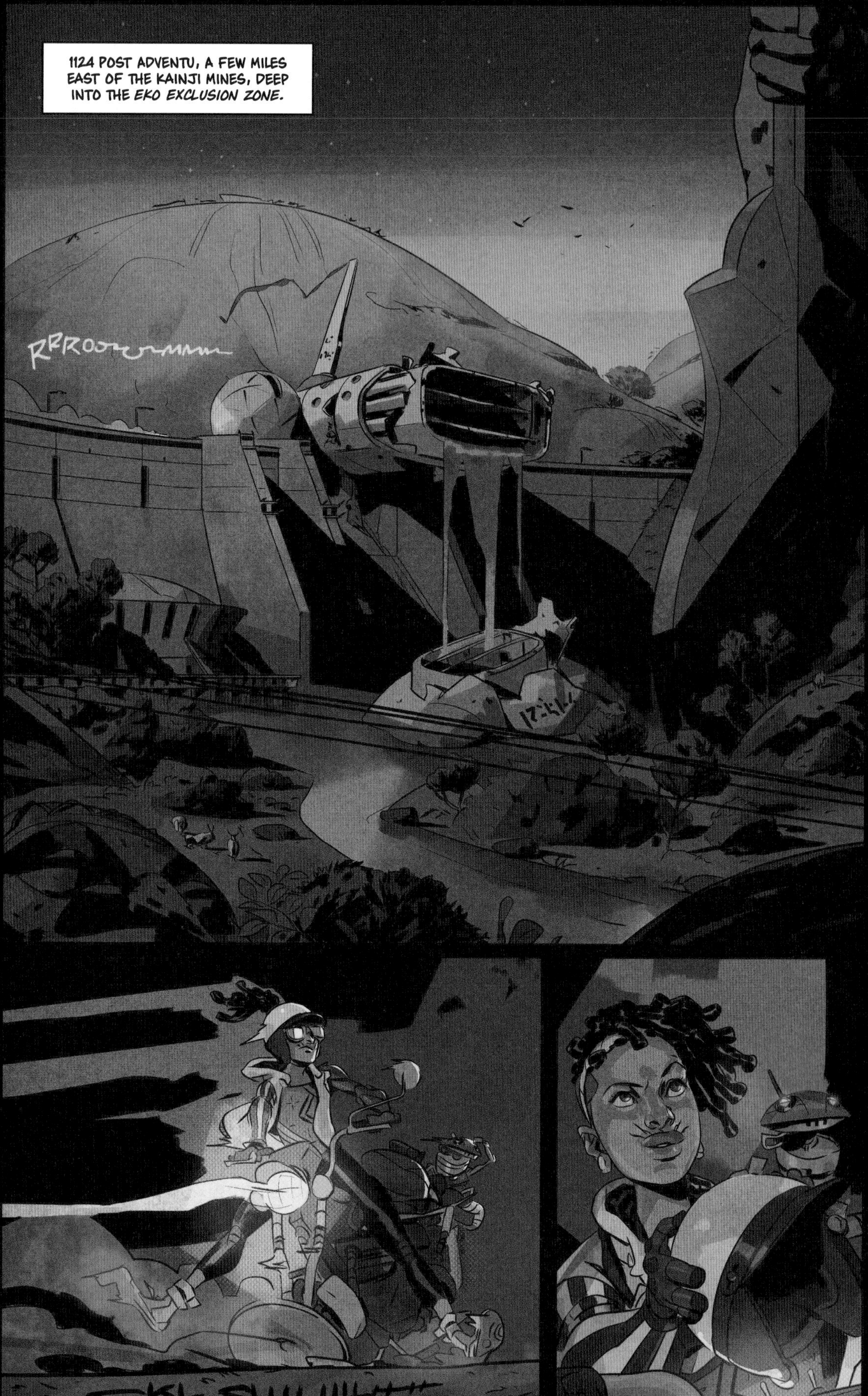
1124 POST ADVENTU, A FEW MILES EAST OF THE KAINJI MINES, DEEP INTO THE *EKO EXCLUSION ZONE.*
RRROOOMMM
SKKSHHH

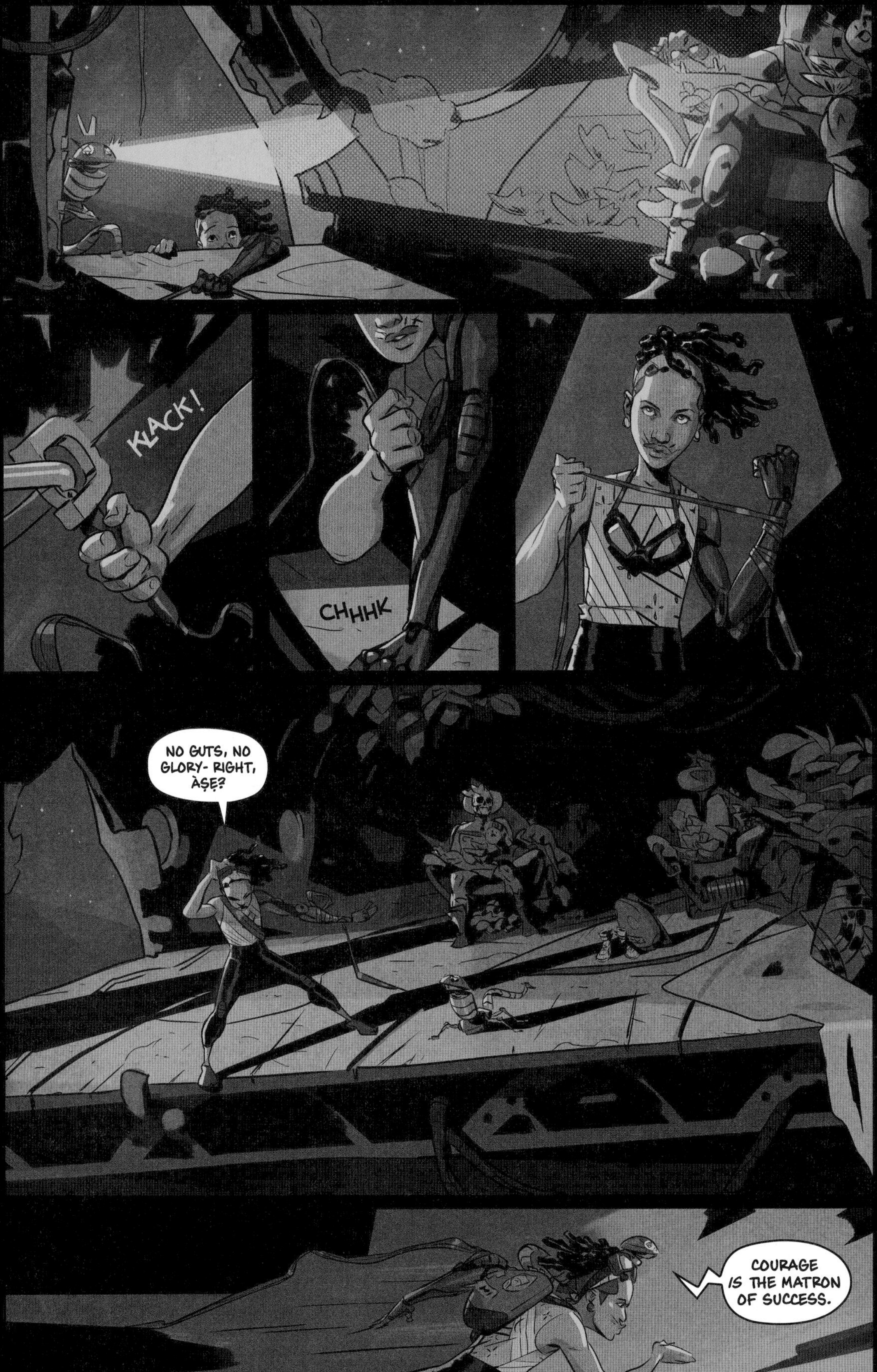
KLACK!
CHHHK
NO GUTS, NO GLORY- RIGHT, ÀṢẸ?
COURAGE IS THE MATRON OF SUCCESS.

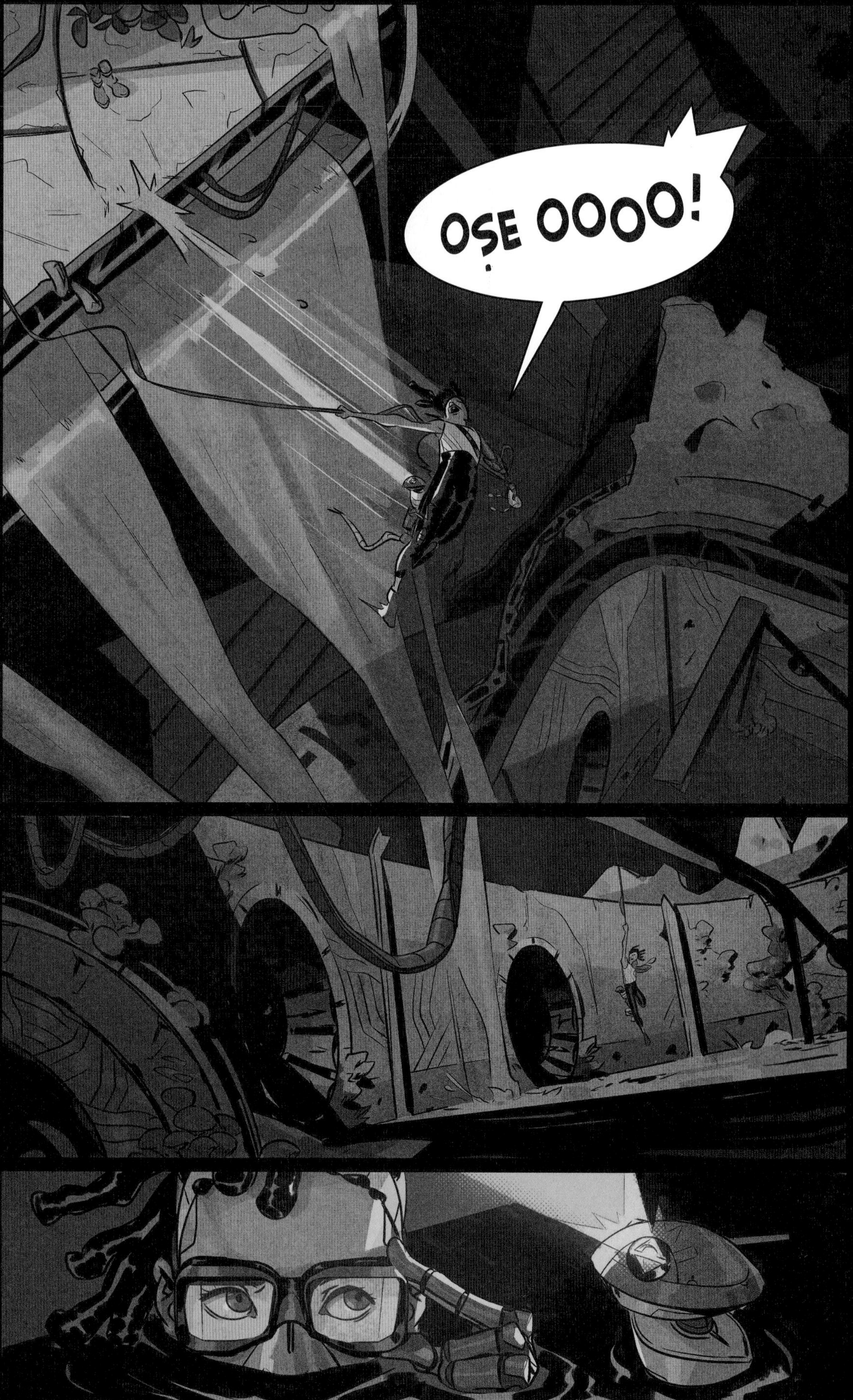
OṢE OOOO!

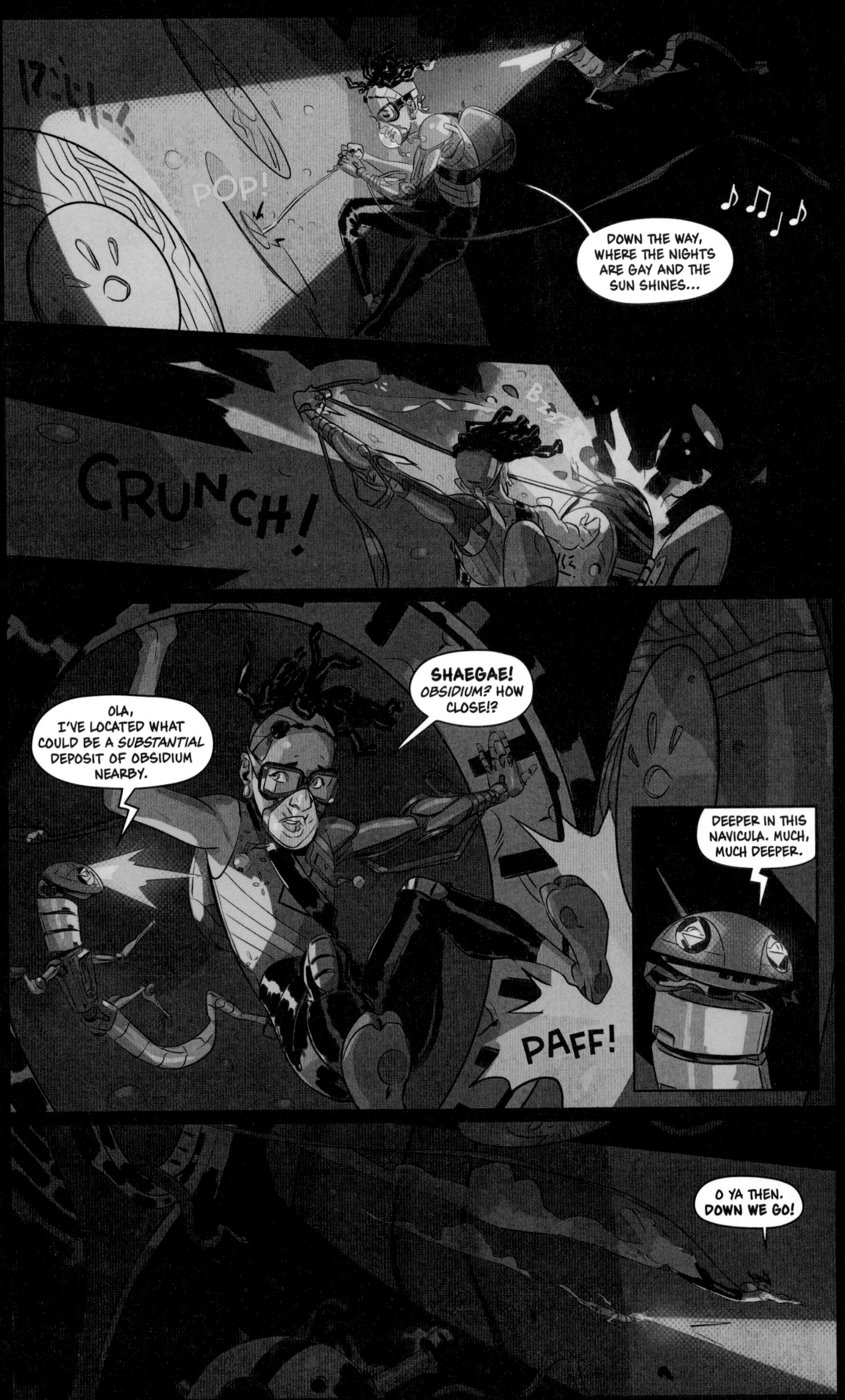
POP!
DOWN THE WAY, WHERE THE NIGHTS ARE GAY AND THE SUN SHINES...
CRUNCH!
OLA, I'VE LOCATED WHAT COULD BE A *SUBSTANTIAL* DEPOSIT OF OBSIDIUM NEARBY.
SHAEGAE! *OBSIDIUM?* HOW CLOSE!?
DEEPER IN THIS NAVICULA. MUCH, MUCH DEEPER.
PAFF!
O YA THEN. DOWN WE GO!

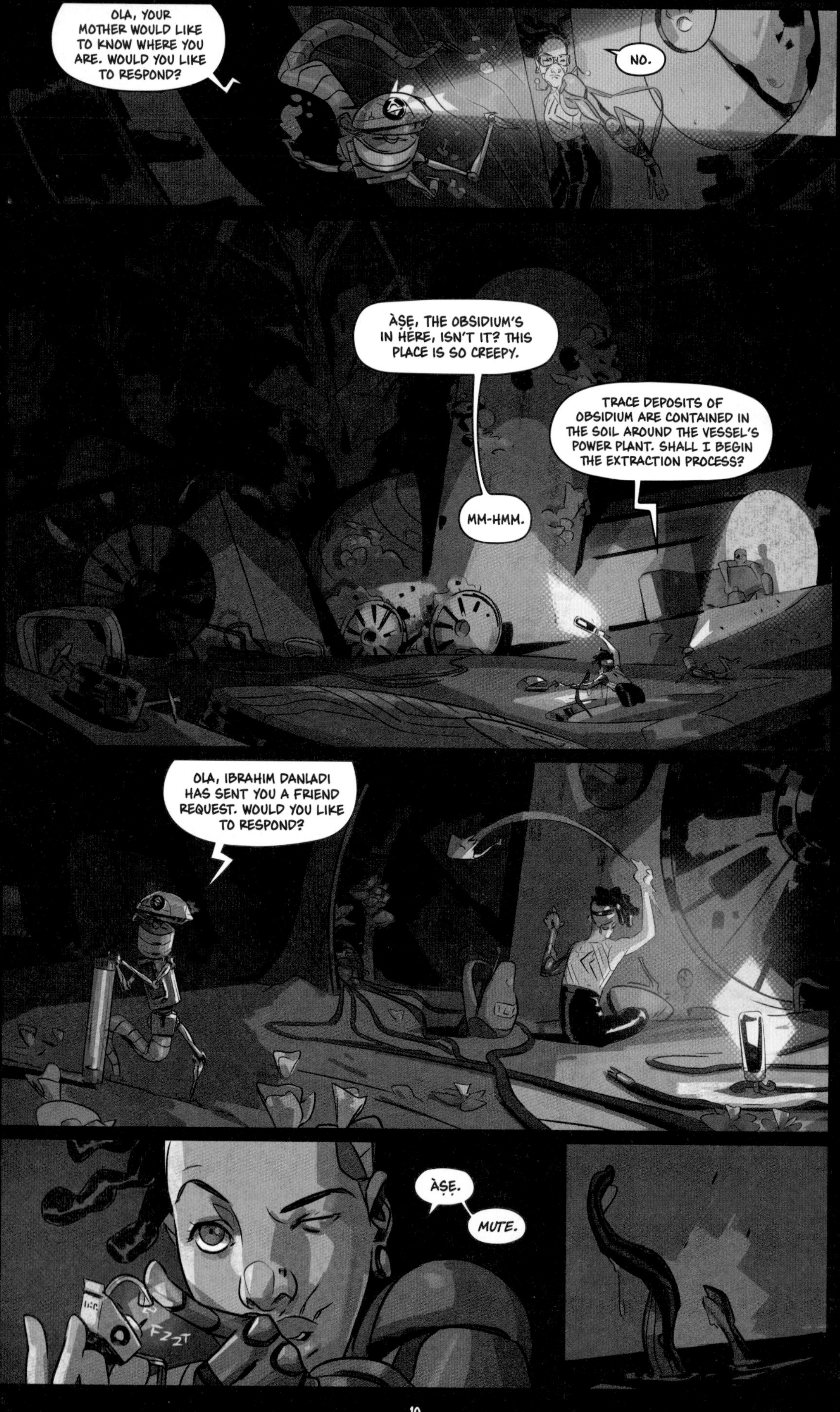
OLA, YOUR MOTHER WOULD LIKE TO KNOW WHERE YOU ARE. WOULD YOU LIKE TO RESPOND?
NO.
ÀṢẸ, THE OBSIDIUM'S IN HERE, ISN'T IT? THIS PLACE IS SO CREEPY.
TRACE DEPOSITS OF OBSIDIUM ARE CONTAINED IN THE SOIL AROUND THE VESSEL'S POWER PLANT. SHALL I BEGIN THE EXTRACTION PROCESS?
MM-HMM.
OLA, IBRAHIM DANLADI HAS SENT YOU A FRIEND REQUEST. WOULD YOU LIKE TO RESPOND?
ÀṢẸ.
MUTE.
FZZT

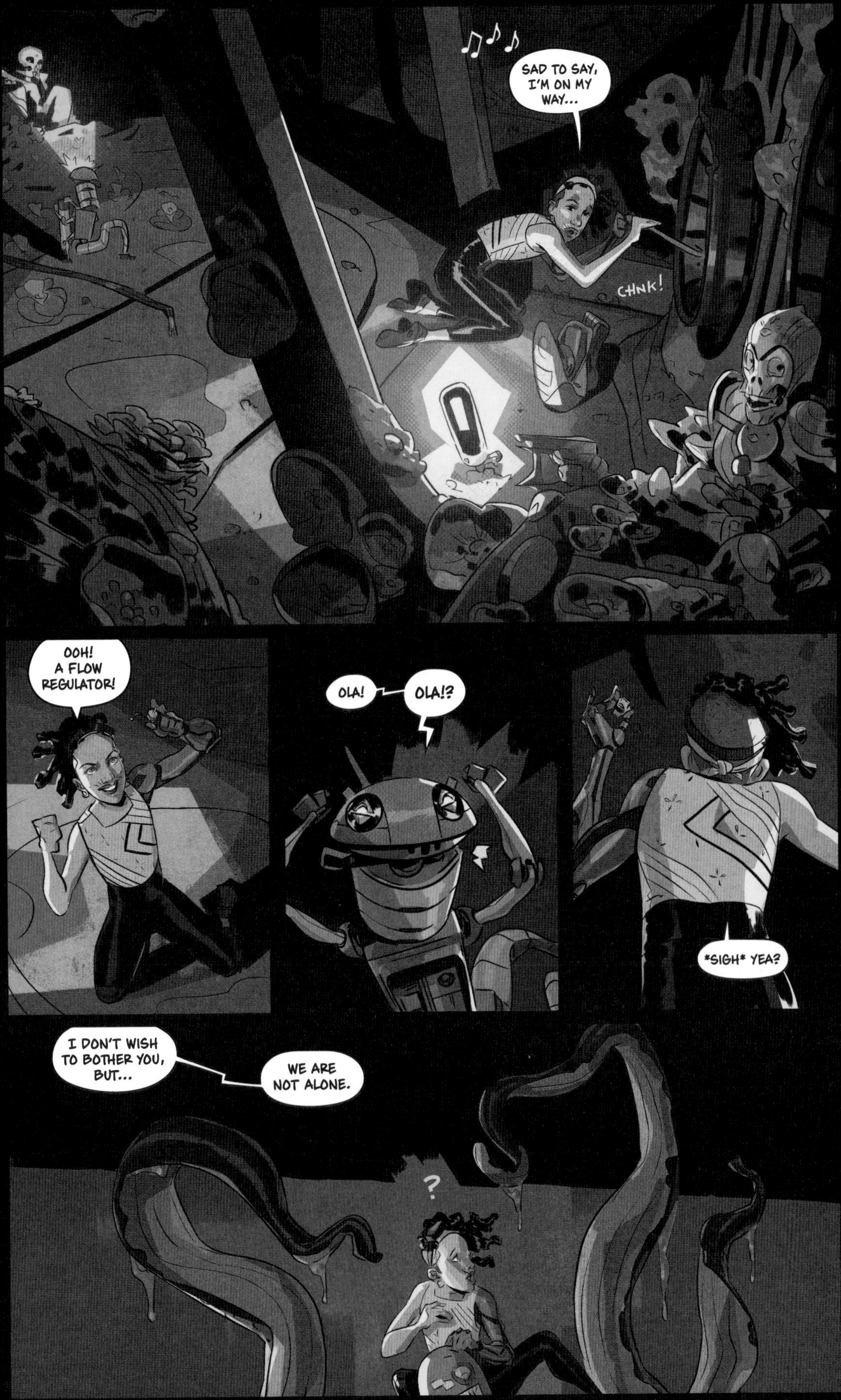
SAD TO SAY, I'M ON MY WAY...
CHNK!
OOH! A FLOW REGULATOR!
OLA!
OLA!?
SIGH YEA?
I DON'T WISH TO BOTHER YOU, BUT...
WE ARE NOT ALONE.
?

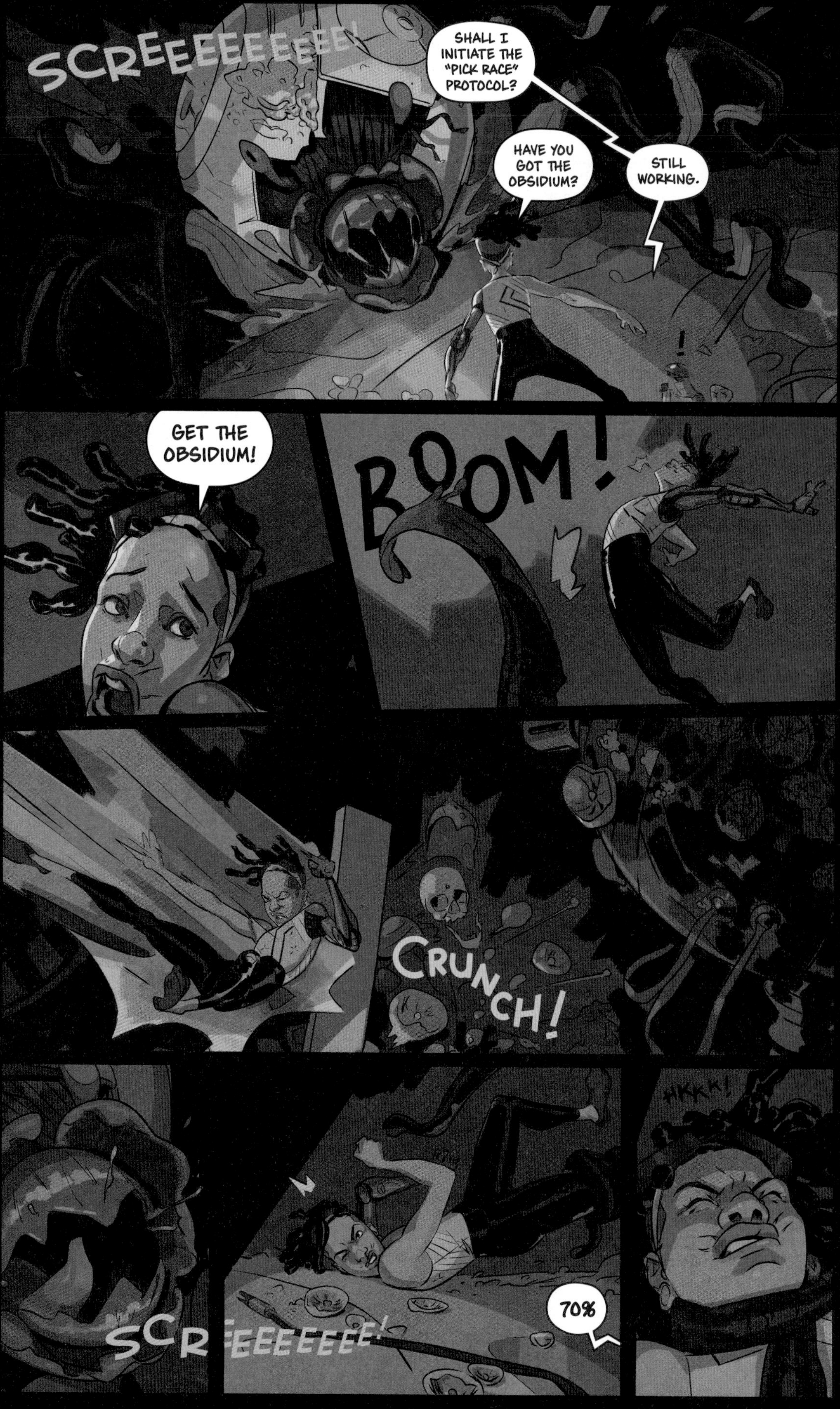
SCREEEEEEEEEE!
SHALL I INITIATE THE "PICK RACE" PROTOCOL?
HAVE YOU GOT THE OBSIDIUM?
STILL WORKING.
!
GET THE OBSIDIUM!
BOOM!
CRUNCH!
HKKK!
SCREEEEEEEEE!
70%

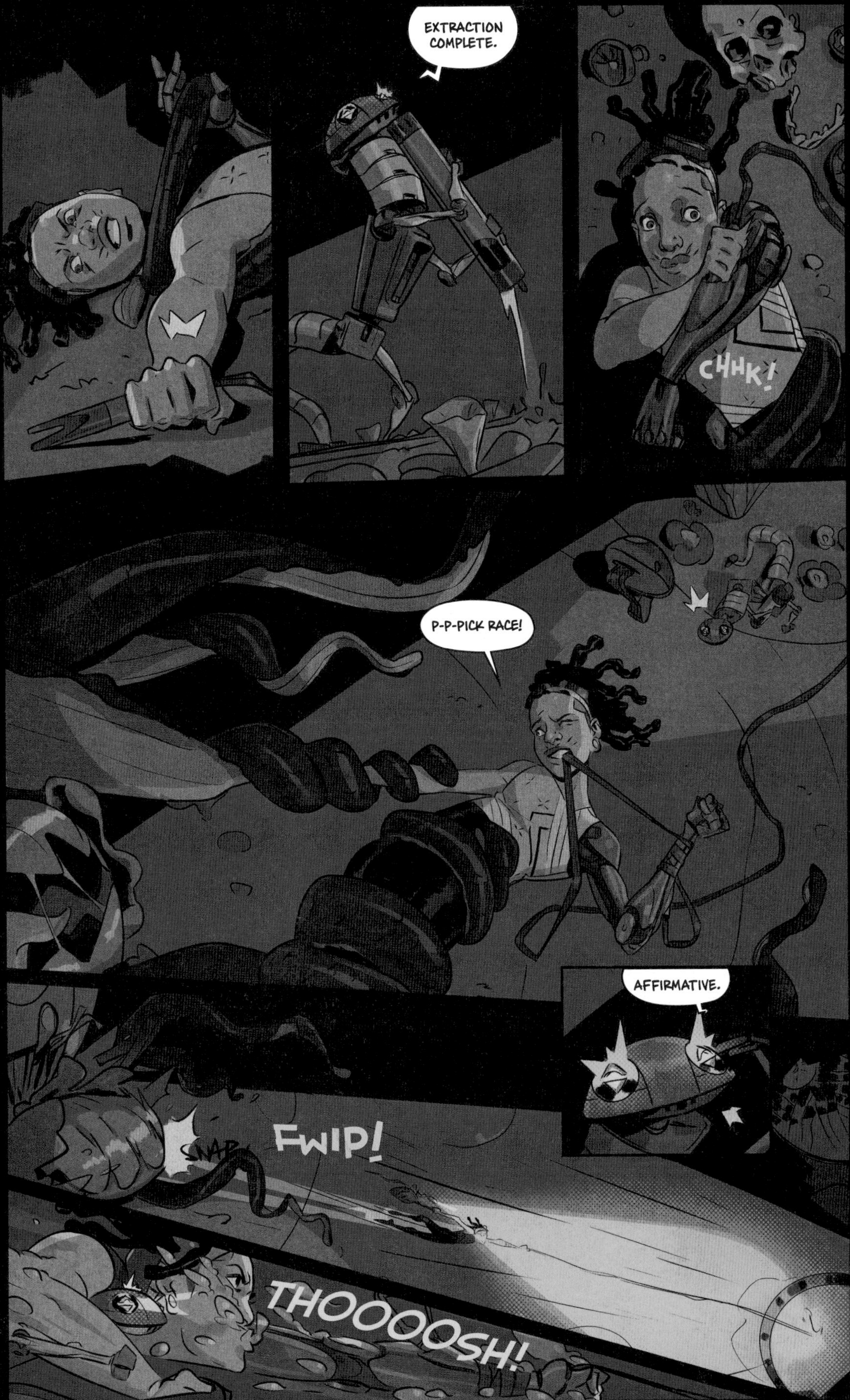
EXTRACTION COMPLETE.
CHHK!
P-P-PICK RACE!
AFFIRMATIVE.
FWIP!
THOOOOSH!

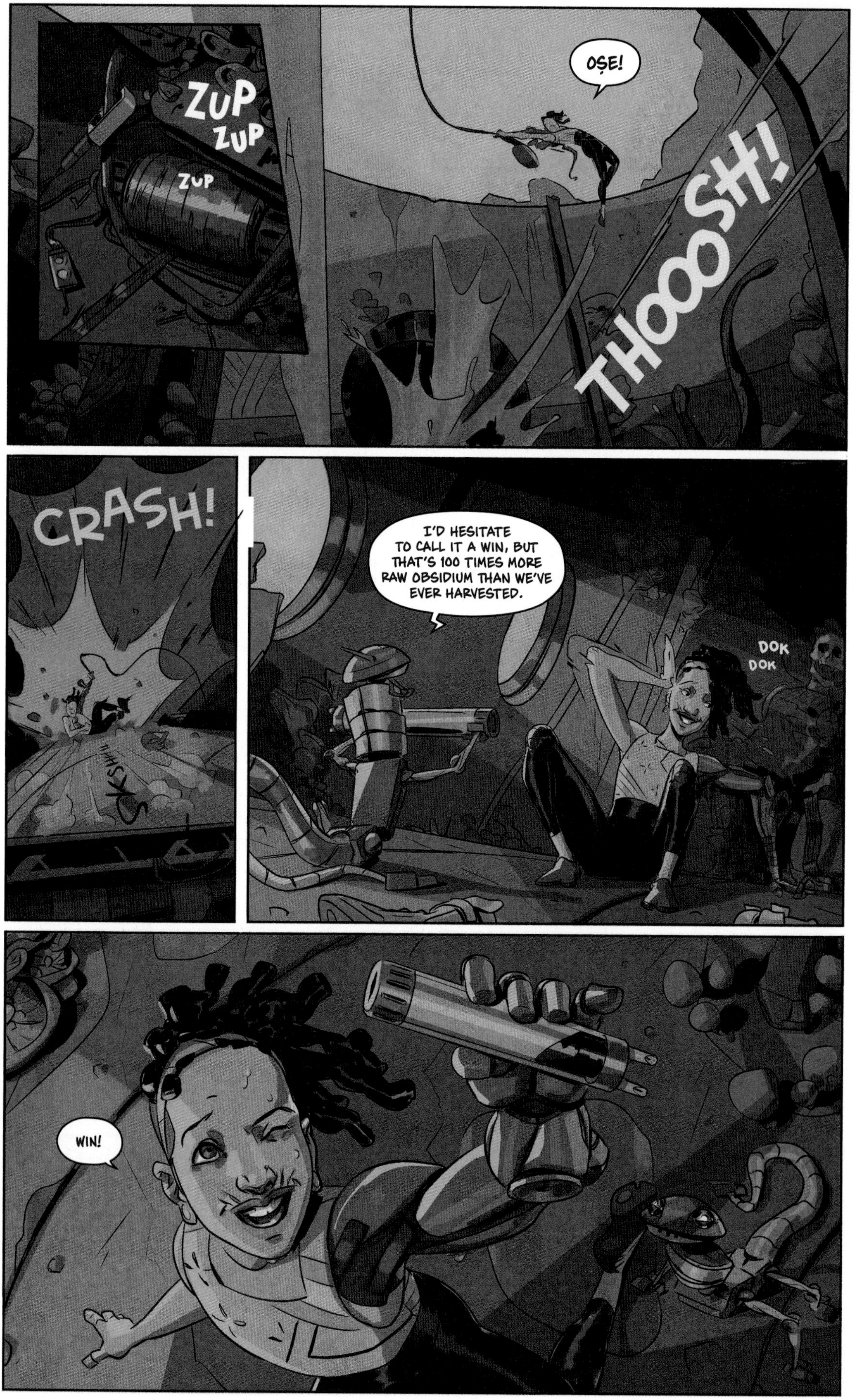
ZUP
ZUP
ZUP
OṢE!
THOOOSH!
CRASH!
I'D HESITATE TO CALL IT A WIN, BUT THAT'S 100 TIMES MORE RAW OBSIDIUM THAN WE'VE EVER HARVESTED.
DOK DOK
WIN!

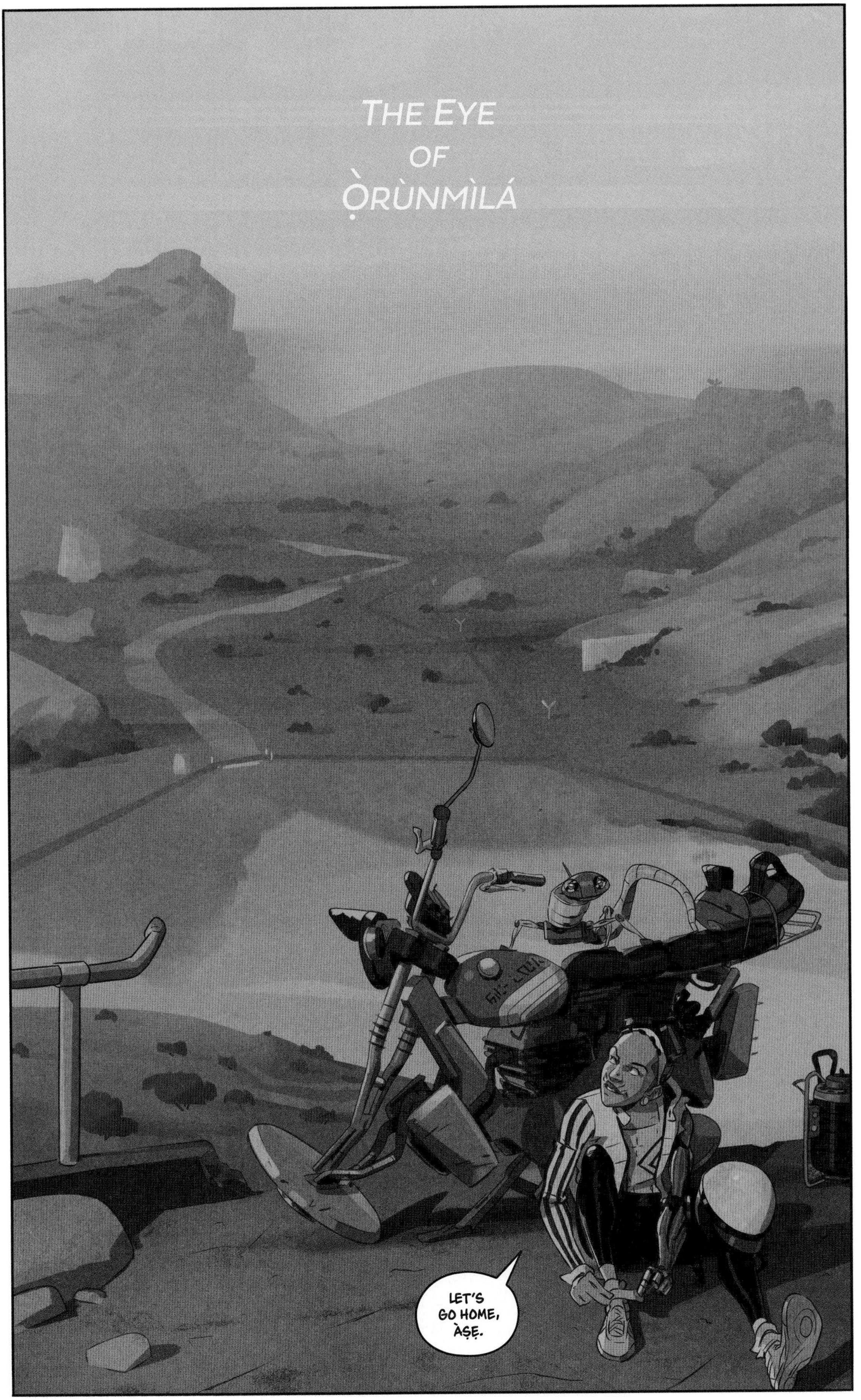
THE EYE
OF
ỌRÙNMÌLÁ
LET'S GO HOME, ÀṢẸ.

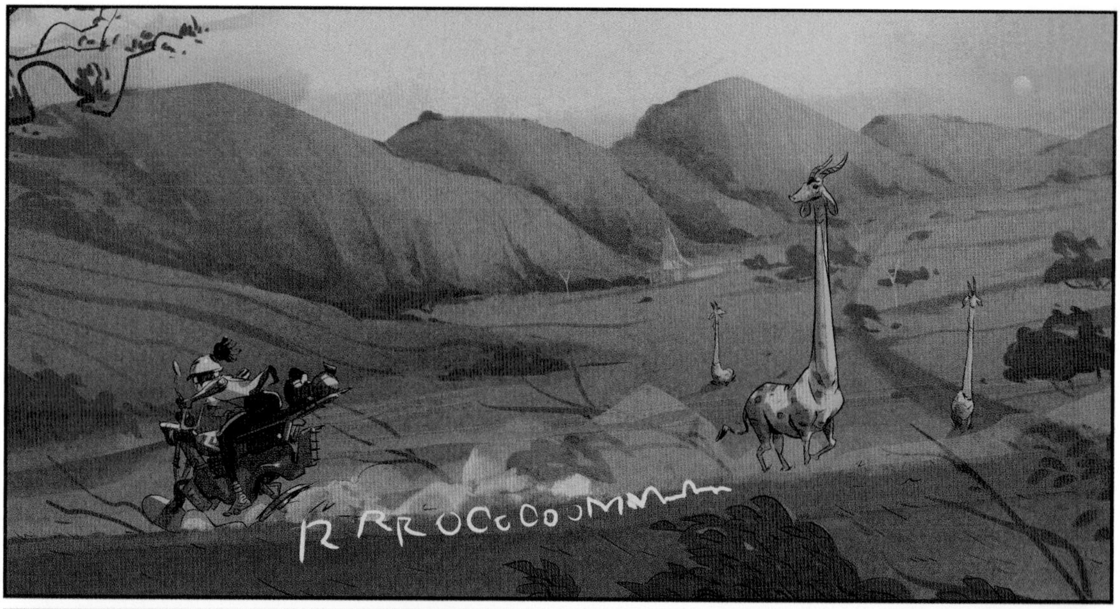
RRROCCCOOOMMM

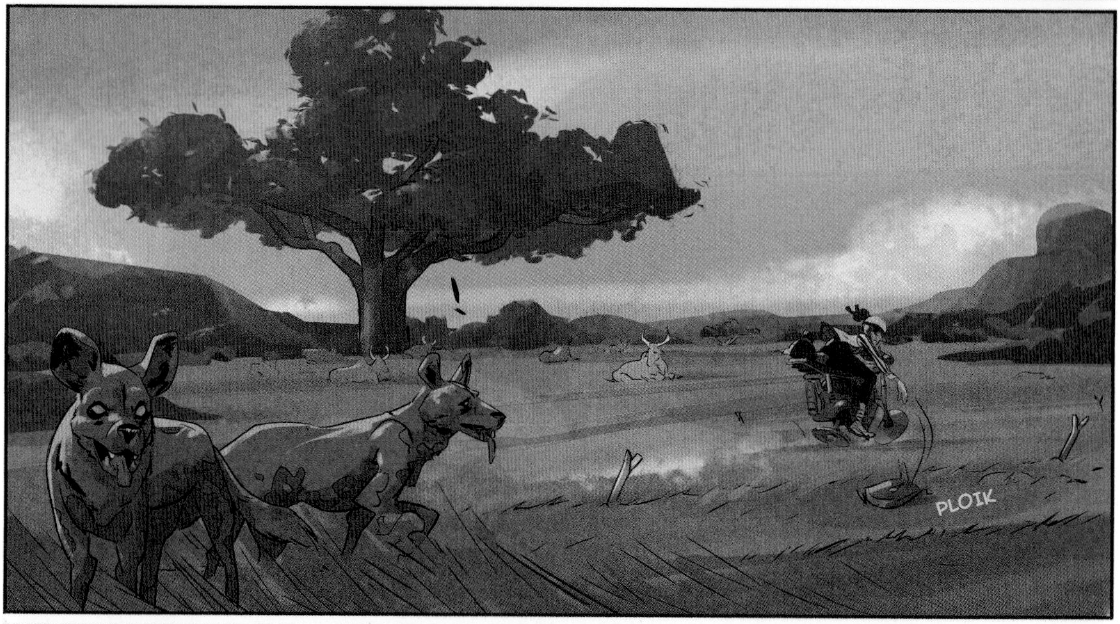
PLOIK

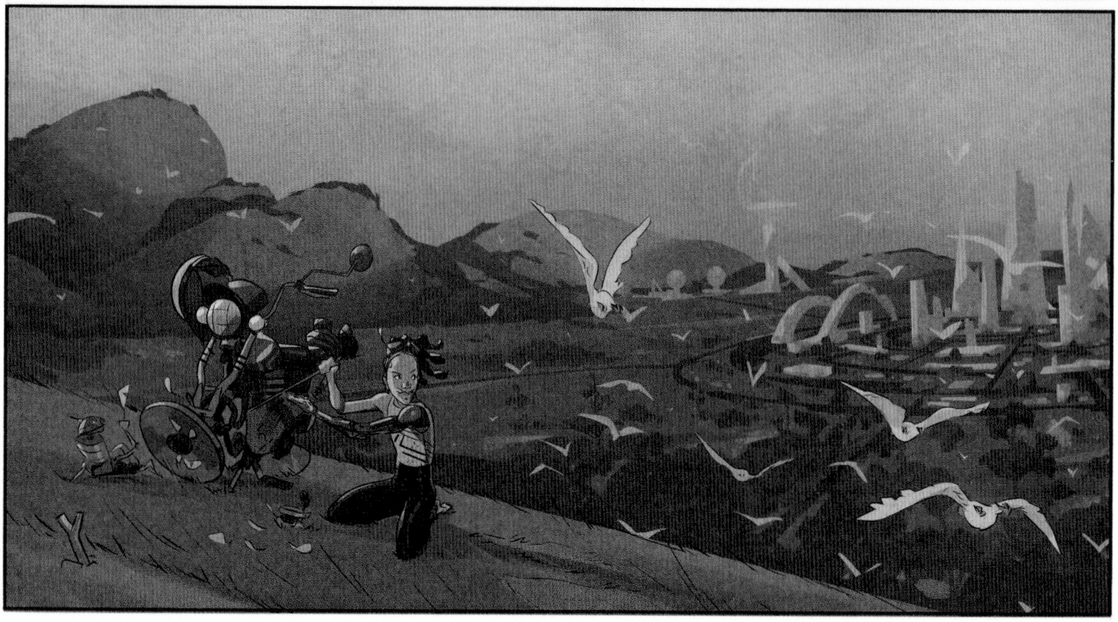

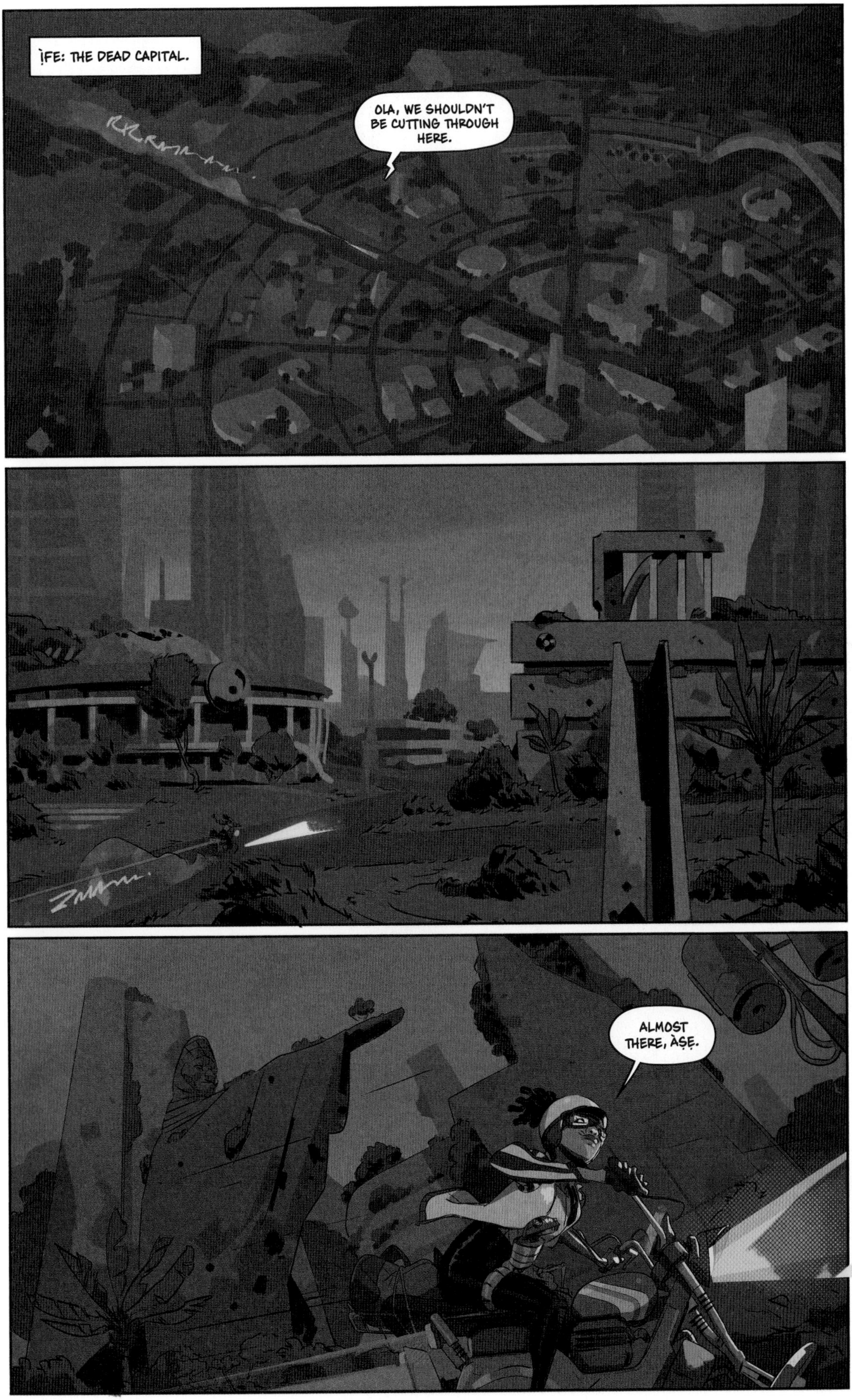
ỊFE: THE DEAD CAPITAL.
OLA, WE SHOULDN'T BE CUTTING THROUGH HERE.
ALMOST THERE, ÀṢẸ.

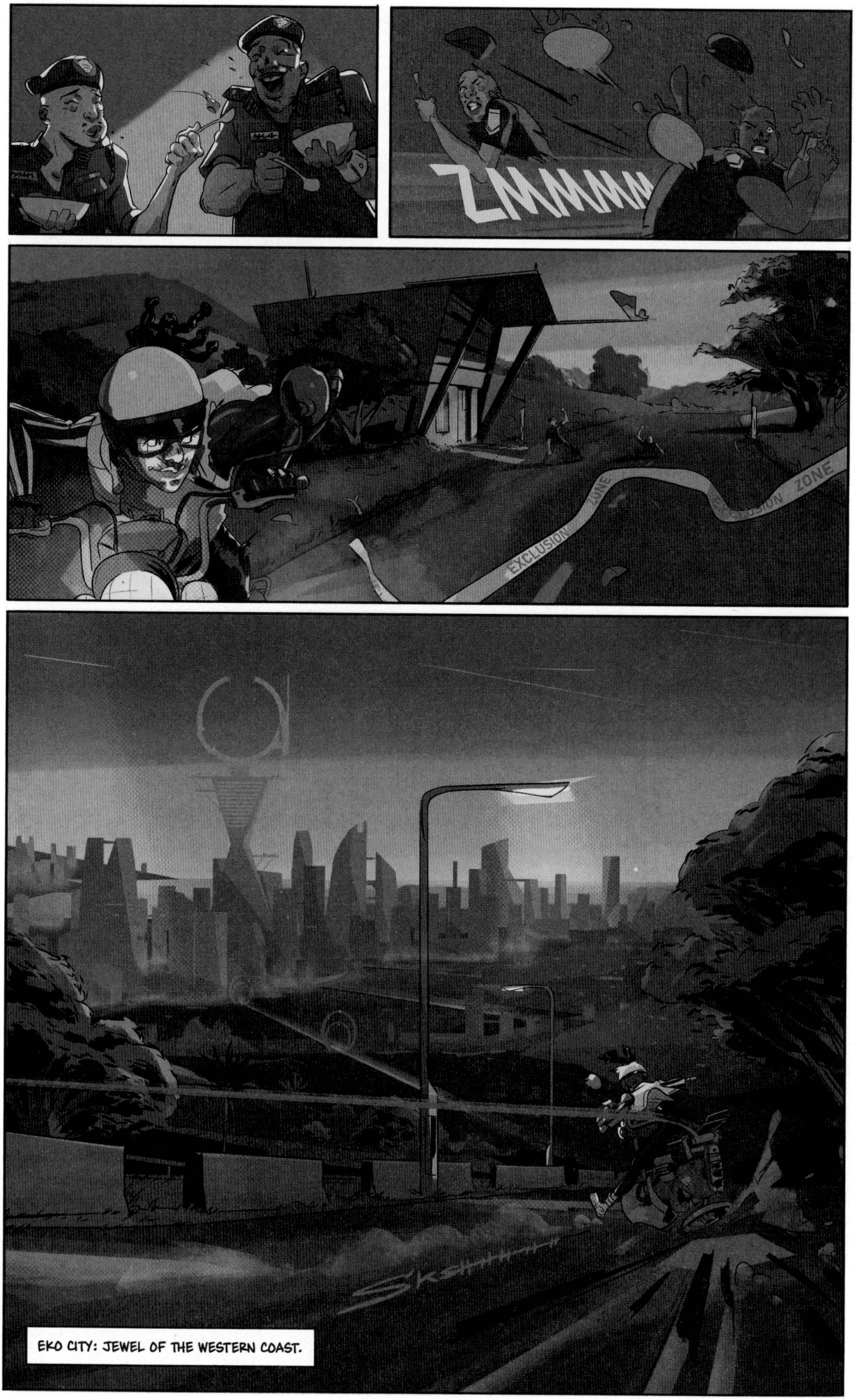
ZMMMM
EXCLUSION ZONE
EXCLUSION ZONE
EKO CITY: JEWEL OF THE WESTERN COAST.

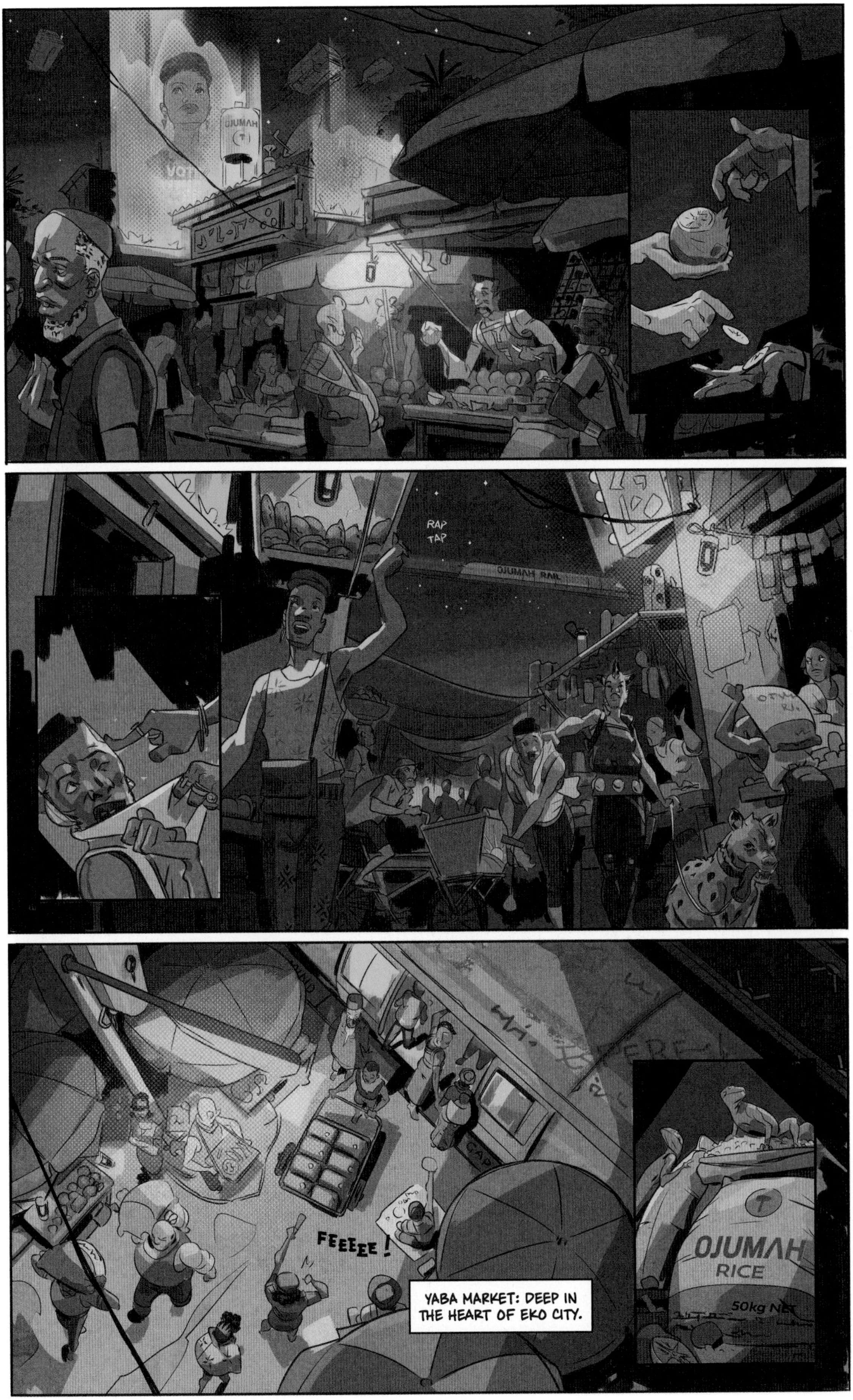
OJUMAH
RAP
TAP
OJUMAH RAIL
FEEEEE!
YABA MARKET: DEEP IN THE HEART OF EKO CITY.
OJUMAH
RICE
50kg NET

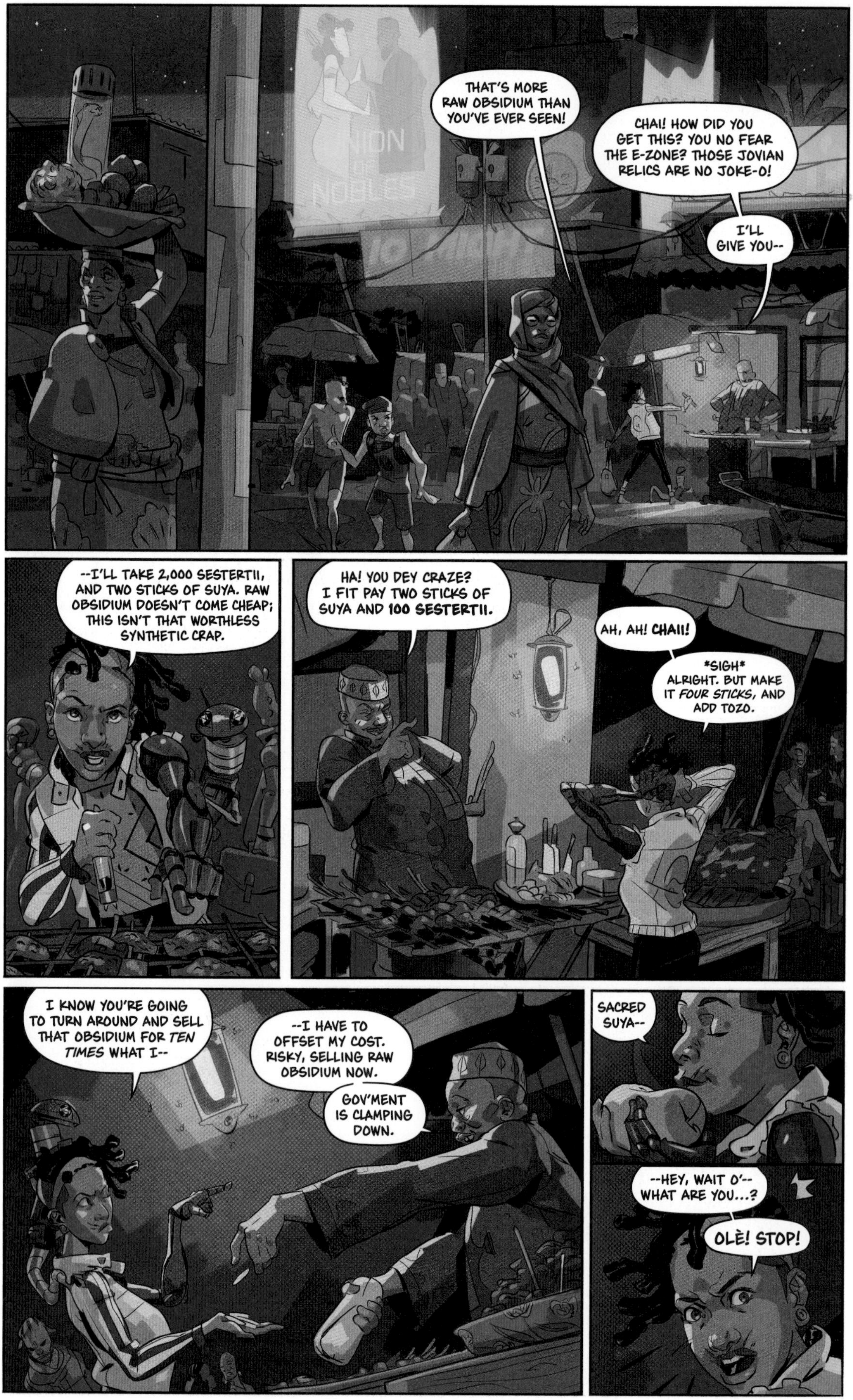
THAT'S MORE RAW OBSIDIUM THAN YOU'VE EVER SEEN!
CHAI! HOW DID YOU GET THIS? YOU NO FEAR THE E-ZONE? THOSE JOVIAN RELICS ARE NO JOKE-O!
I'LL GIVE YOU--
--I'LL TAKE 2,000 SESTERTII, AND TWO STICKS OF SUYA. RAW OBSIDIUM DOESN'T COME CHEAP; THIS ISN'T THAT WORTHLESS SYNTHETIC CRAP.
HA! YOU DEY CRAZE? I FIT PAY TWO STICKS OF SUYA AND **100 SESTERTII.**
AH, AH! **CHAI!**
SIGH ALRIGHT. BUT MAKE IT *FOUR STICKS*, AND ADD TOZO.
I KNOW YOU'RE GOING TO TURN AROUND AND SELL THAT OBSIDIUM FOR *TEN TIMES* WHAT I--
--I HAVE TO OFFSET MY COST. RISKY, SELLING RAW OBSIDIUM NOW.
GOV'MENT IS CLAMPING DOWN.
SACRED SUYA--
--HEY, WAIT O'-- WHAT ARE YOU...?
OLÈ! STOP!

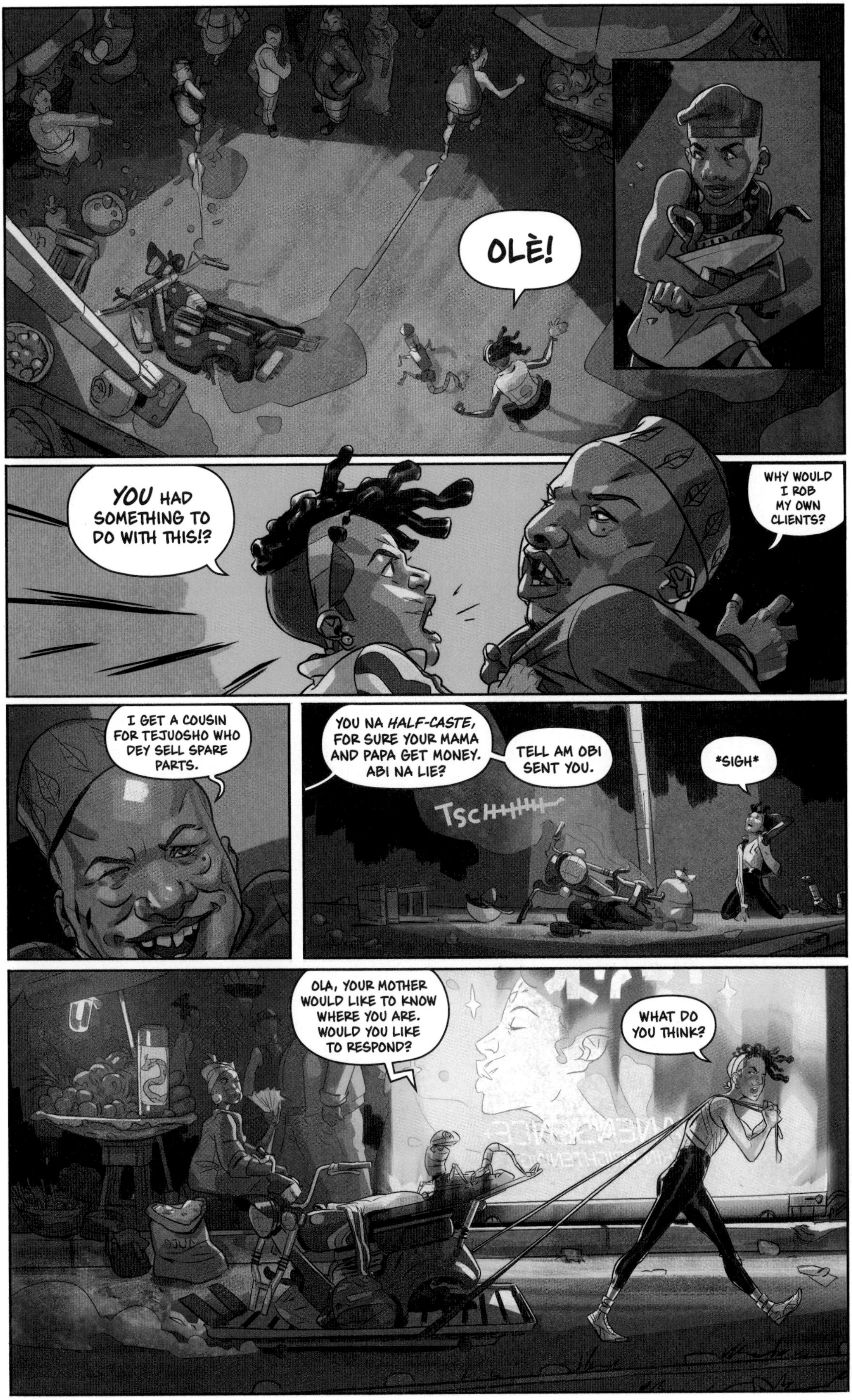
OLÈ!
YOU HAD SOMETHING TO DO WITH THIS!?
WHY WOULD I ROB MY OWN CLIENTS?
I GET A COUSIN FOR TEJUOSHO WHO DEY SELL SPARE PARTS.
YOU NA HALF-CASTE, FOR SURE YOUR MAMA AND PAPA GET MONEY. ABI NA LIE?
TELL AM OBI SENT YOU.
TSCHHHHHH
SIGH
OLA, YOUR MOTHER WOULD LIKE TO KNOW WHERE YOU ARE. WOULD YOU LIKE TO RESPOND?
WHAT DO YOU THINK?

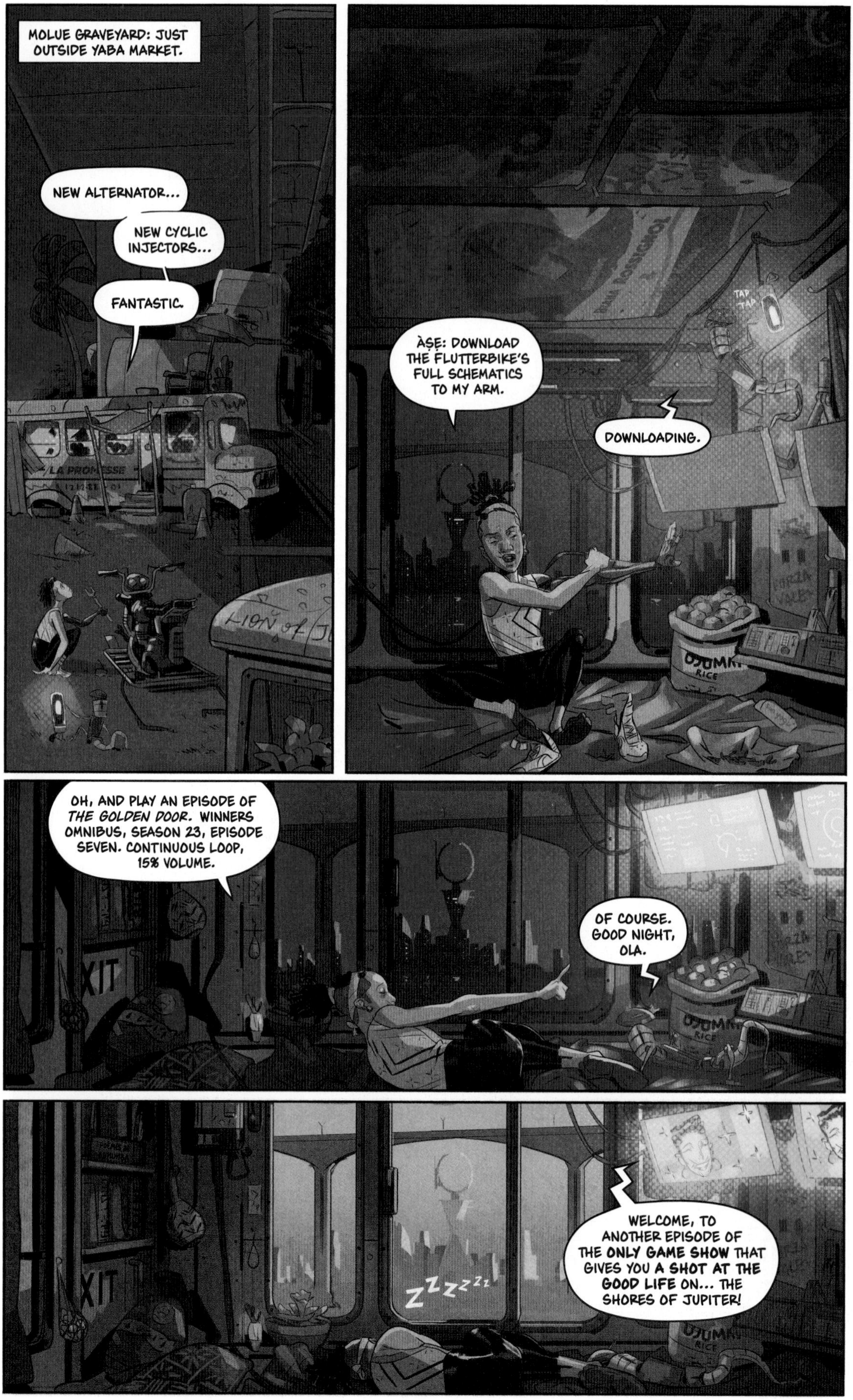
MOLUE GRAVEYARD: JUST OUTSIDE YABA MARKET.
NEW ALTERNATOR...
NEW CYCLIC INJECTORS...
FANTASTIC.
ÀṢẸ: DOWNLOAD THE FLUTTERBIKE'S FULL SCHEMATICS TO MY ARM.
TAP TAP
DOWNLOADING.
OH, AND PLAY AN EPISODE OF *THE GOLDEN DOOR*. WINNERS OMNIBUS, SEASON 23, EPISODE SEVEN. CONTINUOUS LOOP, 15% VOLUME.
OF COURSE. GOOD NIGHT, OLA.
EXIT
ZZZzzz
WELCOME, TO ANOTHER EPISODE OF THE **ONLY GAME SHOW** THAT GIVES YOU **A SHOT AT THE GOOD LIFE** ON... THE SHORES OF JUPITER!

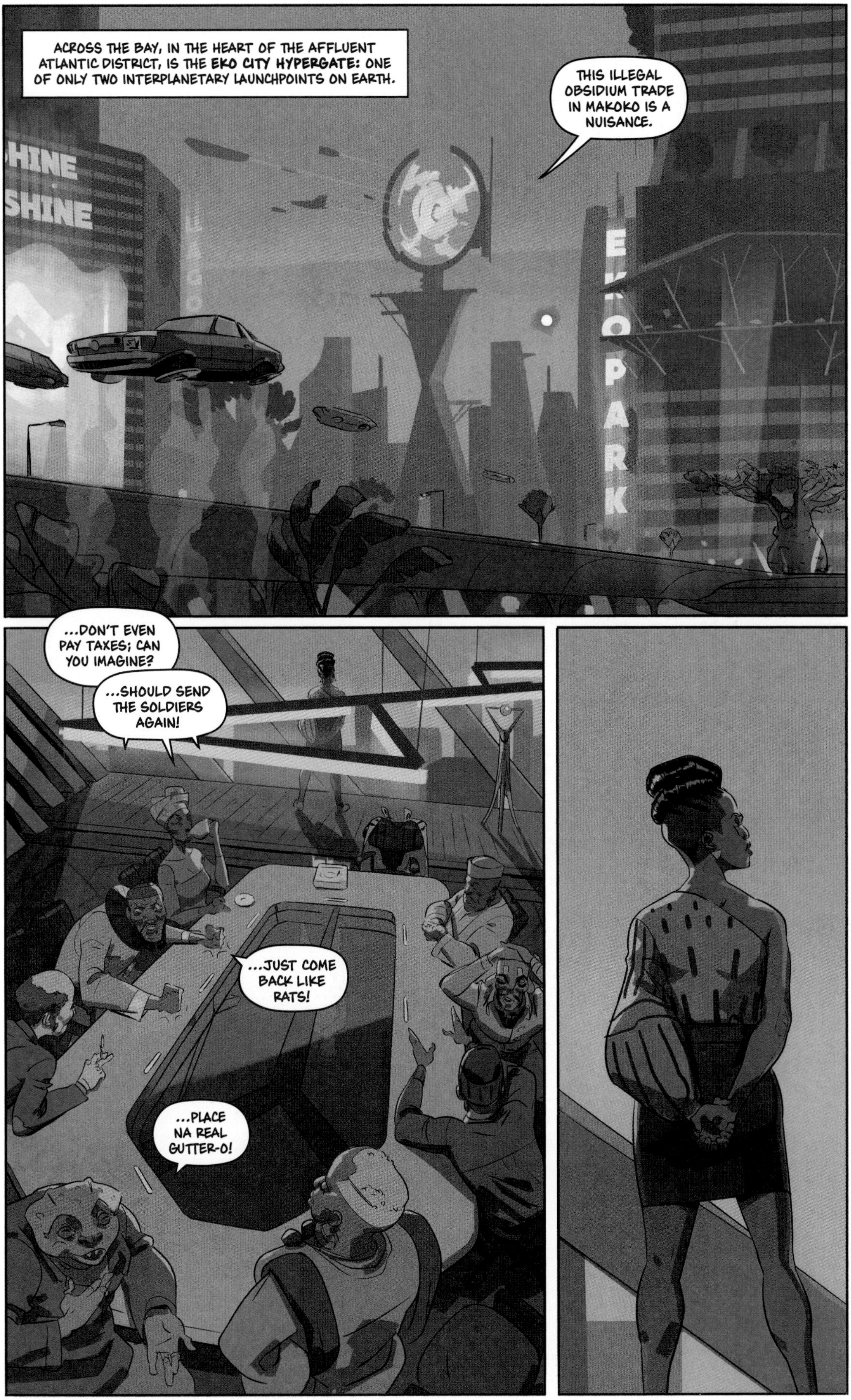
ACROSS THE BAY, IN THE HEART OF THE AFFLUENT ATLANTIC DISTRICT, IS THE **EKO CITY HYPERGATE:** ONE OF ONLY TWO INTERPLANETARY LAUNCHPOINTS ON EARTH.
THIS ILLEGAL OBSIDIUM TRADE IN MAKOKO IS A NUISANCE.
SHINE
SHINE
EKO PARK
...DON'T EVEN PAY TAXES; CAN YOU IMAGINE?
...SHOULD SEND THE SOLDIERS AGAIN!
...JUST COME BACK LIKE RATS!
...PLACE NA REAL GUTTER-O!

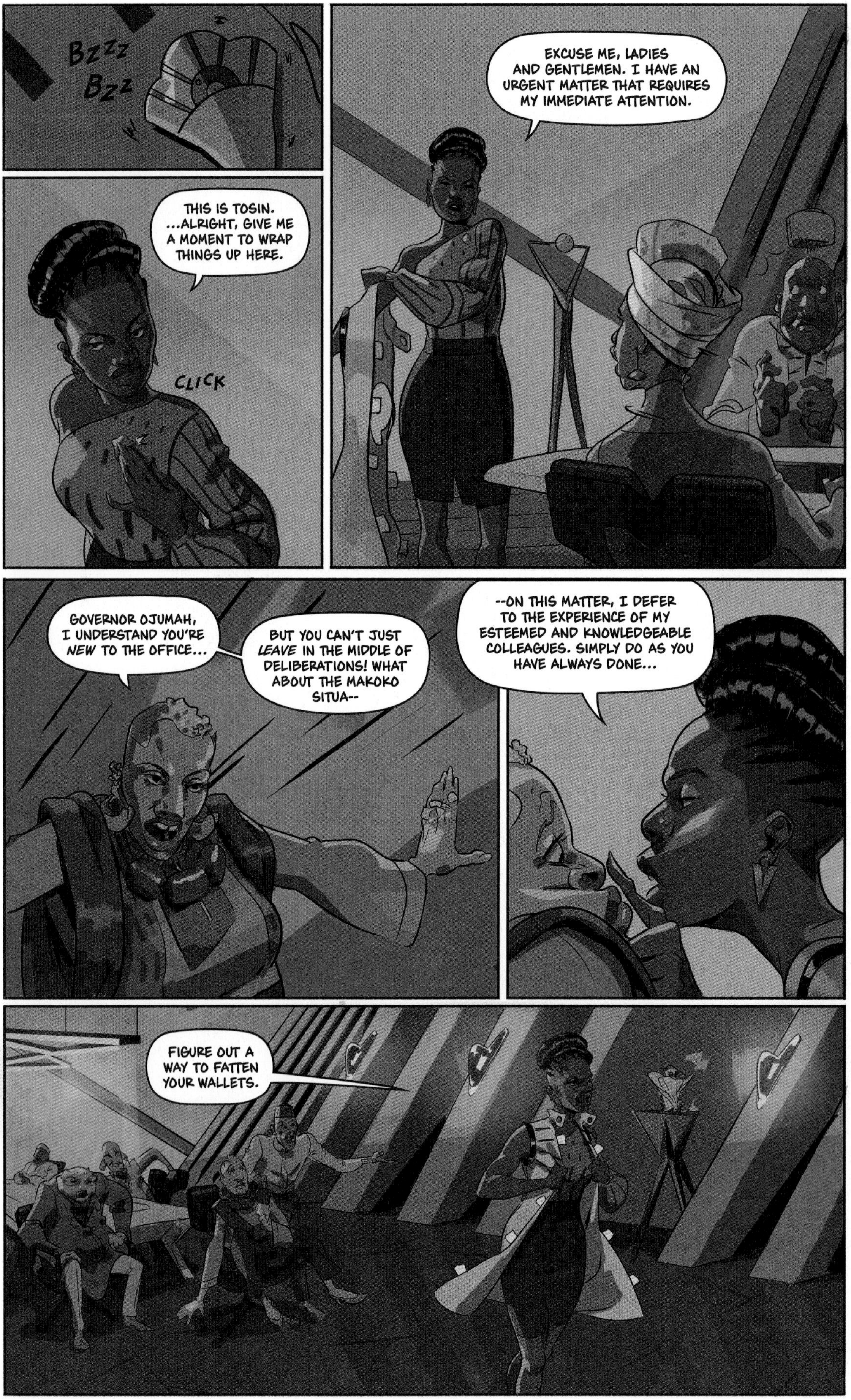

Bzzz
Bzz
EXCUSE ME, LADIES AND GENTLEMEN. I HAVE AN URGENT MATTER THAT REQUIRES MY IMMEDIATE ATTENTION.
THIS IS TOSIN. ...ALRIGHT, GIVE ME A MOMENT TO WRAP THINGS UP HERE.
CLICK
GOVERNOR OJUMAH, I UNDERSTAND YOU'RE NEW TO THE OFFICE...
BUT YOU CAN'T JUST LEAVE IN THE MIDDLE OF DELIBERATIONS! WHAT ABOUT THE MAKOKO SITUA--
--ON THIS MATTER, I DEFER TO THE EXPERIENCE OF MY ESTEEMED AND KNOWLEDGEABLE COLLEAGUES. SIMPLY DO AS YOU HAVE ALWAYS DONE...
FIGURE OUT A WAY TO FATTEN YOUR WALLETS.

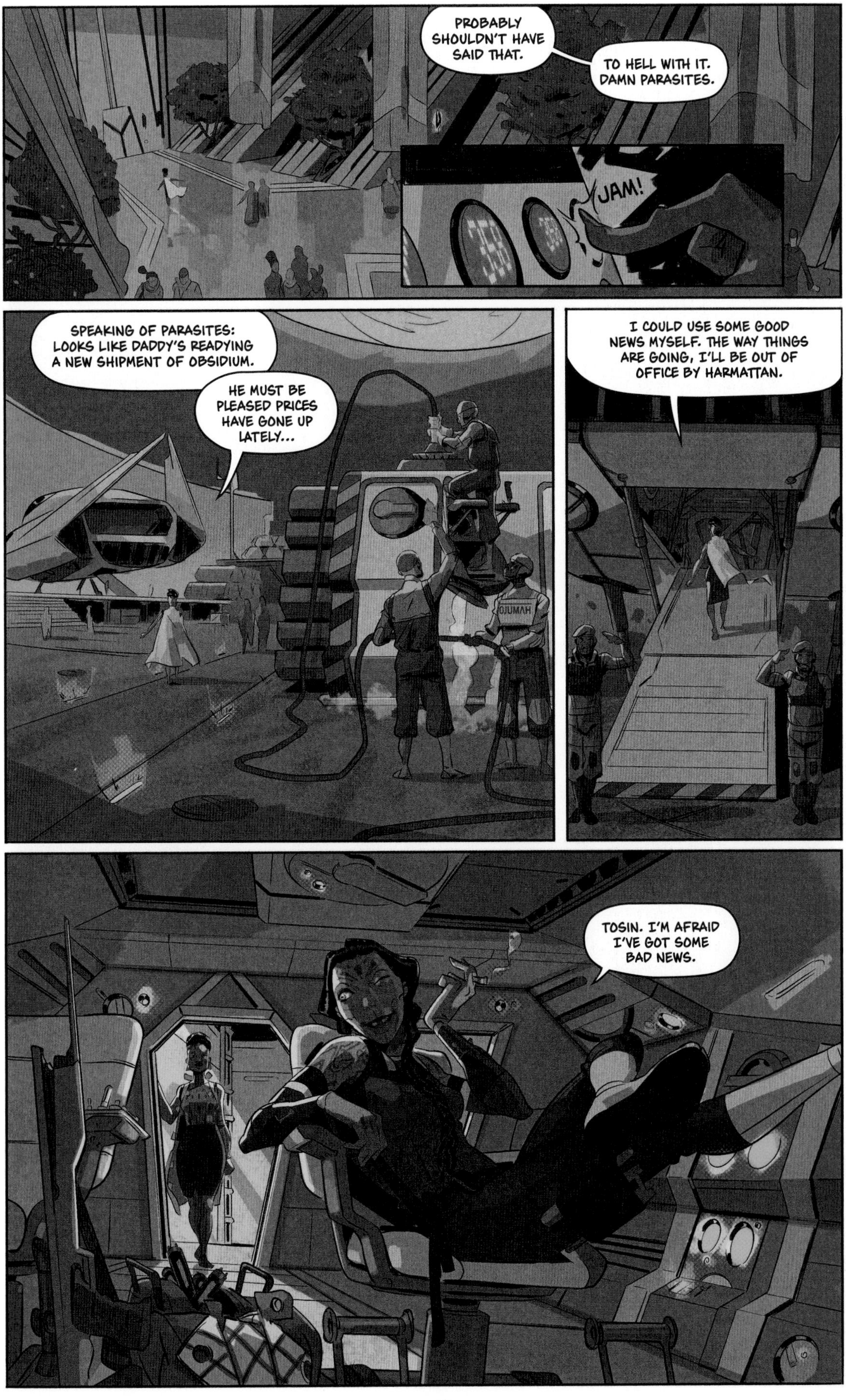
PROBABLY SHOULDN'T HAVE SAID THAT.
TO HELL WITH IT. DAMN PARASITES.
JAM!
SPEAKING OF PARASITES: LOOKS LIKE DADDY'S READYING A NEW SHIPMENT OF OBSIDIUM.
HE MUST BE PLEASED PRICES HAVE GONE UP LATELY...
OJUMAH
I COULD USE SOME GOOD NEWS MYSELF. THE WAY THINGS ARE GOING, I'LL BE OUT OF OFFICE BY HARMATTAN.
TOSIN. I'M AFRAID I'VE GOT SOME BAD NEWS.

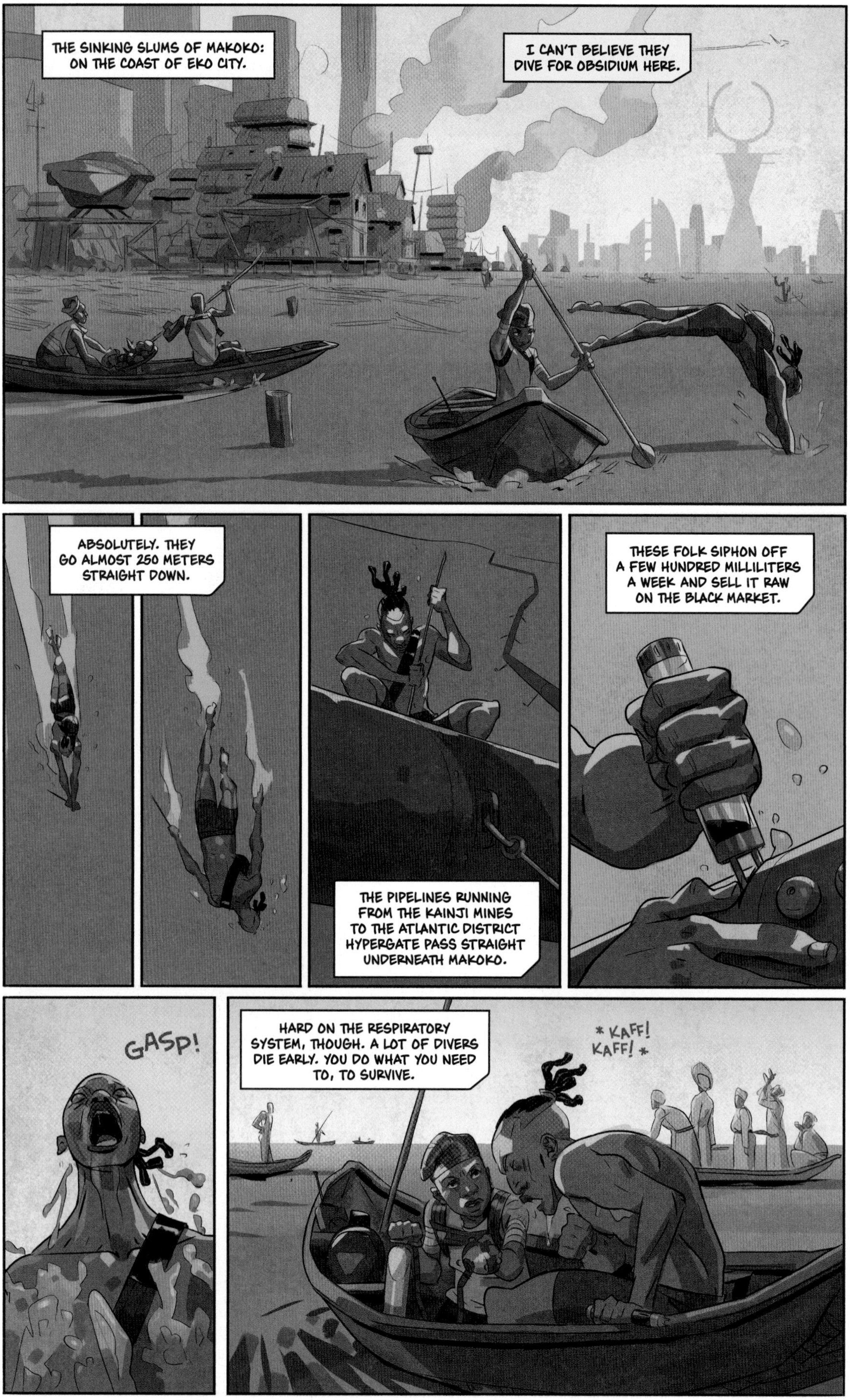
THE SINKING SLUMS OF MAKOKO: ON THE COAST OF EKO CITY.
I CAN'T BELIEVE THEY DIVE FOR OBSIDIUM HERE.
ABSOLUTELY. THEY GO ALMOST 250 METERS STRAIGHT DOWN.
THE PIPELINES RUNNING FROM THE KAINJI MINES TO THE ATLANTIC DISTRICT HYPERGATE PASS STRAIGHT UNDERNEATH MAKOKO.
THESE FOLK SIPHON OFF A FEW HUNDRED MILLILITERS A WEEK AND SELL IT RAW ON THE BLACK MARKET.
GASP!
HARD ON THE RESPIRATORY SYSTEM, THOUGH. A LOT OF DIVERS DIE EARLY. YOU DO WHAT YOU NEED TO, TO SURVIVE.
KAFF! KAFF!

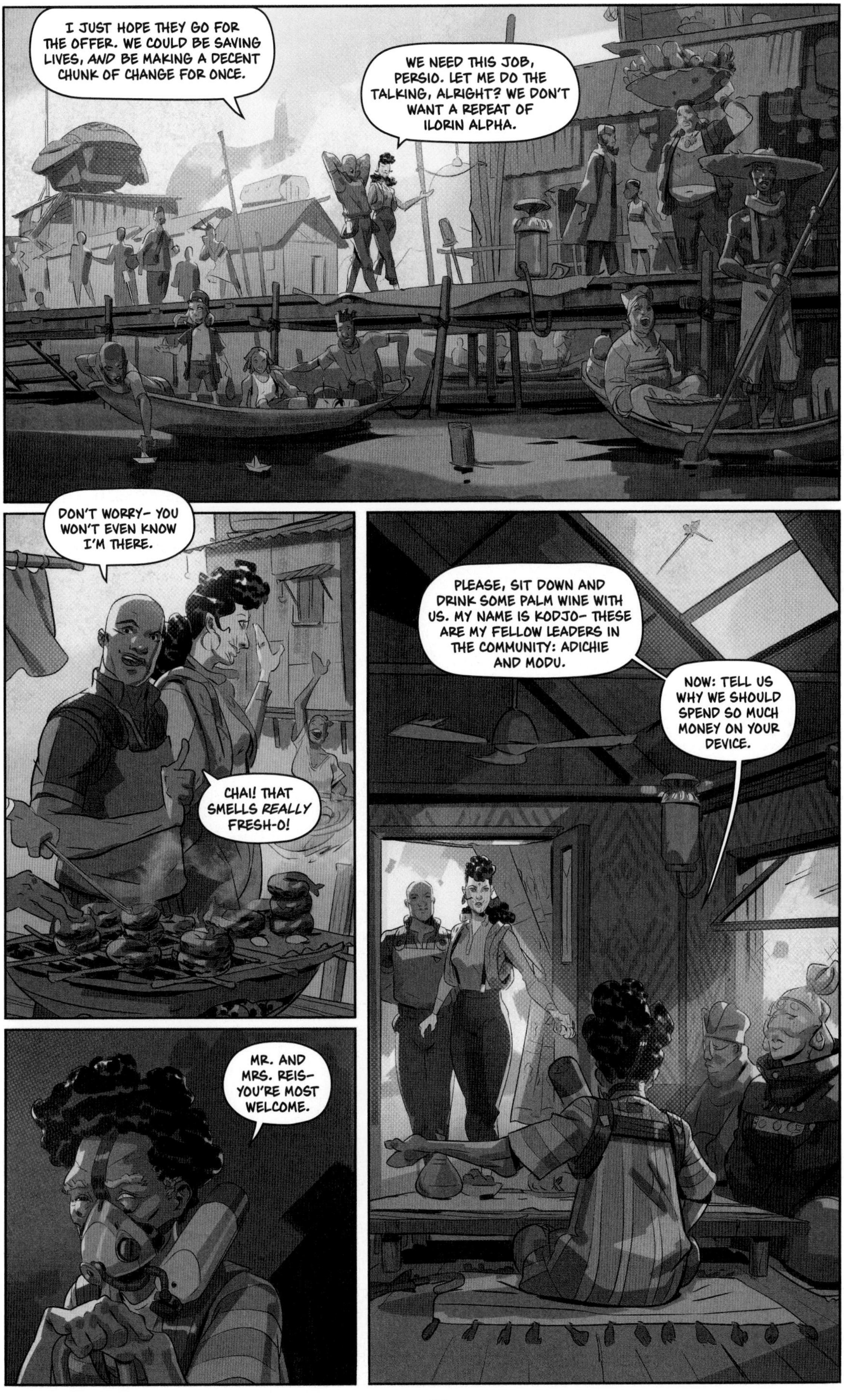
I JUST HOPE THEY GO FOR THE OFFER. WE COULD BE SAVING LIVES, *AND* BE MAKING A DECENT CHUNK OF CHANGE FOR ONCE.
WE NEED THIS JOB, PERSIO. LET ME DO THE TALKING, ALRIGHT? WE DON'T WANT A REPEAT OF ILORIN ALPHA.
DON'T WORRY- YOU WON'T EVEN KNOW I'M THERE.
CHAI! THAT SMELLS *REALLY* FRESH-O!
MR. AND MRS. REIS- YOU'RE MOST WELCOME.
PLEASE, SIT DOWN AND DRINK SOME PALM WINE WITH US. MY NAME IS KODJO- THESE ARE MY FELLOW LEADERS IN THE COMMUNITY: ADICHIE AND MODU.
NOW: TELL US WHY WE SHOULD SPEND SO MUCH MONEY ON YOUR DEVICE.

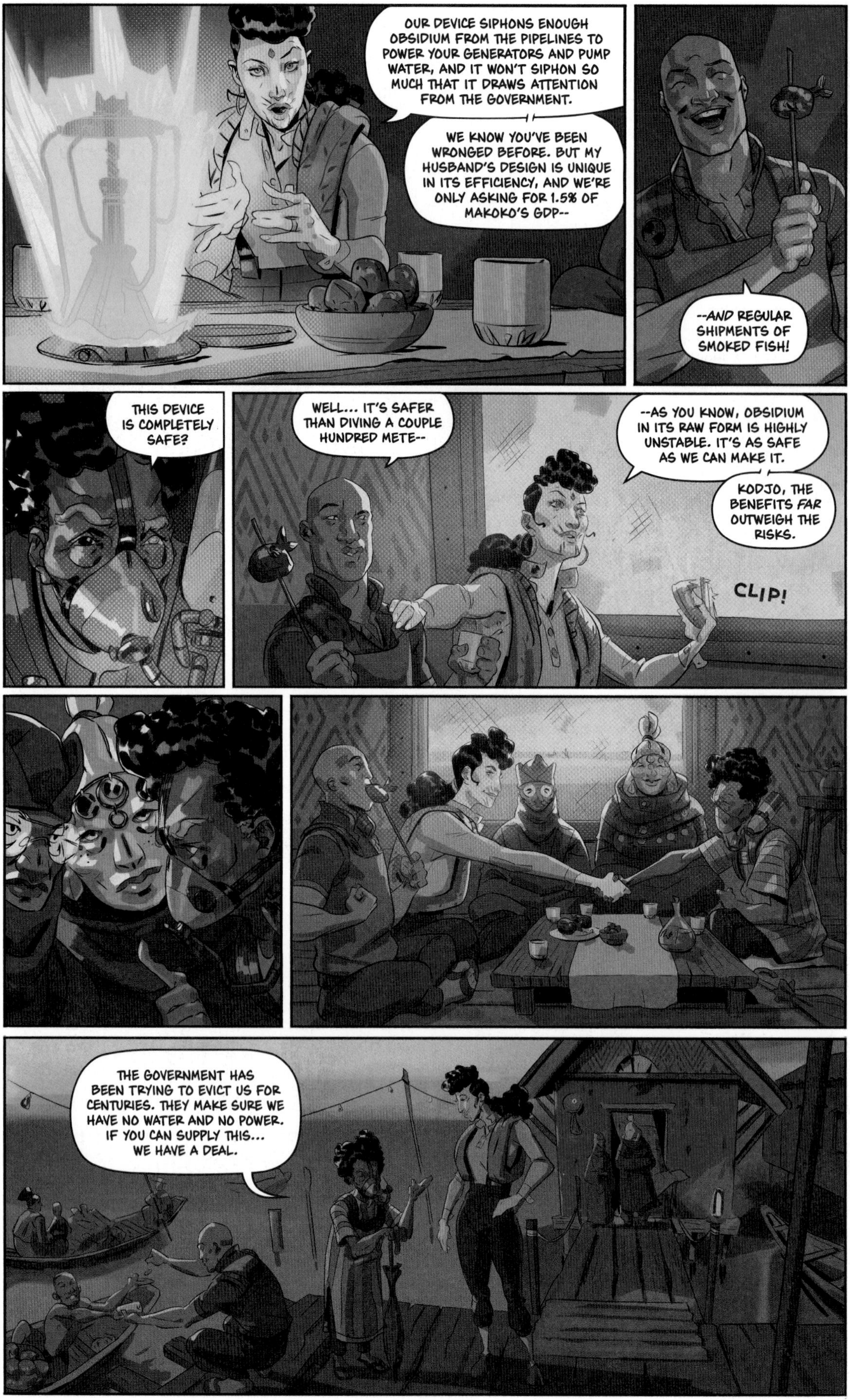
OUR DEVICE SIPHONS ENOUGH OBSIDIUM FROM THE PIPELINES TO POWER YOUR GENERATORS AND PUMP WATER, AND IT WON'T SIPHON SO MUCH THAT IT DRAWS ATTENTION FROM THE GOVERNMENT.
WE KNOW YOU'VE BEEN WRONGED BEFORE. BUT MY HUSBAND'S DESIGN IS UNIQUE IN ITS EFFICIENCY, AND WE'RE ONLY ASKING FOR 1.5% OF MAKOKO'S GDP--
--AND REGULAR SHIPMENTS OF SMOKED FISH!
THIS DEVICE IS COMPLETELY SAFE?
WELL... IT'S SAFER THAN DIVING A COUPLE HUNDRED METE--
--AS YOU KNOW, OBSIDIUM IN ITS RAW FORM IS HIGHLY UNSTABLE. IT'S AS SAFE AS WE CAN MAKE IT.
KODJO, THE BENEFITS FAR OUTWEIGH THE RISKS.
CLIP!
THE GOVERNMENT HAS BEEN TRYING TO EVICT US FOR CENTURIES. THEY MAKE SURE WE HAVE NO WATER AND NO POWER. IF YOU CAN SUPPLY THIS... WE HAVE A DEAL.

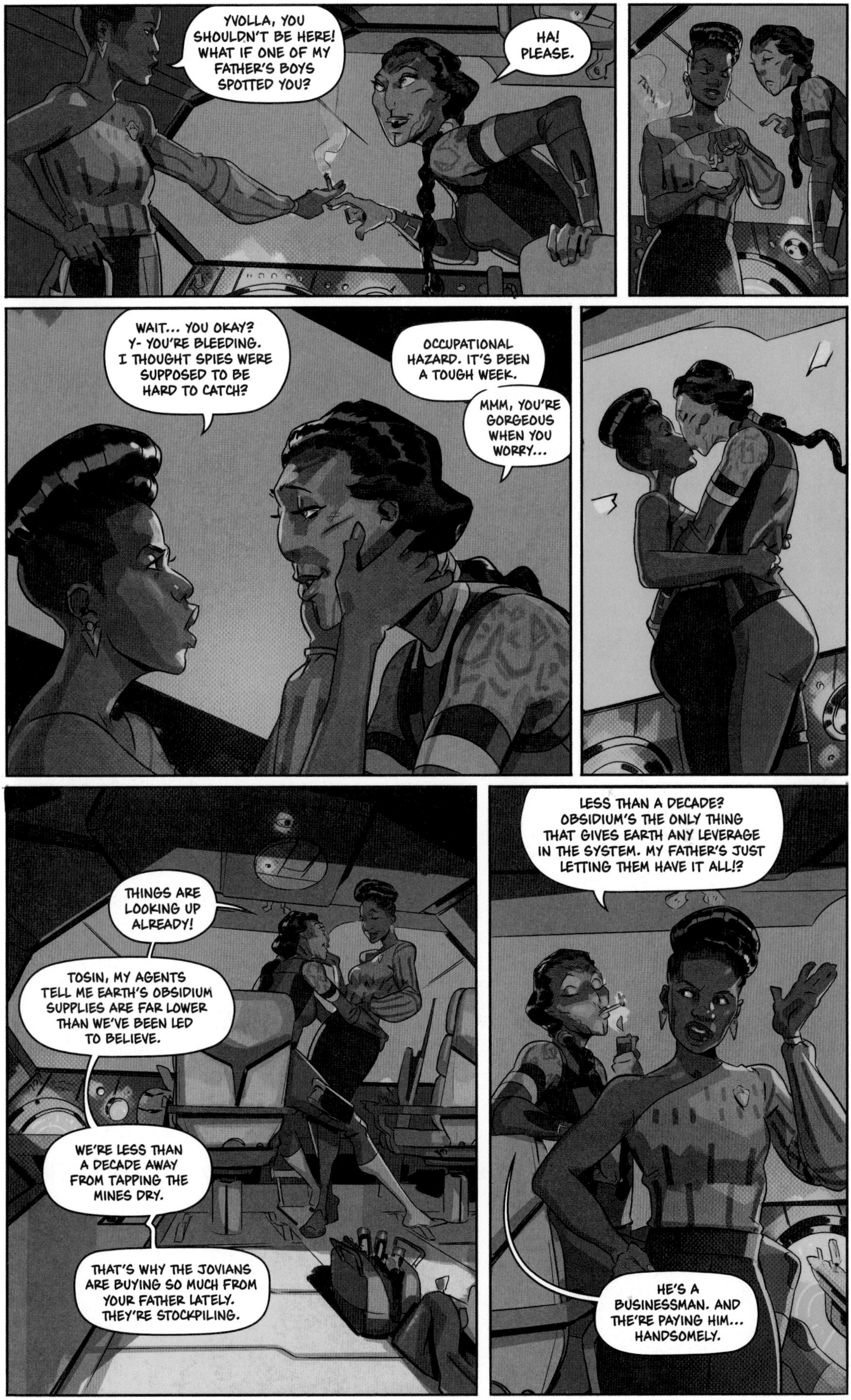
YVOLLA, YOU SHOULDN'T BE HERE! WHAT IF ONE OF MY FATHER'S BOYS SPOTTED YOU?
HA! PLEASE.
WAIT... YOU OKAY? Y- YOU'RE BLEEDING. I THOUGHT SPIES WERE SUPPOSED TO BE HARD TO CATCH?
OCCUPATIONAL HAZARD. IT'S BEEN A TOUGH WEEK.
MMM, YOU'RE GORGEOUS WHEN YOU WORRY...
THINGS ARE LOOKING UP ALREADY!
TOSIN, MY AGENTS TELL ME EARTH'S OBSIDIUM SUPPLIES ARE FAR LOWER THAN WE'VE BEEN LED TO BELIEVE.
WE'RE LESS THAN A DECADE AWAY FROM TAPPING THE MINES DRY.
THAT'S WHY THE JOVIANS ARE BUYING SO MUCH FROM YOUR FATHER LATELY. THEY'RE STOCKPILING.
LESS THAN A DECADE? OBSIDIUM'S THE ONLY THING THAT GIVES EARTH ANY LEVERAGE IN THE SYSTEM. MY FATHER'S JUST LETTING THEM HAVE IT ALL!?
HE'S A BUSINESSMAN. AND THE'RE PAYING HIM... HANDSOMELY.

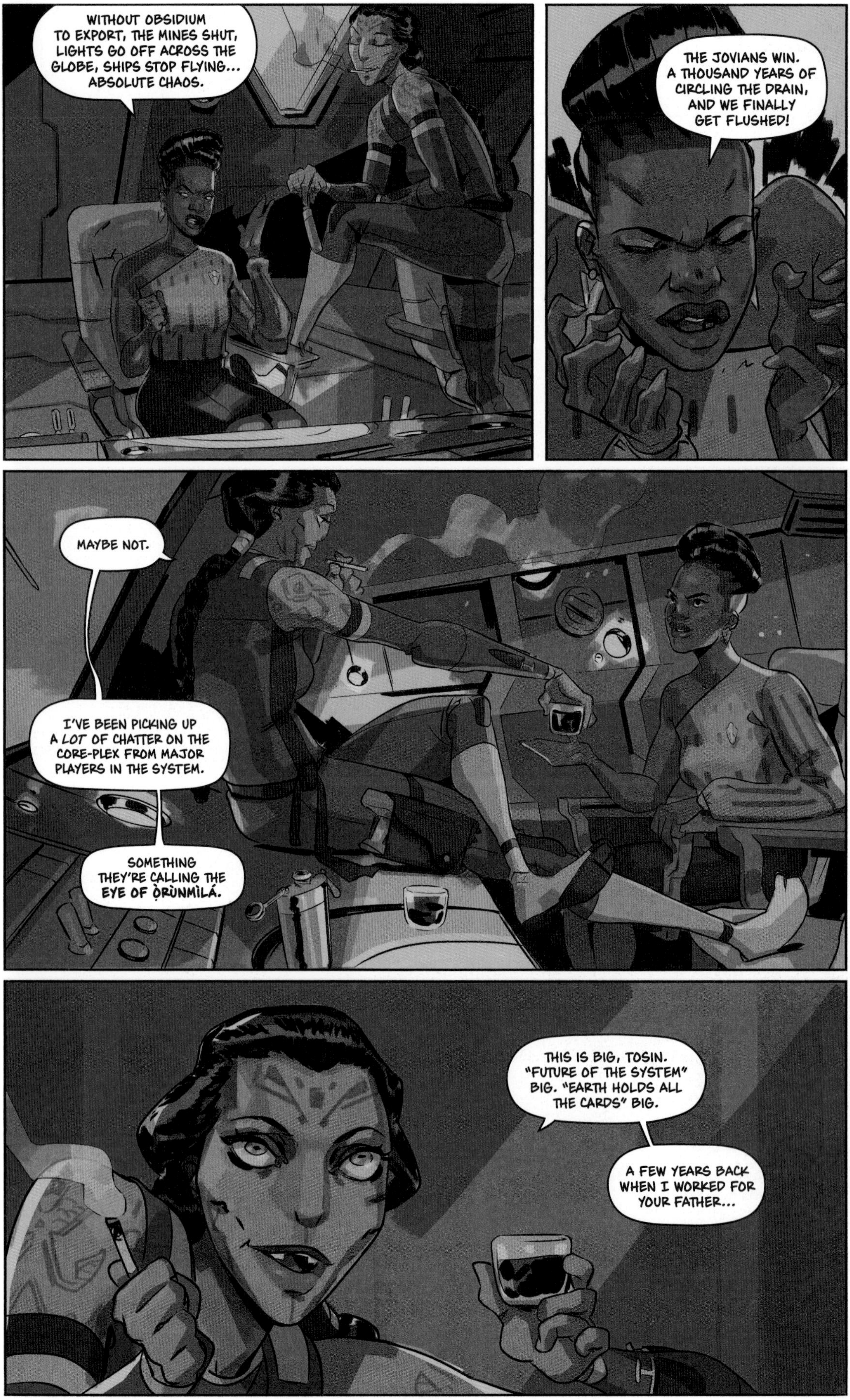
WITHOUT OBSIDIUM TO EXPORT, THE MINES SHUT, LIGHTS GO OFF ACROSS THE GLOBE, SHIPS STOP FLYING... ABSOLUTE CHAOS.
THE JOVIANS WIN. A THOUSAND YEARS OF CIRCLING THE DRAIN, AND WE FINALLY GET FLUSHED!
MAYBE NOT.
I'VE BEEN PICKING UP A *LOT* OF CHATTER ON THE CORE-PLEX FROM MAJOR PLAYERS IN THE SYSTEM.
SOMETHING THEY'RE CALLING THE **EYE OF ỌRÙNMÌLÁ.**
THIS IS BIG, TOSIN. "FUTURE OF THE SYSTEM" BIG. "EARTH HOLDS ALL THE CARDS" BIG.
A FEW YEARS BACK WHEN I WORKED FOR YOUR FATHER...

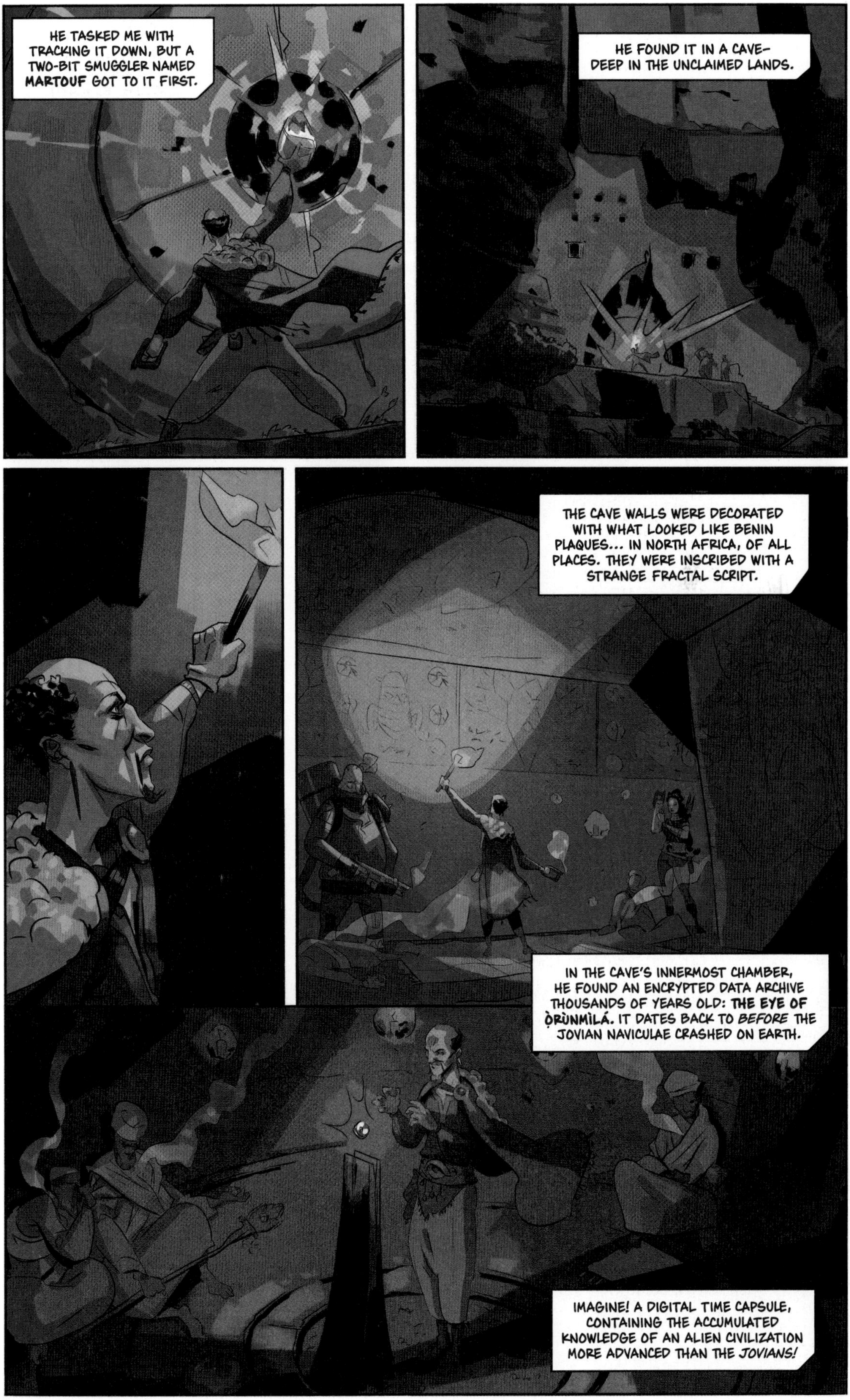
HE TASKED ME WITH TRACKING IT DOWN, BUT A TWO-BIT SMUGGLER NAMED **MARTOUF** GOT TO IT FIRST.
HE FOUND IT IN A CAVE-DEEP IN THE UNCLAIMED LANDS.
THE CAVE WALLS WERE DECORATED WITH WHAT LOOKED LIKE BENIN PLAQUES... IN NORTH AFRICA, OF ALL PLACES. THEY WERE INSCRIBED WITH A STRANGE FRACTAL SCRIPT.
IN THE CAVE'S INNERMOST CHAMBER, HE FOUND AN ENCRYPTED DATA ARCHIVE THOUSANDS OF YEARS OLD: **THE EYE OF ỌRÙNMÌLÁ**. IT DATES BACK TO *BEFORE* THE JOVIAN NAVICULAE CRASHED ON EARTH.
IMAGINE! A DIGITAL TIME CAPSULE, CONTAINING THE ACCUMULATED KNOWLEDGE OF AN ALIEN CIVILIZATION MORE ADVANCED THAN THE *JOVIANS!*

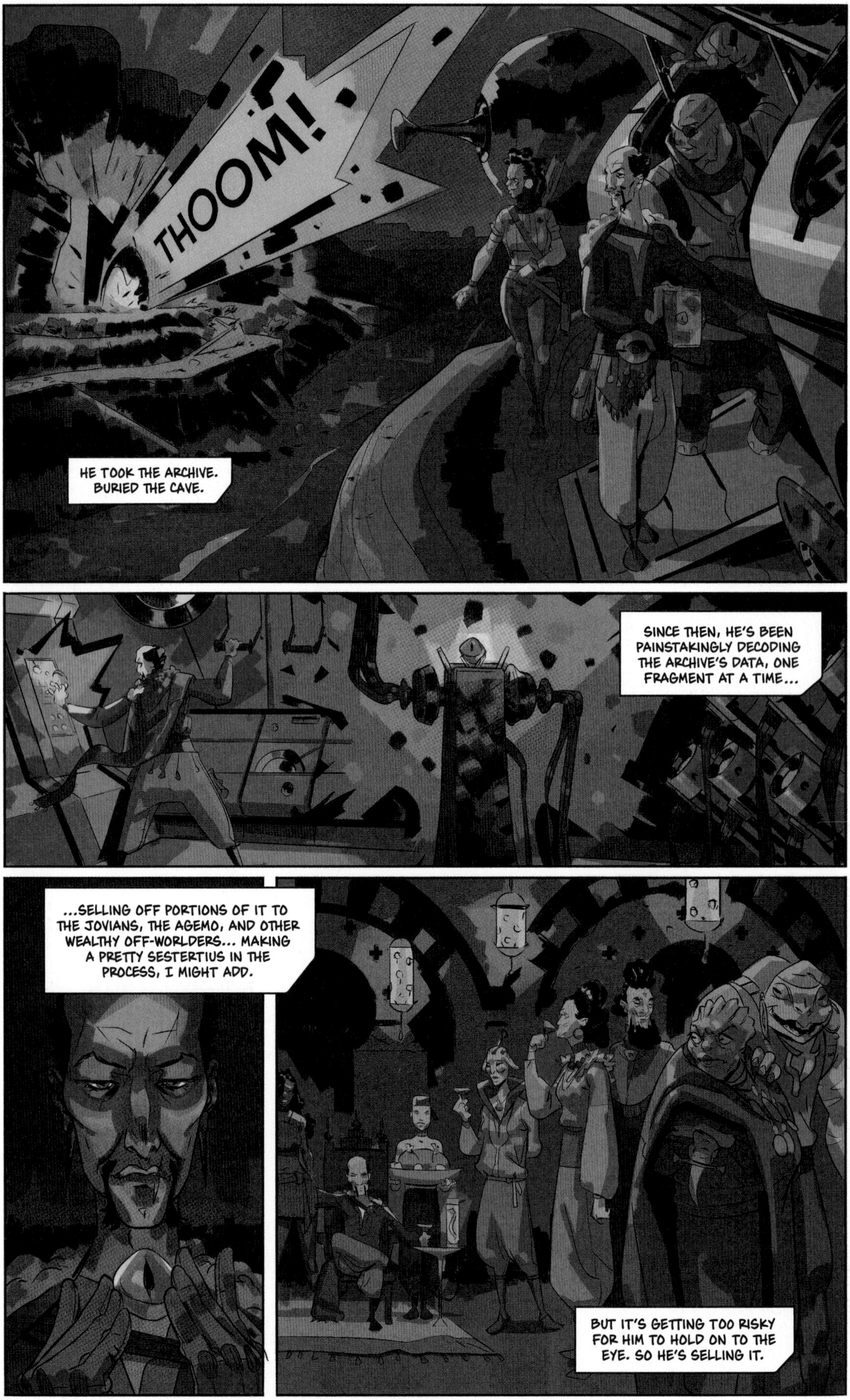
THOOM!
HE TOOK THE ARCHIVE. BURIED THE CAVE.
SINCE THEN, HE'S BEEN PAINSTAKINGLY DECODING THE ARCHIVE'S DATA, ONE FRAGMENT AT A TIME...
...SELLING OFF PORTIONS OF IT TO THE JOVIANS, THE AGEMO, AND OTHER WEALTHY OFF-WORLDERS... MAKING A PRETTY SESTERTIUS IN THE PROCESS, I MIGHT ADD.
BUT IT'S GETTING TOO RISKY FOR HIM TO HOLD ON TO THE EYE. SO HE'S SELLING IT.

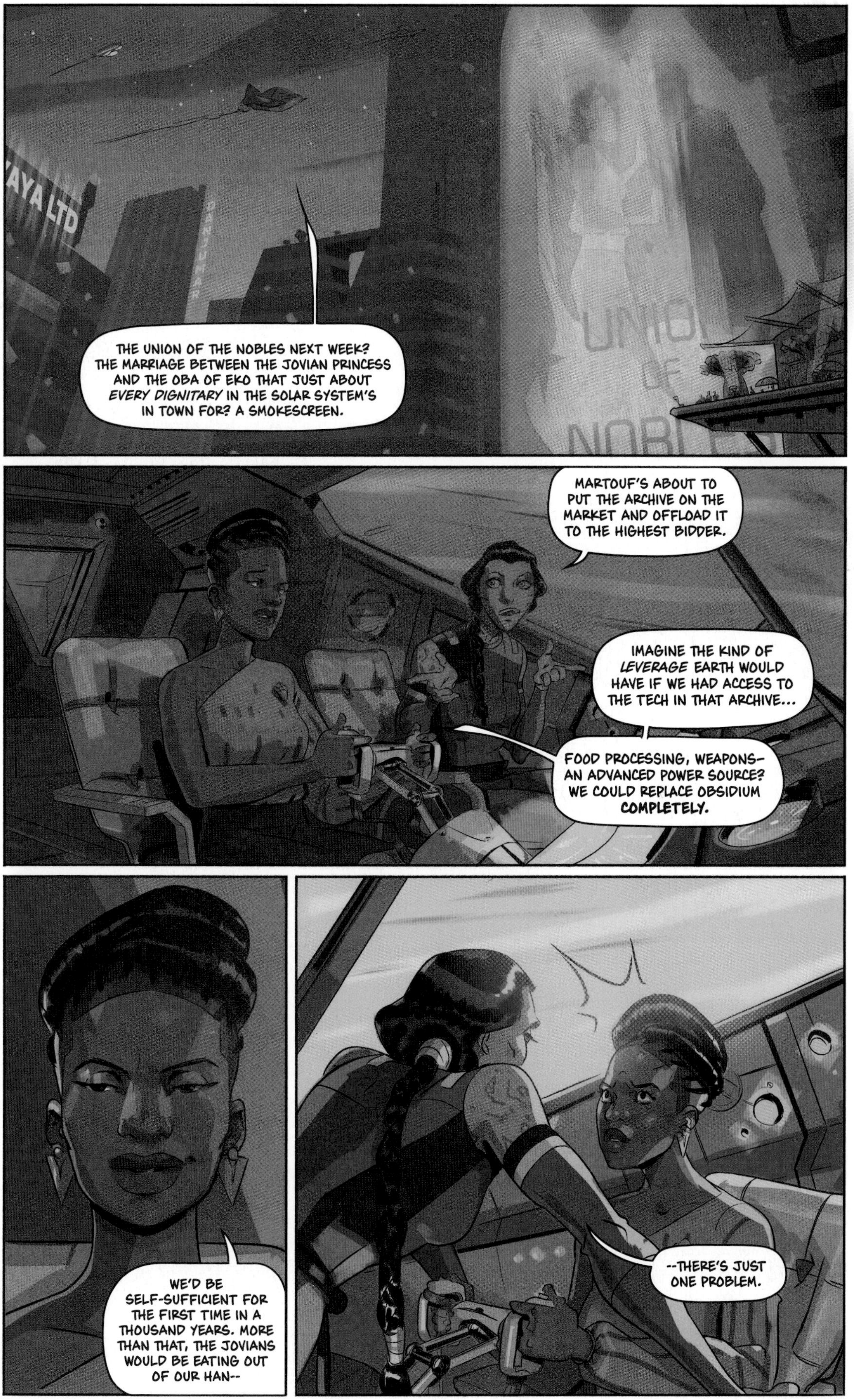
THE UNION OF THE NOBLES NEXT WEEK? THE MARRIAGE BETWEEN THE JOVIAN PRINCESS AND THE OBA OF EKO THAT JUST ABOUT *EVERY DIGNITARY* IN THE SOLAR SYSTEM'S IN TOWN FOR? A SMOKESCREEN.
MARTOUF'S ABOUT TO PUT THE ARCHIVE ON THE MARKET AND OFFLOAD IT TO THE HIGHEST BIDDER.
IMAGINE THE KIND OF *LEVERAGE* EARTH WOULD HAVE IF WE HAD ACCESS TO THE TECH IN THAT ARCHIVE...
FOOD PROCESSING, WEAPONS-AN ADVANCED POWER SOURCE? WE COULD REPLACE OBSIDIUM **COMPLETELY.**
WE'D BE SELF-SUFFICIENT FOR THE FIRST TIME IN A THOUSAND YEARS. MORE THAN THAT, THE JOVIANS WOULD BE EATING OUT OF OUR HAN--
--THERE'S JUST ONE PROBLEM.

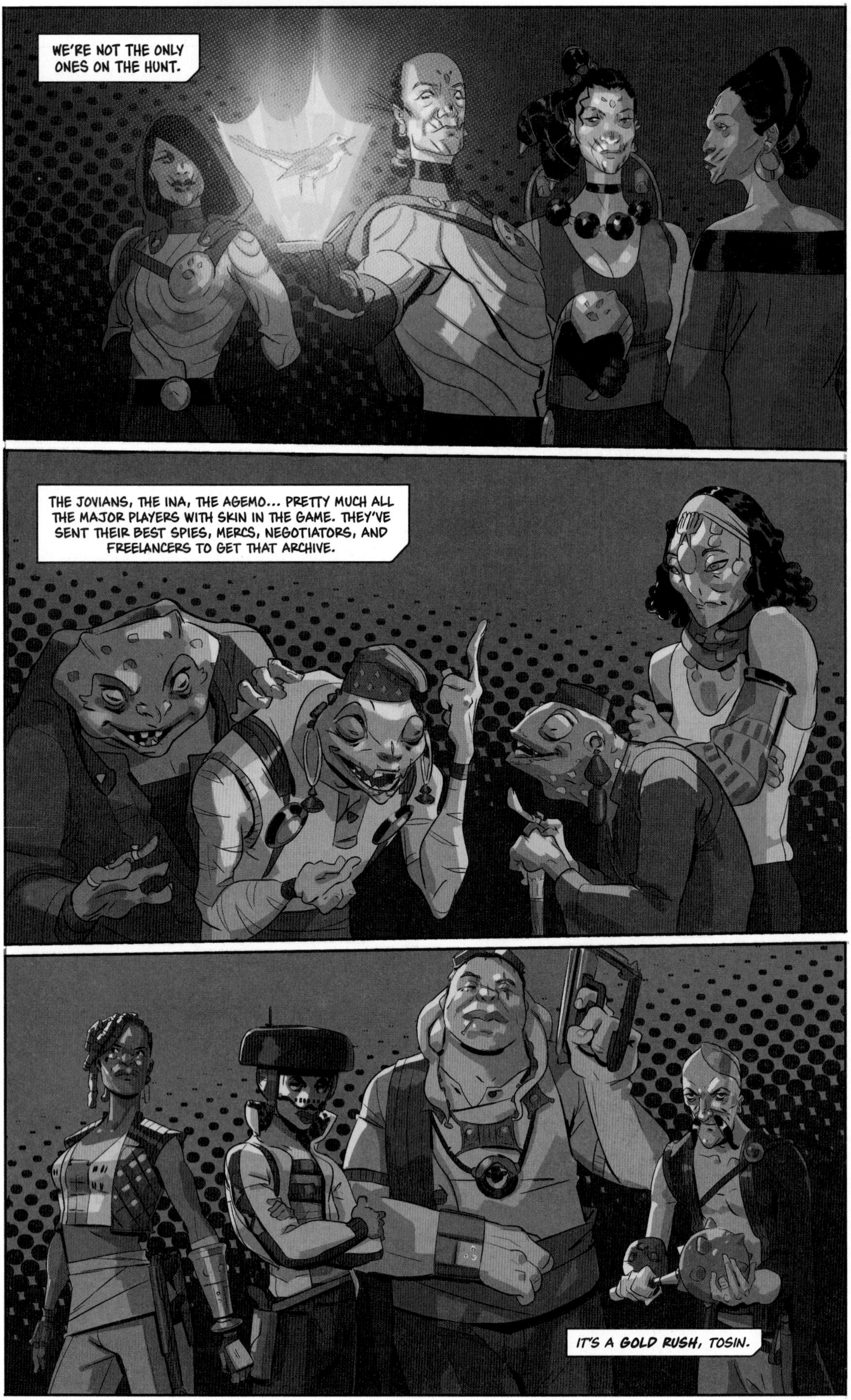
WE'RE NOT THE ONLY ONES ON THE HUNT.
THE JOVIANS, THE INA, THE AGEMO... PRETTY MUCH ALL THE MAJOR PLAYERS WITH SKIN IN THE GAME. THEY'VE SENT THEIR BEST SPIES, MERCS, NEGOTIATORS, AND FREELANCERS TO GET THAT ARCHIVE.
IT'S A GOLD RUSH, TOSIN.

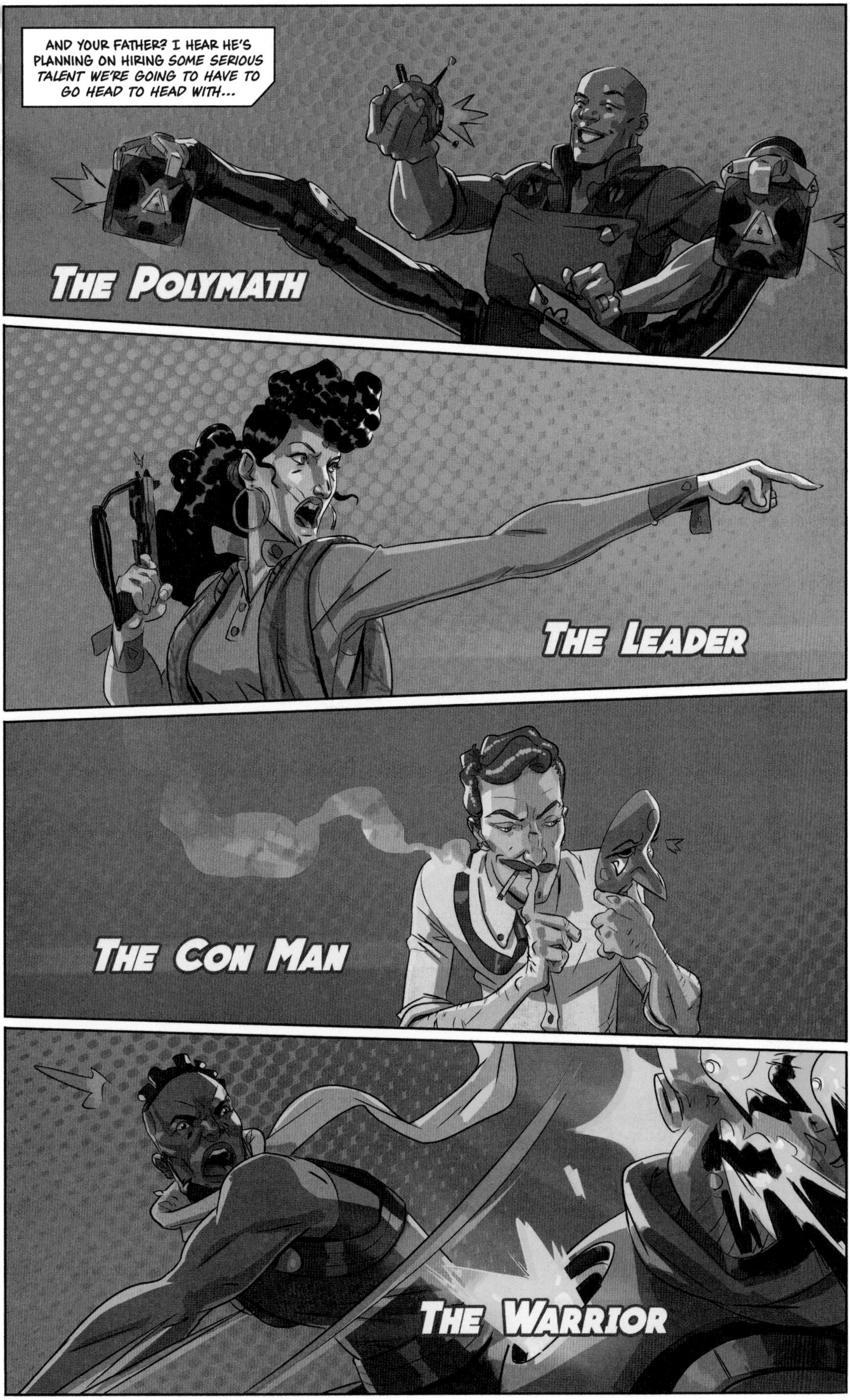
AND YOUR FATHER? I HEAR HE'S PLANNING ON HIRING SOME SERIOUS TALENT WE'RE GOING TO HAVE TO GO HEAD TO HEAD WITH...
THE POLYMATH
THE LEADER
THE CON MAN
THE WARRIOR

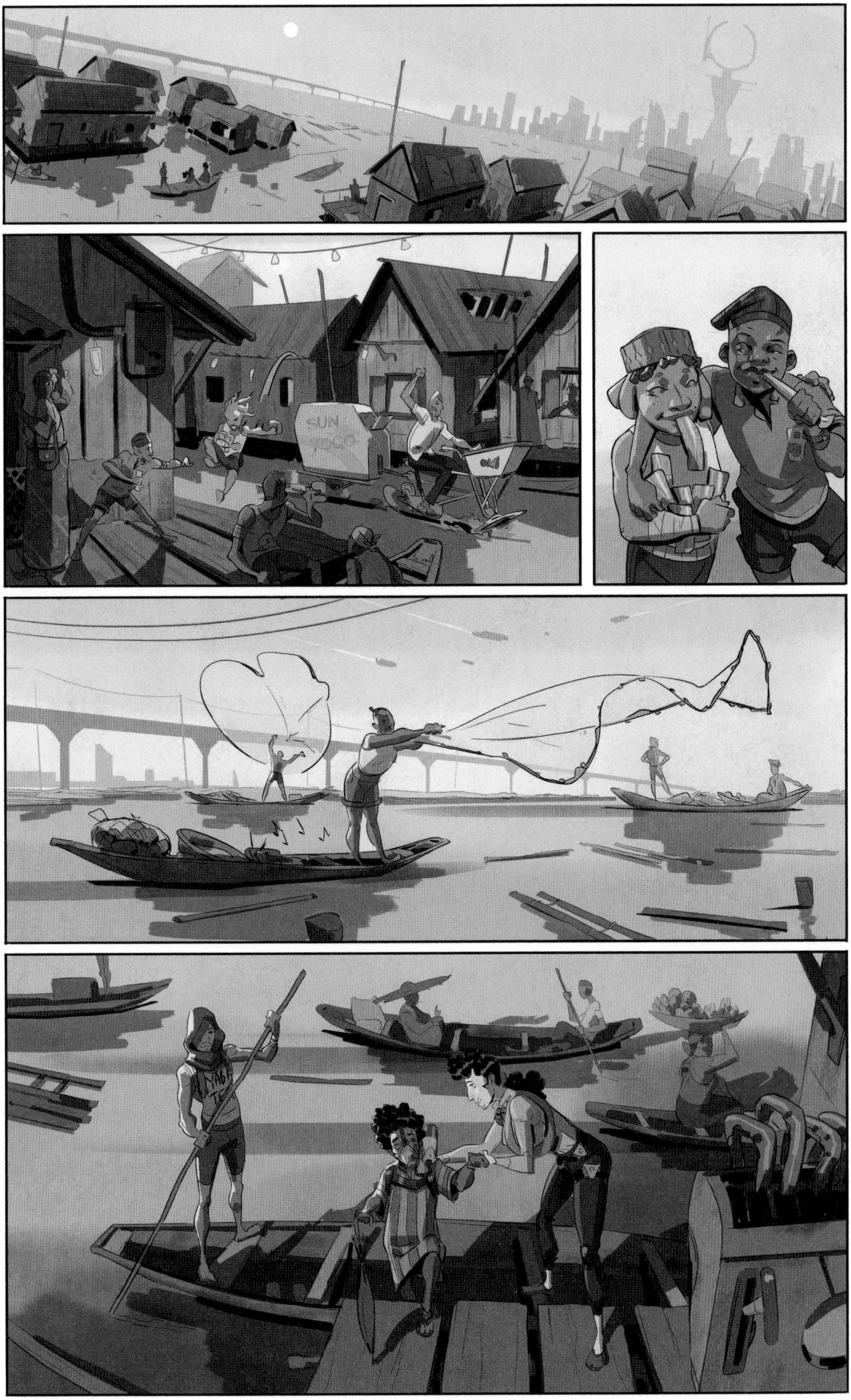
SUN
YOGO

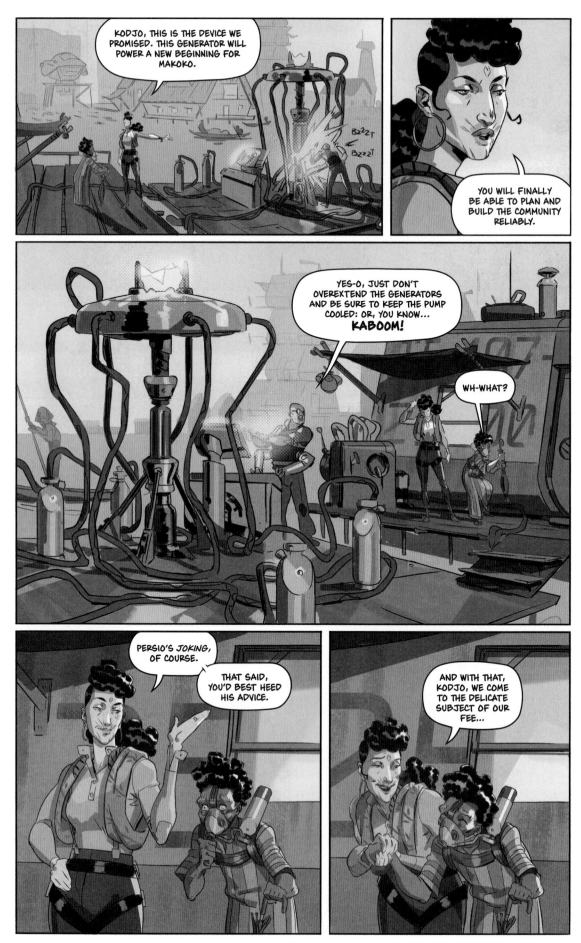

KODJO, THIS IS THE DEVICE WE PROMISED. THIS GENERATOR WILL POWER A NEW BEGINNING FOR MAKOKO.

BZZZT
BZZZT

YOU WILL FINALLY BE ABLE TO PLAN AND BUILD THE COMMUNITY RELIABLY.

YES-O, JUST DON'T OVEREXTEND THE GENERATORS AND BE SURE TO KEEP THE PUMP COOLED; OR, YOU KNOW... KABOOM!

WH-WHAT?

PERSIO'S JOKING, OF COURSE.

THAT SAID, YOU'D BEST HEED HIS ADVICE.

AND WITH THAT, KODJO, WE COME TO THE DELICATE SUBJECT OF OUR FEE...

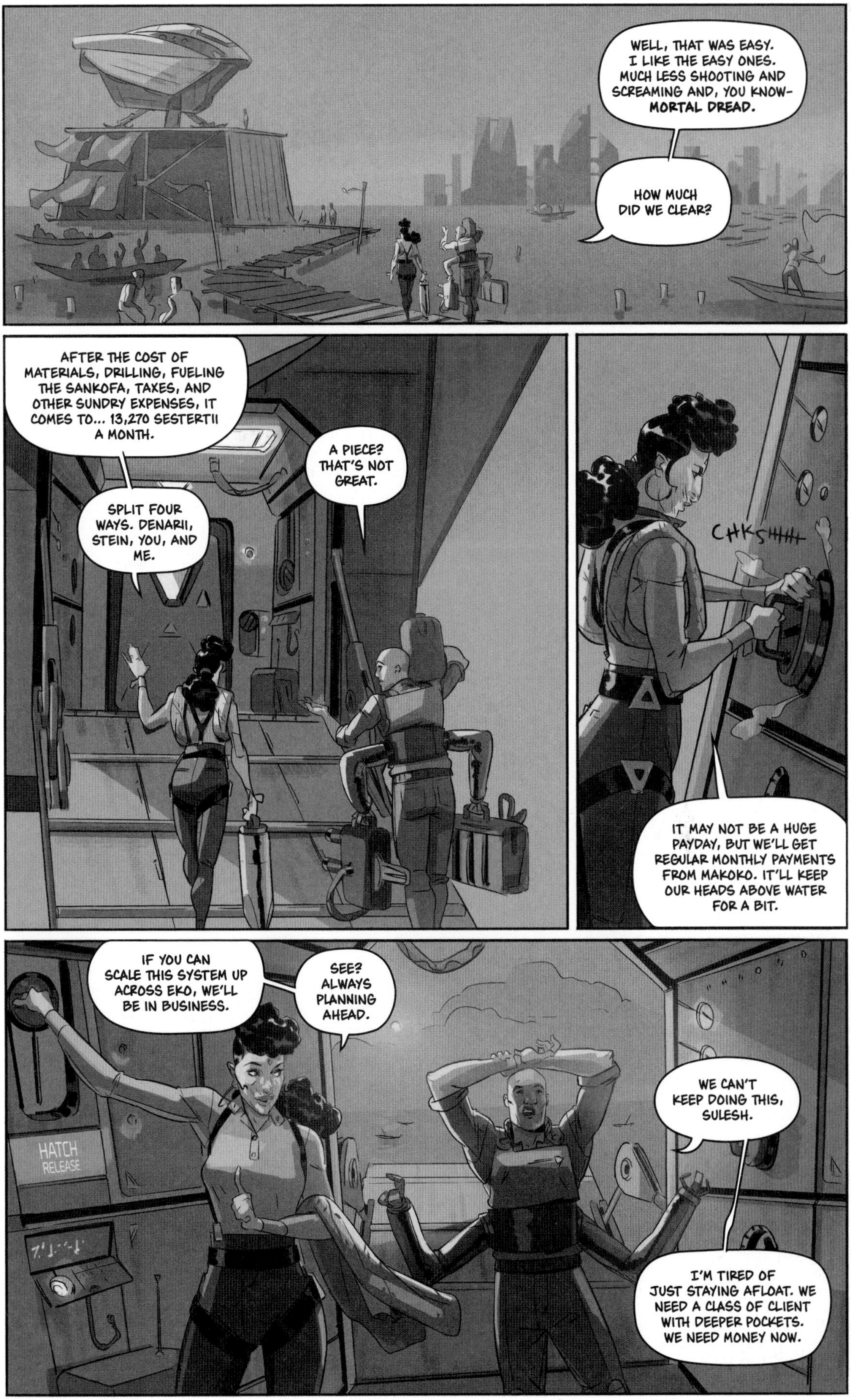
WELL, THAT WAS EASY. I LIKE THE EASY ONES. MUCH LESS SHOOTING AND SCREAMING AND, YOU KNOW- MORTAL DREAD.
HOW MUCH DID WE CLEAR?
AFTER THE COST OF MATERIALS, DRILLING, FUELING THE SANKOFA, TAXES, AND OTHER SUNDRY EXPENSES, IT COMES TO... 13,270 SESTERTII A MONTH.
SPLIT FOUR WAYS. DENARII, STEIN, YOU, AND ME.
A PIECE? THAT'S NOT GREAT.
CHKSHHHH
IT MAY NOT BE A HUGE PAYDAY, BUT WE'LL GET REGULAR MONTHLY PAYMENTS FROM MAKOKO. IT'LL KEEP OUR HEADS ABOVE WATER FOR A BIT.
IF YOU CAN SCALE THIS SYSTEM UP ACROSS EKO, WE'LL BE IN BUSINESS.
SEE? ALWAYS PLANNING AHEAD.
HATCH RELEASE
WE CAN'T KEEP DOING THIS, SULESH.
I'M TIRED OF JUST STAYING AFLOAT. WE NEED A CLASS OF CLIENT WITH DEEPER POCKETS. WE NEED MONEY NOW.

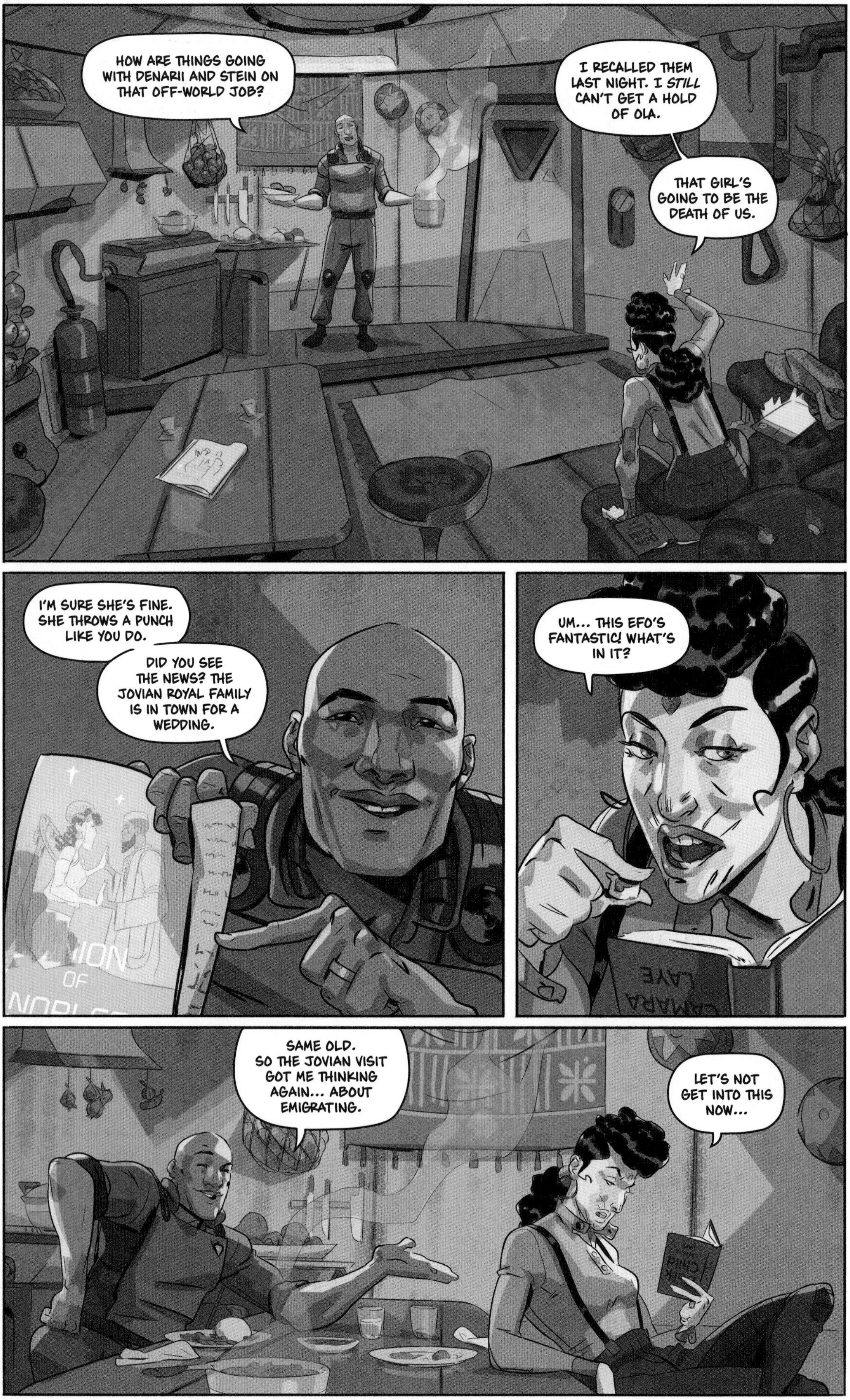
HOW ARE THINGS GOING WITH DENARII AND STEIN ON THAT OFF-WORLD JOB?
I RECALLED THEM LAST NIGHT. I *STILL* CAN'T GET A HOLD OF OLA.
THAT GIRL'S GOING TO BE THE DEATH OF US.
I'M SURE SHE'S FINE. SHE THROWS A PUNCH LIKE YOU DO.
DID YOU SEE THE NEWS? THE JOVIAN ROYAL FAMILY IS IN TOWN FOR A WEDDING.
UM... THIS EFO'S FANTASTIC! WHAT'S IN IT?
SAME OLD. SO THE JOVIAN VISIT GOT ME THINKING AGAIN... ABOUT EMIGRATING.
LET'S NOT GET INTO THIS NOW...

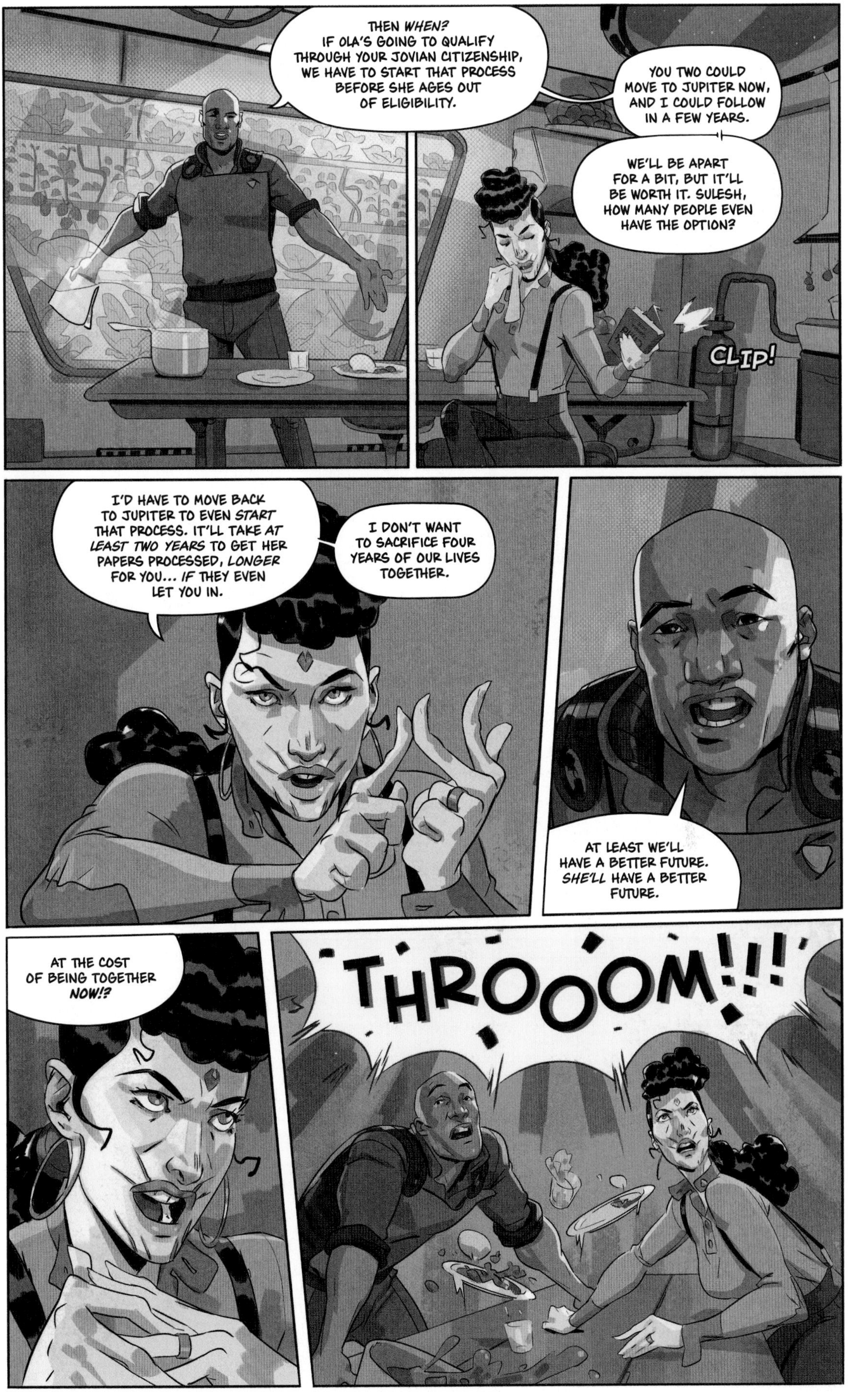
THEN *WHEN?* IF OLA'S GOING TO QUALIFY THROUGH YOUR JOVIAN CITIZENSHIP, WE HAVE TO START THAT PROCESS BEFORE SHE AGES OUT OF ELIGIBILITY.
YOU TWO COULD MOVE TO JUPITER NOW, AND I COULD FOLLOW IN A FEW YEARS.
WE'LL BE APART FOR A BIT, BUT IT'LL BE WORTH IT. SULESH, HOW MANY PEOPLE EVEN HAVE THE OPTION?
CLIP!
I'D HAVE TO MOVE BACK TO JUPITER TO EVEN *START* THAT PROCESS. IT'LL TAKE *AT LEAST TWO YEARS* TO GET HER PAPERS PROCESSED, *LONGER* FOR YOU... *IF* THEY EVEN LET YOU IN.
I DON'T WANT TO SACRIFICE FOUR YEARS OF OUR LIVES TOGETHER.
AT LEAST WE'LL HAVE A BETTER FUTURE. *SHE'LL* HAVE A BETTER FUTURE.
AT THE COST OF BEING TOGETHER *NOW!?*
THROOOM!!!

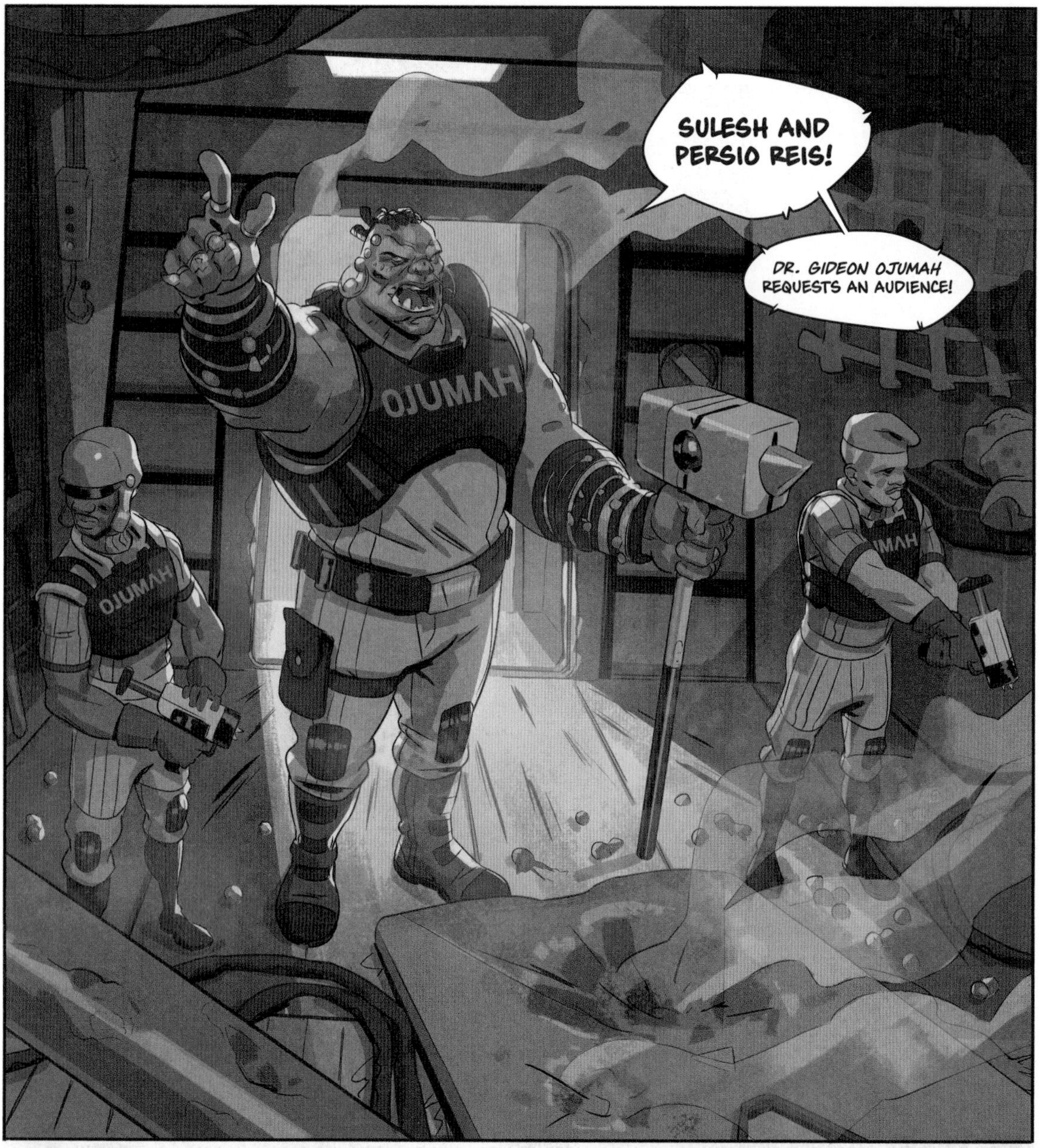
SULESH AND PERSIO REIS!
DR. GIDEON OJUMAH REQUESTS AN AUDIENCE!
OJUMAH

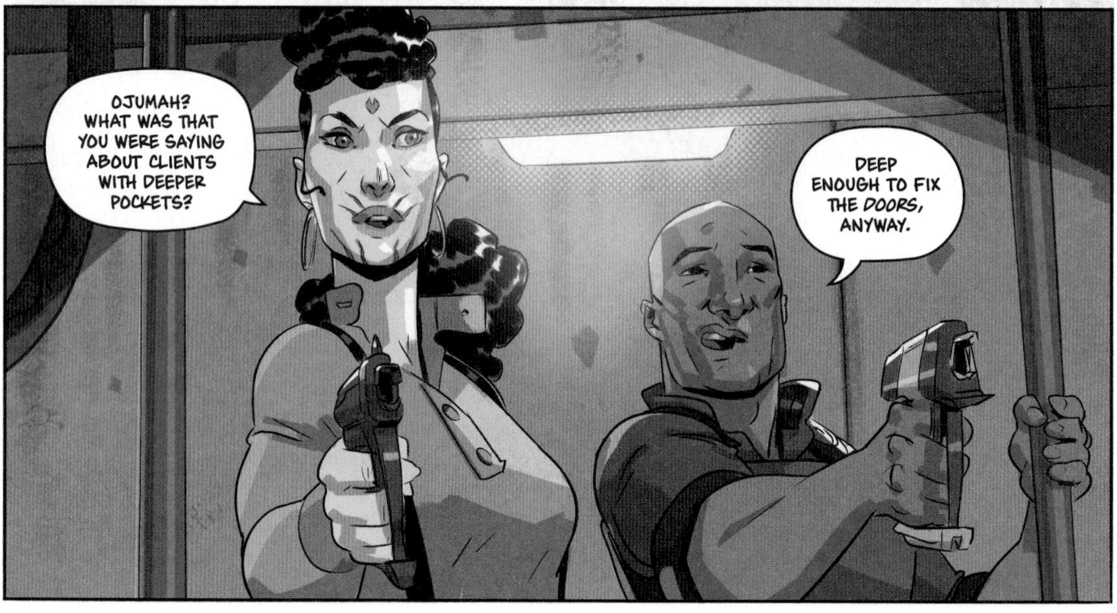
OJUMAH? WHAT WAS THAT YOU WERE SAYING ABOUT CLIENTS WITH DEEPER POCKETS?
DEEP ENOUGH TO FIX THE DOORS, ANYWAY.

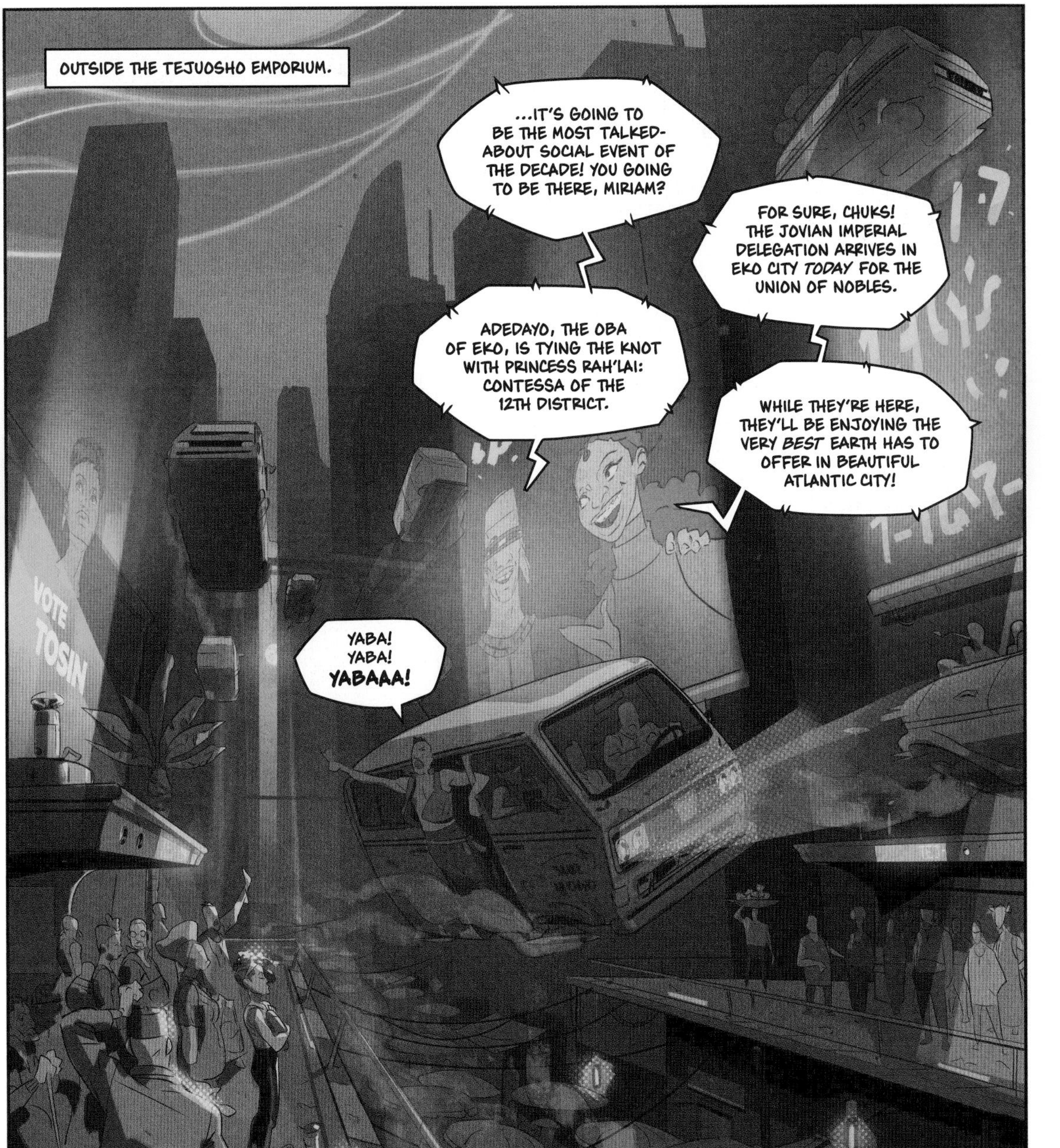
OUTSIDE THE TEJUOSHO EMPORIUM.
...IT'S GOING TO BE THE MOST TALKED-ABOUT SOCIAL EVENT OF THE DECADE! YOU GOING TO BE THERE, MIRIAM?
ADEDAYO, THE OBA OF EKO, IS TYING THE KNOT WITH PRINCESS RAH'LAI: CONTESSA OF THE 12TH DISTRICT.
FOR SURE, CHUKS! THE JOVIAN IMPERIAL DELEGATION ARRIVES IN EKO CITY *TODAY* FOR THE UNION OF NOBLES.
WHILE THEY'RE HERE, THEY'LL BE ENJOYING THE VERY *BEST* EARTH HAS TO OFFER IN BEAUTIFUL ATLANTIC CITY!
YABA! YABA! **YABAAA!**
VOTE TOSIN

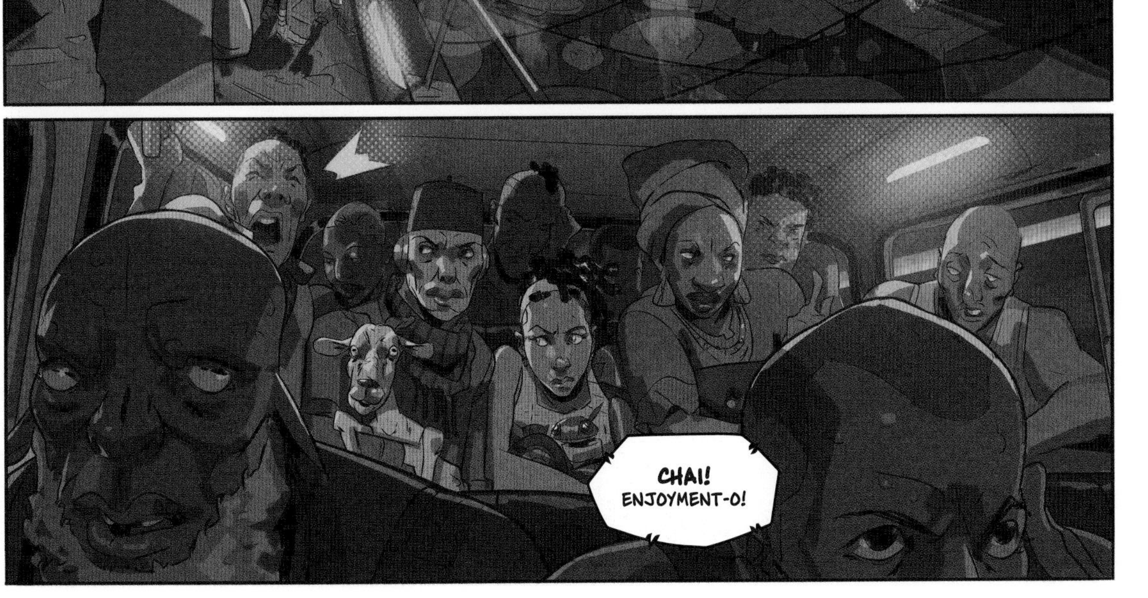
CHAI! ENJOYMENT-O!

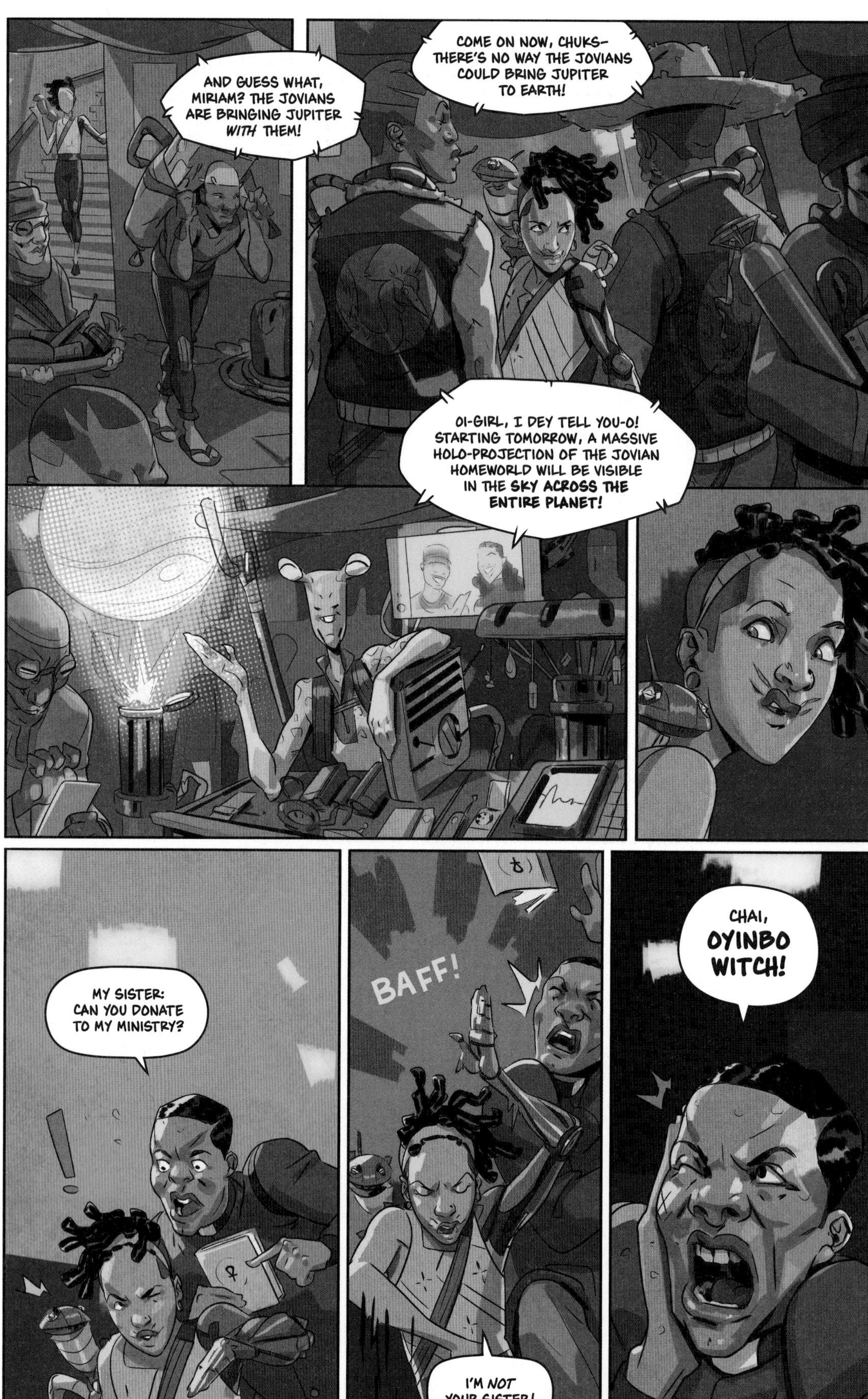
AND GUESS WHAT, MIRIAM? THE JOVIANS ARE BRINGING JUPITER *WITH* THEM!
COME ON NOW, CHUKS- THERE'S NO WAY THE JOVIANS COULD BRING JUPITER TO EARTH!
OI-GIRL, I DEY TELL YOU-O! STARTING TOMORROW, A MASSIVE HOLO-PROJECTION OF THE JOVIAN HOMEWORLD WILL BE VISIBLE IN THE **SKY ACROSS THE ENTIRE PLANET!**
MY SISTER: CAN YOU DONATE TO MY MINISTRY?
BAFF!
I'M *NOT* YOUR SISTER!
CHAI, **OYINBO WITCH!**

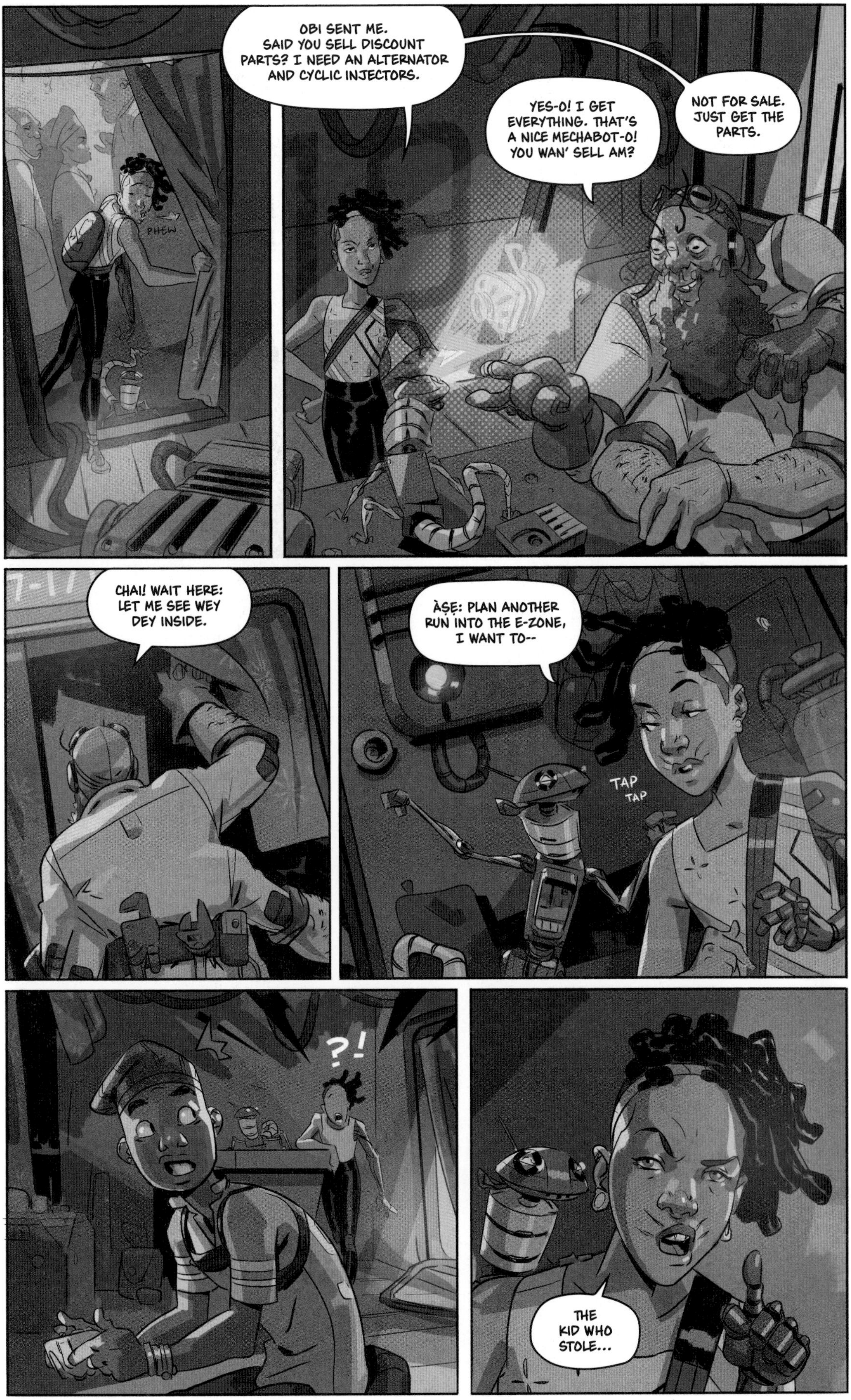
PHEW
OBI SENT ME. SAID YOU SELL DISCOUNT PARTS? I NEED AN ALTERNATOR AND CYCLIC INJECTORS.
YES-O! I GET EVERYTHING. THAT'S A NICE MECHABOT-O! YOU WAN' SELL AM?
NOT FOR SALE. JUST GET THE PARTS.
CHAI! WAIT HERE: LET ME SEE WEY DEY INSIDE.
ÀṢẸ: PLAN ANOTHER RUN INTO THE E-ZONE, I WANT TO--
TAP TAP
?!
THE KID WHO STOLE...

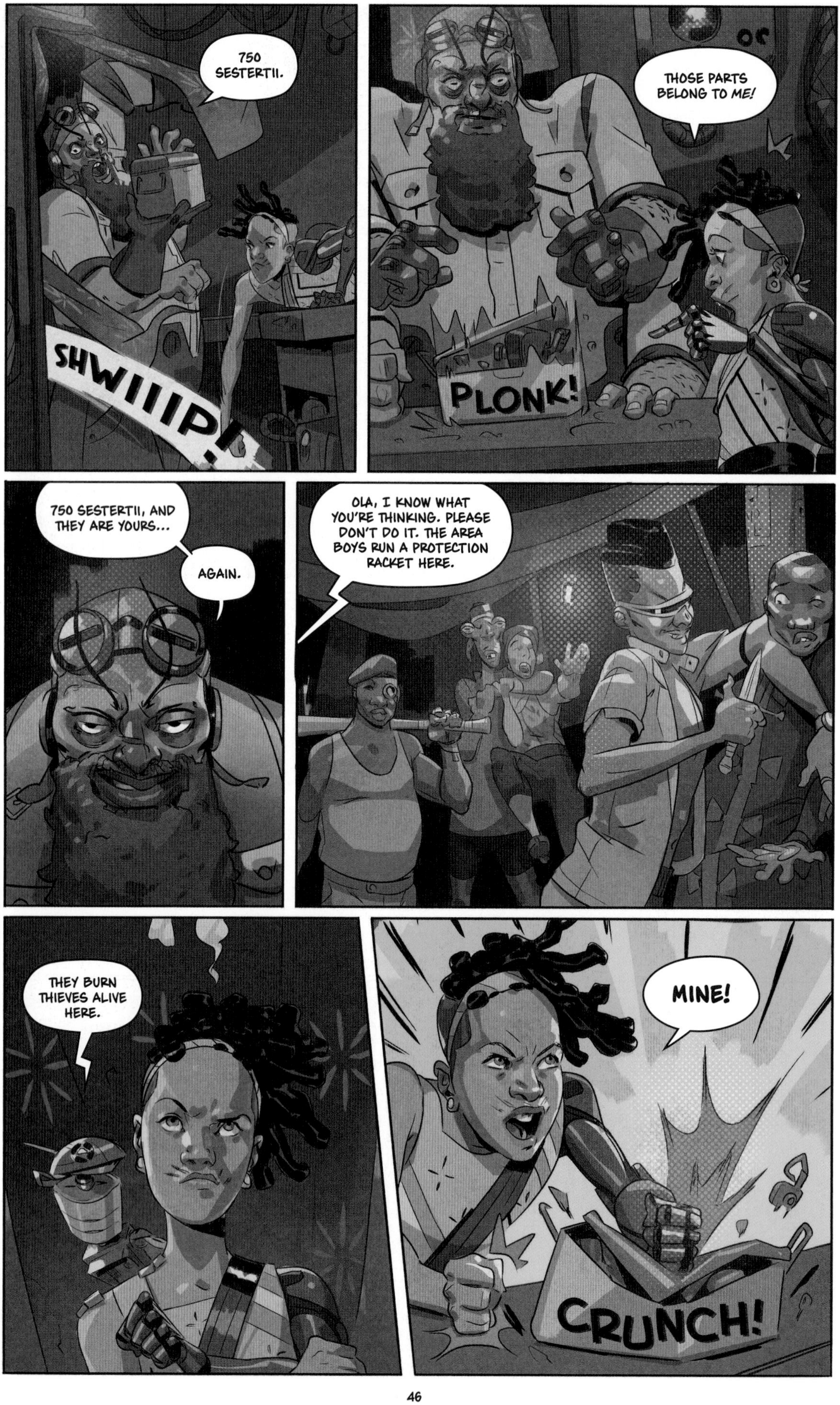
750 SESTERTII.
SHWIIIP!
THOSE PARTS BELONG TO ME!
PLONK!
750 SESTERTII, AND THEY ARE YOURS...
AGAIN.
OLA, I KNOW WHAT YOU'RE THINKING. PLEASE DON'T DO IT. THE AREA BOYS RUN A PROTECTION RACKET HERE.
THEY BURN THIEVES ALIVE HERE.
MINE!
CRUNCH!

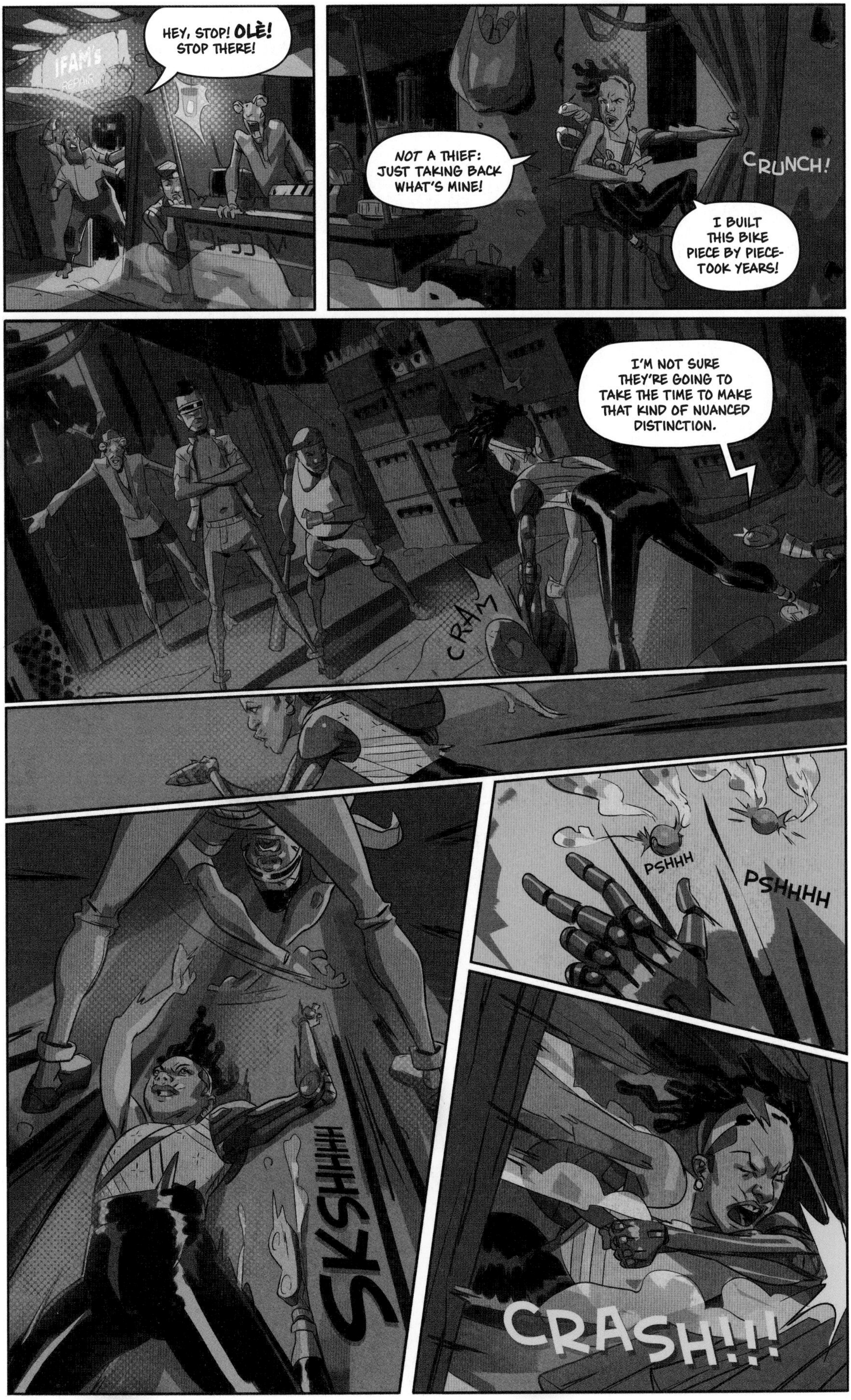
IFAM'S
REPAIR
HEY, STOP! OLÈ! STOP THERE!
NOT A THIEF: JUST TAKING BACK WHAT'S MINE!
CRUNCH!
I BUILT THIS BIKE PIECE BY PIECE- TOOK YEARS!
I'M NOT SURE THEY'RE GOING TO TAKE THE TIME TO MAKE THAT KIND OF NUANCED DISTINCTION.
CRAM
PSHHH
PSHHHH
SKSHHHHH
CRASH!!!

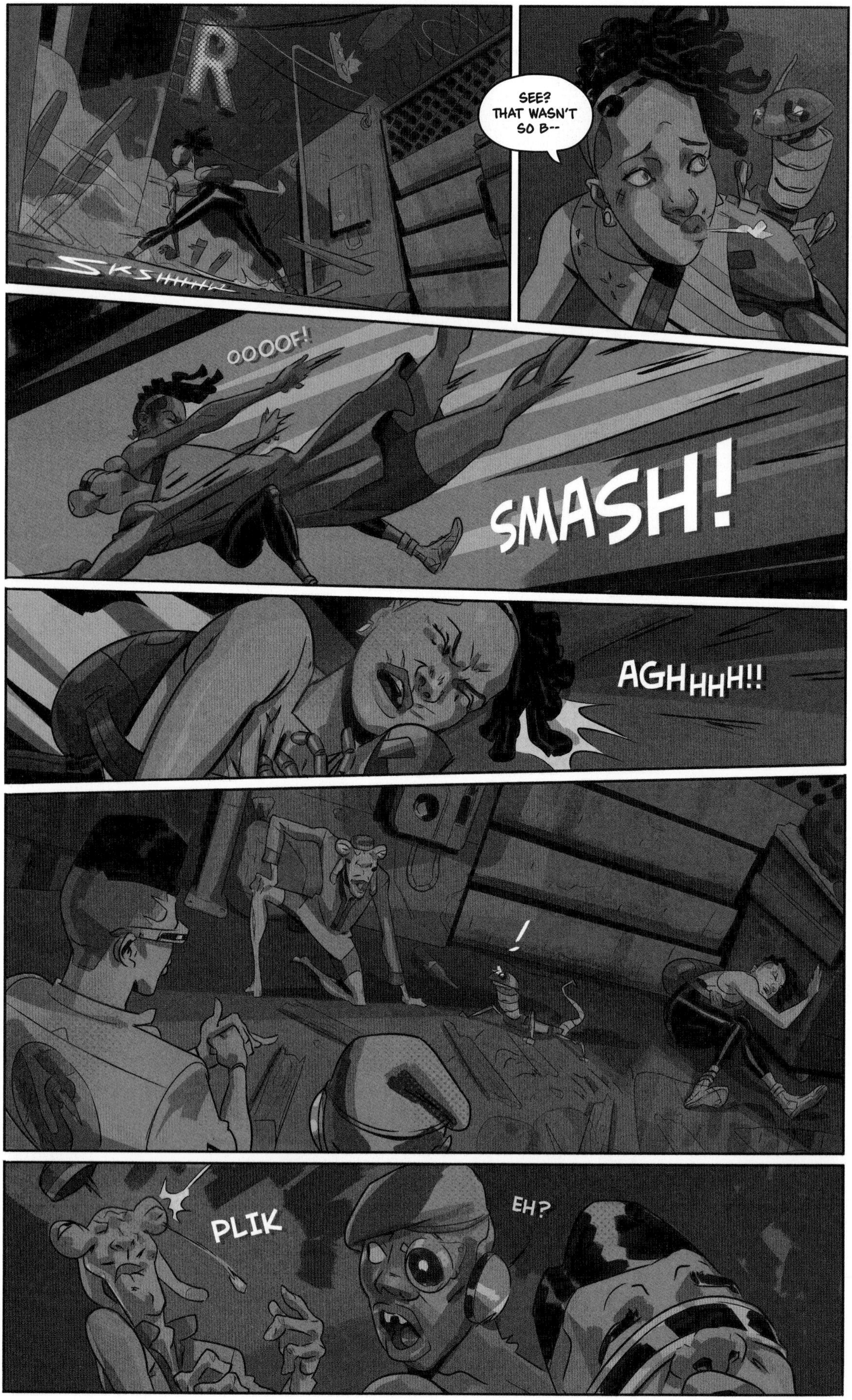
SKSHHHHH
SEE? THAT WASN'T SO B--
OOOOF!
SMASH!
AGHHHH!!
!
PLIK
EH?

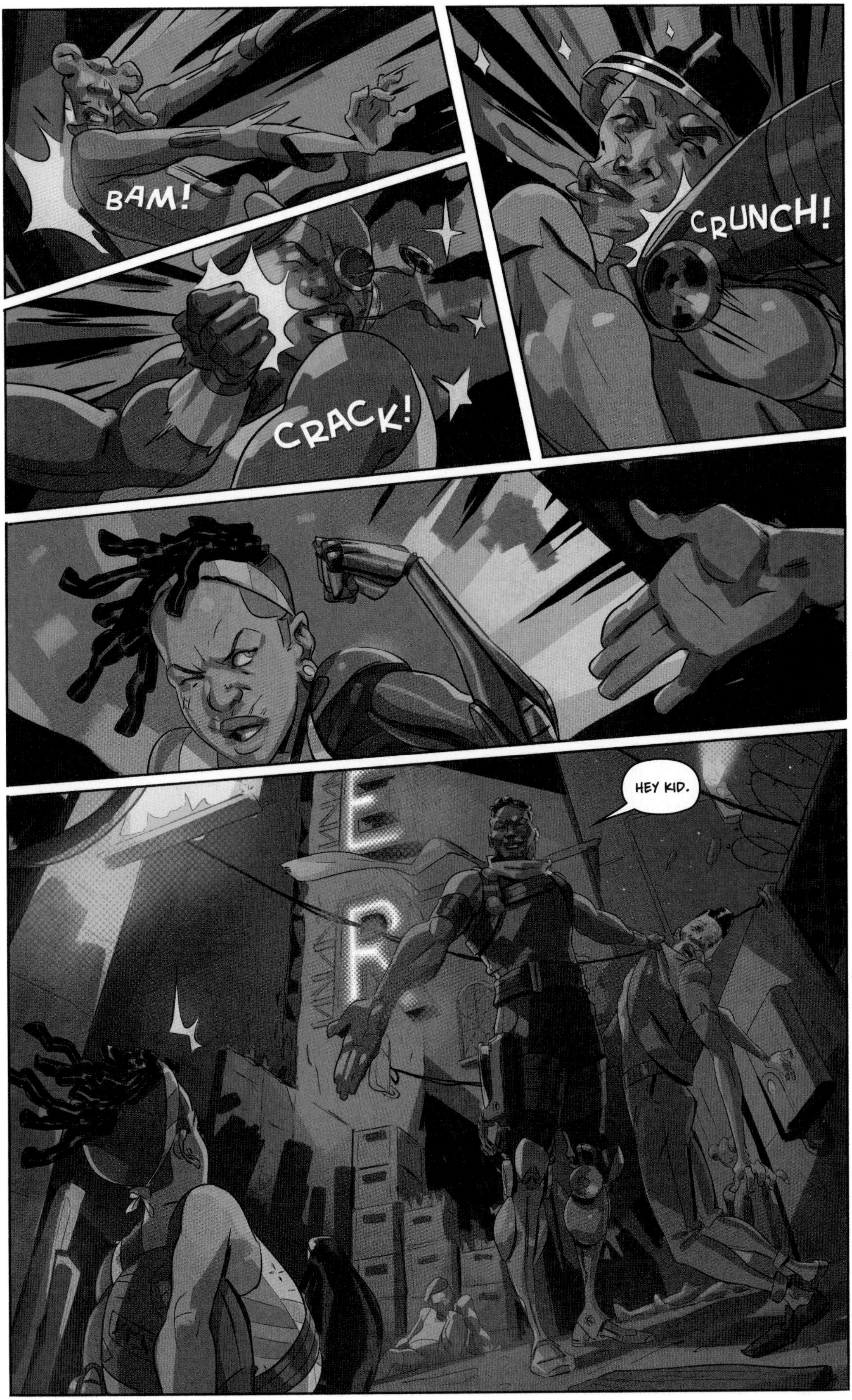
BAM!
CRACK!
CRUNCH!
HEY KID.

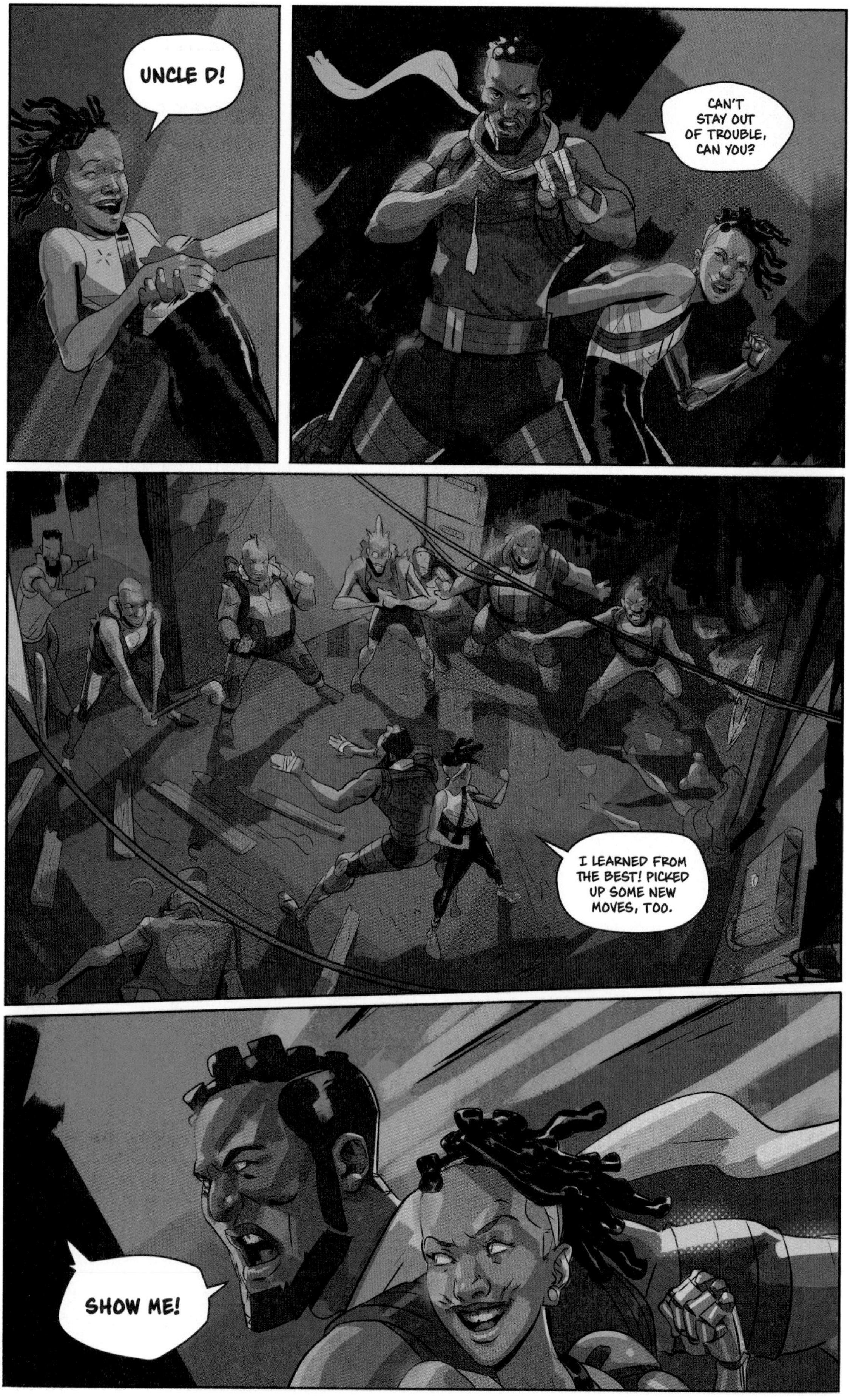
UNCLE D!
CAN'T STAY OUT OF TROUBLE, CAN YOU?
I LEARNED FROM THE BEST! PICKED UP SOME NEW MOVES, TOO.
SHOW ME!

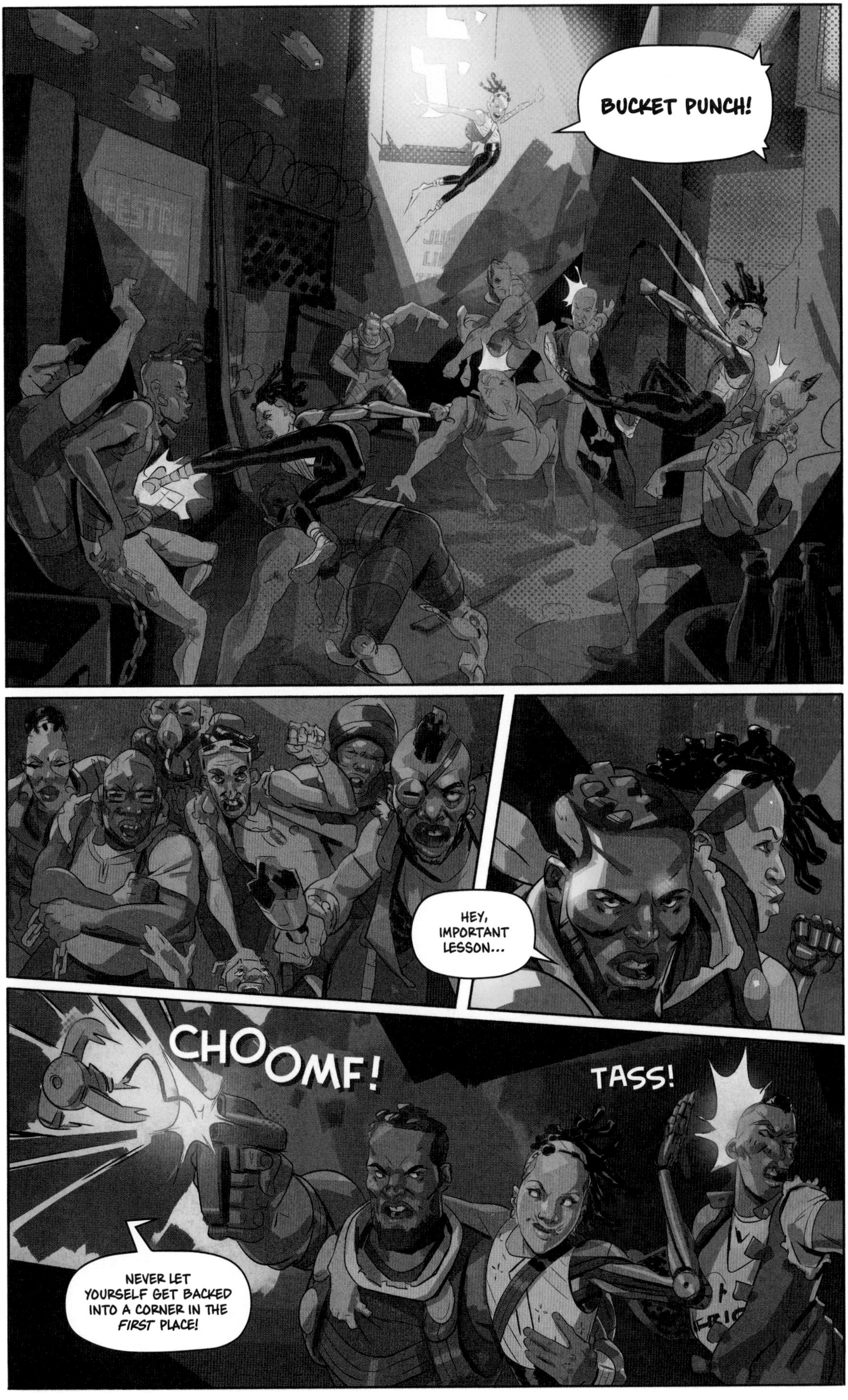
BUCKET PUNCH!
HEY, IMPORTANT LESSON...
CHOOMF!
TASS!
NEVER LET YOURSELF GET BACKED INTO A CORNER IN THE *FIRST* PLACE!

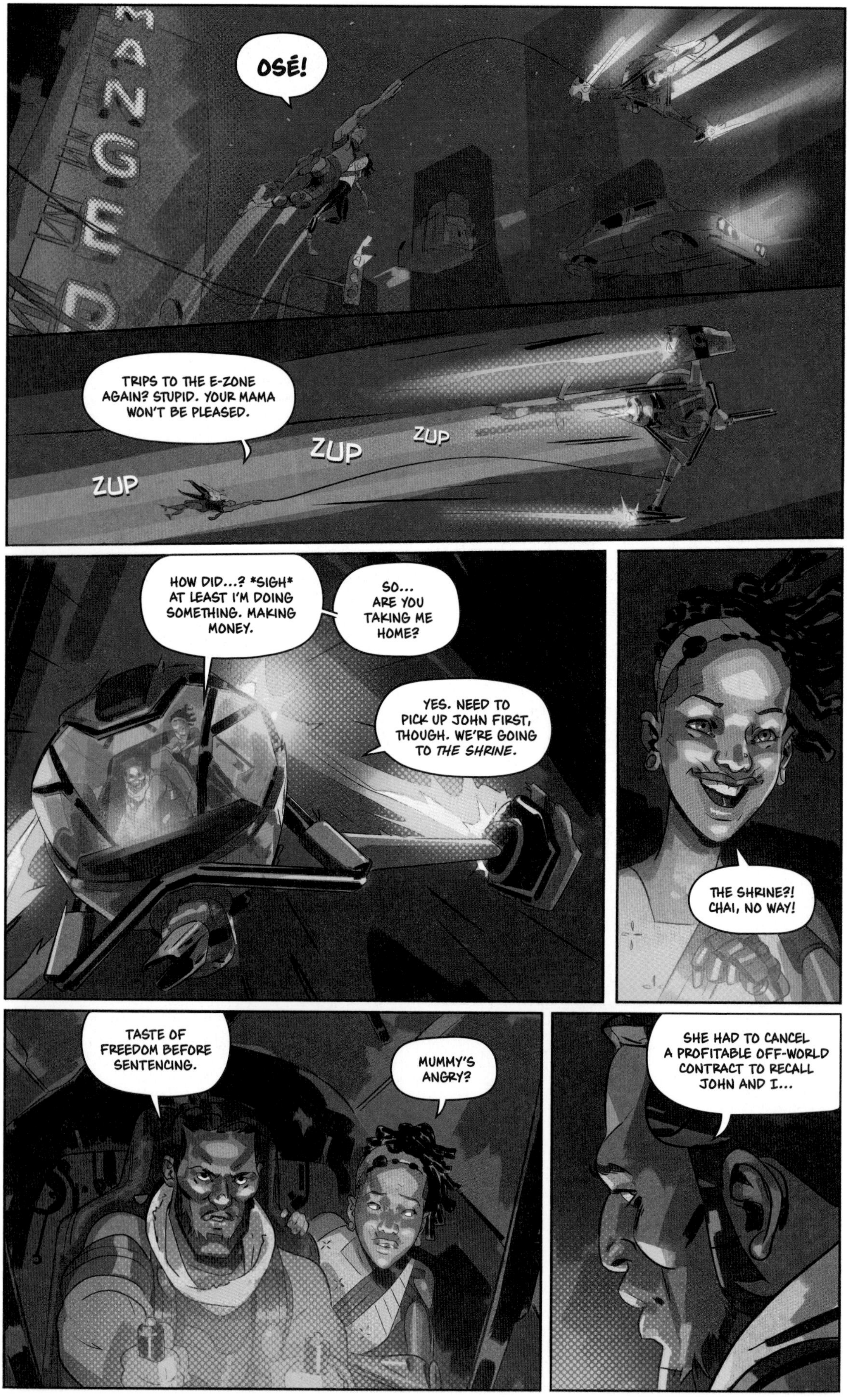
OSÉ!
TRIPS TO THE E-ZONE AGAIN? STUPID. YOUR MAMA WON'T BE PLEASED.
ZUP
ZUP
ZUP
HOW DID...? *SIGH* AT LEAST I'M DOING SOMETHING. MAKING MONEY.
SO... ARE YOU TAKING ME HOME?
YES. NEED TO PICK UP JOHN FIRST, THOUGH. WE'RE GOING TO *THE SHRINE*.
THE SHRINE?! CHAI, NO WAY!
TASTE OF FREEDOM BEFORE SENTENCING.
MUMMY'S ANGRY?
SHE HAD TO CANCEL A PROFITABLE OFF-WORLD CONTRACT TO RECALL JOHN AND I...

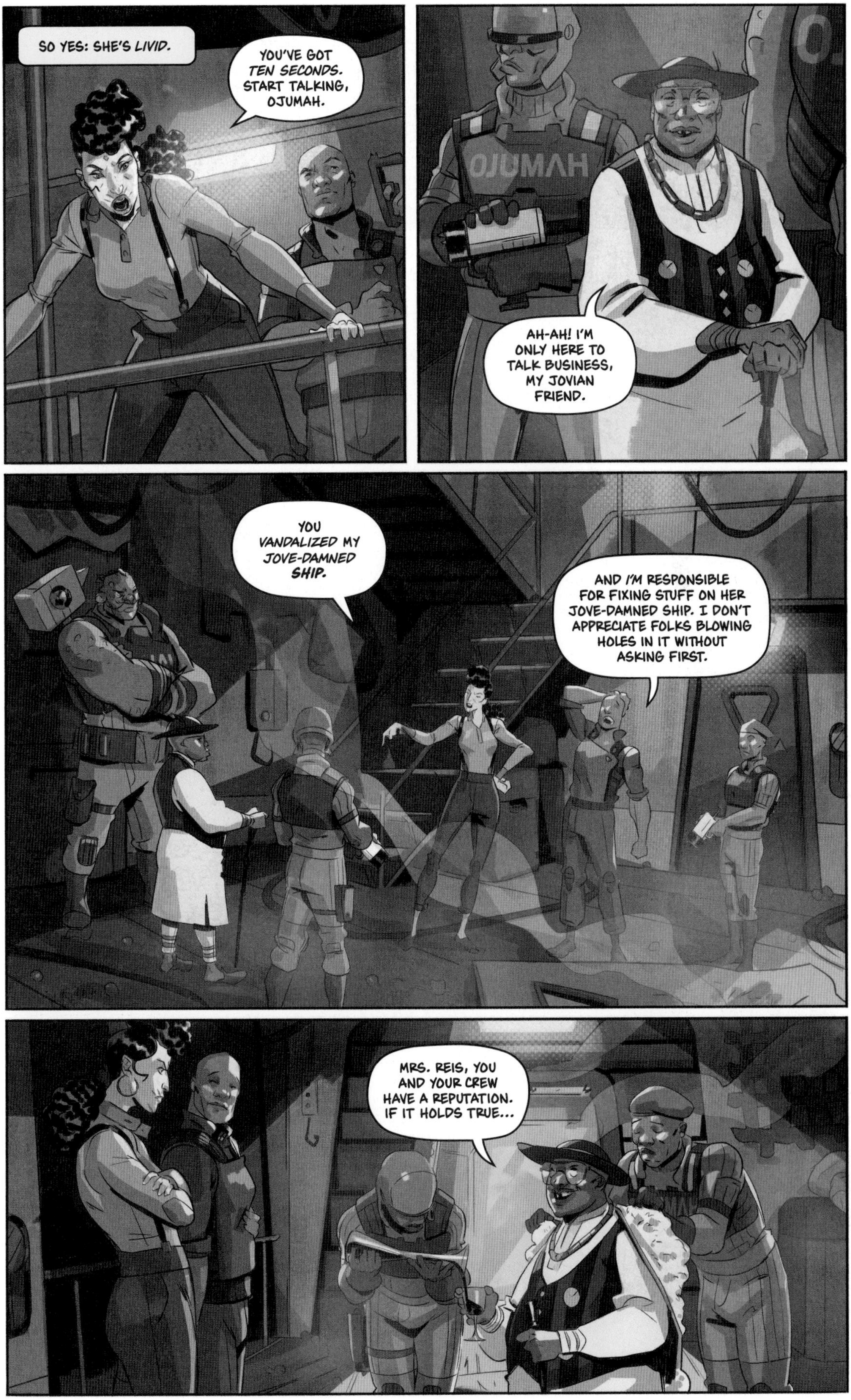
SO YES: SHE'S LIVID.
YOU'VE GOT TEN SECONDS. START TALKING, OJUMAH.
OJUMAH
AH-AH! I'M ONLY HERE TO TALK BUSINESS, MY JOVIAN FRIEND.
YOU VANDALIZED MY JOVE-DAMNED SHIP.
AND I'M RESPONSIBLE FOR FIXING STUFF ON HER JOVE-DAMNED SHIP. I DON'T APPRECIATE FOLKS BLOWING HOLES IN IT WITHOUT ASKING FIRST.
MRS. REIS, YOU AND YOUR CREW HAVE A REPUTATION. IF IT HOLDS TRUE...

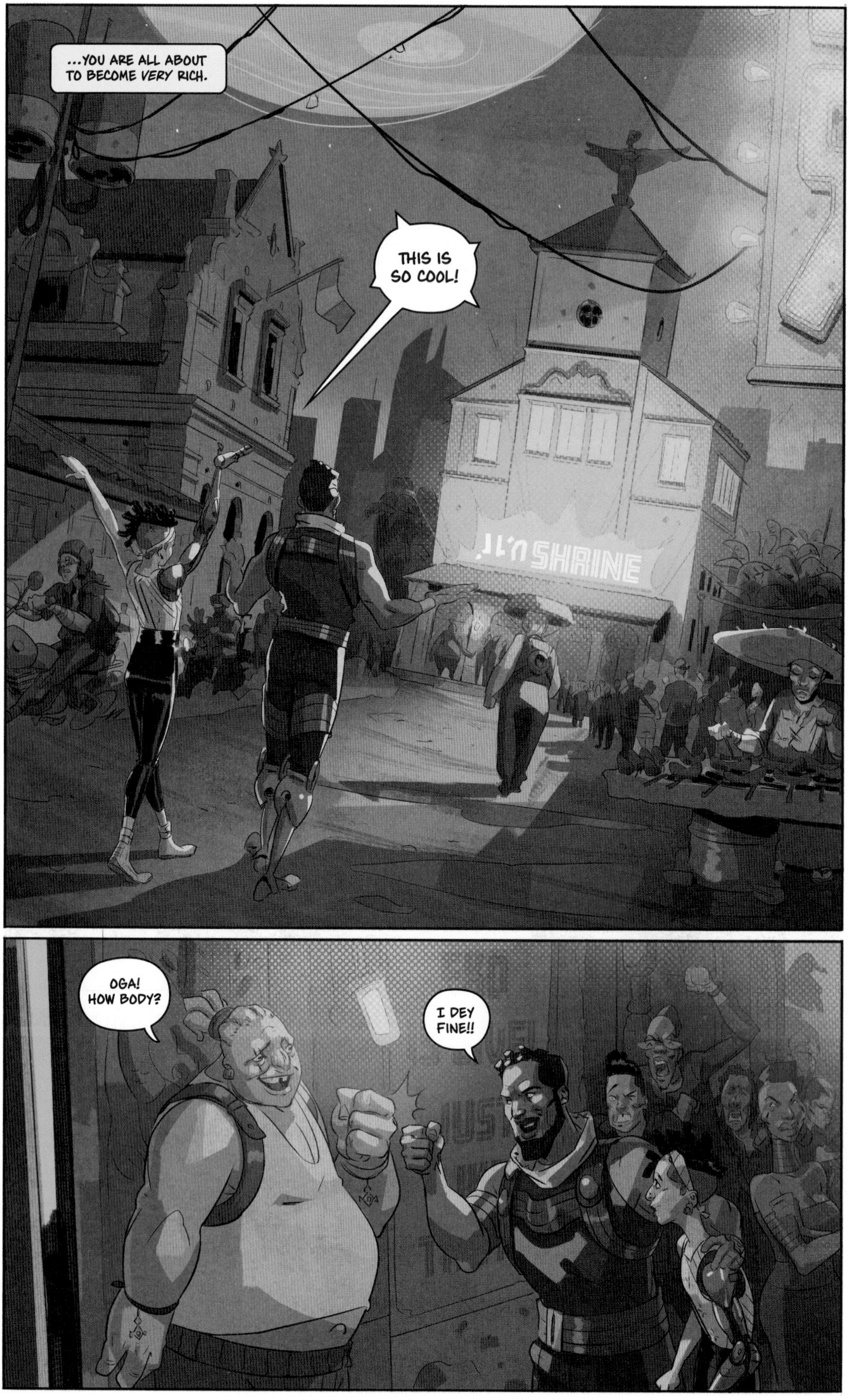
...YOU ARE ALL ABOUT TO BECOME *VERY* RICH.
THIS IS SO COOL!
SHRINE
OGA! HOW BODY?
I DEY FINE!!

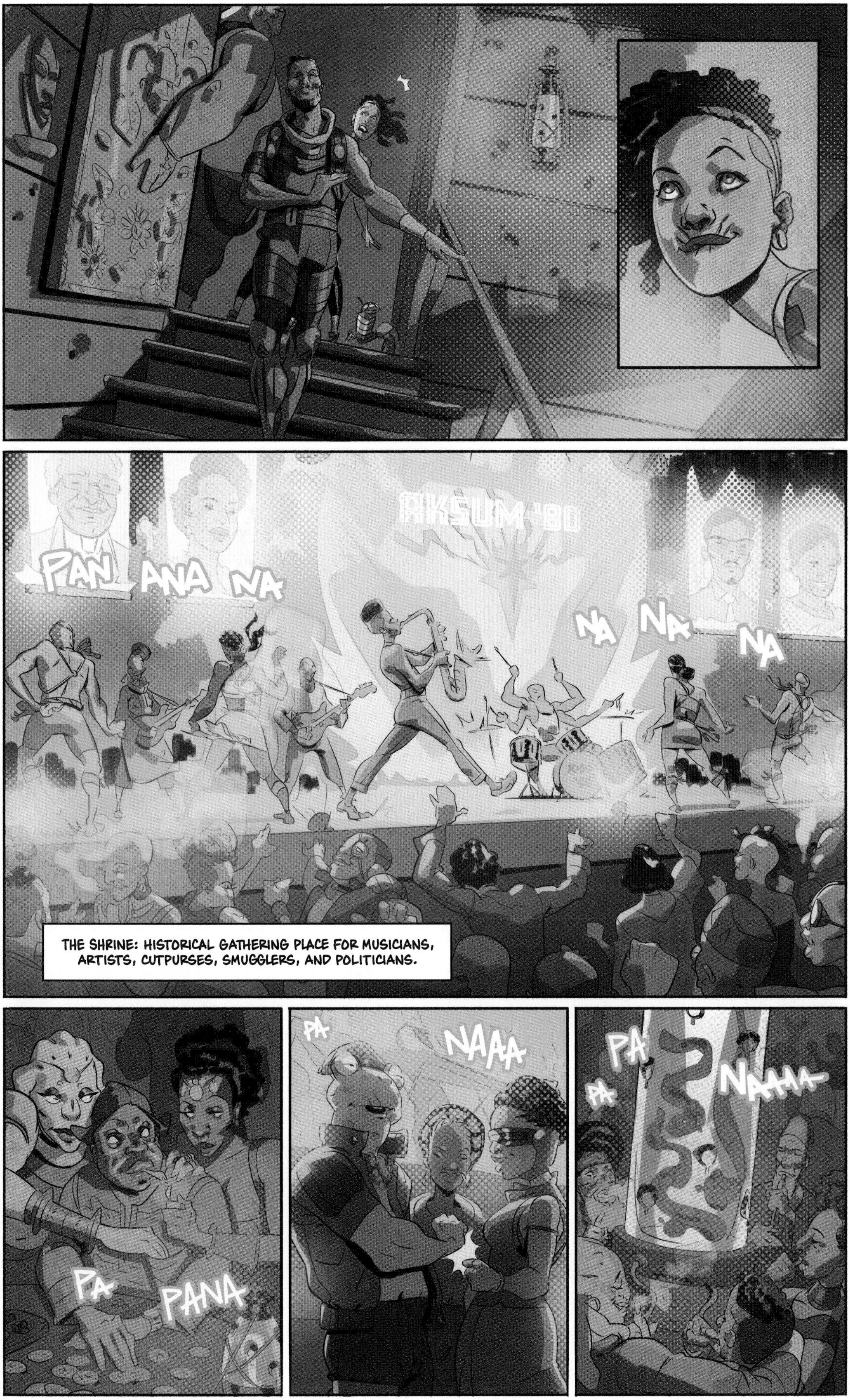
AKSUM '80
PAN ANA NA
NA NA NA
THE SHRINE: HISTORICAL GATHERING PLACE FOR MUSICIANS, ARTISTS, CUTPURSES, SMUGGLERS, AND POLITICIANS.
PA PANA
PA
NAAA
PA
PA
NAAAA-

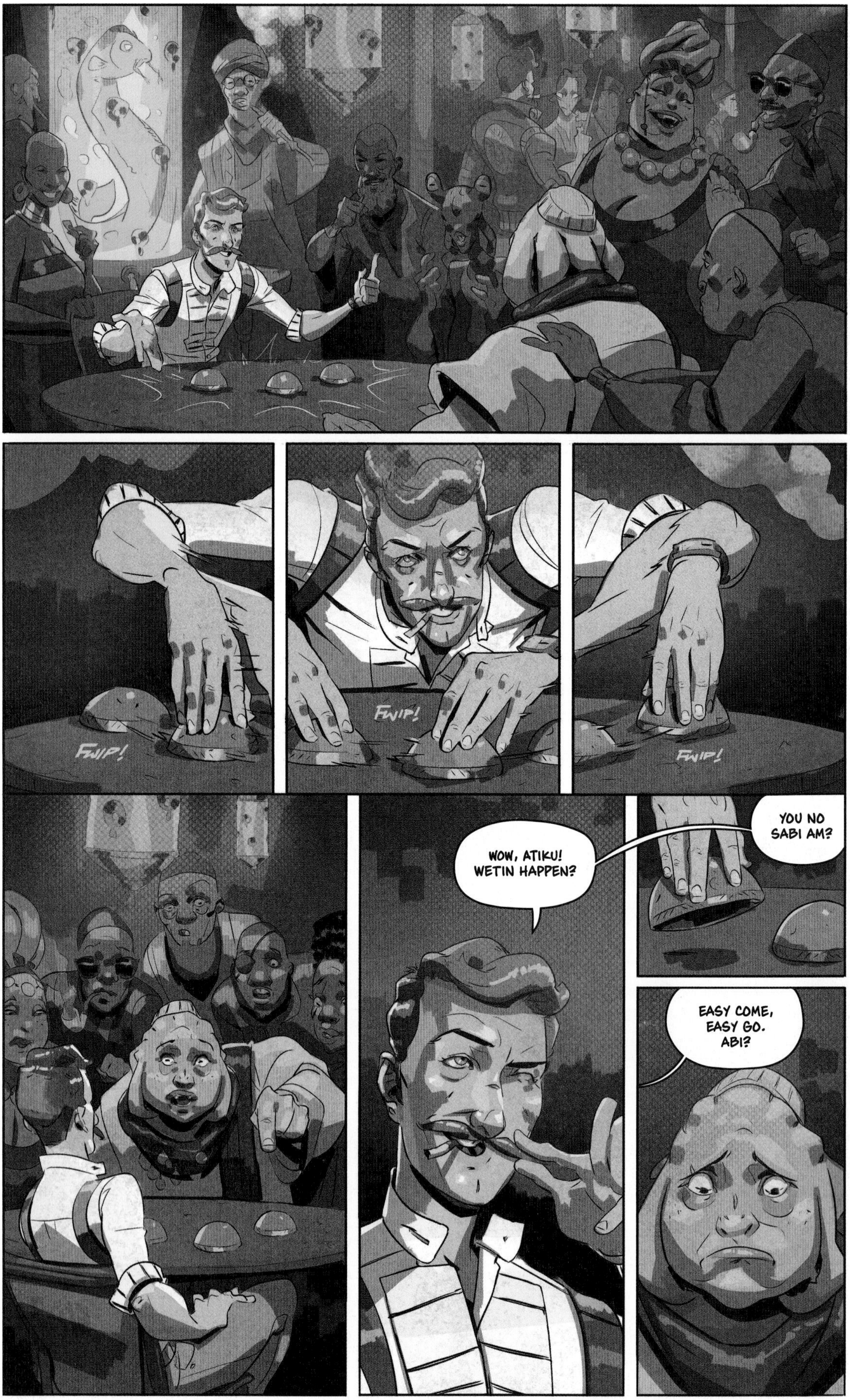
FWIP!
FWIP!
FWIP!
WOW, ATIKU! WETIN HAPPEN?
YOU NO SABI AM?
EASY COME, EASY GO. ABI?

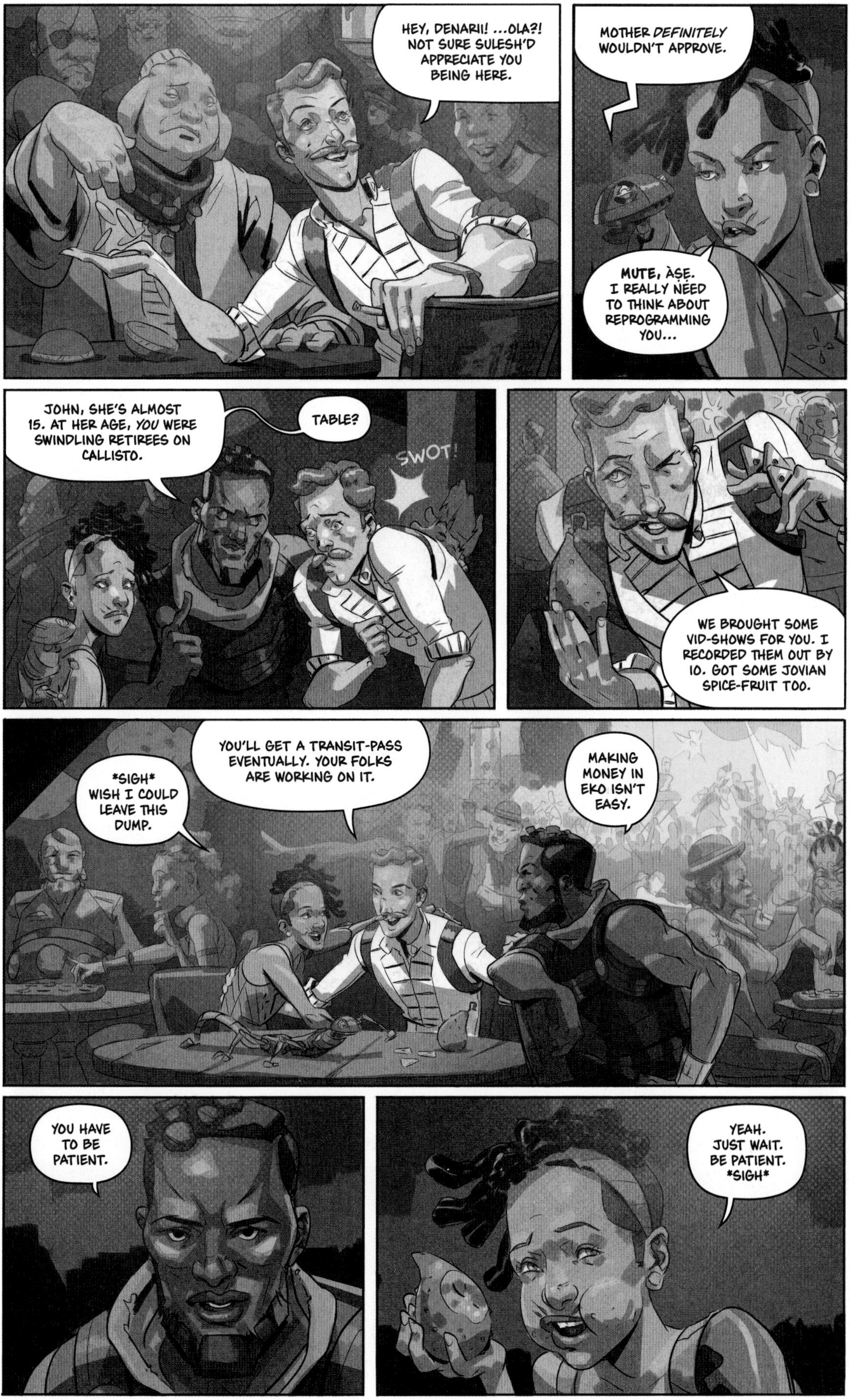
HEY, DENARII! ...OLA?! NOT SURE SULESH'D APPRECIATE YOU BEING HERE.
MOTHER DEFINITELY WOULDN'T APPROVE.
MUTE, ÀṢẸ. I REALLY NEED TO THINK ABOUT REPROGRAMMING YOU...
JOHN, SHE'S ALMOST 15. AT HER AGE, YOU WERE SWINDLING RETIREES ON CALLISTO.
TABLE?
SWOT!
WE BROUGHT SOME VID-SHOWS FOR YOU. I RECORDED THEM OUT BY IO. GOT SOME JOVIAN SPICE-FRUIT TOO.
SIGH WISH I COULD LEAVE THIS DUMP.
YOU'LL GET A TRANSIT-PASS EVENTUALLY. YOUR FOLKS ARE WORKING ON IT.
MAKING MONEY IN EKO ISN'T EASY.
YOU HAVE TO BE PATIENT.
YEAH. JUST WAIT. BE PATIENT. *SIGH*

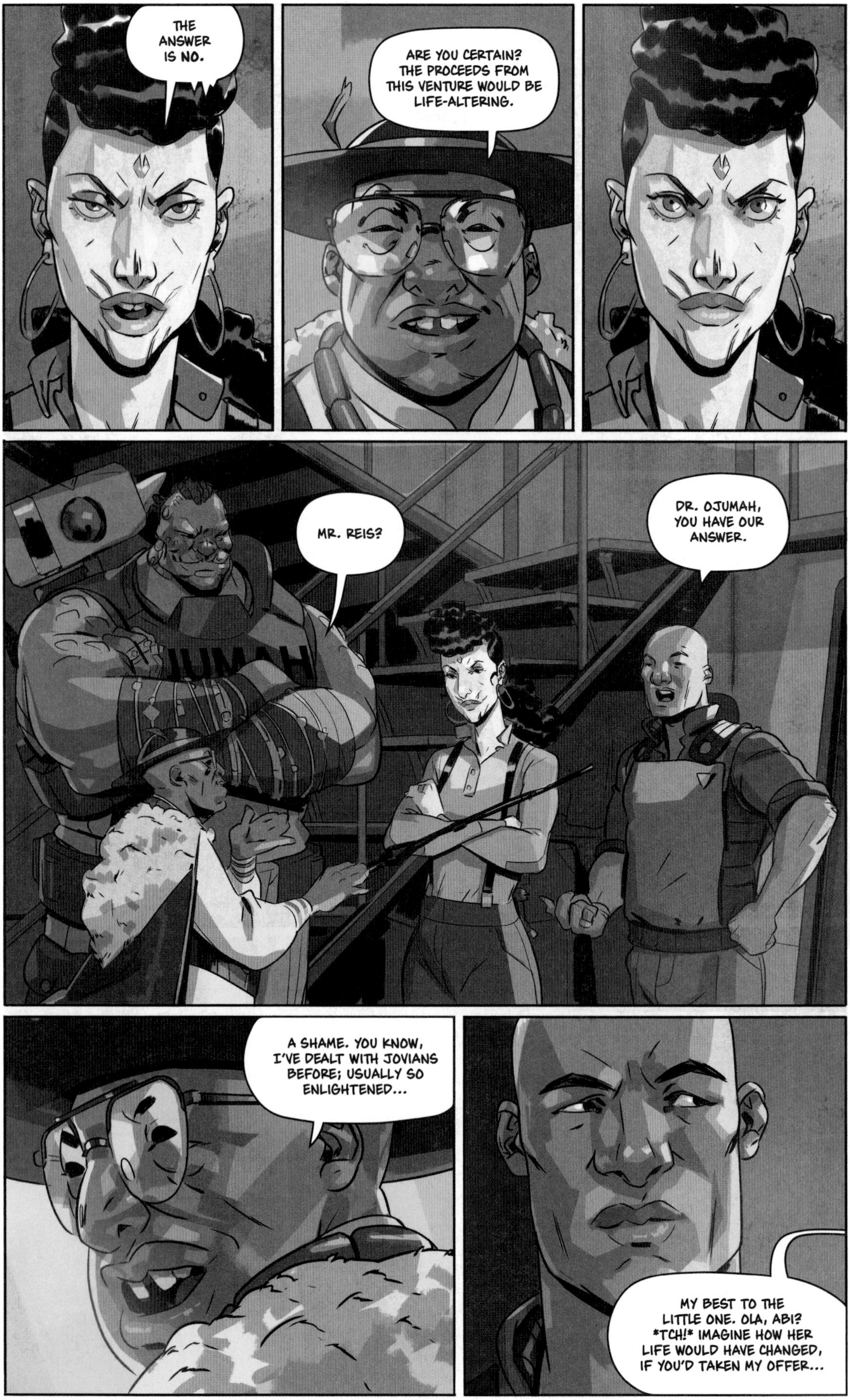
THE ANSWER IS NO.
ARE YOU CERTAIN? THE PROCEEDS FROM THIS VENTURE WOULD BE LIFE-ALTERING.
MR. REIS?
DR. OJUMAH, YOU HAVE OUR ANSWER.
A SHAME. YOU KNOW, I'VE DEALT WITH JOVIANS BEFORE; USUALLY SO ENLIGHTENED...
MY BEST TO THE LITTLE ONE. OLA, ABI? *TCH!* IMAGINE HOW HER LIFE WOULD HAVE CHANGED, IF YOU'D TAKEN MY OFFER...

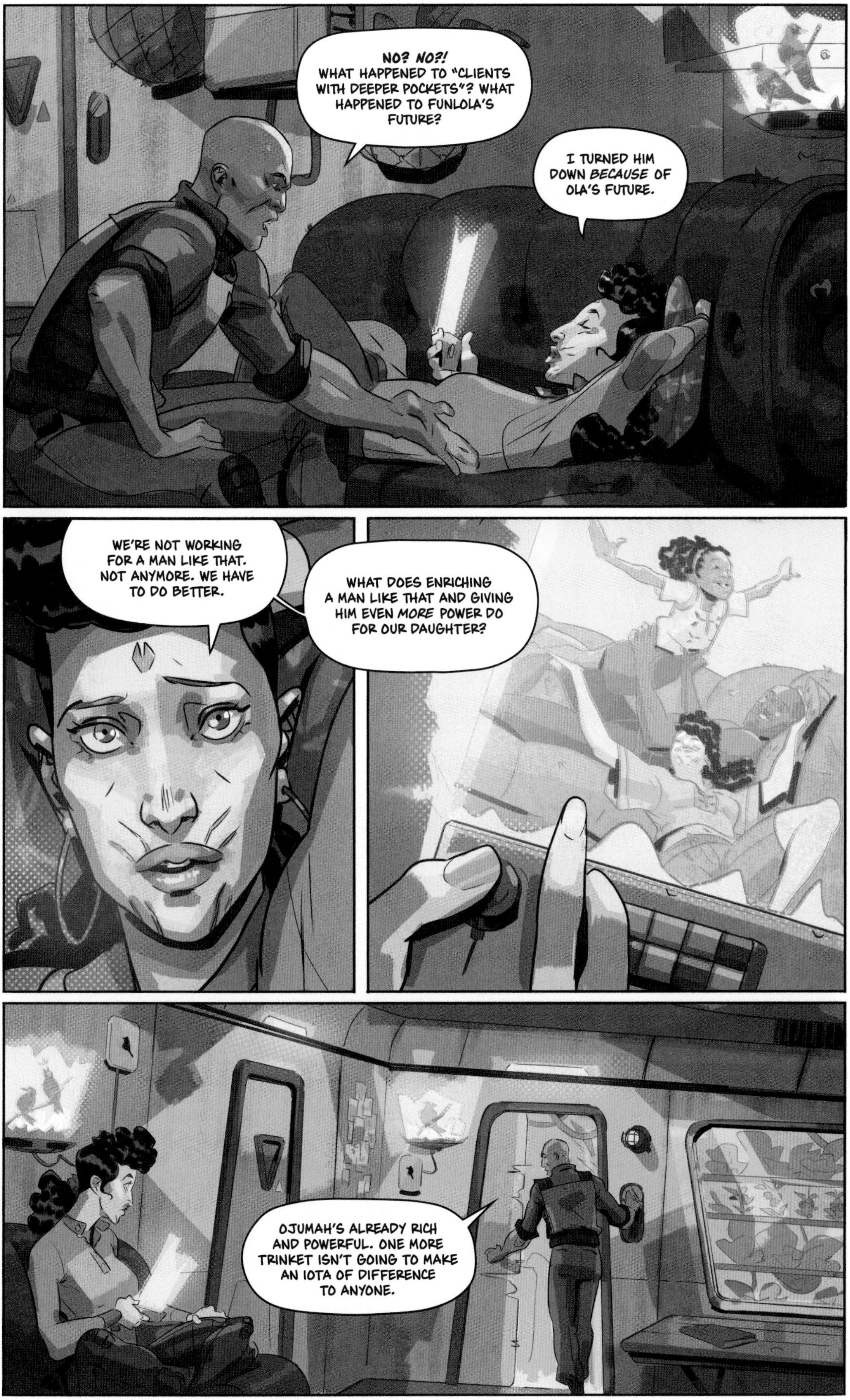
NO? NO?! WHAT HAPPENED TO "CLIENTS WITH DEEPER POCKETS"? WHAT HAPPENED TO FUNLOLA'S FUTURE?
I TURNED HIM DOWN *BECAUSE* OF OLA'S FUTURE.
WE'RE NOT WORKING FOR A MAN LIKE THAT. NOT ANYMORE. WE HAVE TO DO BETTER.
WHAT DOES ENRICHING A MAN LIKE THAT AND GIVING HIM EVEN *MORE* POWER DO FOR OUR DAUGHTER?
OJUMAH'S ALREADY RICH AND POWERFUL. ONE MORE TRINKET ISN'T GOING TO MAKE AN IOTA OF DIFFERENCE TO ANYONE.

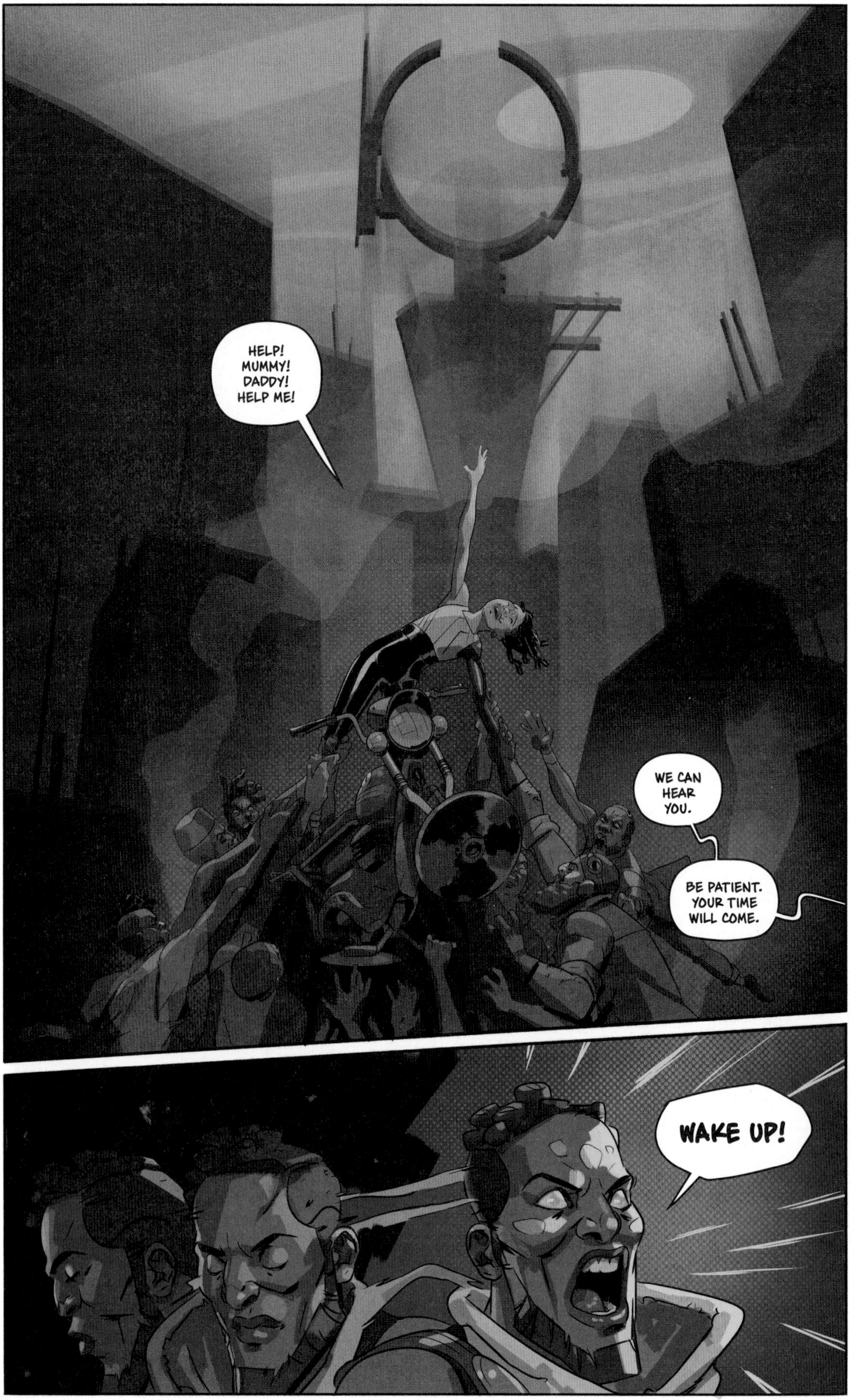
HELP! MUMMY! DADDY! HELP ME!
WE CAN HEAR YOU.
BE PATIENT. YOUR TIME WILL COME.
WAKE UP!

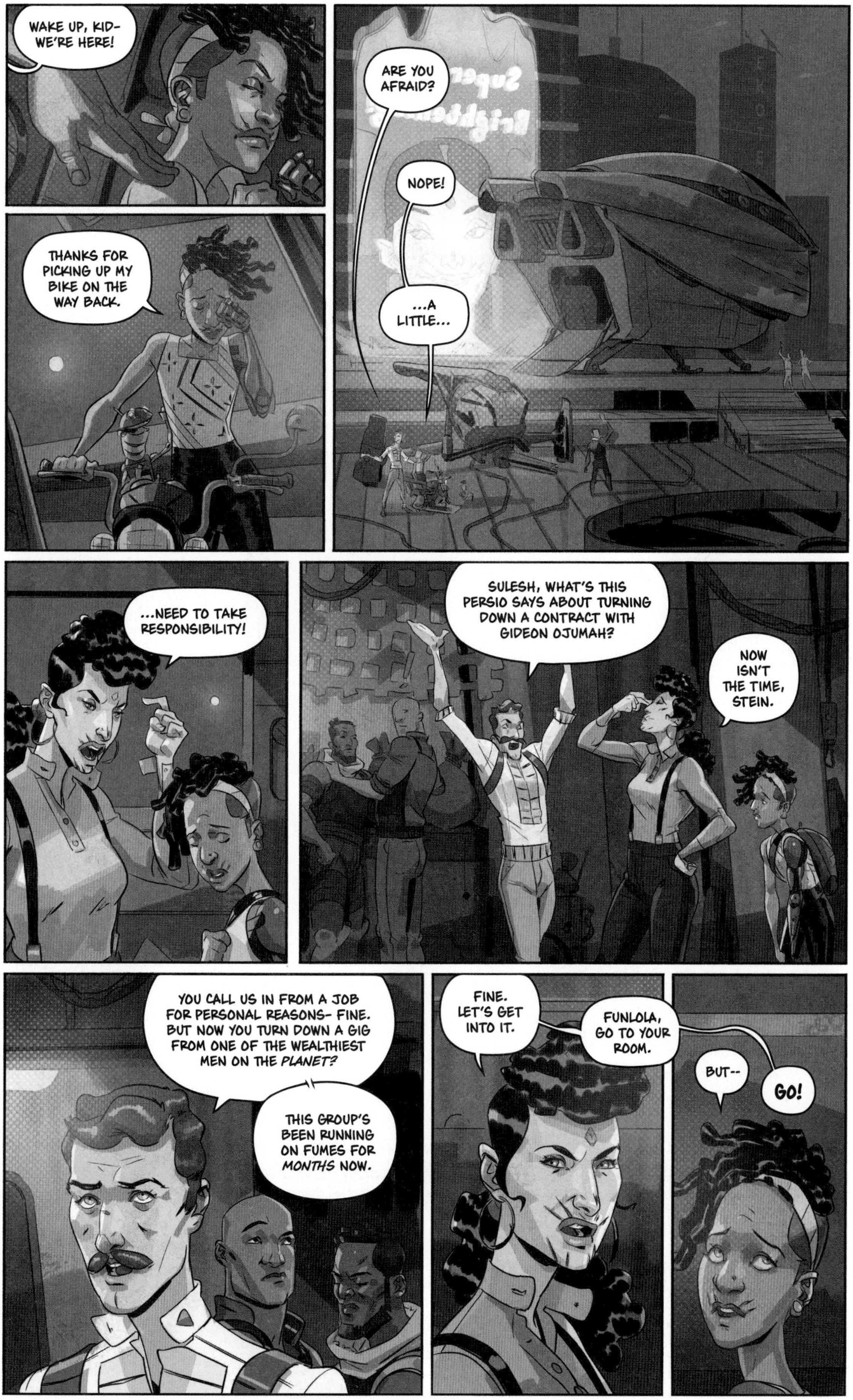
WAKE UP, KID- WE'RE HERE!
ARE YOU AFRAID?
NOPE!
...A LITTLE...
THANKS FOR PICKING UP MY BIKE ON THE WAY BACK.
...NEED TO TAKE RESPONSIBILITY!
SULESH, WHAT'S THIS PERSIO SAYS ABOUT TURNING DOWN A CONTRACT WITH GIDEON OJUMAH?
NOW ISN'T THE TIME, STEIN.
YOU CALL US IN FROM A JOB FOR PERSONAL REASONS- FINE. BUT NOW YOU TURN DOWN A GIG FROM ONE OF THE WEALTHIEST MEN ON THE *PLANET?*
THIS GROUP'S BEEN RUNNING ON FUMES FOR *MONTHS* NOW.
FINE. LET'S GET INTO IT.
FUNLOLA, GO TO YOUR ROOM.
BUT--
GO!

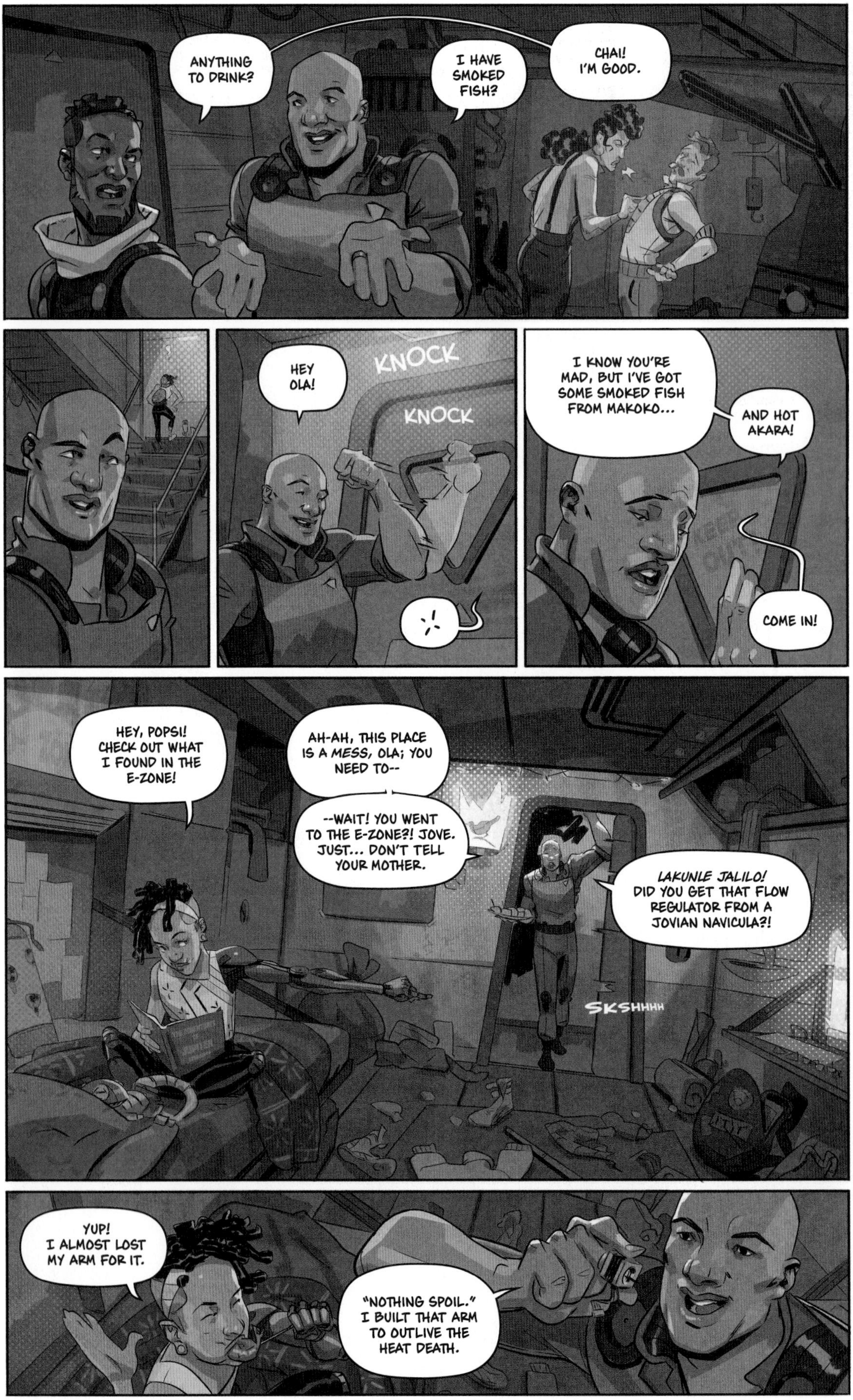
ANYTHING TO DRINK?
I HAVE SMOKED FISH?
CHAI! I'M GOOD.
HEY OLA!
KNOCK
KNOCK
I KNOW YOU'RE MAD, BUT I'VE GOT SOME SMOKED FISH FROM MAKOKO...
AND HOT AKARA!
COME IN!
HEY, POPSI! CHECK OUT WHAT I FOUND IN THE E-ZONE!
AH-AH, THIS PLACE IS A MESS, OLA; YOU NEED TO--
--WAIT! YOU WENT TO THE E-ZONE?! JOVE. JUST... DON'T TELL YOUR MOTHER.
LAKUNLE JALILO! DID YOU GET THAT FLOW REGULATOR FROM A JOVIAN NAVICULA?!
SKSHHHH
YUP! I ALMOST LOST MY ARM FOR IT.
"NOTHING SPOIL." I BUILT THAT ARM TO OUTLIVE THE HEAT DEATH.

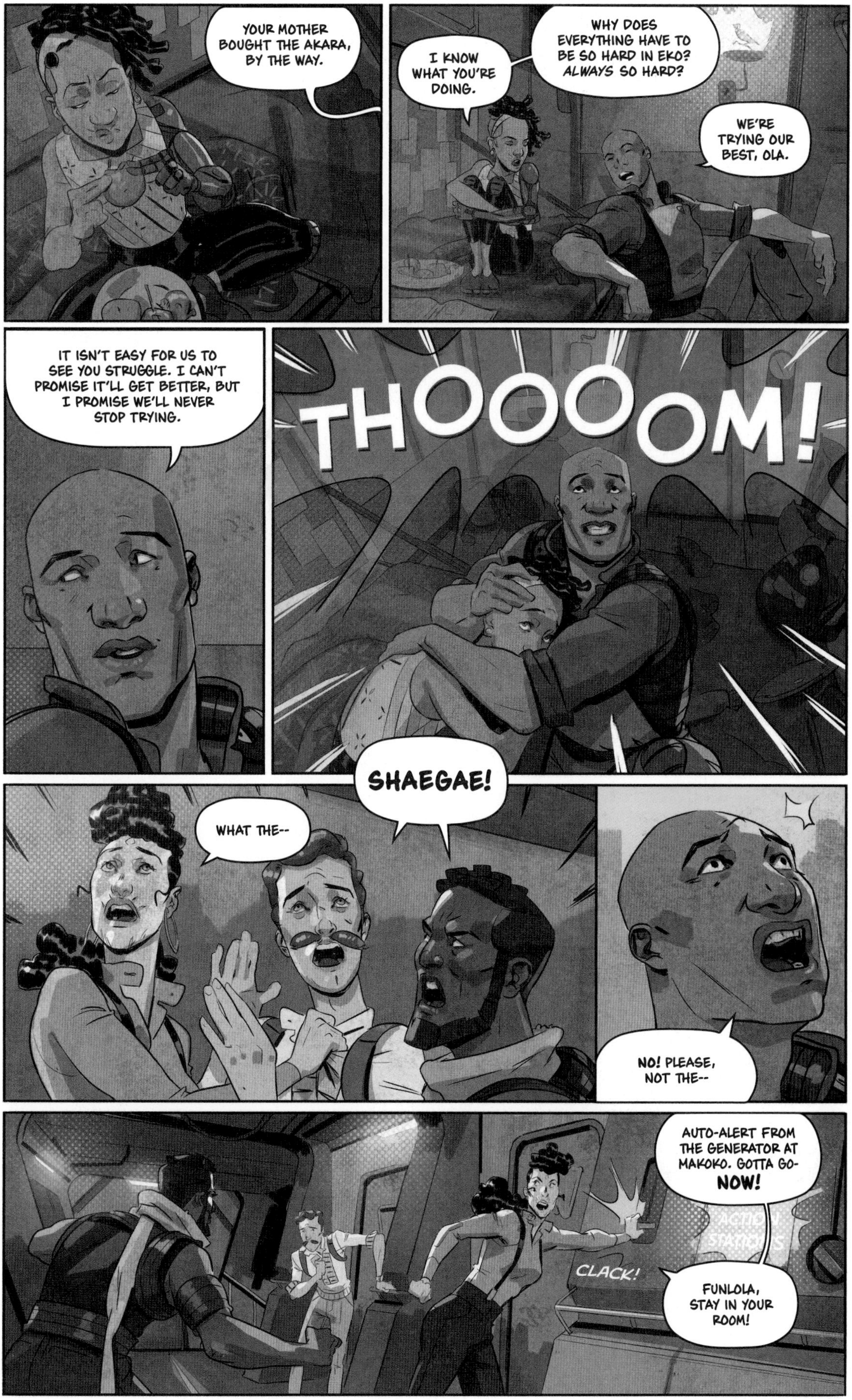
YOUR MOTHER BOUGHT THE AKARA, BY THE WAY.
I KNOW WHAT YOU'RE DOING.
WHY DOES EVERYTHING HAVE TO BE SO HARD IN EKO? *ALWAYS* SO HARD?
WE'RE TRYING OUR BEST, OLA.
IT ISN'T EASY FOR US TO SEE YOU STRUGGLE. I CAN'T PROMISE IT'LL GET BETTER, BUT I PROMISE WE'LL NEVER STOP TRYING.
THOOOOM!
WHAT THE--
SHAEGAE!
NO! PLEASE, NOT THE--
AUTO-ALERT FROM THE GENERATOR AT MAKOKO. GOTTA GO- **NOW!**
CLACK!
FUNLOLA, STAY IN YOUR ROOM!

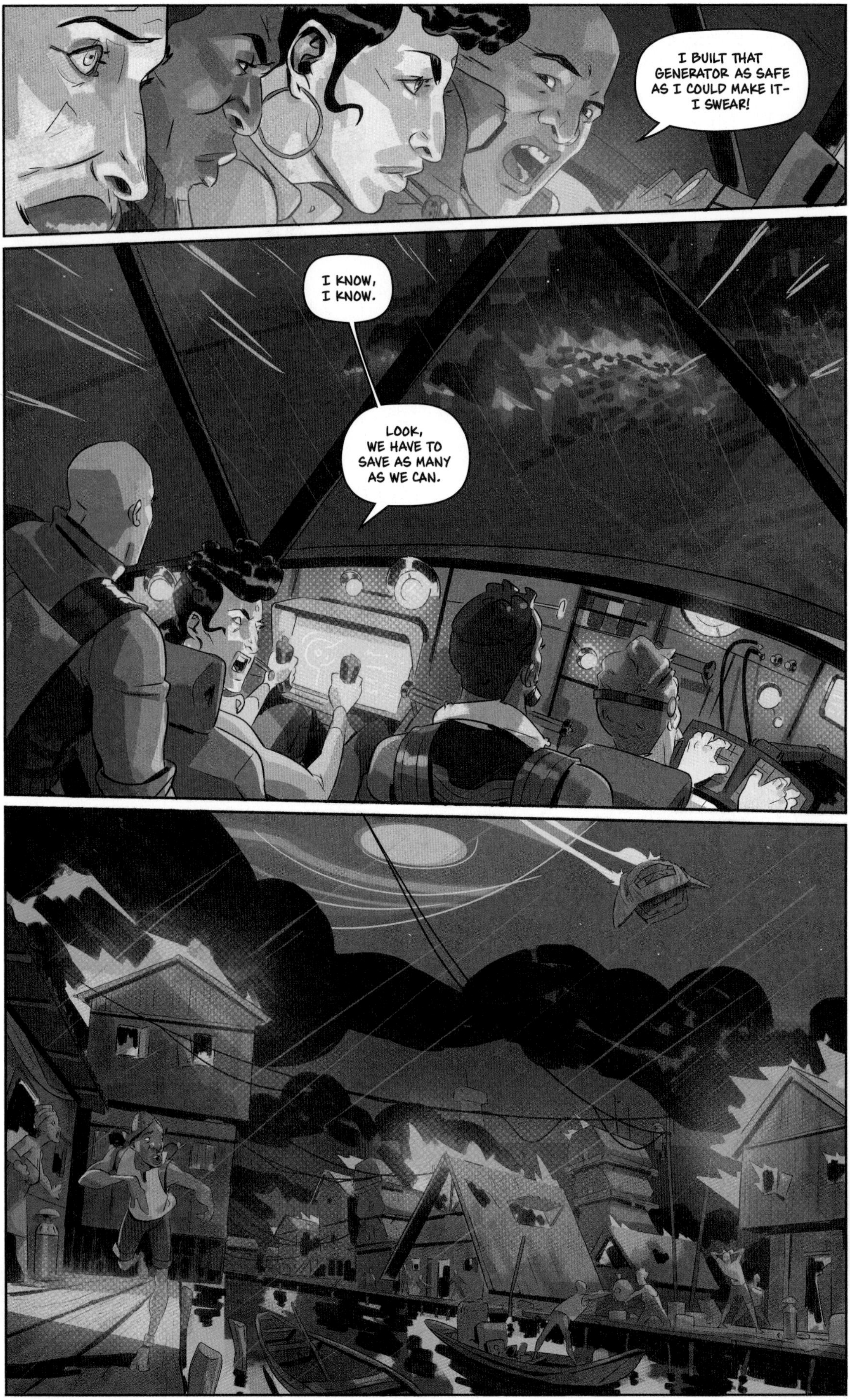
I BUILT THAT GENERATOR AS SAFE AS I COULD MAKE IT- I SWEAR!
I KNOW, I KNOW.
LOOK, WE HAVE TO SAVE AS MANY AS WE CAN.

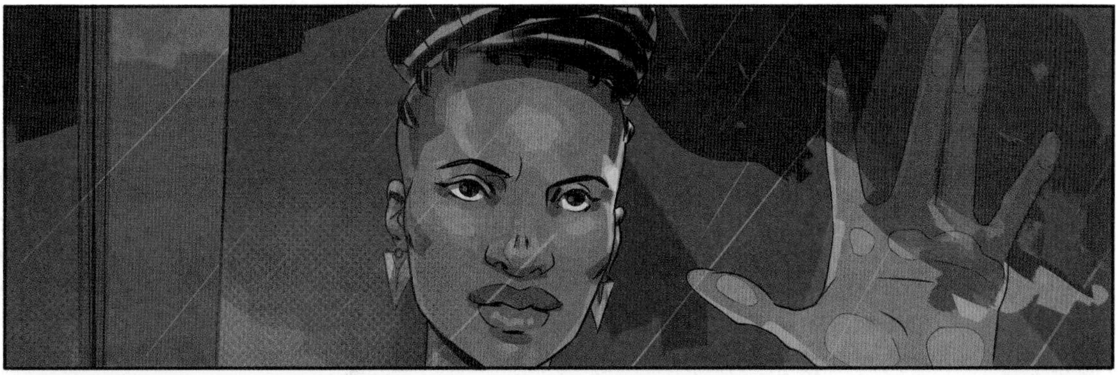

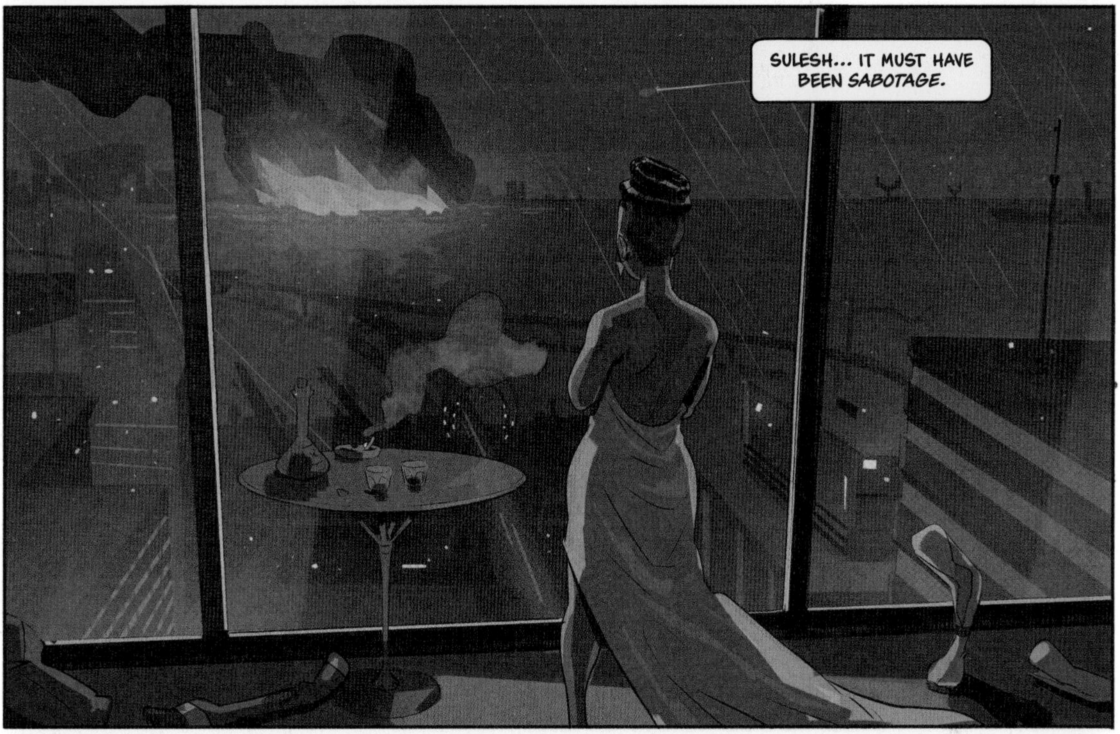
SULESH... IT MUST HAVE BEEN SABOTAGE.

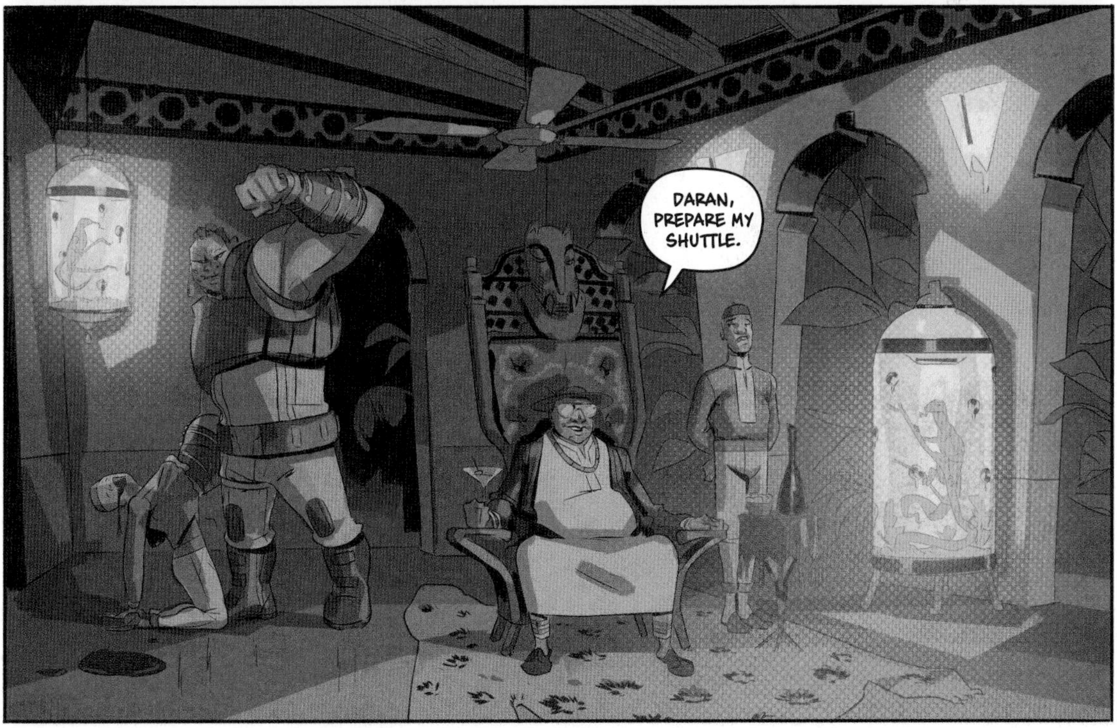
DARAN, PREPARE MY SHUTTLE.

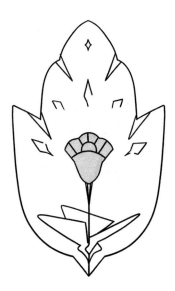

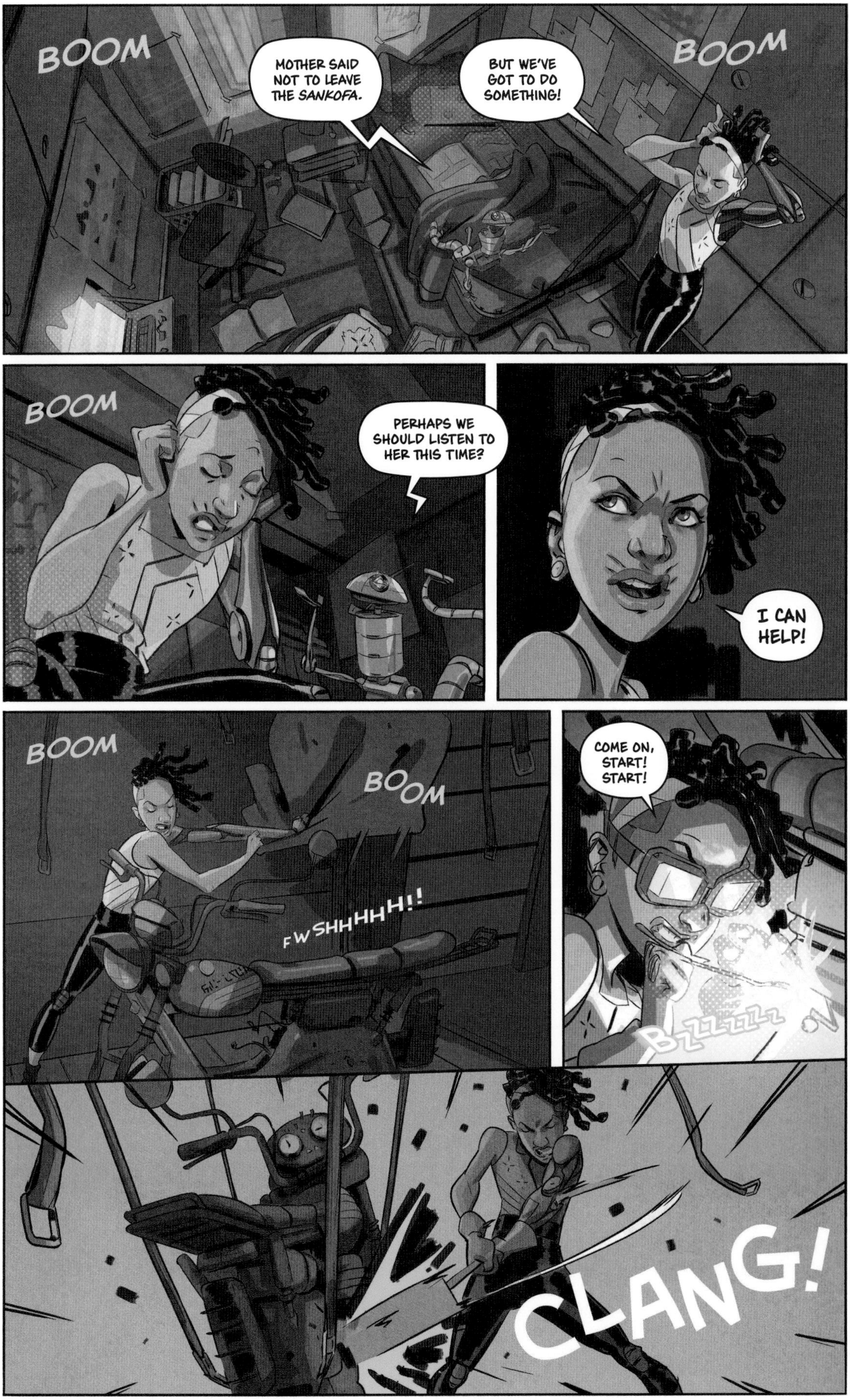
BOOM
MOTHER SAID NOT TO LEAVE THE SANKOFA.
BUT WE'VE GOT TO DO SOMETHING!
BOOM
BOOM
PERHAPS WE SHOULD LISTEN TO HER THIS TIME?
I CAN HELP!
BOOM
BOOM
FWSHHHHH!!
COME ON, START! START!
BZZZZZZ
CLANG!

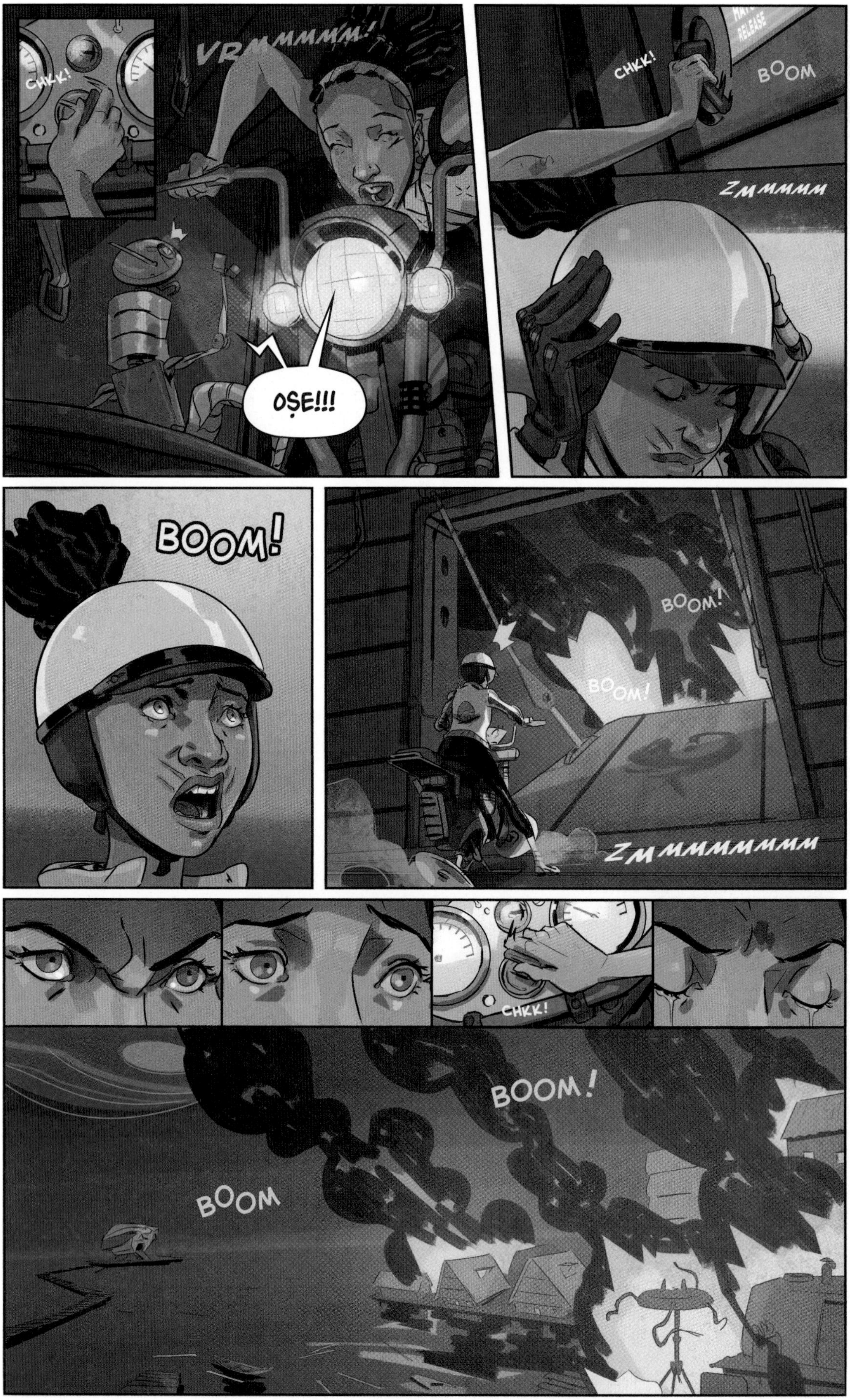
VRMMMMMM!
CHKK!
OȘE!!!
CHKK!
RELEASE
BOOM
ZMMMMM
BOOM!
BOOM!
BOOM!
ZMMMMMMMM
CHKK!
BOOM!
BOOM

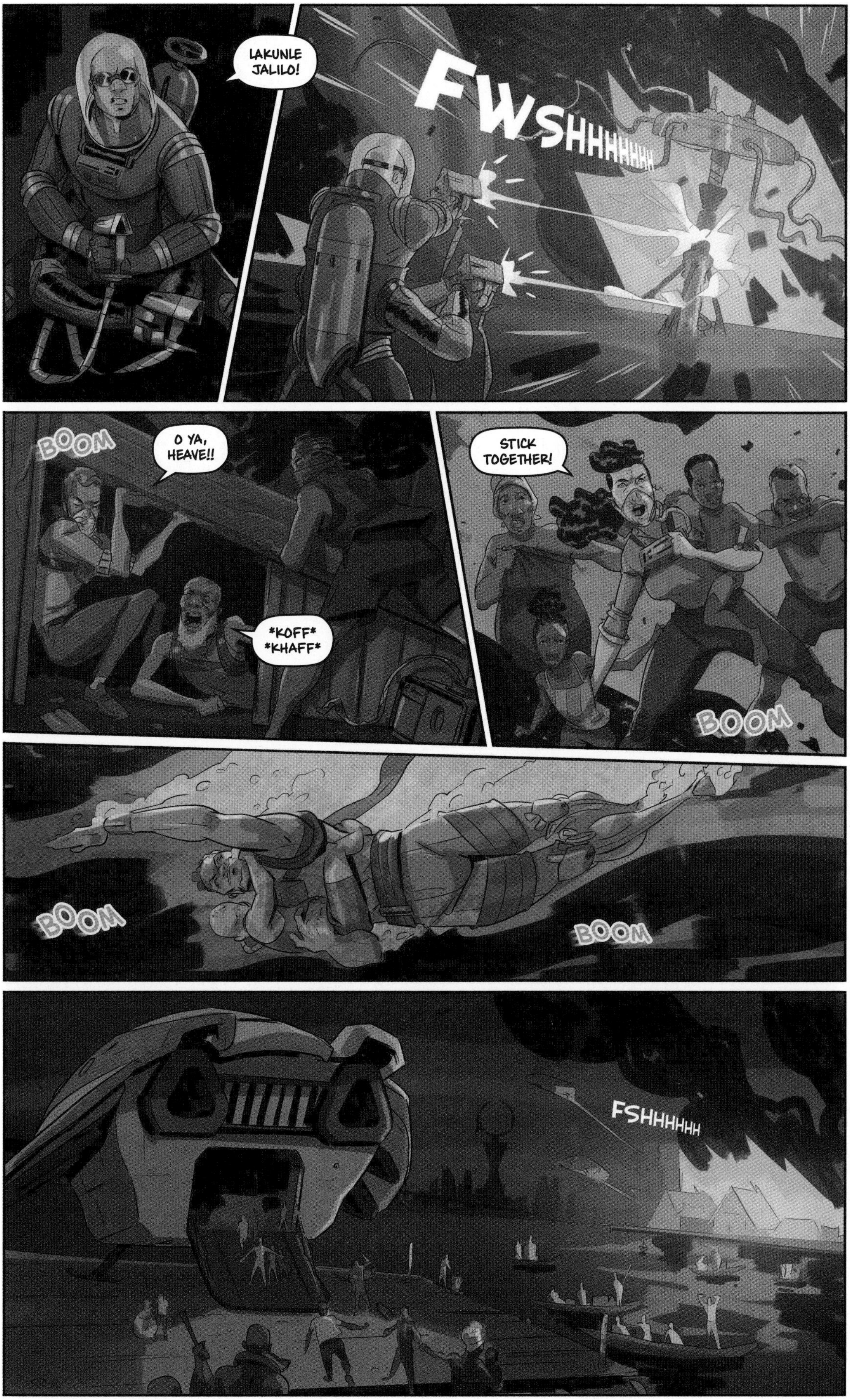
LAKUNLE JALILO!
FWSHHHHHHH
BOOM
O YA, HEAVE!!
KOFF *KHAFF*
STICK TOGETHER!
BOOM
BOOM
BOOM
FSHHHHHH

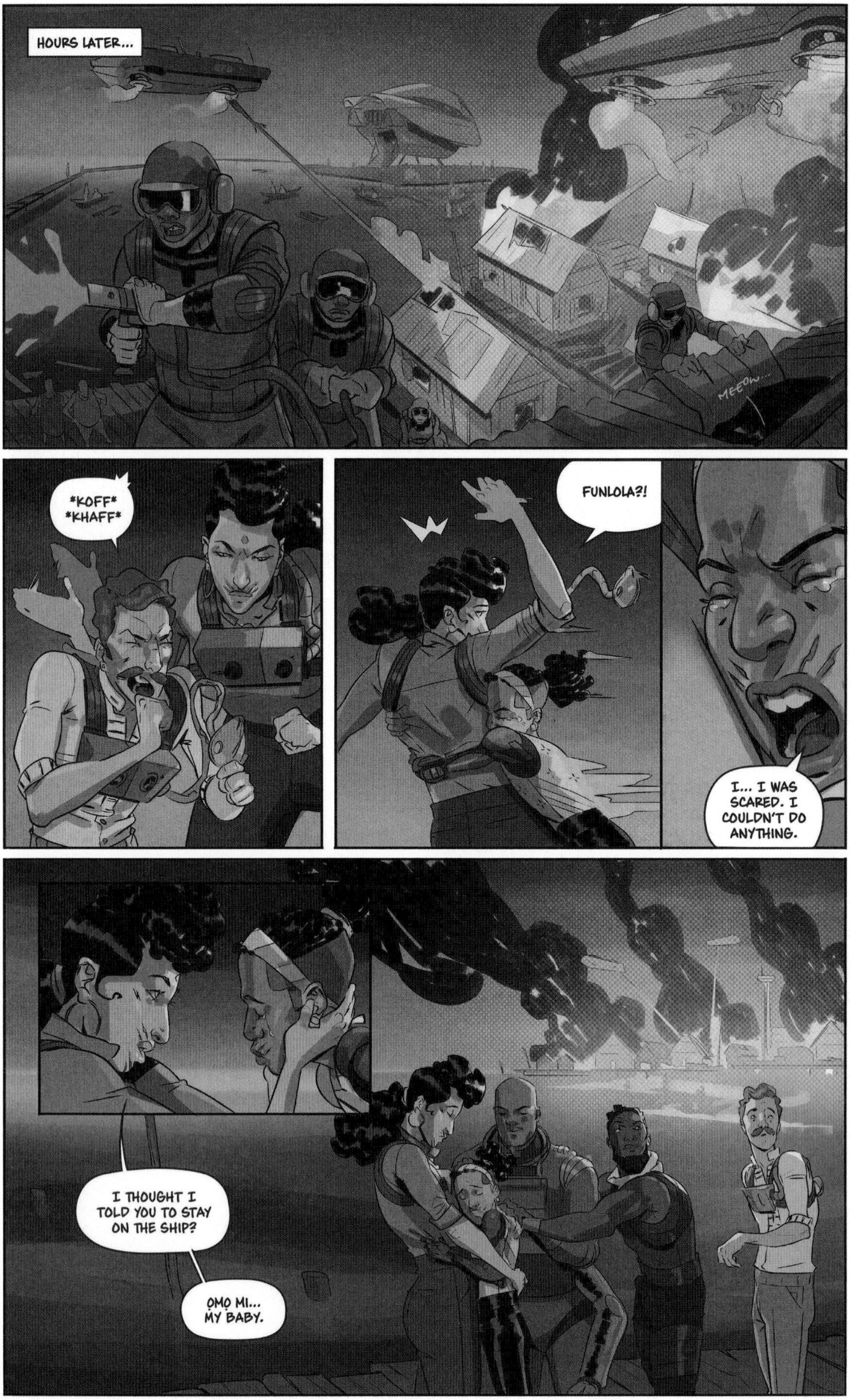
HOURS LATER...
MEEOW...
KOFF
KHAFF
FUNLOLA?!
I... I WAS SCARED. I COULDN'T DO ANYTHING.
I THOUGHT I TOLD YOU TO STAY ON THE SHIP?
OMO MI... MY BABY.

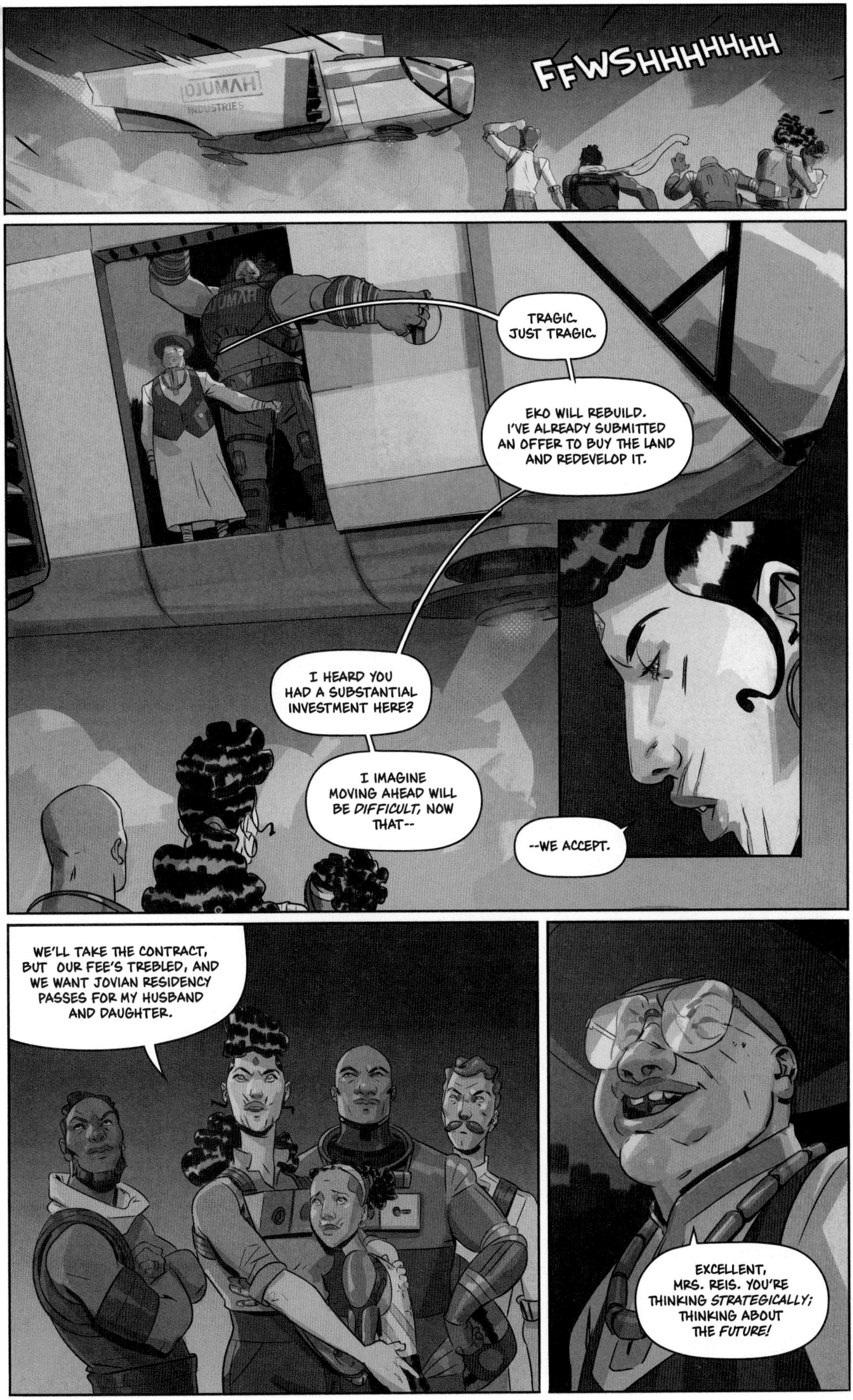

FFWSHHHHHHH
OJUMAH INDUSTRIES
TRAGIC. JUST TRAGIC.
EKO WILL REBUILD. I'VE ALREADY SUBMITTED AN OFFER TO BUY THE LAND AND REDEVELOP IT.
I HEARD YOU HAD A SUBSTANTIAL INVESTMENT HERE?
I IMAGINE MOVING AHEAD WILL BE *DIFFICULT*, NOW THAT--
--WE ACCEPT.
WE'LL TAKE THE CONTRACT, BUT OUR FEE'S TREBLED, AND WE WANT JOVIAN RESIDENCY PASSES FOR MY HUSBAND AND DAUGHTER.
EXCELLENT, MRS. REIS. YOU'RE THINKING *STRATEGICALLY*; THINKING ABOUT THE *FUTURE*!

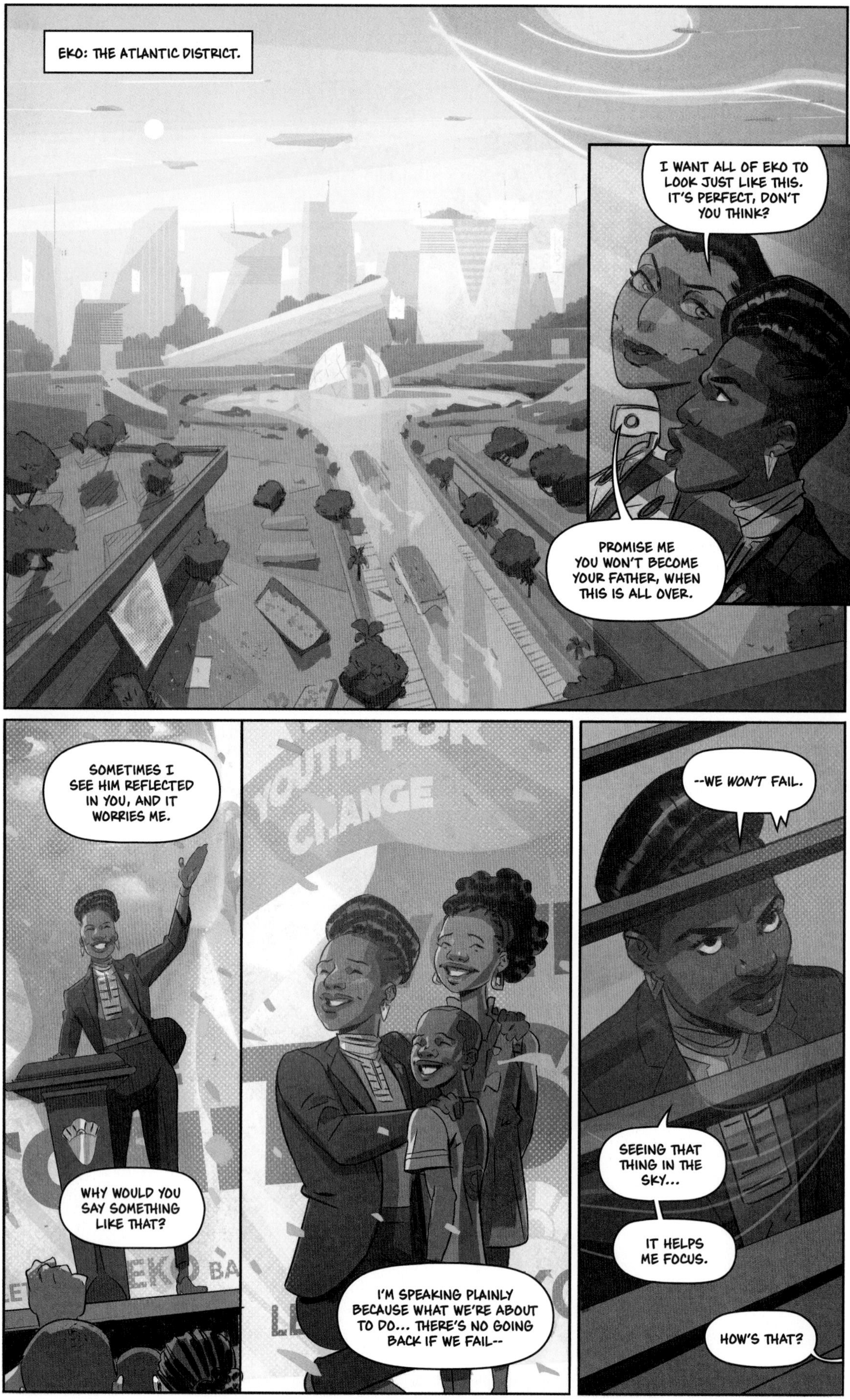
EKO: THE ATLANTIC DISTRICT.
I WANT ALL OF EKO TO LOOK JUST LIKE THIS. IT'S PERFECT, DON'T YOU THINK?
PROMISE ME YOU WON'T BECOME YOUR FATHER, WHEN THIS IS ALL OVER.
SOMETIMES I SEE HIM REFLECTED IN YOU, AND IT WORRIES ME.
WHY WOULD YOU SAY SOMETHING LIKE THAT?
I'M SPEAKING PLAINLY BECAUSE WHAT WE'RE ABOUT TO DO... THERE'S NO GOING BACK IF WE FAIL--
--WE *WON'T* FAIL.
SEEING THAT THING IN THE SKY...
IT HELPS ME FOCUS.
HOW'S THAT?

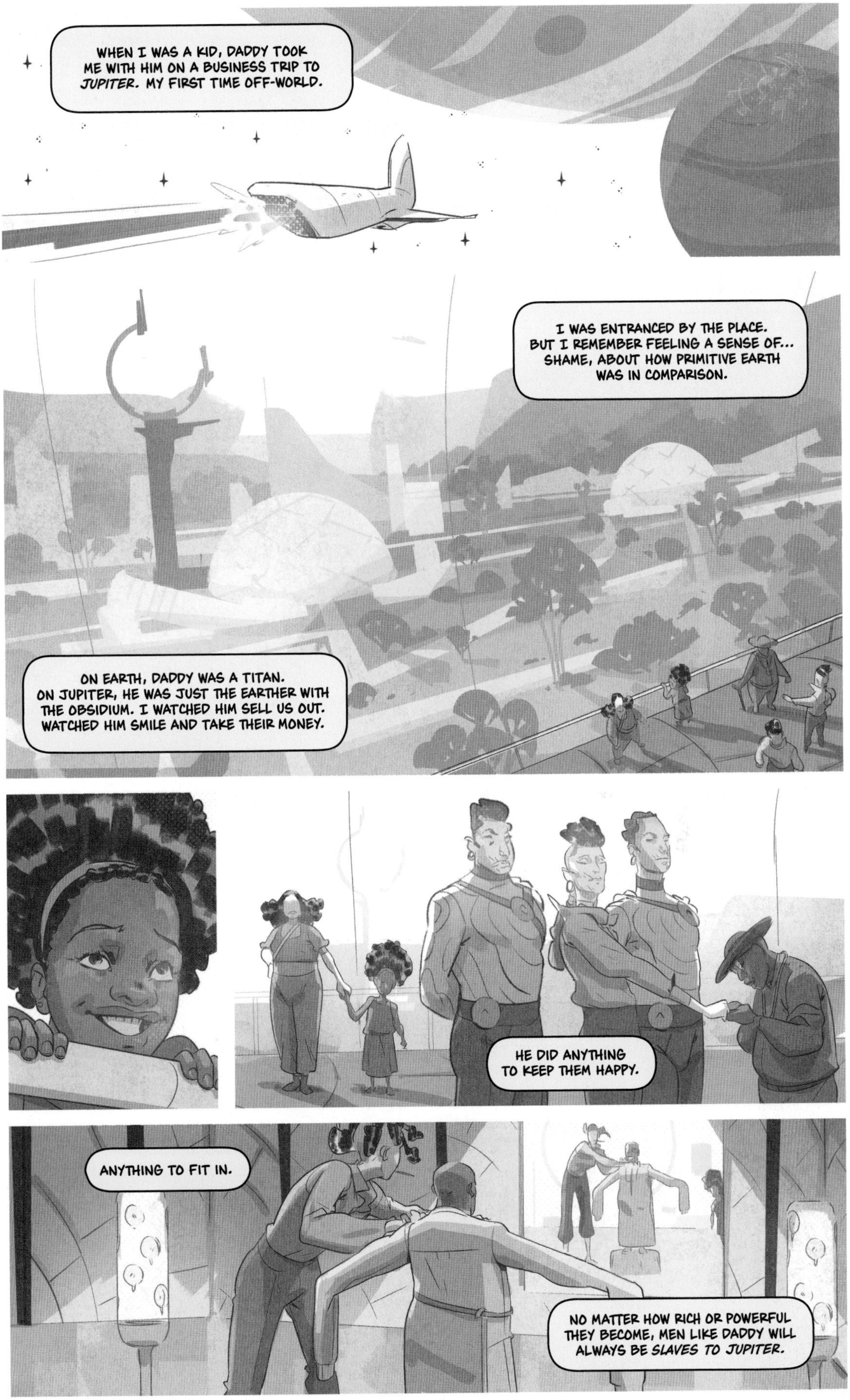
WHEN I WAS A KID, DADDY TOOK ME WITH HIM ON A BUSINESS TRIP TO *JUPITER.* MY FIRST TIME OFF-WORLD.
I WAS ENTRANCED BY THE PLACE. BUT I REMEMBER FEELING A SENSE OF... SHAME, ABOUT HOW PRIMITIVE EARTH WAS IN COMPARISON.
ON EARTH, DADDY WAS A TITAN. ON JUPITER, HE WAS JUST THE EARTHER WITH THE OBSIDIUM. I WATCHED HIM SELL US OUT. WATCHED HIM SMILE AND TAKE THEIR MONEY.
HE DID ANYTHING TO KEEP THEM HAPPY.
ANYTHING TO FIT IN.
NO MATTER HOW RICH OR POWERFUL THEY BECOME, MEN LIKE DADDY WILL ALWAYS BE *SLAVES* TO *JUPITER.*

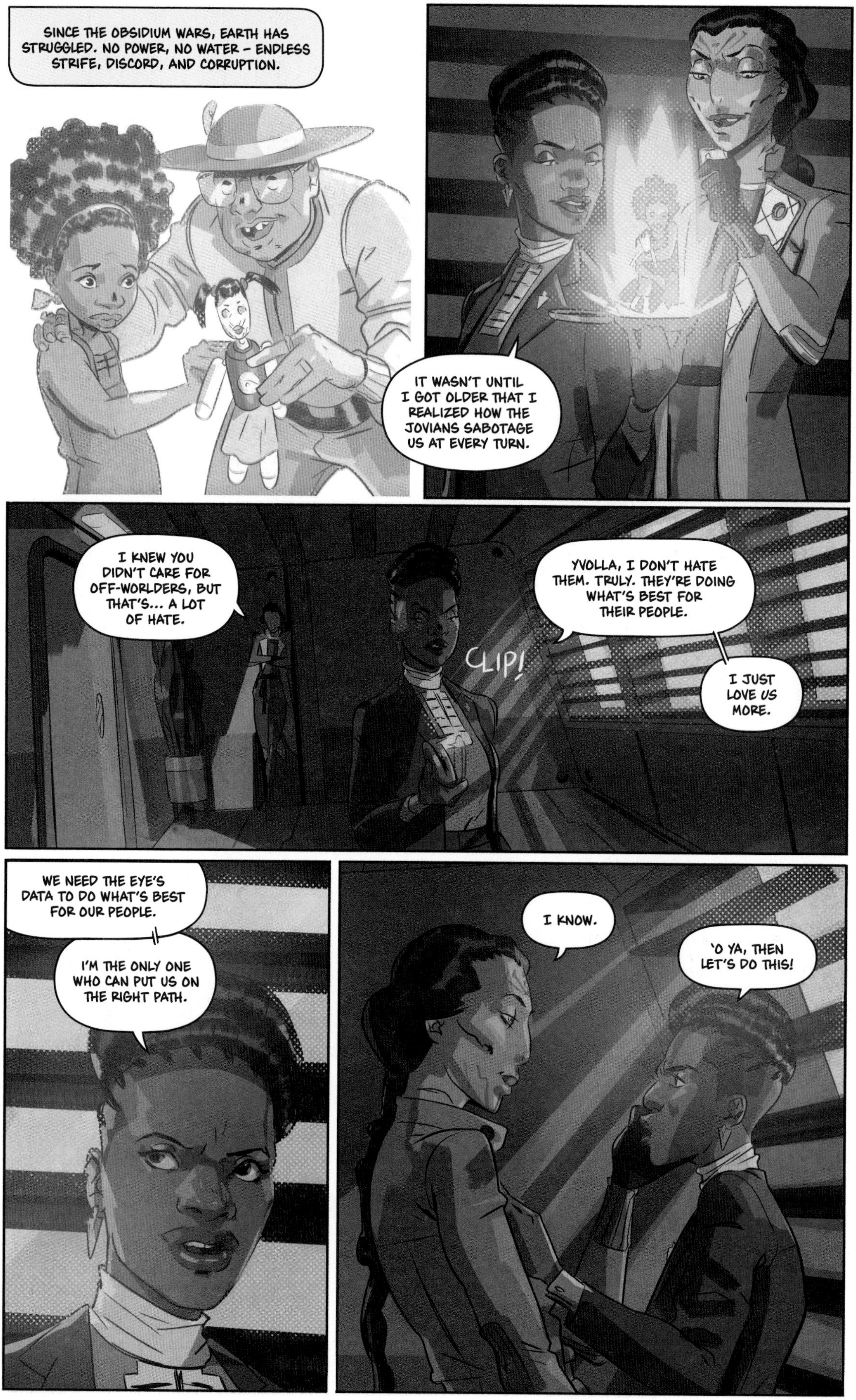
SINCE THE OBSIDIUM WARS, EARTH HAS STRUGGLED. NO POWER, NO WATER – ENDLESS STRIFE, DISCORD, AND CORRUPTION.
IT WASN'T UNTIL I GOT OLDER THAT I REALIZED HOW THE JOVIANS SABOTAGE US AT EVERY TURN.
I KNEW YOU DIDN'T CARE FOR OFF-WORLDERS, BUT THAT'S... A LOT OF HATE.
CLIP!
YVOLLA, I DON'T HATE THEM. TRULY. THEY'RE DOING WHAT'S BEST FOR THEIR PEOPLE.
I JUST LOVE US MORE.
WE NEED THE EYE'S DATA TO DO WHAT'S BEST FOR OUR PEOPLE.
I'M THE ONLY ONE WHO CAN PUT US ON THE RIGHT PATH.
I KNOW.
'O YA, THEN LET'S DO THIS!

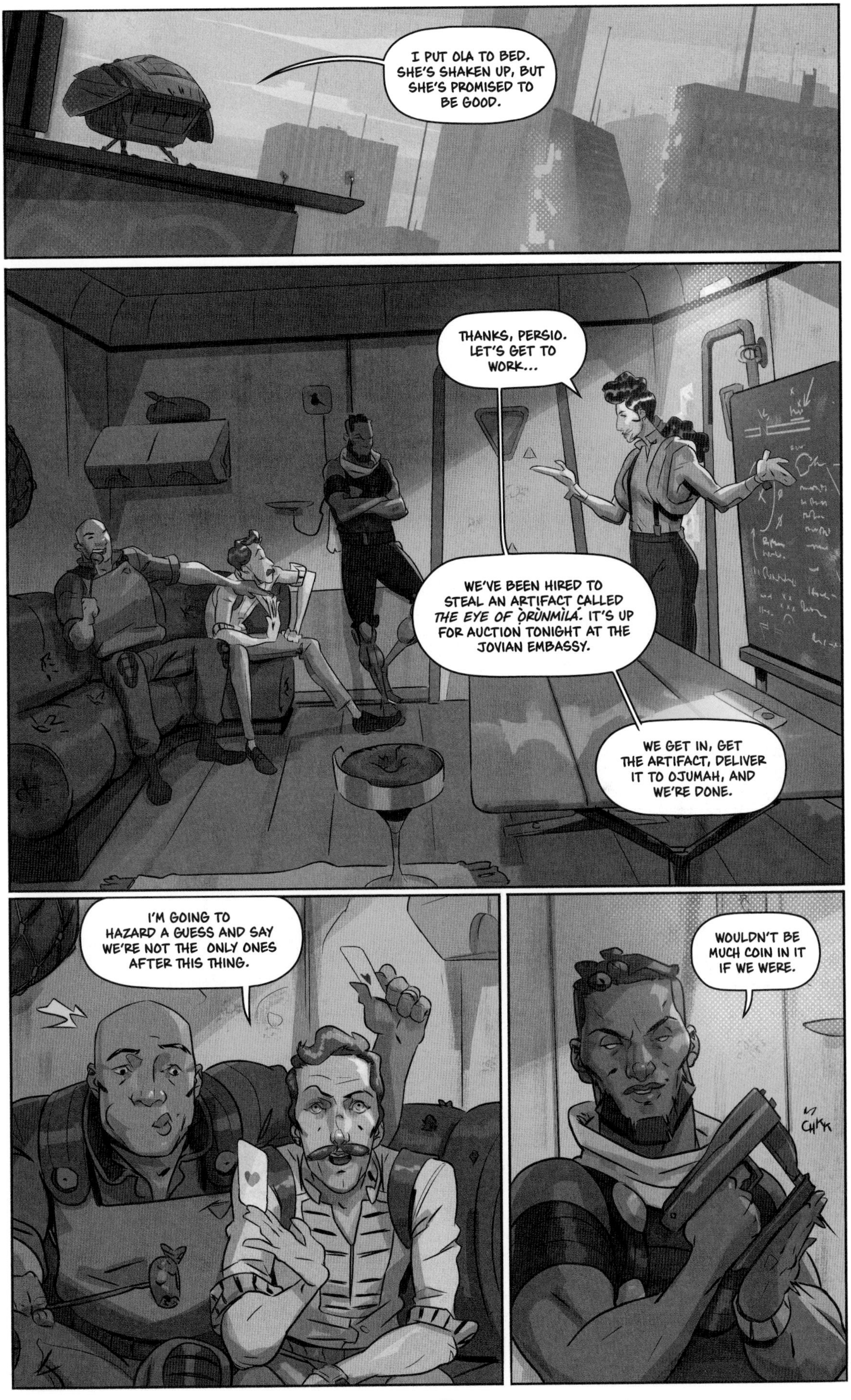
I PUT OLA TO BED. SHE'S SHAKEN UP, BUT SHE'S PROMISED TO BE GOOD.
THANKS, PERSIO. LET'S GET TO WORK...
WE'VE BEEN HIRED TO STEAL AN ARTIFACT CALLED *THE EYE OF Ọ̀RÙNMÌLÁ*. IT'S UP FOR AUCTION TONIGHT AT THE JOVIAN EMBASSY.
WE GET IN, GET THE ARTIFACT, DELIVER IT TO OJUMAH, AND WE'RE DONE.
I'M GOING TO HAZARD A GUESS AND SAY WE'RE NOT THE ONLY ONES AFTER THIS THING.
WOULDN'T BE MUCH COIN IN IT IF WE WERE.
CHKK

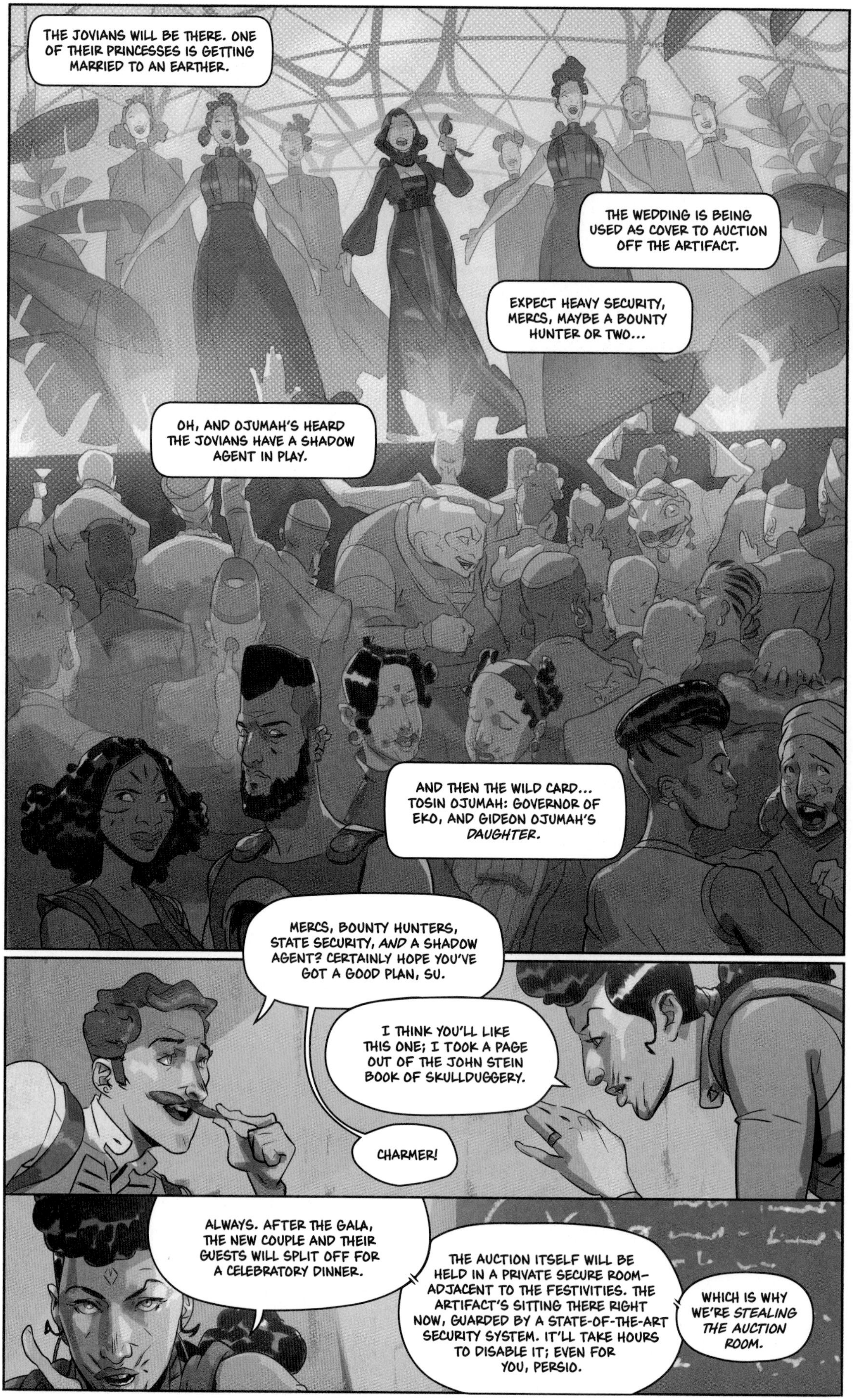
THE JOVIANS WILL BE THERE. ONE OF THEIR PRINCESSES IS GETTING MARRIED TO AN EARTHER.
THE WEDDING IS BEING USED AS COVER TO AUCTION OFF THE ARTIFACT.
EXPECT HEAVY SECURITY, MERCS, MAYBE A BOUNTY HUNTER OR TWO...
OH, AND OJUMAH'S HEARD THE JOVIANS HAVE A SHADOW AGENT IN PLAY.
AND THEN THE WILD CARD... TOSIN OJUMAH: GOVERNOR OF EKO, AND GIDEON OJUMAH'S *DAUGHTER.*
MERCS, BOUNTY HUNTERS, STATE SECURITY, *AND* A SHADOW AGENT? CERTAINLY HOPE YOU'VE GOT A GOOD PLAN, SU.
I THINK YOU'LL LIKE THIS ONE; I TOOK A PAGE OUT OF THE JOHN STEIN BOOK OF SKULLDUGGERY.
CHARMER!
ALWAYS. AFTER THE GALA, THE NEW COUPLE AND THEIR GUESTS WILL SPLIT OFF FOR A CELEBRATORY DINNER.
THE AUCTION ITSELF WILL BE HELD IN A PRIVATE SECURE ROOM–ADJACENT TO THE FESTIVITIES. THE ARTIFACT'S SITTING THERE RIGHT NOW, GUARDED BY A STATE-OF-THE-ART SECURITY SYSTEM. IT'LL TAKE HOURS TO DISABLE IT; EVEN FOR YOU, PERSIO.
WHICH IS WHY WE'RE *STEALING THE AUCTION ROOM.*

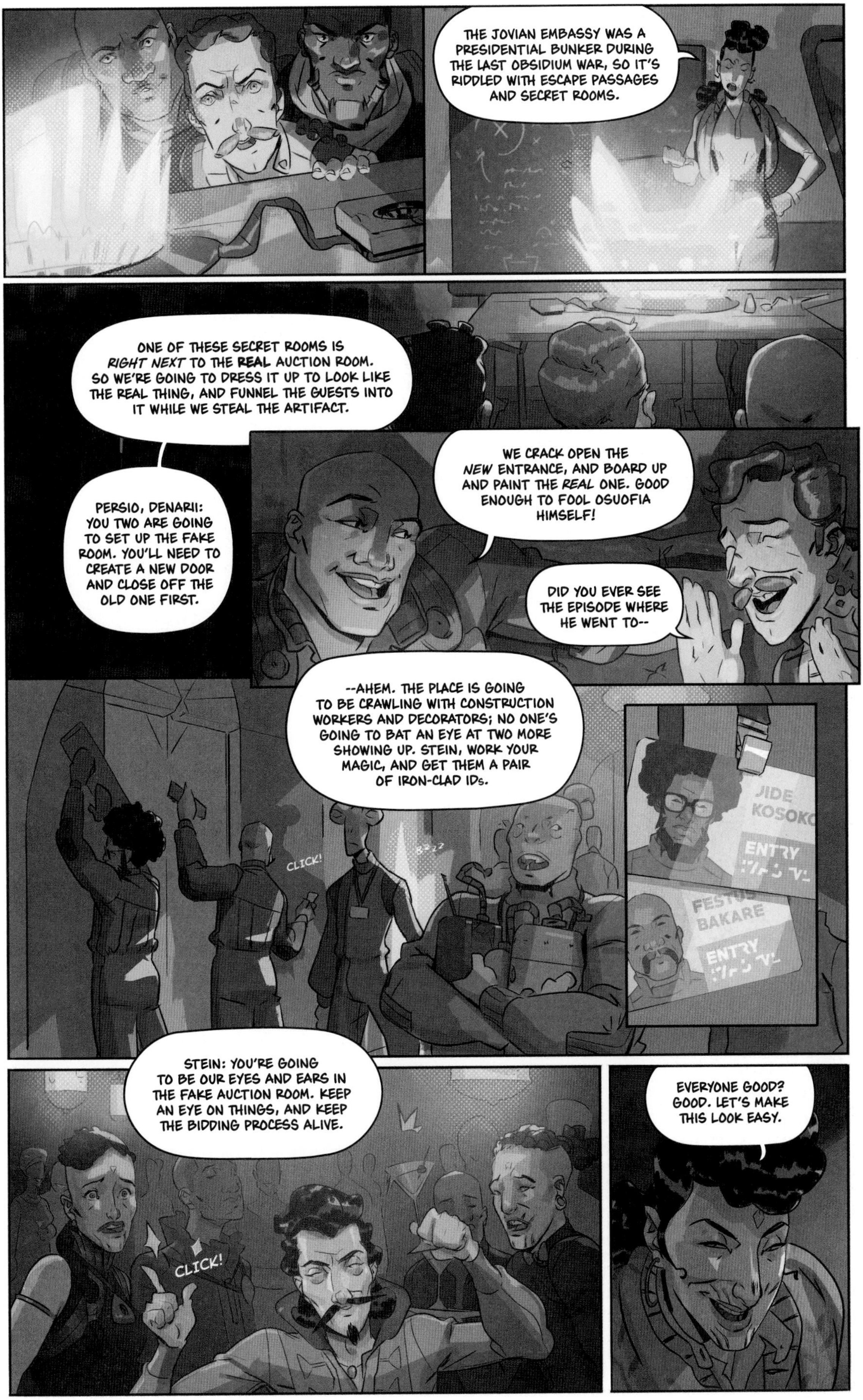
THE JOVIAN EMBASSY WAS A PRESIDENTIAL BUNKER DURING THE LAST OBSIDIUM WAR, SO IT'S RIDDLED WITH ESCAPE PASSAGES AND SECRET ROOMS.
ONE OF THESE SECRET ROOMS IS *RIGHT NEXT* TO THE **REAL** AUCTION ROOM. SO WE'RE GOING TO DRESS IT UP TO LOOK LIKE THE REAL THING, AND FUNNEL THE GUESTS INTO IT WHILE WE STEAL THE ARTIFACT.
PERSIO, DENARII: YOU TWO ARE GOING TO SET UP THE FAKE ROOM. YOU'LL NEED TO CREATE A NEW DOOR AND CLOSE OFF THE OLD ONE FIRST.
WE CRACK OPEN THE *NEW* ENTRANCE, AND BOARD UP AND PAINT THE *REAL* ONE. GOOD ENOUGH TO FOOL OSUOFIA HIMSELF!
DID YOU EVER SEE THE EPISODE WHERE HE WENT TO--
--AHEM. THE PLACE IS GOING TO BE CRAWLING WITH CONSTRUCTION WORKERS AND DECORATORS; NO ONE'S GOING TO BAT AN EYE AT TWO MORE SHOWING UP. STEIN, WORK YOUR MAGIC, AND GET THEM A PAIR OF IRON-CLAD IDs.
CLICK!
JIDE
ENTRY
BAKARE
ENTRY
STEIN: YOU'RE GOING TO BE OUR EYES AND EARS IN THE FAKE AUCTION ROOM. KEEP AN EYE ON THINGS, AND KEEP THE BIDDING PROCESS ALIVE.
CLICK!
EVERYONE GOOD? GOOD. LET'S MAKE THIS LOOK EASY.

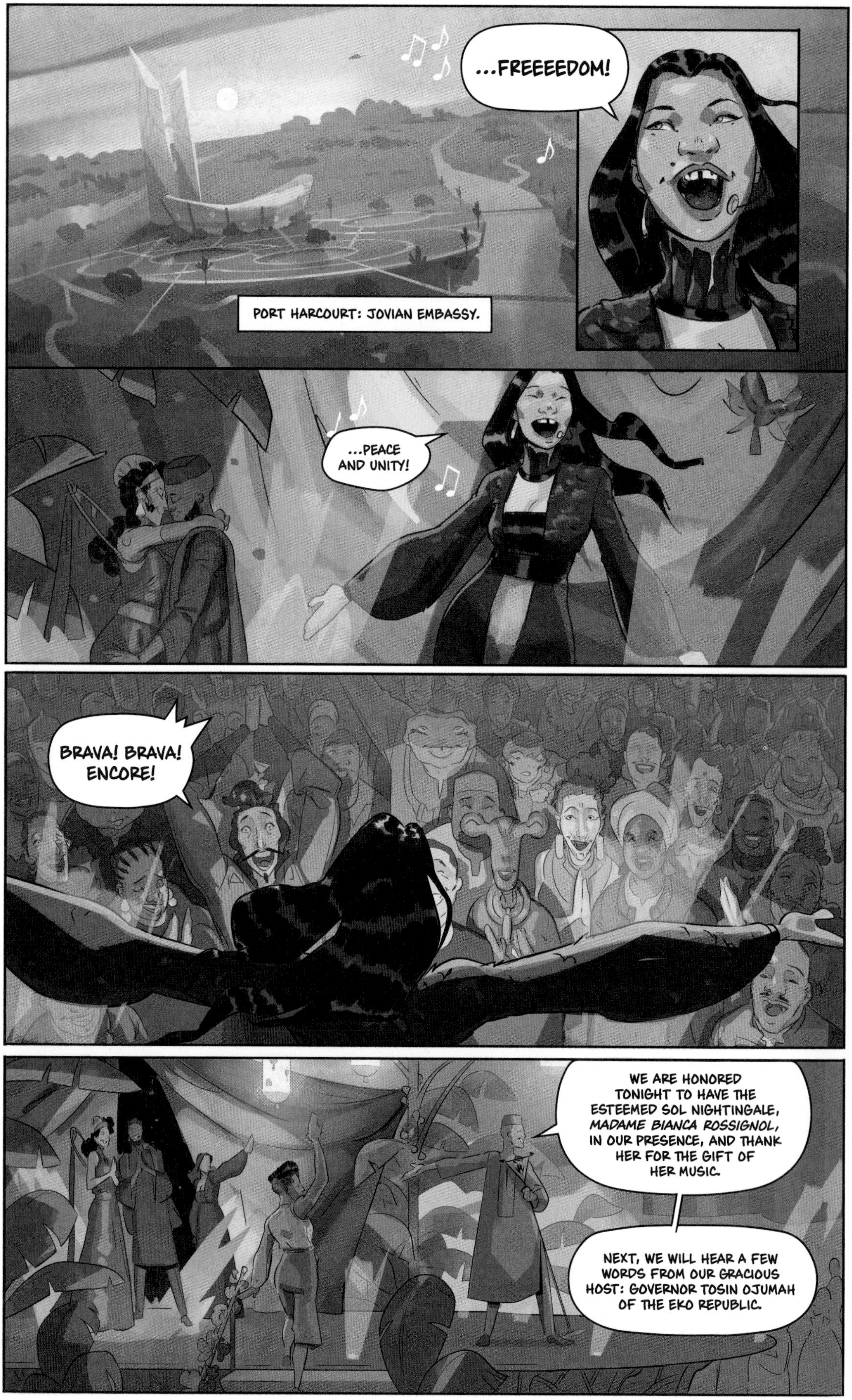
...FREEEEDOM!
PORT HARCOURT: JOVIAN EMBASSY.
...PEACE AND UNITY!
BRAVA! BRAVA! ENCORE!
WE ARE HONORED TONIGHT TO HAVE THE ESTEEMED SOL NIGHTINGALE, *MADAME BIANCA ROSSIGNOL,* IN OUR PRESENCE, AND THANK HER FOR THE GIFT OF HER MUSIC.
NEXT, WE WILL HEAR A FEW WORDS FROM OUR GRACIOUS HOST: GOVERNOR TOSIN OJUMAH OF THE EKO REPUBLIC.

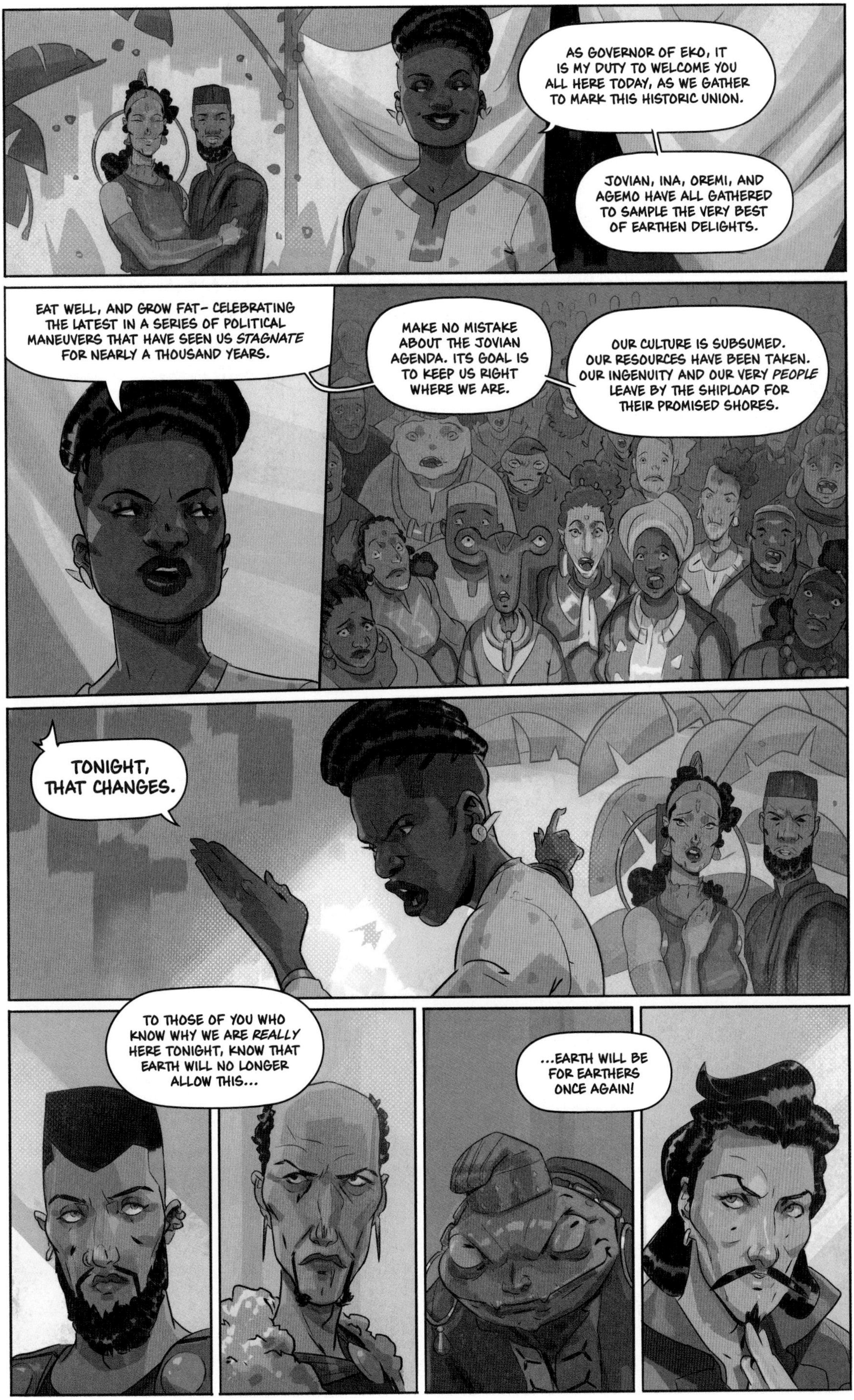

AS GOVERNOR OF EKO, IT IS MY DUTY TO WELCOME YOU ALL HERE TODAY, AS WE GATHER TO MARK THIS HISTORIC UNION.
JOVIAN, INA, OREMI, AND AGEMO HAVE ALL GATHERED TO SAMPLE THE VERY BEST OF EARTHEN DELIGHTS.
EAT WELL, AND GROW FAT- CELEBRATING THE LATEST IN A SERIES OF POLITICAL MANEUVERS THAT HAVE SEEN US *STAGNATE* FOR NEARLY A THOUSAND YEARS.
MAKE NO MISTAKE ABOUT THE JOVIAN AGENDA. ITS GOAL IS TO KEEP US RIGHT WHERE WE ARE.
OUR CULTURE IS SUBSUMED. OUR RESOURCES HAVE BEEN TAKEN. OUR INGENUITY AND OUR VERY *PEOPLE* LEAVE BY THE SHIPLOAD FOR THEIR PROMISED SHORES.
TONIGHT, THAT CHANGES.
TO THOSE OF YOU WHO KNOW WHY WE ARE *REALLY* HERE TONIGHT, KNOW THAT EARTH WILL NO LONGER ALLOW THIS...
...EARTH WILL BE FOR EARTHERS ONCE AGAIN!

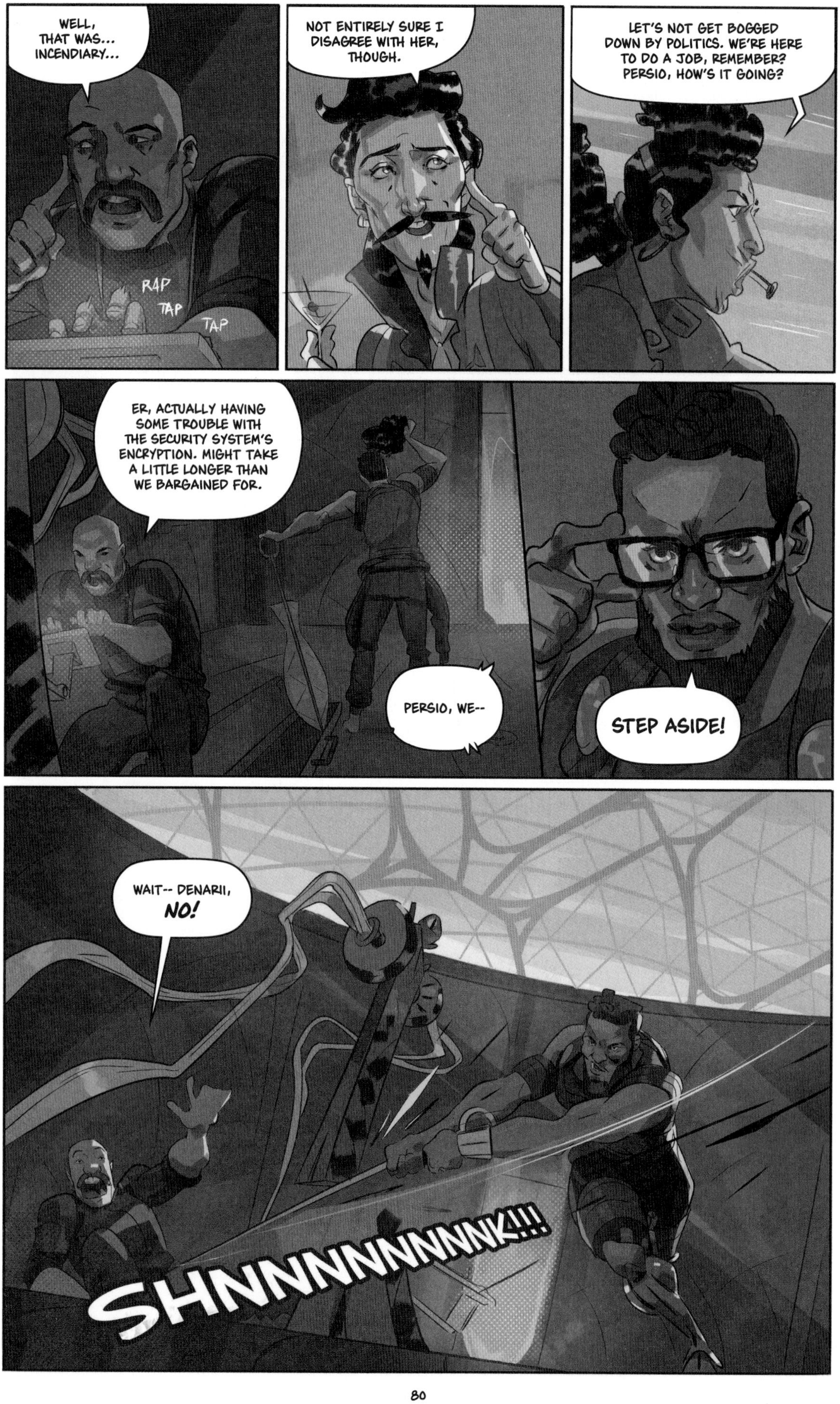
WELL, THAT WAS... INCENDIARY...
RAP TAP TAP
NOT ENTIRELY SURE I DISAGREE WITH HER, THOUGH.
LET'S NOT GET BOGGED DOWN BY POLITICS. WE'RE HERE TO DO A JOB, REMEMBER? PERSIO, HOW'S IT GOING?
ER, ACTUALLY HAVING SOME TROUBLE WITH THE SECURITY SYSTEM'S ENCRYPTION. MIGHT TAKE A LITTLE LONGER THAN WE BARGAINED FOR.
PERSIO, WE--
STEP ASIDE!
WAIT-- DENARII, NO!
SHNNNNNNNNNK!!!

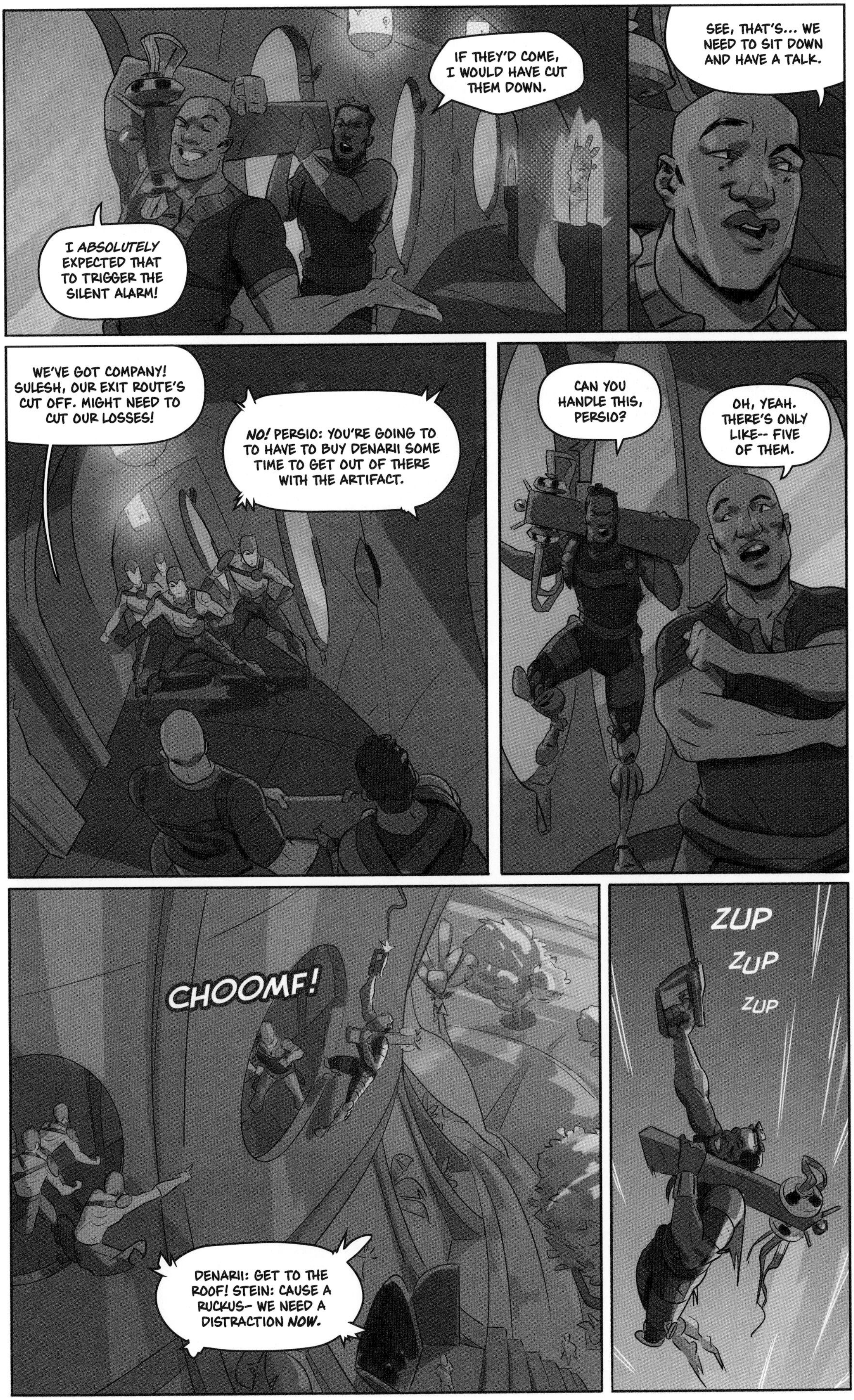
I *ABSOLUTELY* EXPECTED THAT TO TRIGGER THE SILENT ALARM!
IF THEY'D COME, I WOULD HAVE CUT THEM DOWN.
SEE, THAT'S... WE NEED TO SIT DOWN AND HAVE A TALK.
WE'VE GOT COMPANY! SULESH, OUR EXIT ROUTE'S CUT OFF. MIGHT NEED TO CUT OUR LOSSES!
NO! PERSIO: YOU'RE GOING TO TO HAVE TO BUY DENARII SOME TIME TO GET OUT OF THERE WITH THE ARTIFACT.
CAN YOU HANDLE THIS, PERSIO?
OH, YEAH. THERE'S ONLY LIKE-- FIVE OF THEM.
CHOOMF!
DENARII: GET TO THE ROOF! STEIN: CAUSE A RUCKUS- WE NEED A DISTRACTION *NOW*.
ZUP
ZUP
ZUP

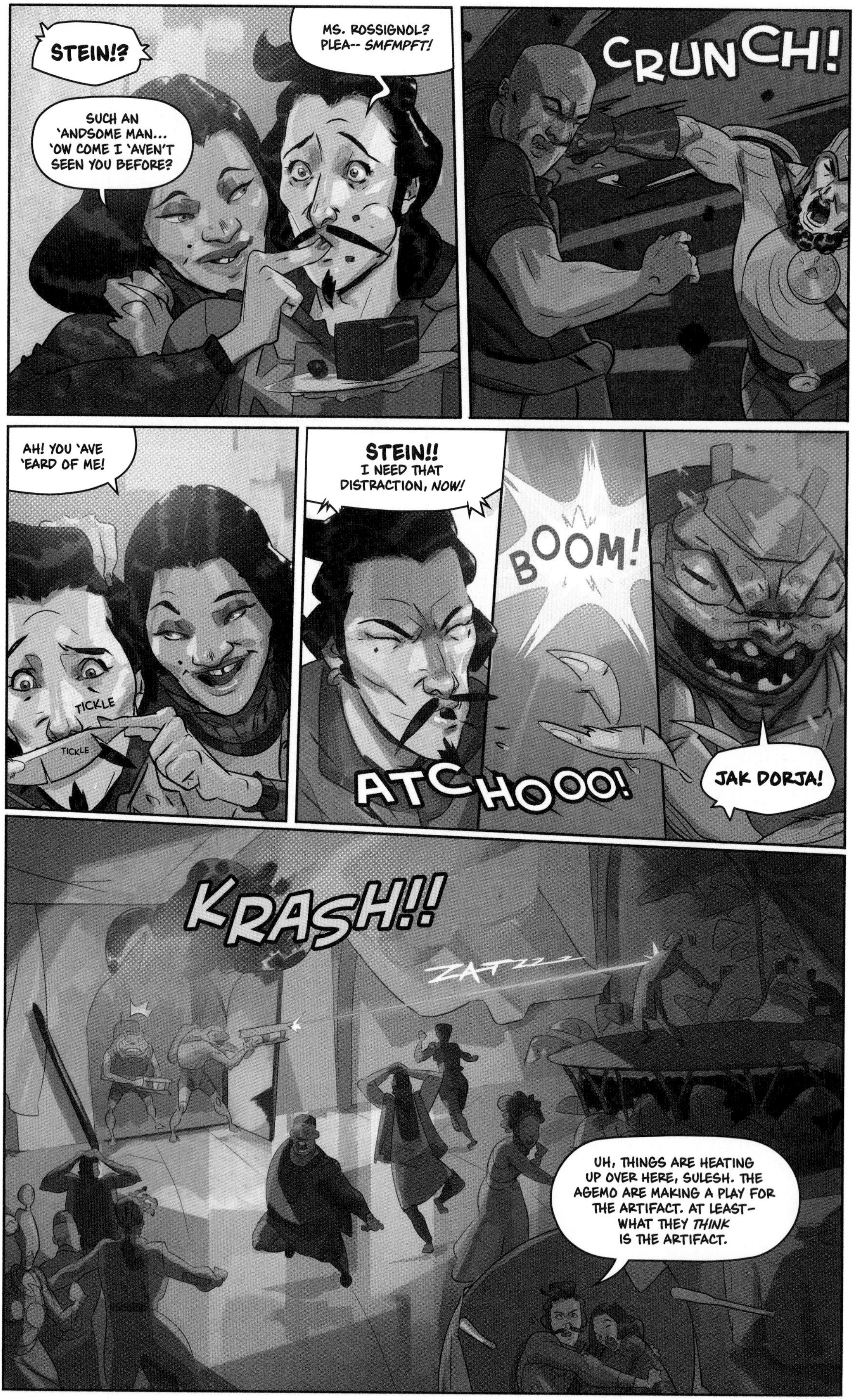
STEIN!?
MS. ROSSIGNOL? PLEA-- SMFMPFT!
SUCH AN 'ANDSOME MAN... 'OW COME I 'AVEN'T SEEN YOU BEFORE?
CRUNCH!
AH! YOU 'AVE 'EARD OF ME!
TICKLE
TICKLE
STEIN!! I NEED THAT DISTRACTION, NOW!
ATCHOOO!
BOOM!
JAK DORJA!
KRASH!!
ZATZZZ
UH, THINGS ARE HEATING UP OVER HERE, SULESH. THE AGEMO ARE MAKING A PLAY FOR THE ARTIFACT. AT LEAST-WHAT THEY THINK IS THE ARTIFACT.

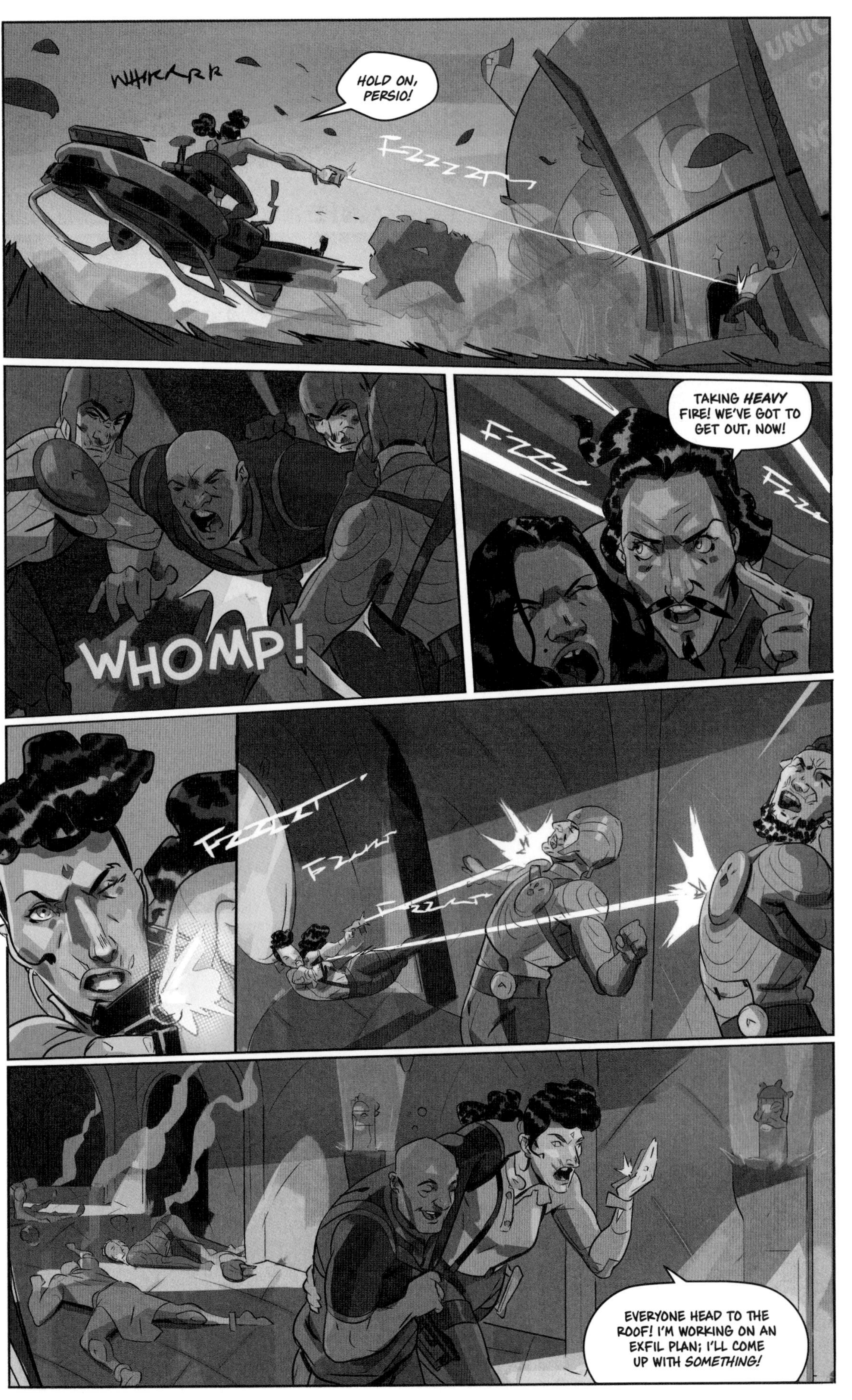
WHKARR
HOLD ON, PERSIO!
FZZZZZT
WHOMP!
FZZZZ
TAKING HEAVY FIRE! WE'VE GOT TO GET OUT, NOW!
FZZZT
FZZZT
FZZZT
FZZZT
EVERYONE HEAD TO THE ROOF! I'M WORKING ON AN EXFIL PLAN; I'LL COME UP WITH SOMETHING!

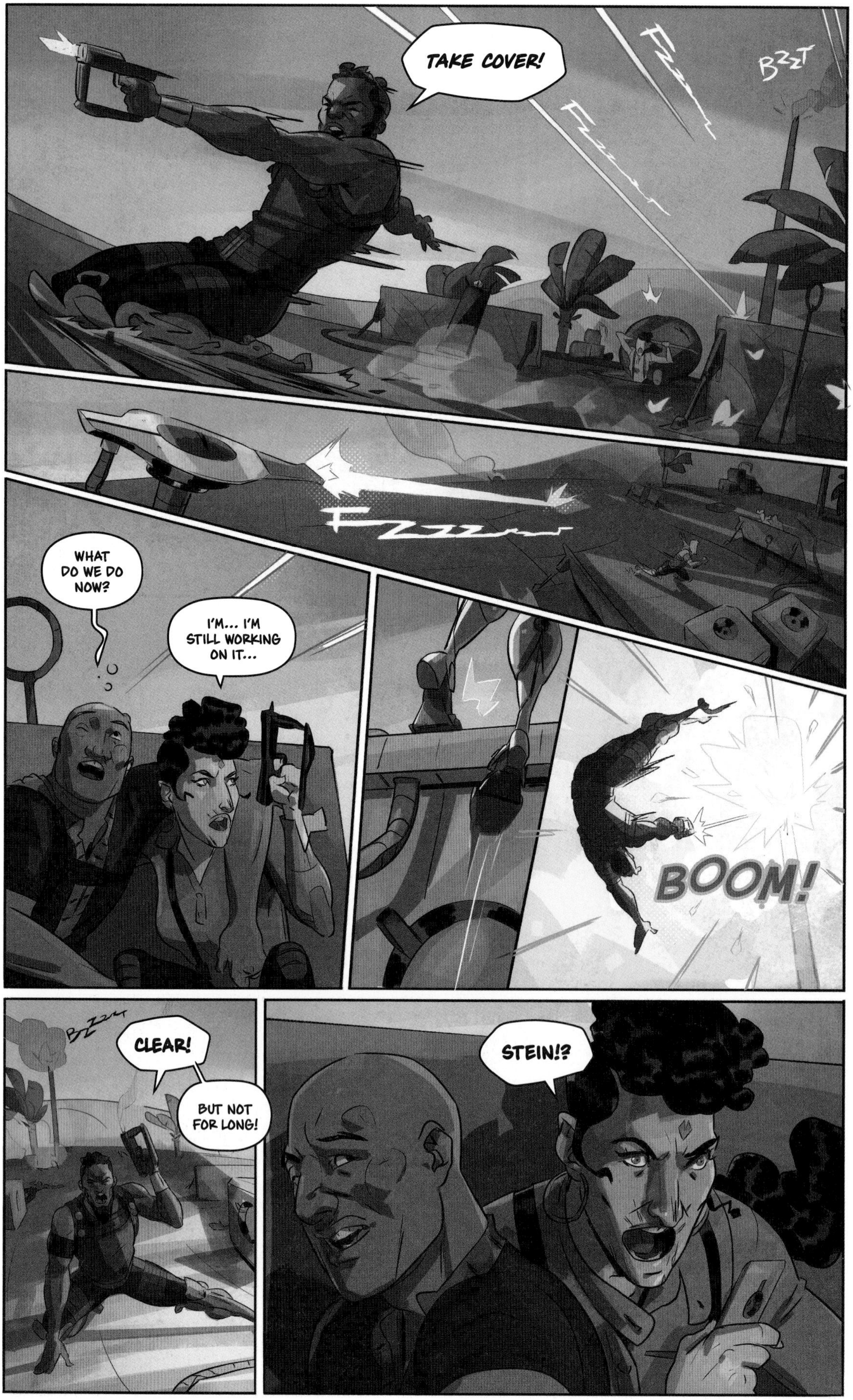
TAKE COVER!
FZZZT
FZZZT
BZZT
FZZZZ
WHAT DO WE DO NOW?
I'M... I'M STILL WORKING ON IT...
BOOM!
CLEAR!
BUT NOT FOR LONG!
STEIN!?

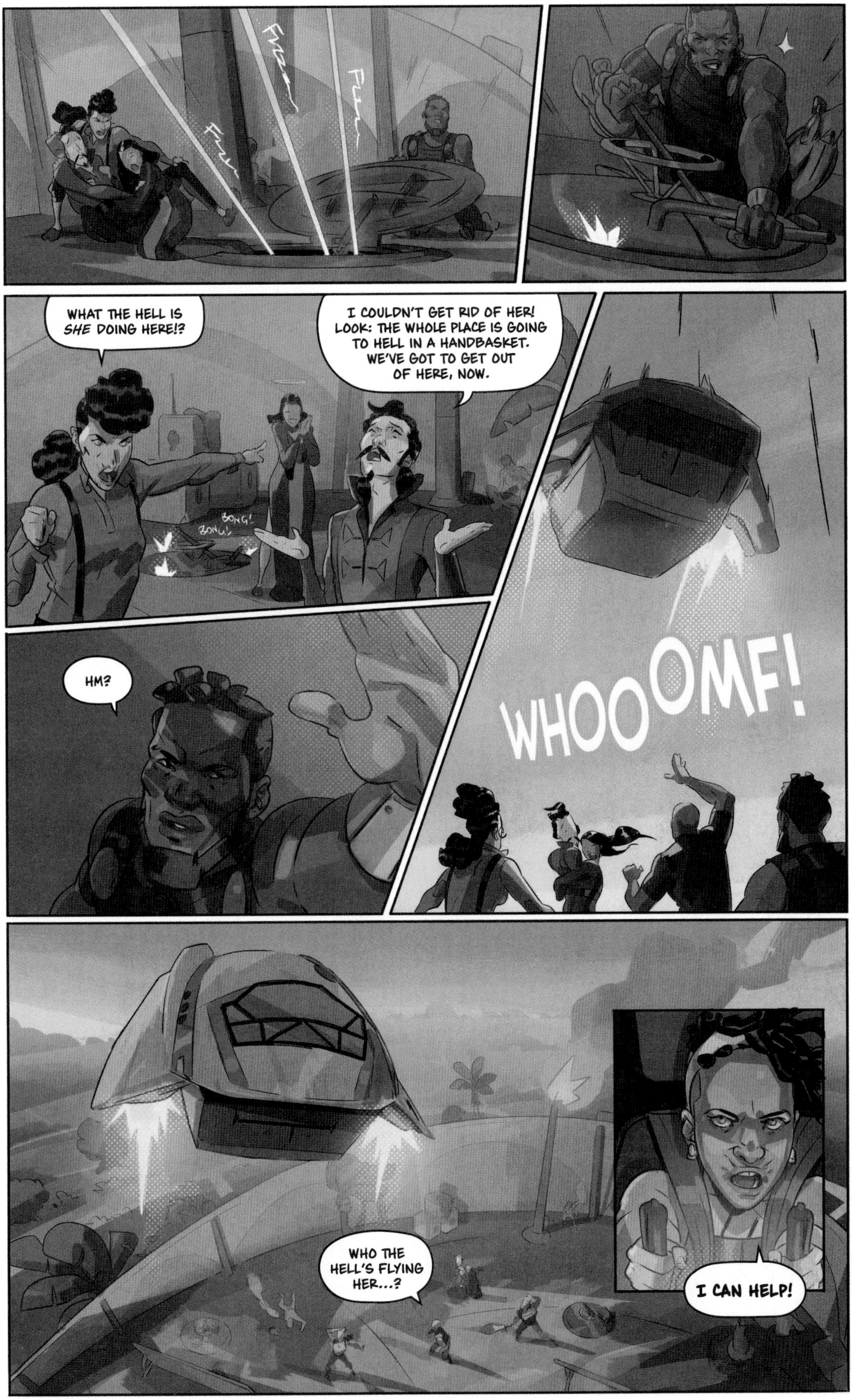
WHAT THE HELL IS *SHE* DOING HERE!?
I COULDN'T GET RID OF HER! LOOK: THE WHOLE PLACE IS GOING TO HELL IN A HANDBASKET. WE'VE GOT TO GET OUT OF HERE, NOW.
BONG! BONG!
HM?
WHOOOMF!
WHO THE HELL'S FLYING HER...?
I CAN HELP!

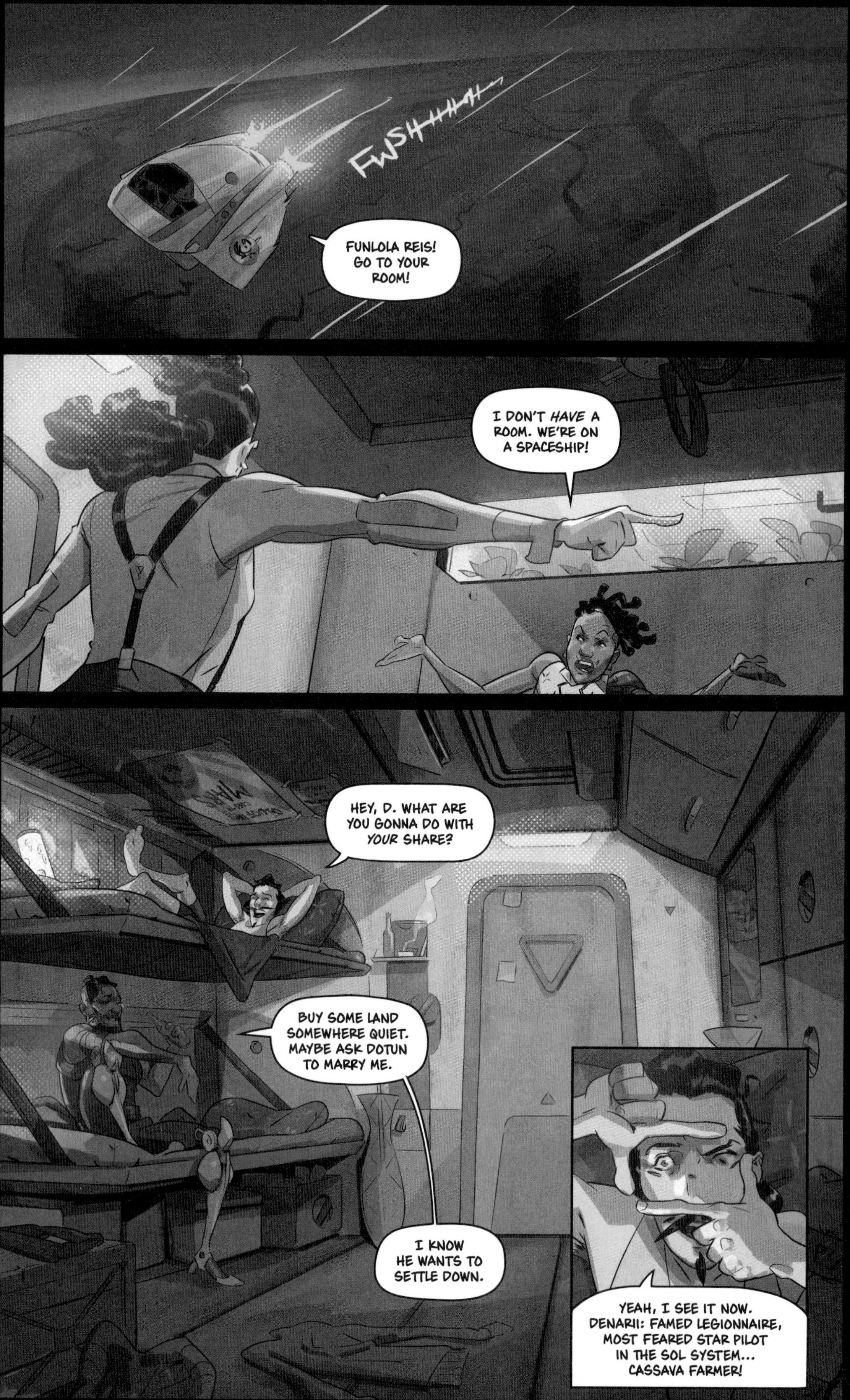
FWSHHHHH
FUNLOLA REIS! GO TO YOUR ROOM!
I DON'T *HAVE* A ROOM. WE'RE ON A SPACESHIP!
HEY, D. WHAT ARE YOU GONNA DO WITH *YOUR* SHARE?
BUY SOME LAND SOMEWHERE QUIET. MAYBE ASK DOTUN TO MARRY ME.
I KNOW HE WANTS TO SETTLE DOWN.
YEAH, I SEE IT NOW. DENARII: FAMED LEGIONNAIRE, MOST FEARED STAR PILOT IN THE SOL SYSTEM... CASSAVA FARMER!

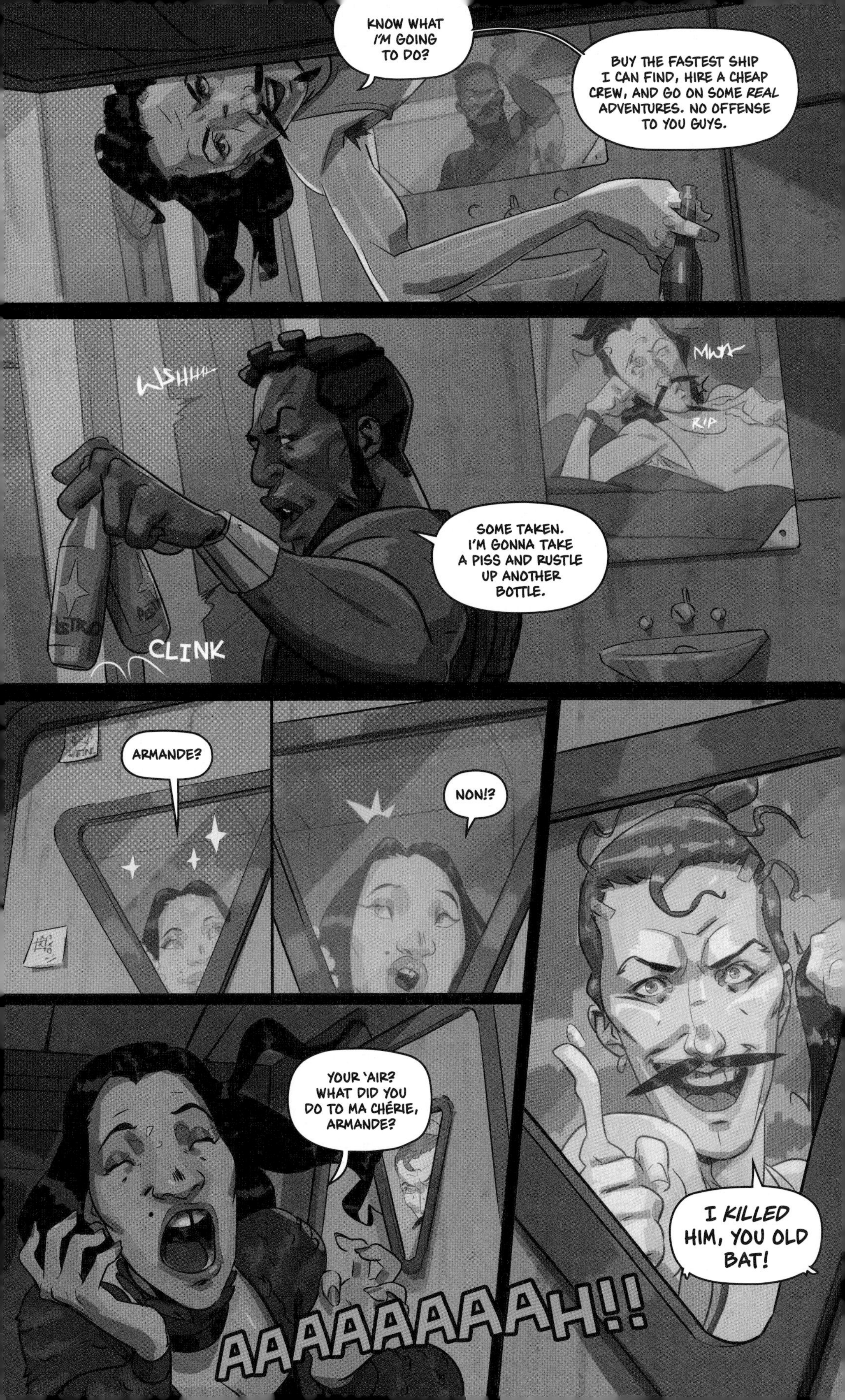
KNOW WHAT I'M GOING TO DO?
BUY THE FASTEST SHIP I CAN FIND, HIRE A CHEAP CREW, AND GO ON SOME REAL ADVENTURES. NO OFFENSE TO YOU GUYS.
MWA
RIP
SOME TAKEN. I'M GONNA TAKE A PISS AND RUSTLE UP ANOTHER BOTTLE.
CLINK
ARMANDE?
NON!?
YOUR 'AIR? WHAT DID YOU DO TO MA CHÉRIE, ARMANDE?
I KILLED HIM, YOU OLD BAT!
AAAAAAAAAH!!

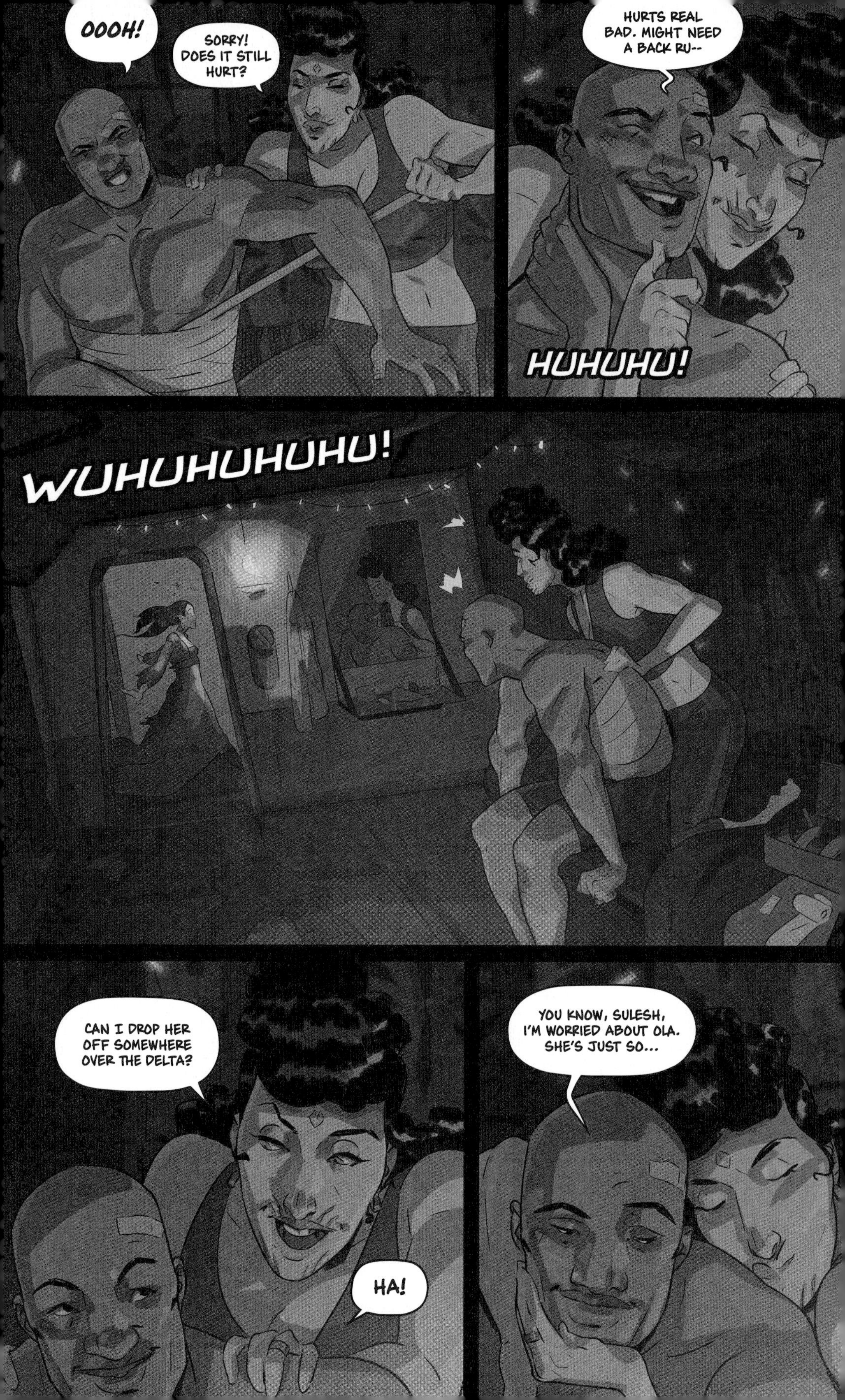
OOOH!
SORRY! DOES IT STILL HURT?
HURTS REAL BAD. MIGHT NEED A BACK RU--
HUHUHU!
WUHUHUHUHU!
CAN I DROP HER OFF SOMEWHERE OVER THE DELTA?
HA!
YOU KNOW, SULESH, I'M WORRIED ABOUT OLA. SHE'S JUST SO...

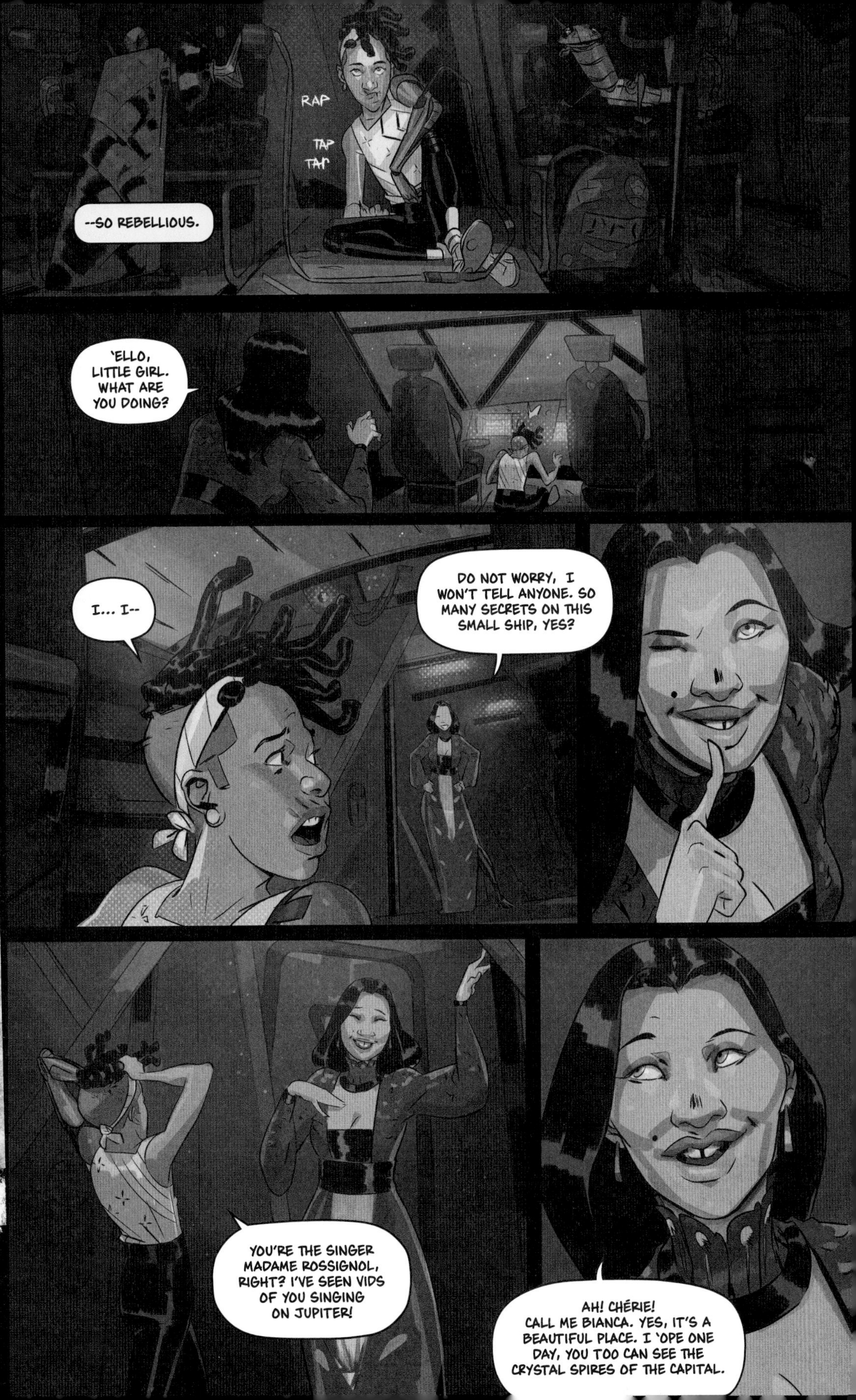
RAP
TAP
TAP
--SO REBELLIOUS.
'ELLO, LITTLE GIRL. WHAT ARE YOU DOING?
I... I--
DO NOT WORRY, I WON'T TELL ANYONE. SO MANY SECRETS ON THIS SMALL SHIP, YES?
YOU'RE THE SINGER MADAME ROSSIGNOL, RIGHT? I'VE SEEN VIDS OF YOU SINGING ON JUPITER!
AH! CHÉRIE! CALL ME BIANCA. YES, IT'S A BEAUTIFUL PLACE. I 'OPE ONE DAY, YOU TOO CAN SEE THE CRYSTAL SPIRES OF THE CAPITAL.

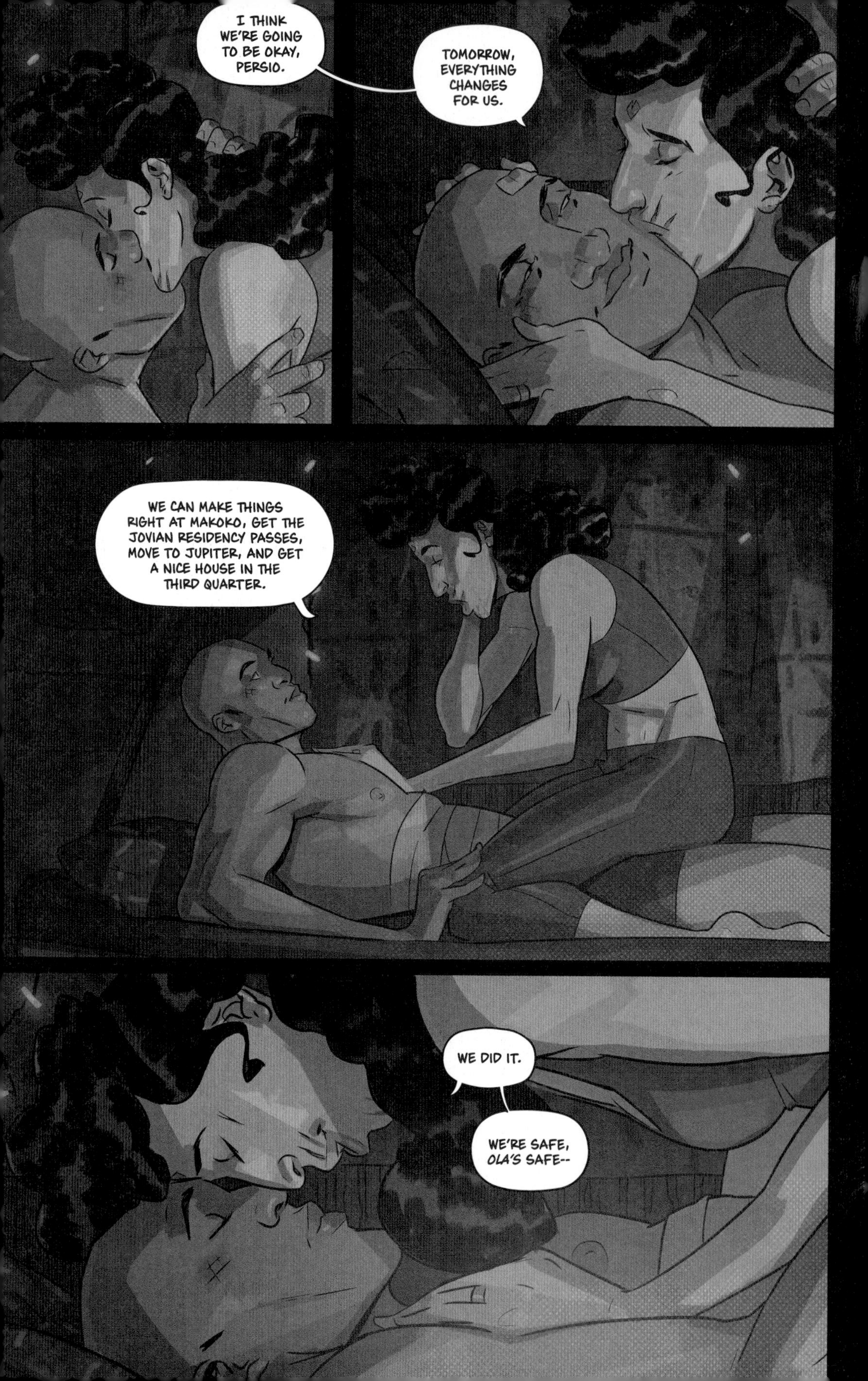
I THINK WE'RE GOING TO BE OKAY, PERSIO.
TOMORROW, EVERYTHING CHANGES FOR US.
WE CAN MAKE THINGS RIGHT AT MAKOKO, GET THE JOVIAN RESIDENCY PASSES, MOVE TO JUPITER, AND GET A NICE HOUSE IN THE THIRD QUARTER.
WE DID IT.
WE'RE SAFE, OLA'S SAFE--

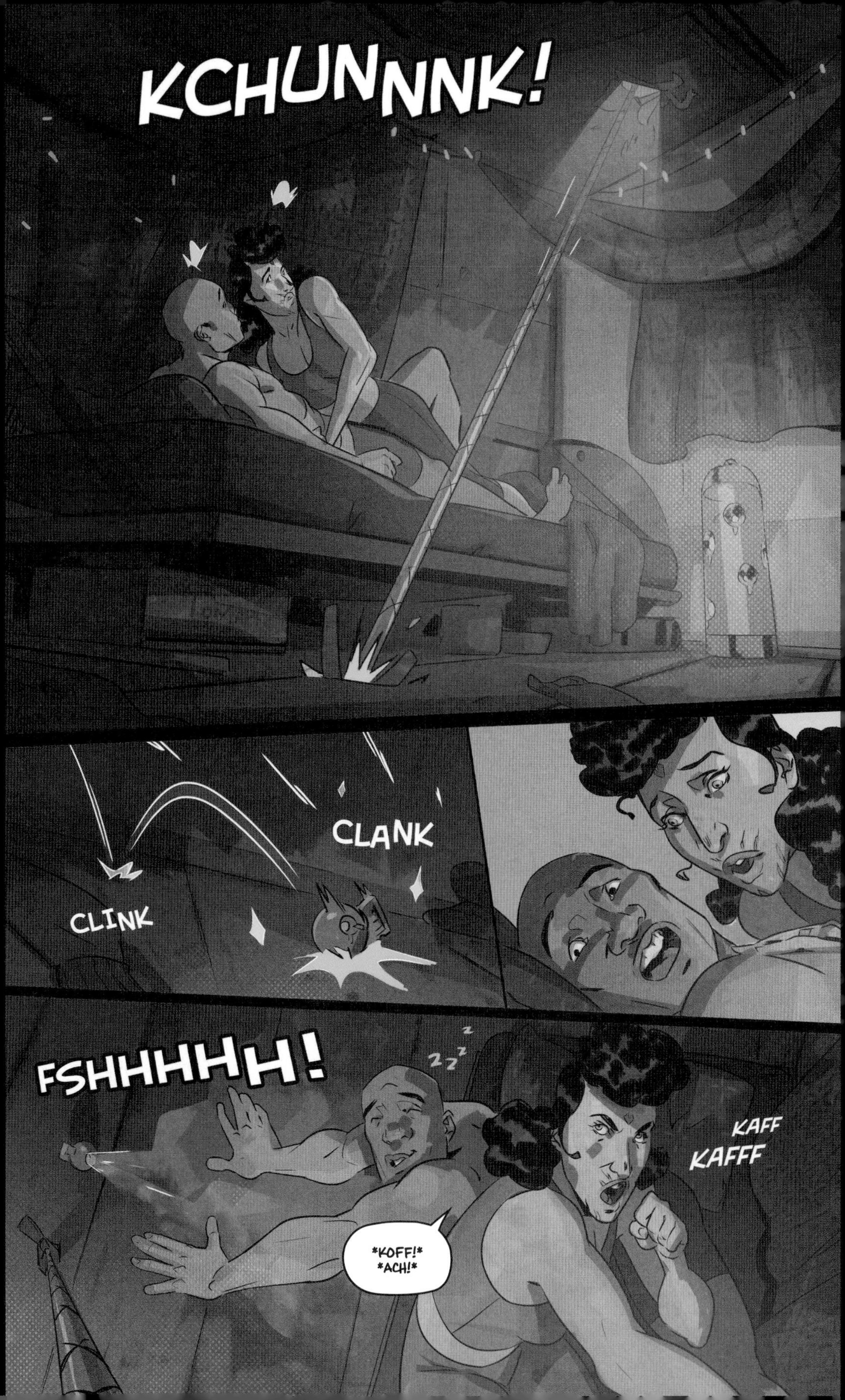
KCHUNNNK!
CLANK
CLINK
FSHHHHH!
Z Z Z
KAFF
KAFFF
KOFF!
ACH!

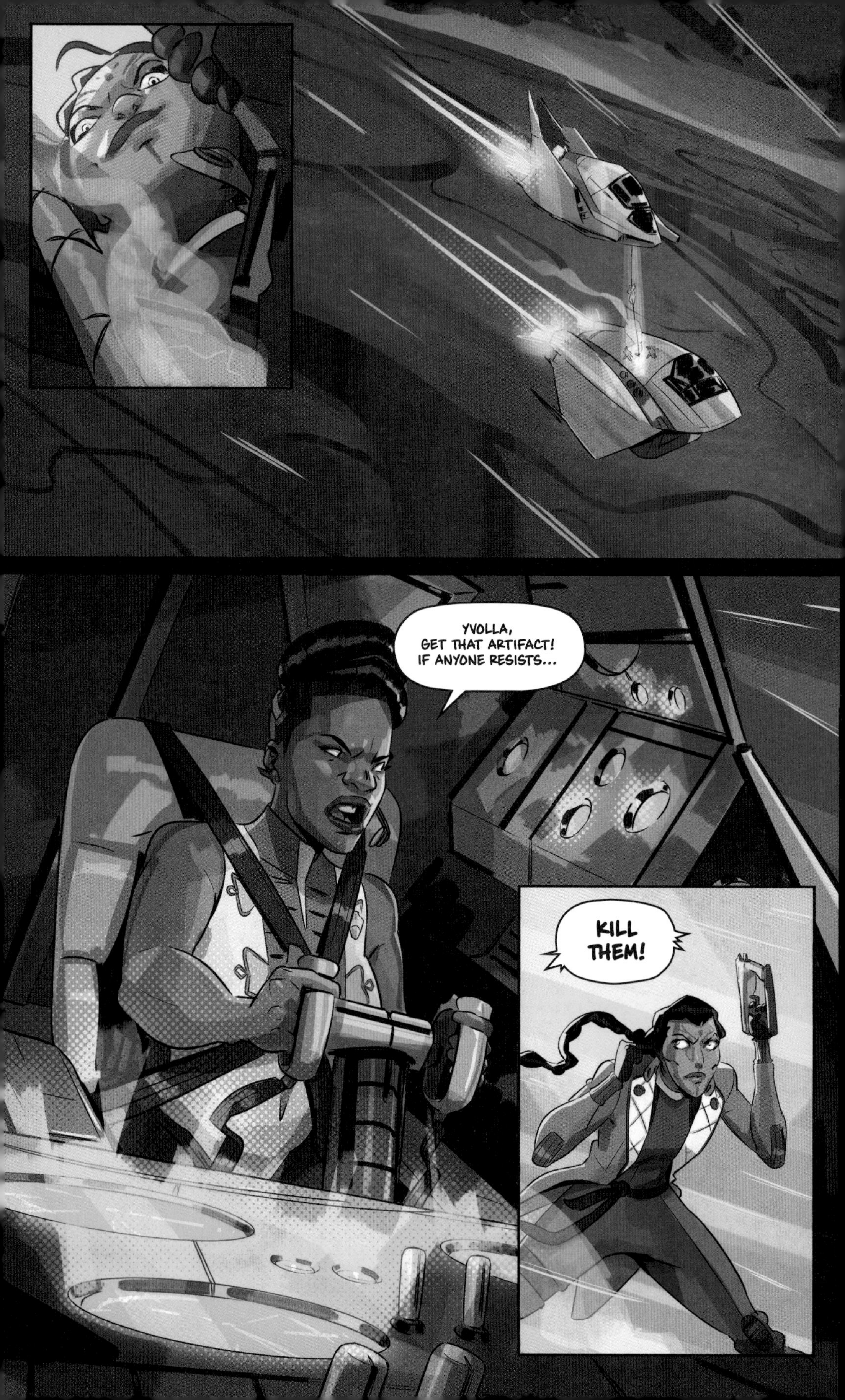
YVOLLA,
GET THAT ARTIFACT!
IF ANYONE RESISTS...
KILL
THEM!

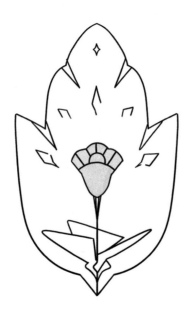

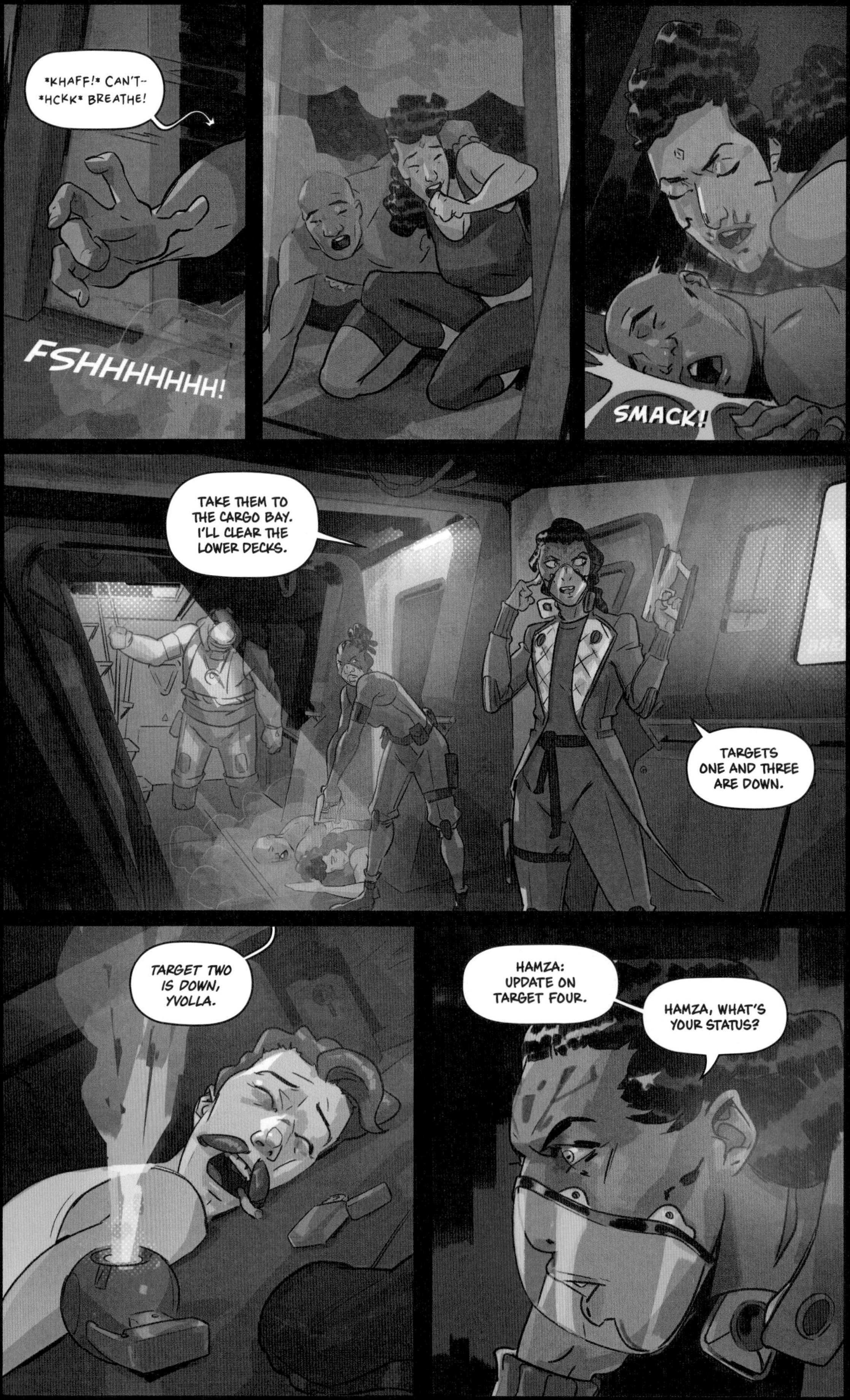
KHAFF! CAN'T--
HCKK BREATHE!
FSHHHHHHH!
SMACK!
TAKE THEM TO THE CARGO BAY. I'LL CLEAR THE LOWER DECKS.
TARGETS ONE AND THREE ARE DOWN.
TARGET TWO IS DOWN, YVOLLA.
HAMZA: UPDATE ON TARGET FOUR.
HAMZA, WHAT'S YOUR STATUS?

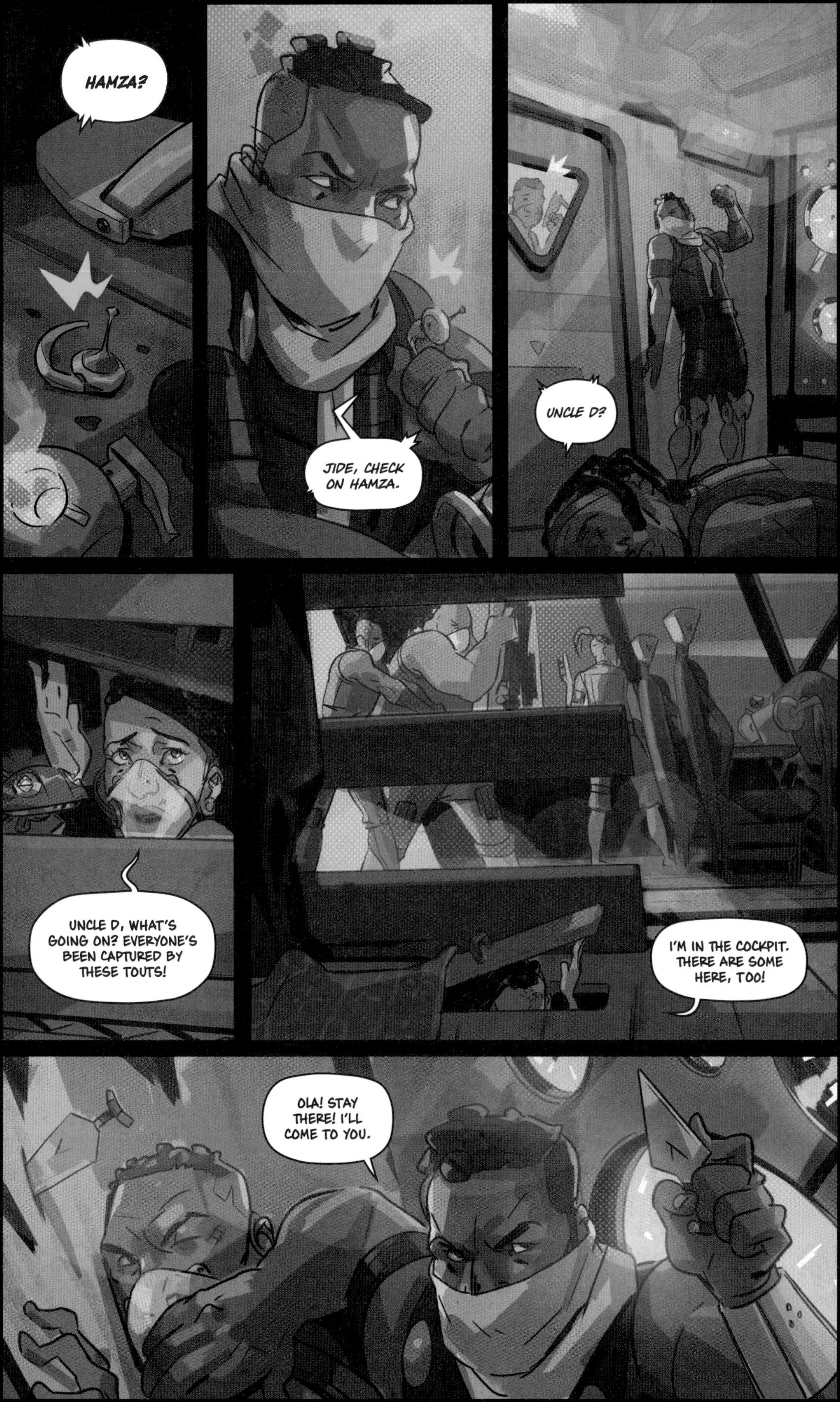
HAMZA?
JIDE, CHECK ON HAMZA.
UNCLE D?
UNCLE D, WHAT'S GOING ON? EVERYONE'S BEEN CAPTURED BY THESE TOUTS!
I'M IN THE COCKPIT. THERE ARE SOME HERE, TOO!
OLA! STAY THERE! I'LL COME TO YOU.

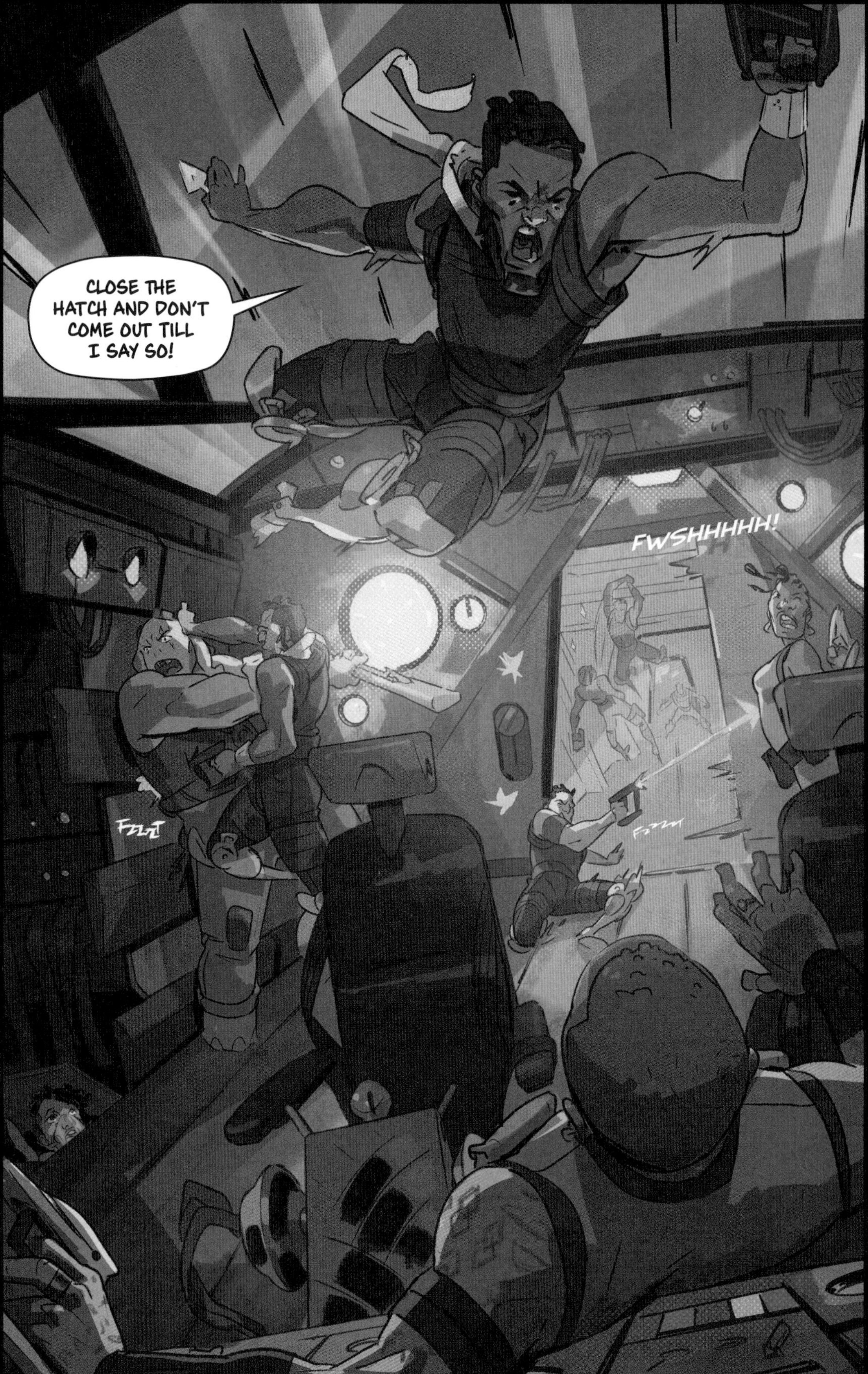
CLOSE THE HATCH AND DON'T COME OUT TILL I SAY SO!
FWSHHHHH!
FZZZT

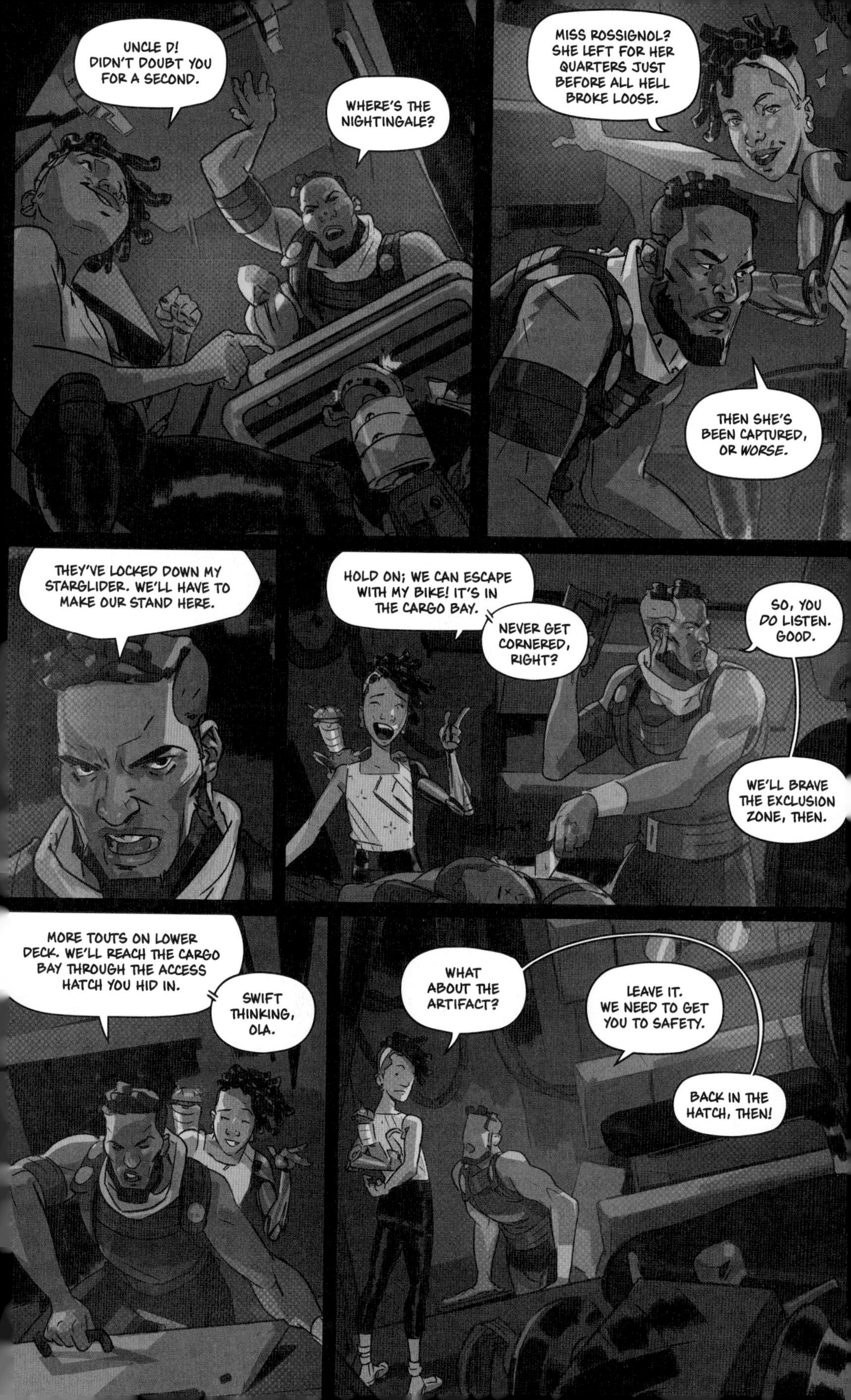
UNCLE D! DIDN'T DOUBT YOU FOR A SECOND.
WHERE'S THE NIGHTINGALE?
MISS ROSSIGNOL? SHE LEFT FOR HER QUARTERS JUST BEFORE ALL HELL BROKE LOOSE.
THEN SHE'S BEEN CAPTURED, OR *WORSE*.
THEY'VE LOCKED DOWN MY STARGLIDER. WE'LL HAVE TO MAKE OUR STAND HERE.
HOLD ON; WE CAN ESCAPE WITH MY BIKE! IT'S IN THE CARGO BAY.
NEVER GET CORNERED, RIGHT?
SO, YOU *DO* LISTEN. GOOD.
WE'LL BRAVE THE EXCLUSION ZONE, THEN.
MORE TOUTS ON LOWER DECK. WE'LL REACH THE CARGO BAY THROUGH THE ACCESS HATCH YOU HID IN.
SWIFT THINKING, OLA.
WHAT ABOUT THE ARTIFACT?
LEAVE IT. WE NEED TO GET YOU TO SAFETY.
BACK IN THE HATCH, THEN!

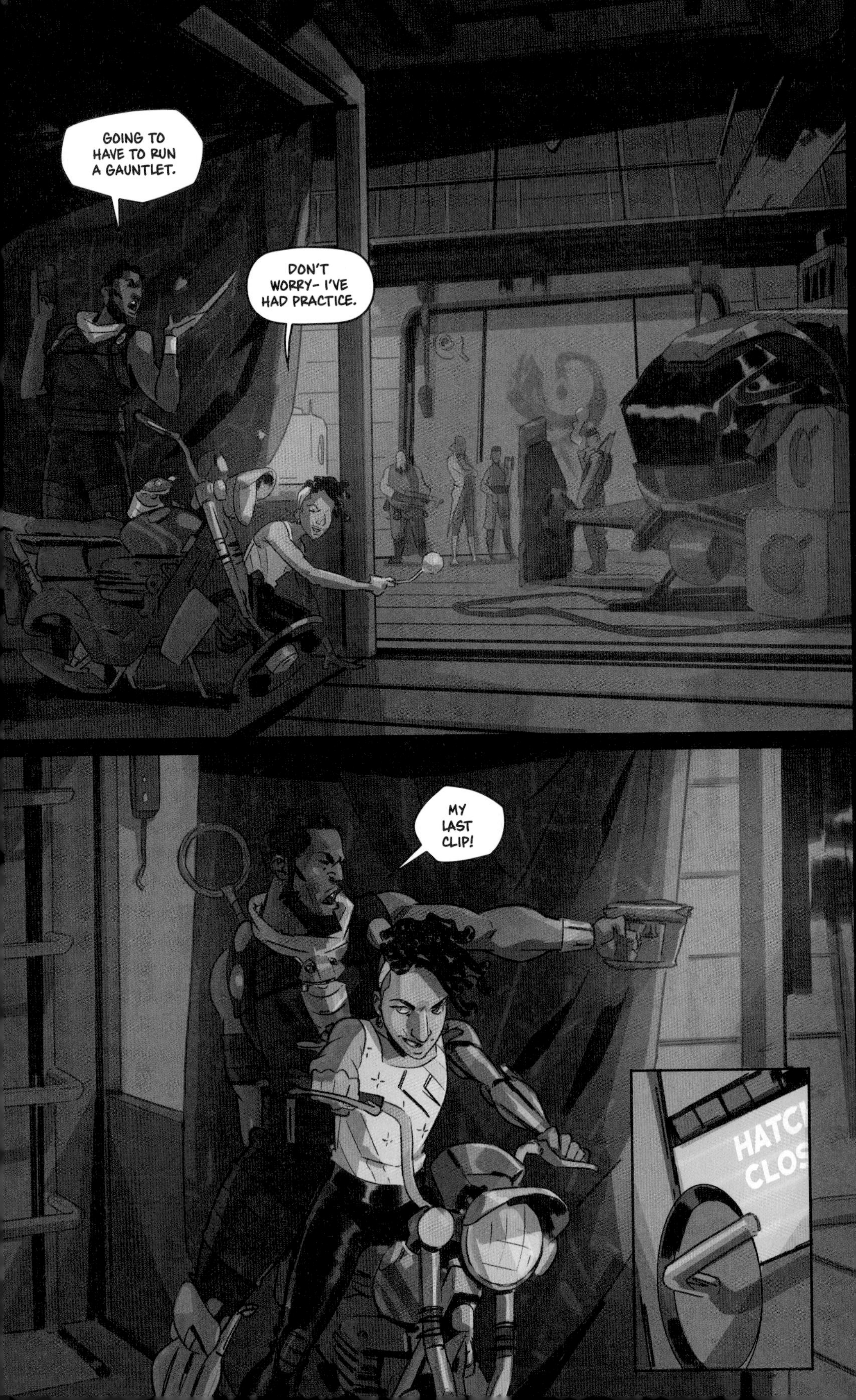
GOING TO HAVE TO RUN A GAUNTLET.
DON'T WORRY- I'VE HAD PRACTICE.
MY LAST CLIP!
HATC
CLOS

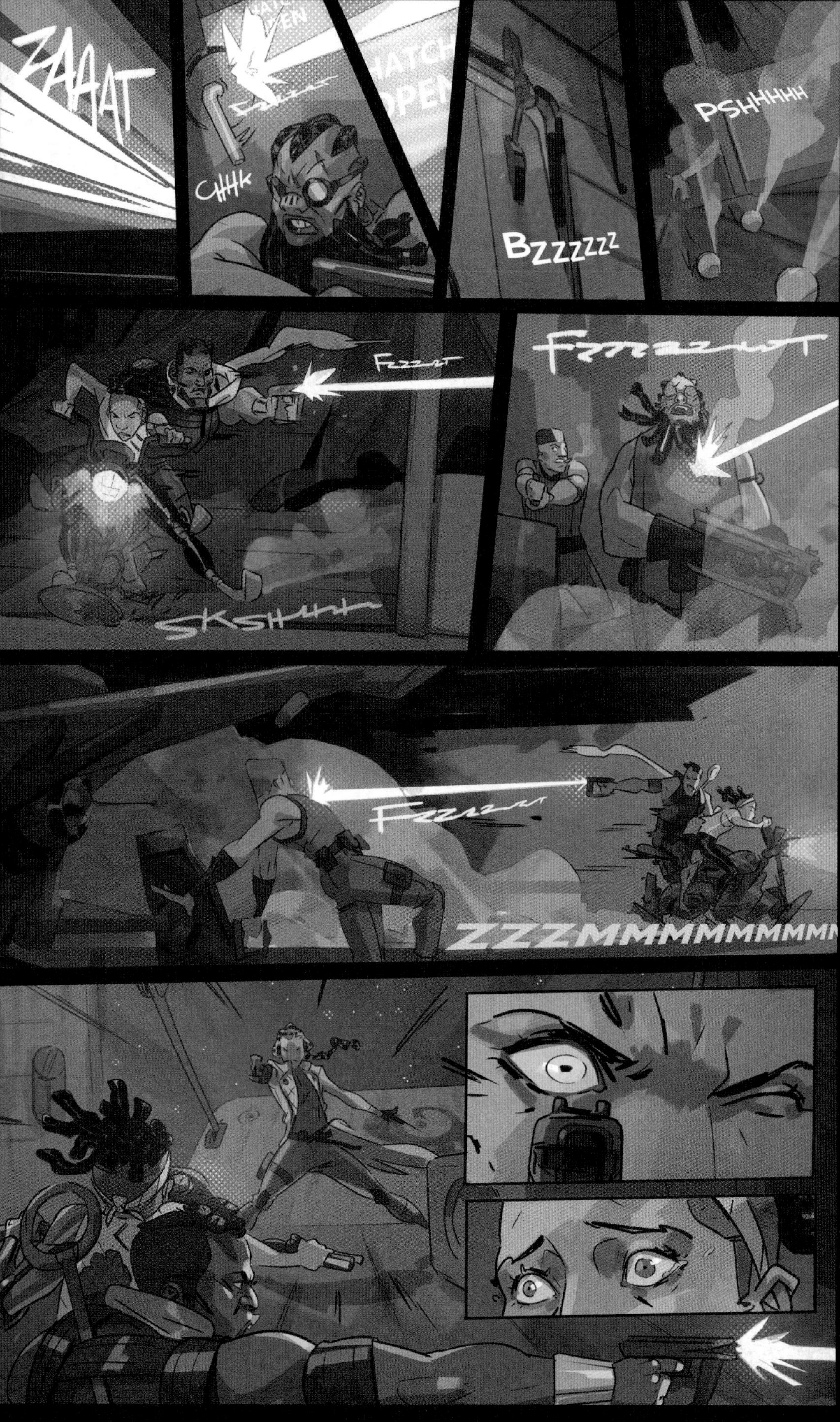
ZAAAT
CHHK
HATCH OPEN
BZZZZZZ
PSHHHHH
SKSHHHH
ZZZMMMMMMMMM

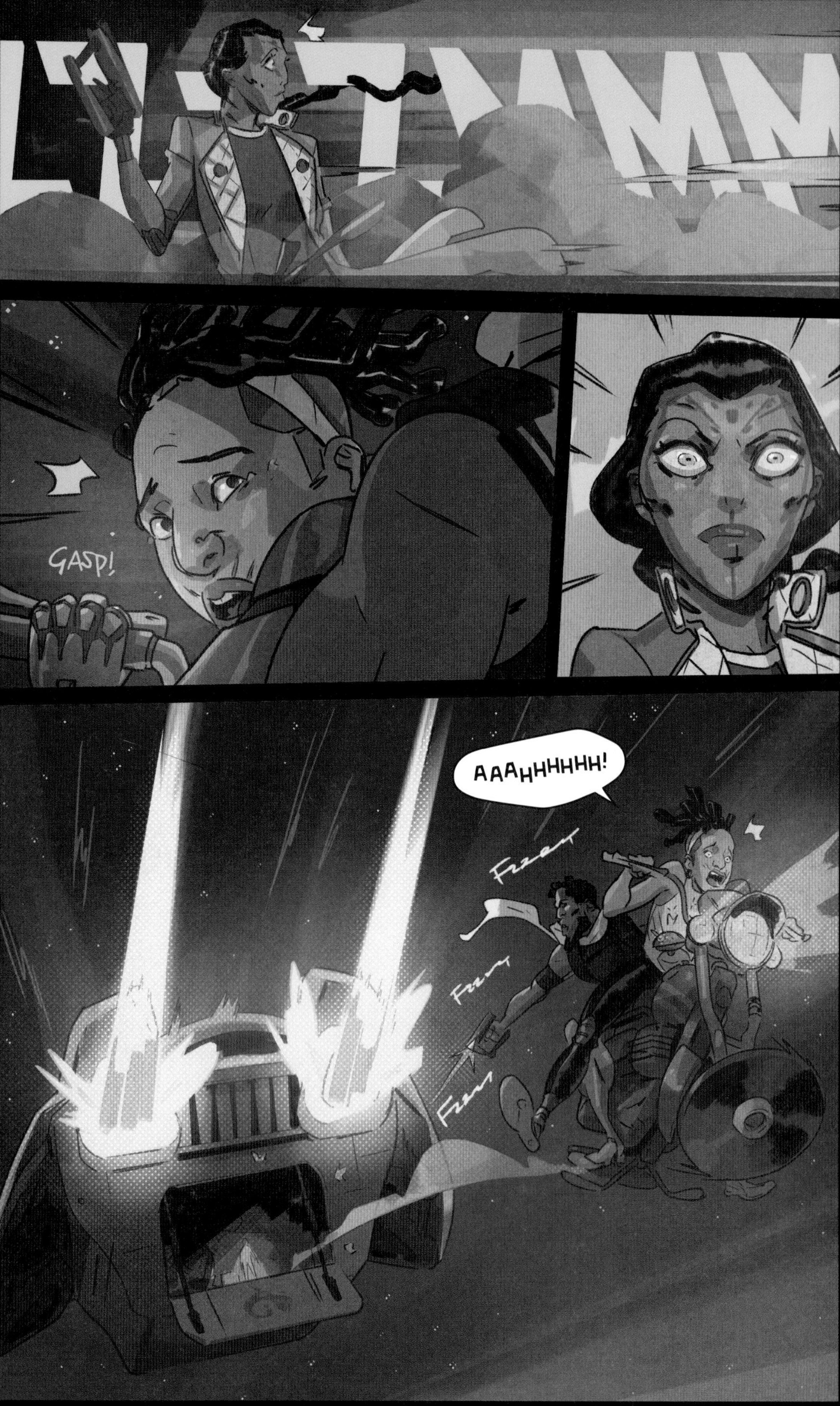
GASP!
AAAHHHHHH!
Frrrr
Frrrr
Frrrr

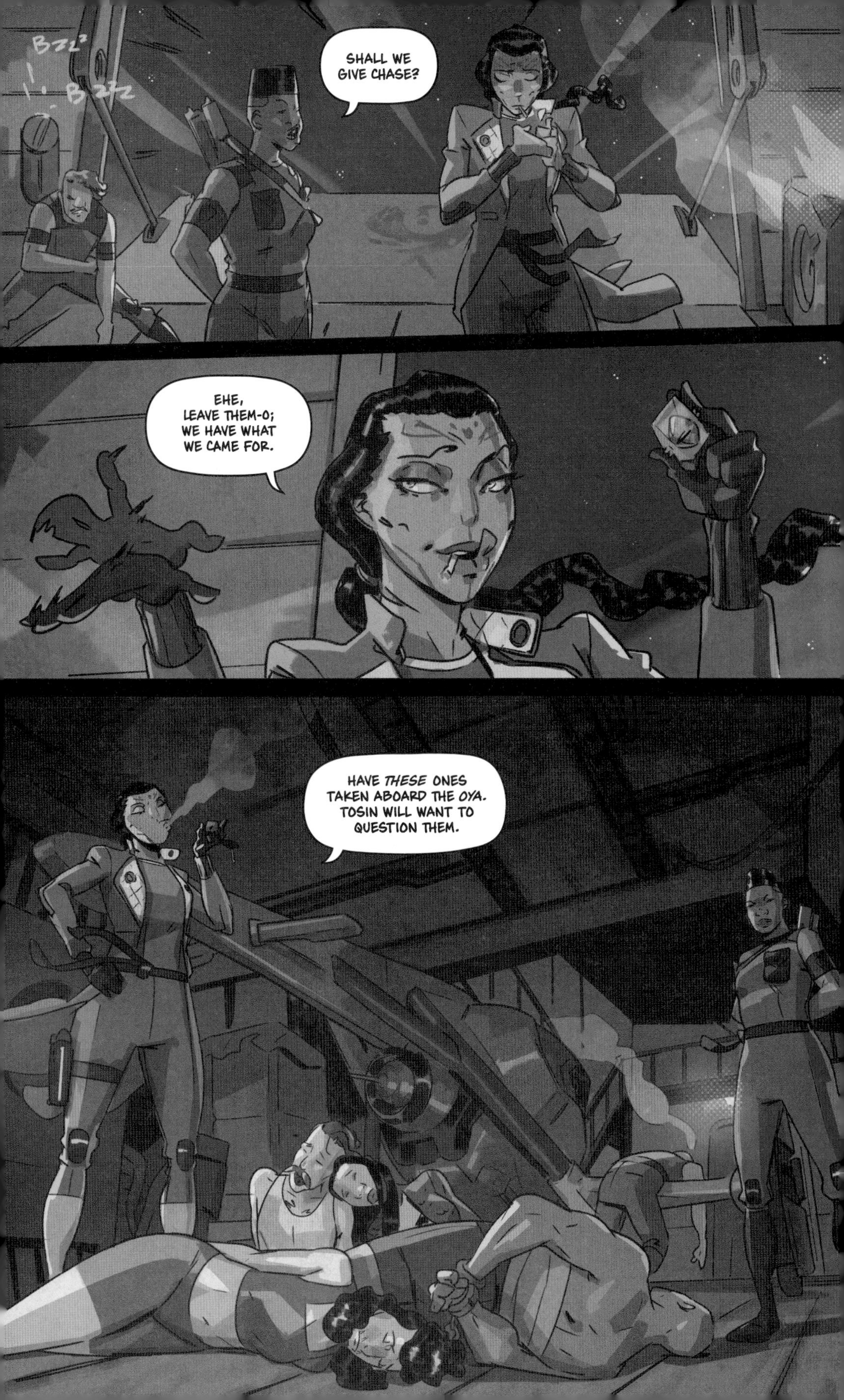
BZZZ
BZZZ
SHALL WE GIVE CHASE?
EHE, LEAVE THEM-O; WE HAVE WHAT WE CAME FOR.
HAVE *THESE* ONES TAKEN ABOARD THE *OYA*. TOSIN WILL WANT TO QUESTION THEM.

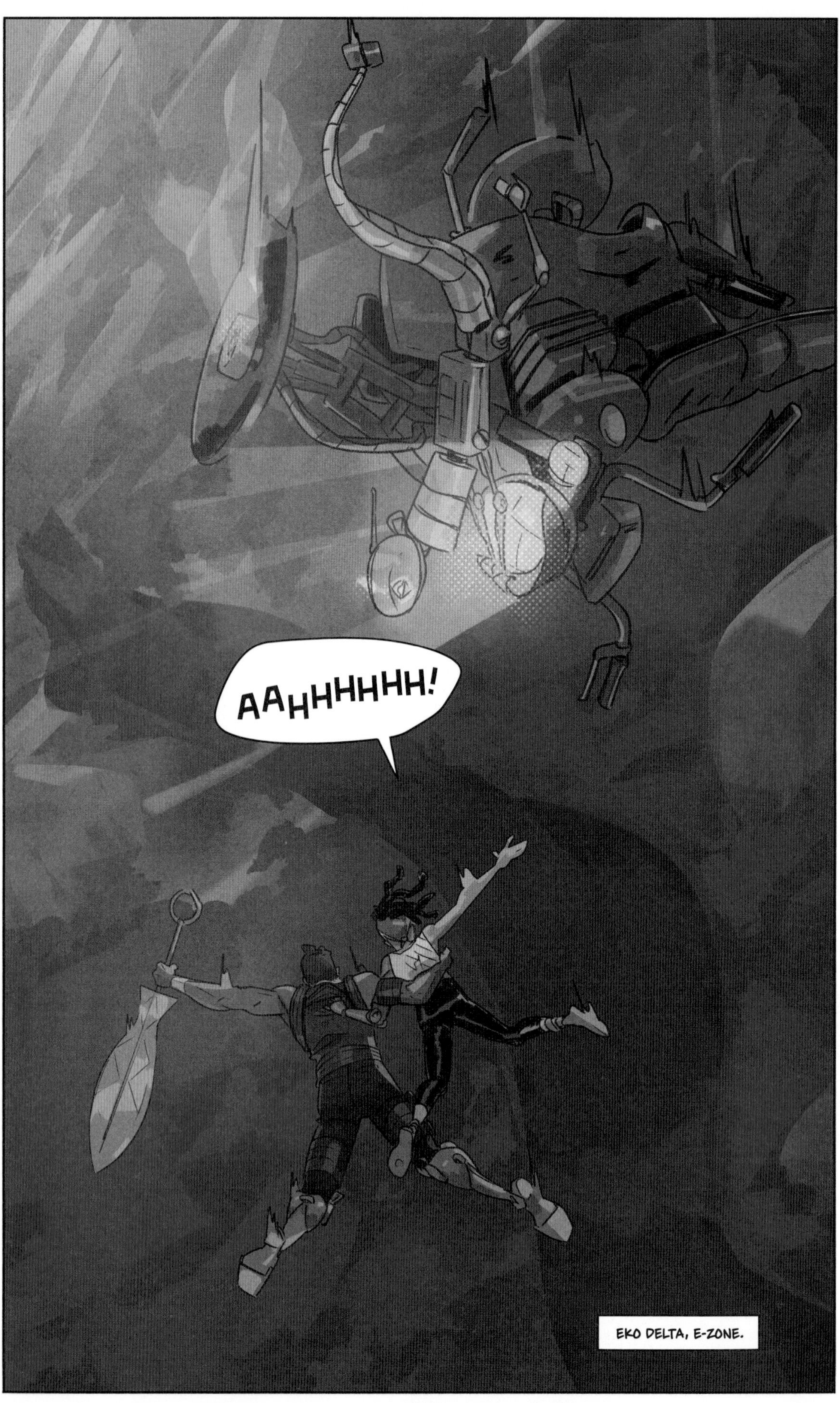
AAHHHHHH!
EKO DELTA, E-ZONE.

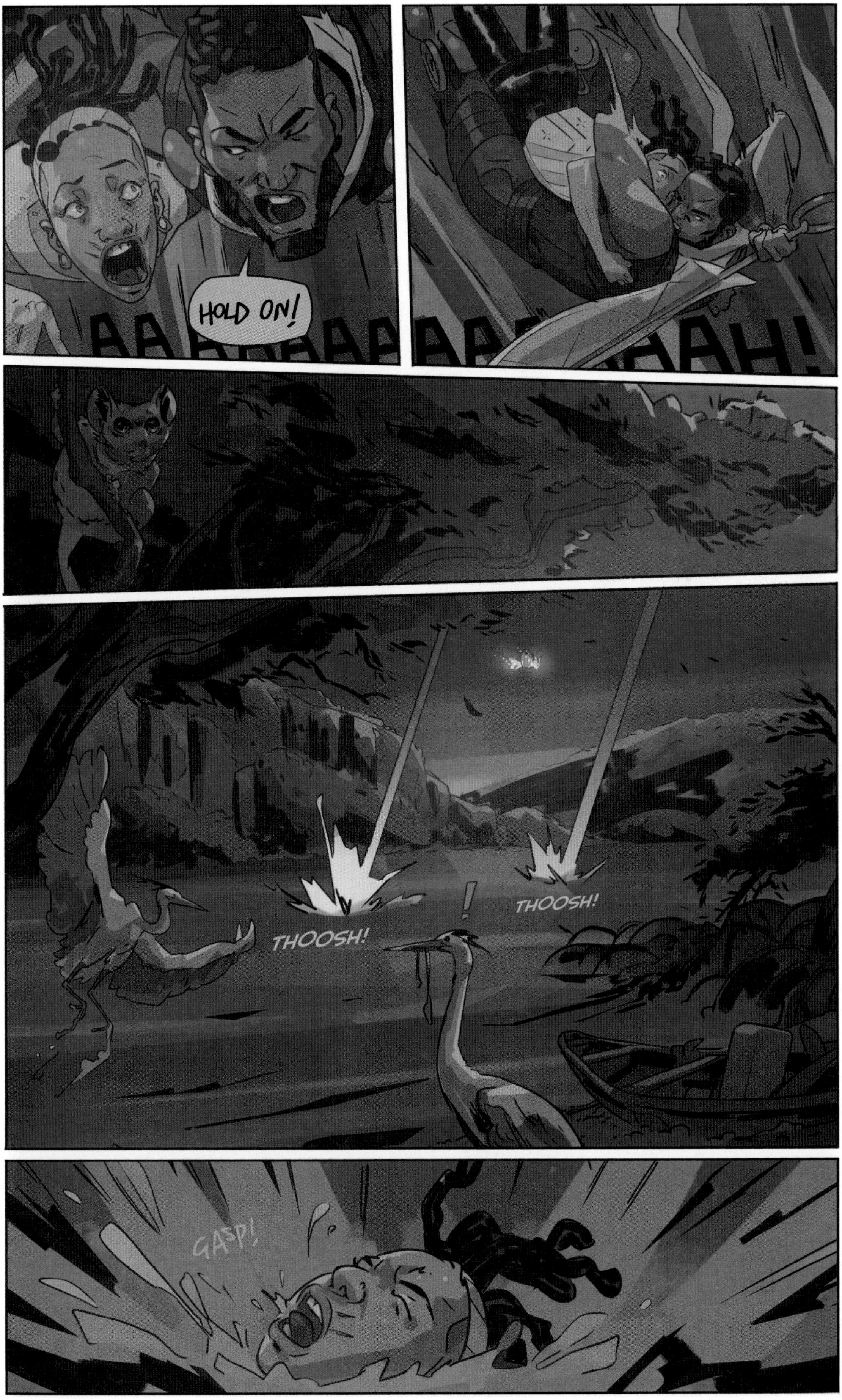
HOLD ON!
AAAAAAAAAAAAH!
THOOSH!
!
THOOSH!
GASP!

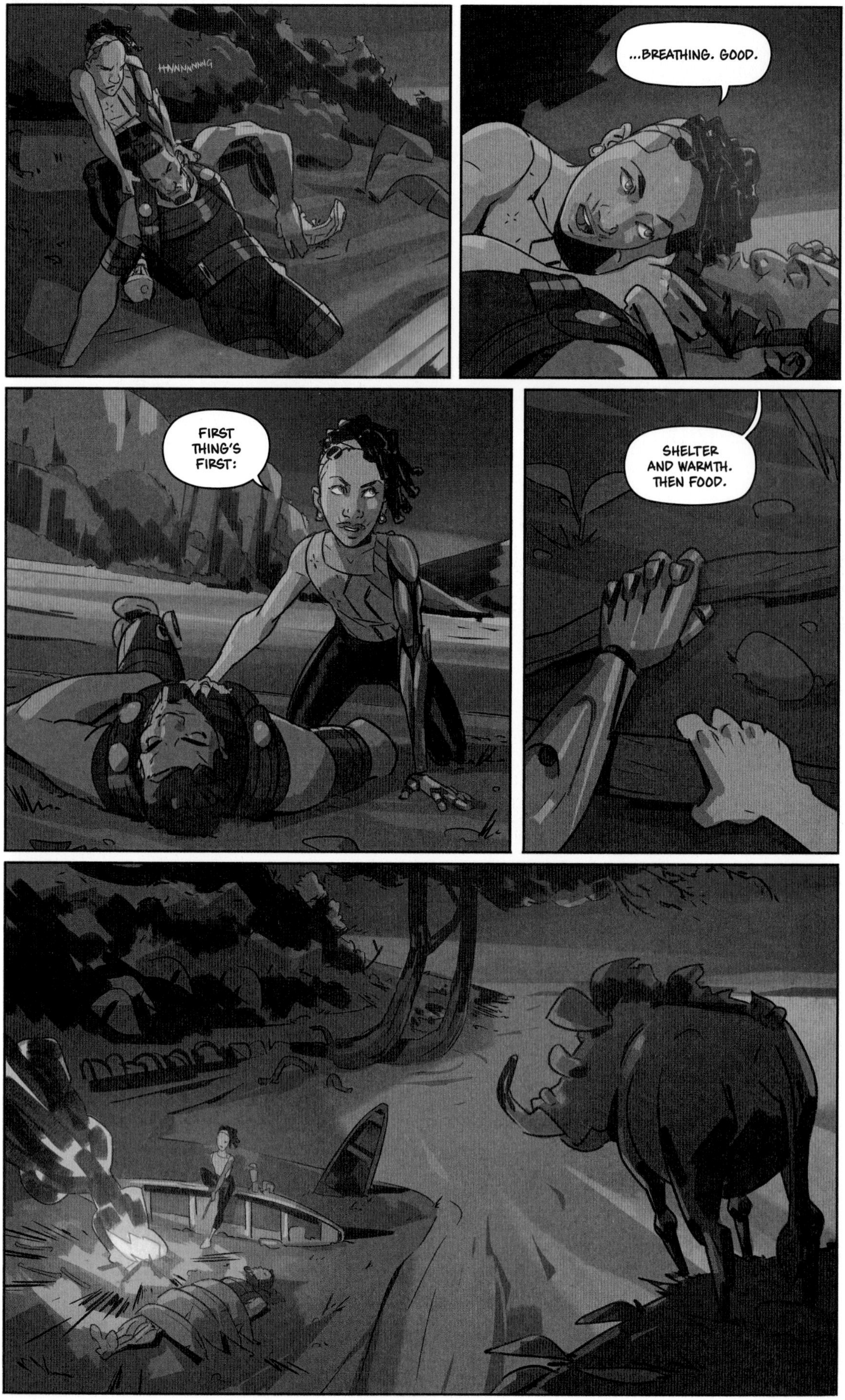
HNNNNNNG
...BREATHING. GOOD.
FIRST THING'S FIRST:
SHELTER AND WARMTH. THEN FOOD.

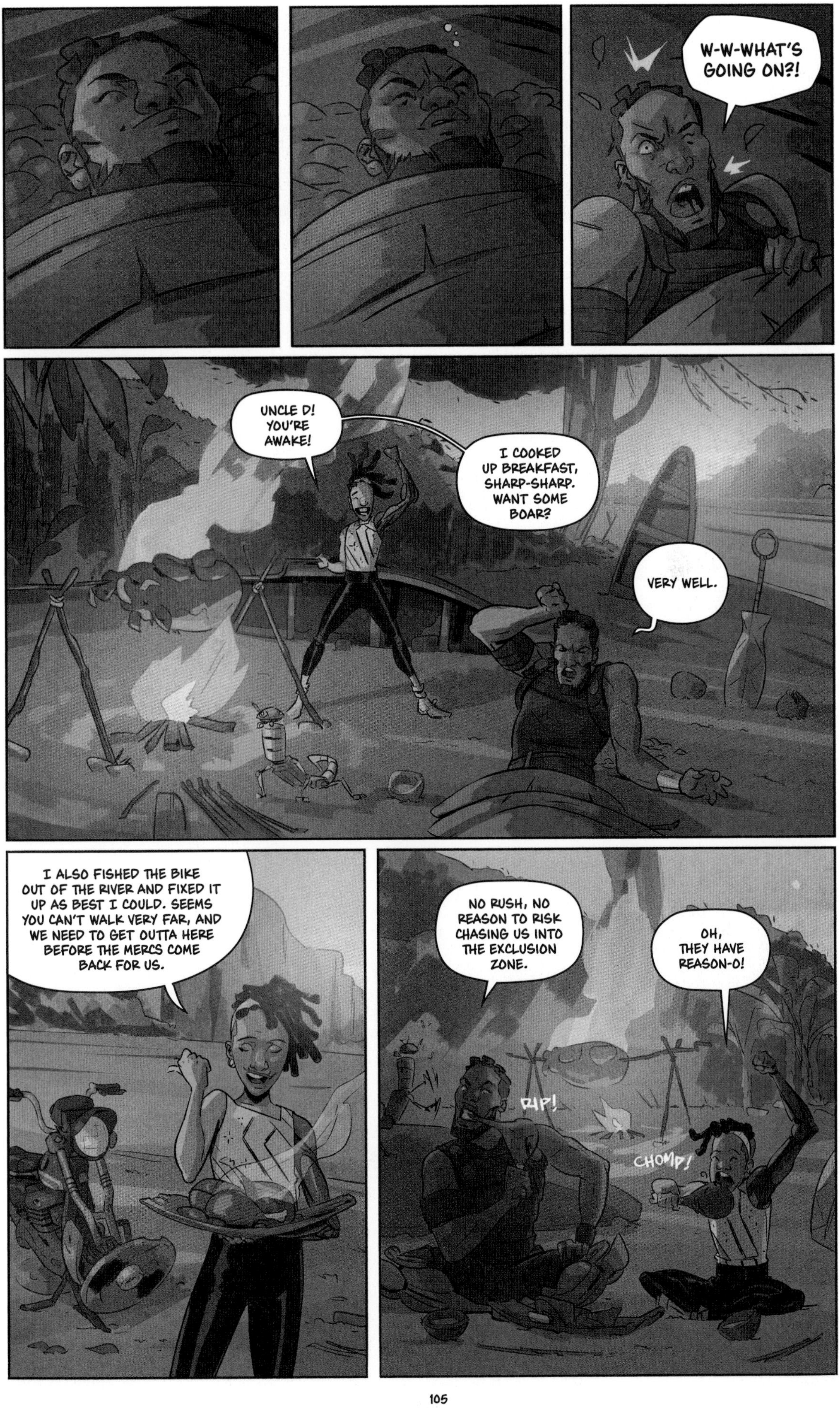
W-W-WHAT'S GOING ON?!
UNCLE D! YOU'RE AWAKE!
I COOKED UP BREAKFAST, SHARP-SHARP. WANT SOME BOAR?
VERY WELL.
I ALSO FISHED THE BIKE OUT OF THE RIVER AND FIXED IT UP AS BEST I COULD. SEEMS YOU CAN'T WALK VERY FAR, AND WE NEED TO GET OUTTA HERE BEFORE THE MERCS COME BACK FOR US.
NO RUSH, NO REASON TO RISK CHASING US INTO THE EXCLUSION ZONE.
OH, THEY HAVE REASON-O!
RIP!
CHOMP!

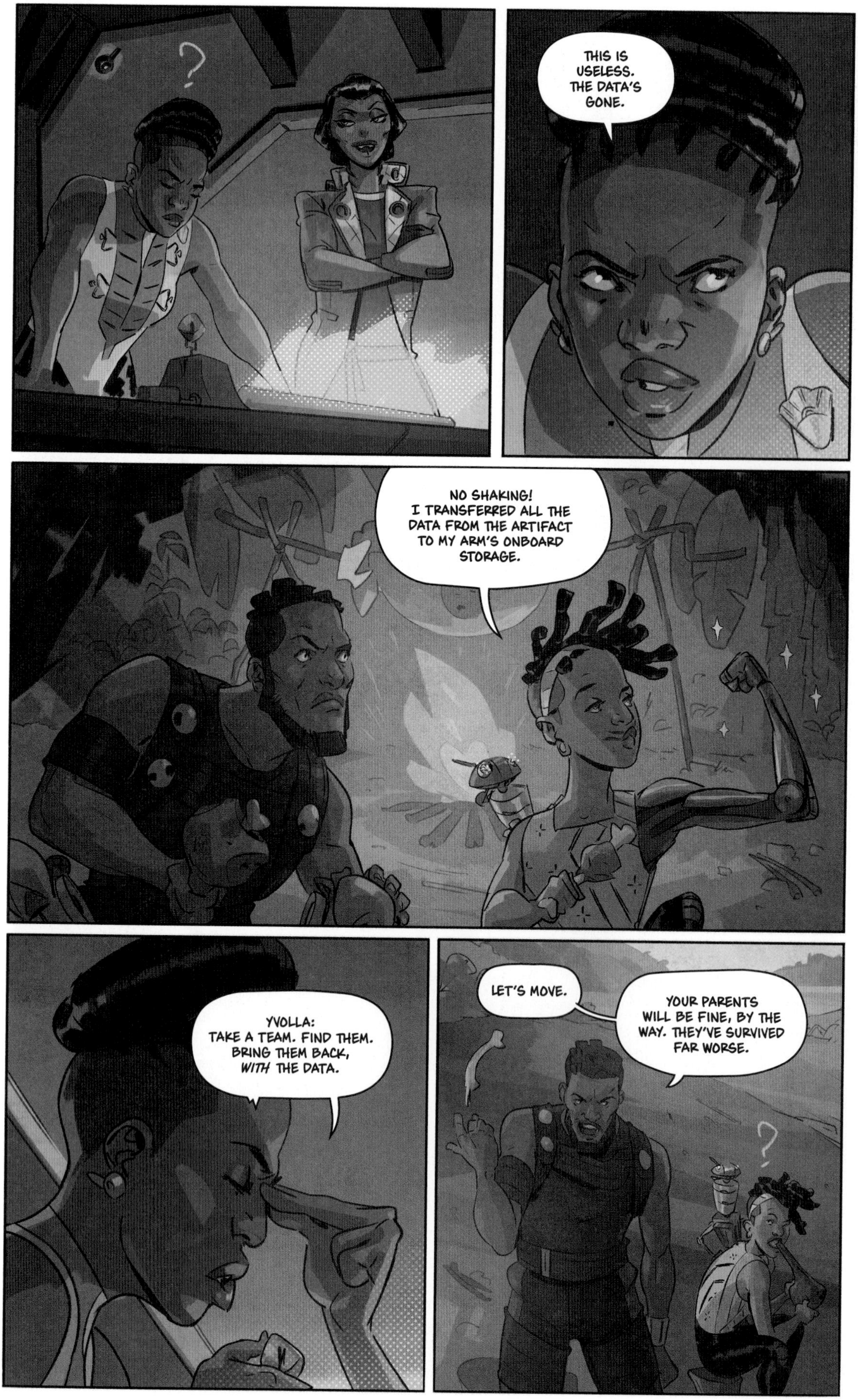
?
THIS IS USELESS. THE DATA'S GONE.
NO SHAKING! I TRANSFERRED ALL THE DATA FROM THE ARTIFACT TO MY ARM'S ONBOARD STORAGE.
YVOLLA: TAKE A TEAM. FIND THEM. BRING THEM BACK, *WITH* THE DATA.
LET'S MOVE.
YOUR PARENTS WILL BE FINE, BY THE WAY. THEY'VE SURVIVED FAR WORSE.
?

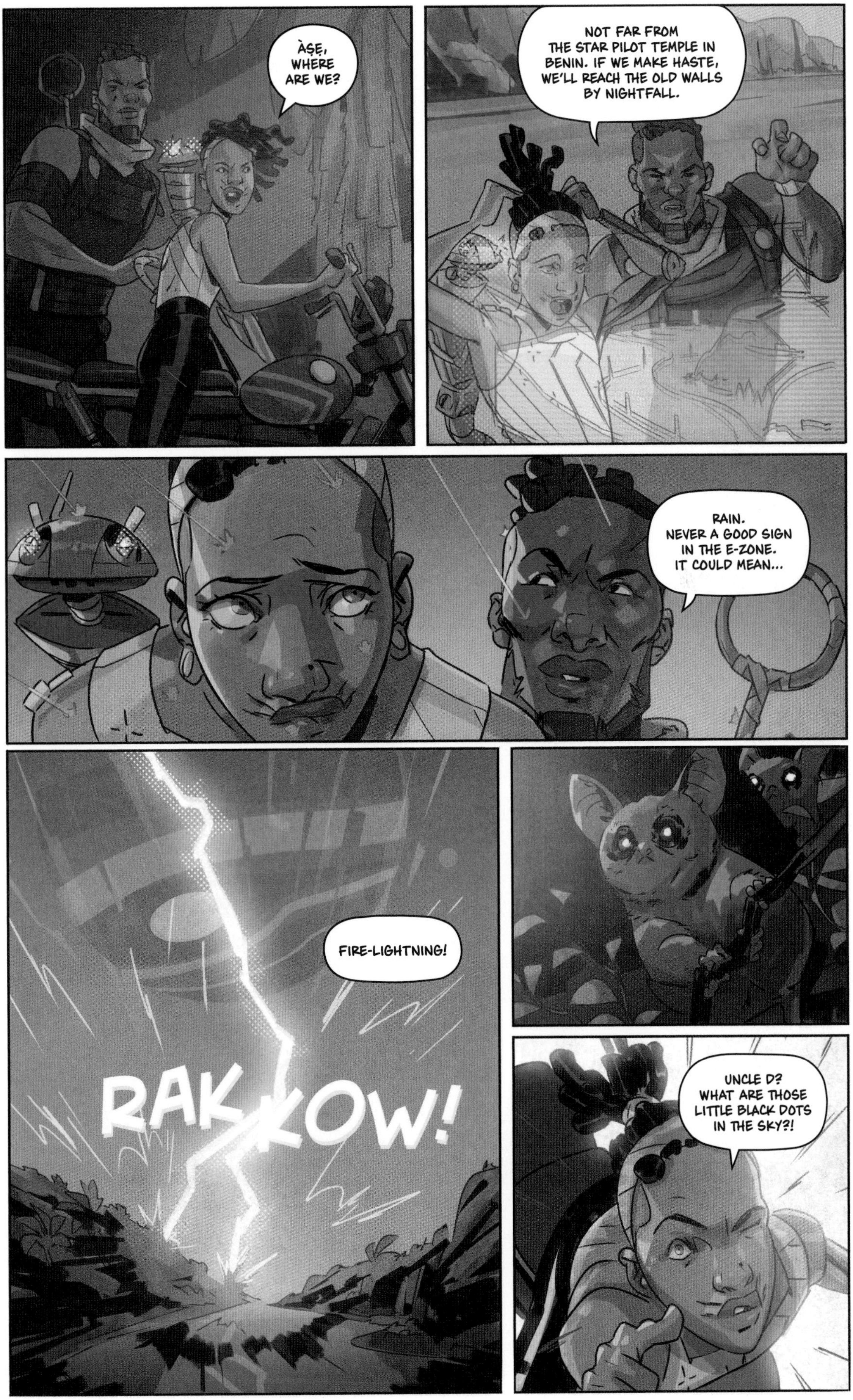
ÀṢẸ, WHERE ARE WE?
NOT FAR FROM THE STAR PILOT TEMPLE IN BENIN. IF WE MAKE HASTE, WE'LL REACH THE OLD WALLS BY NIGHTFALL.
RAIN. NEVER A GOOD SIGN IN THE E-ZONE. IT COULD MEAN...
FIRE-LIGHTNING!
RAKKOW!
UNCLE D? WHAT ARE THOSE LITTLE BLACK DOTS IN THE SKY?!

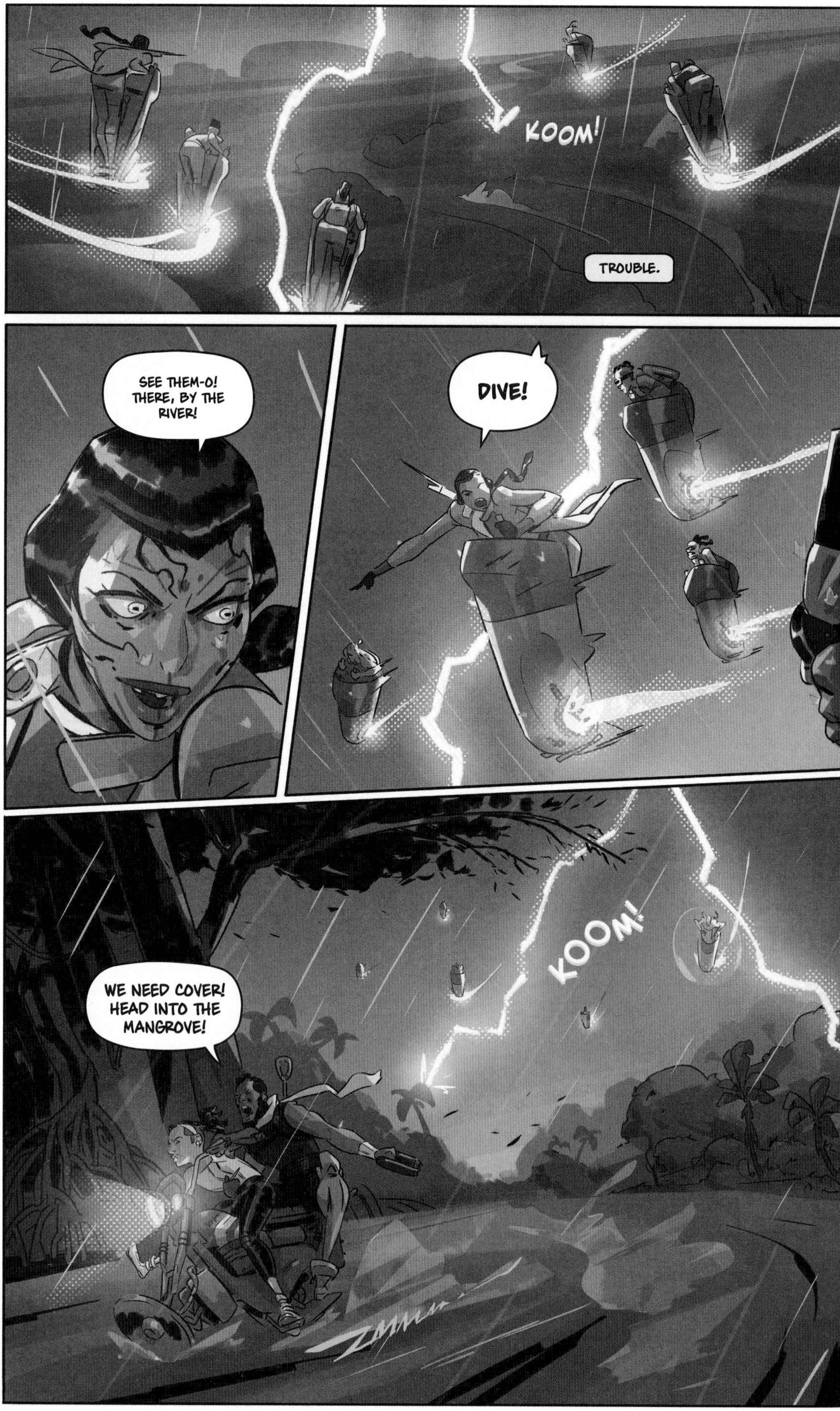
KOOM!
TROUBLE.
SEE THEM-O! THERE, BY THE RIVER!
DIVE!
KOOM!
WE NEED COVER! HEAD INTO THE MANGROVE!

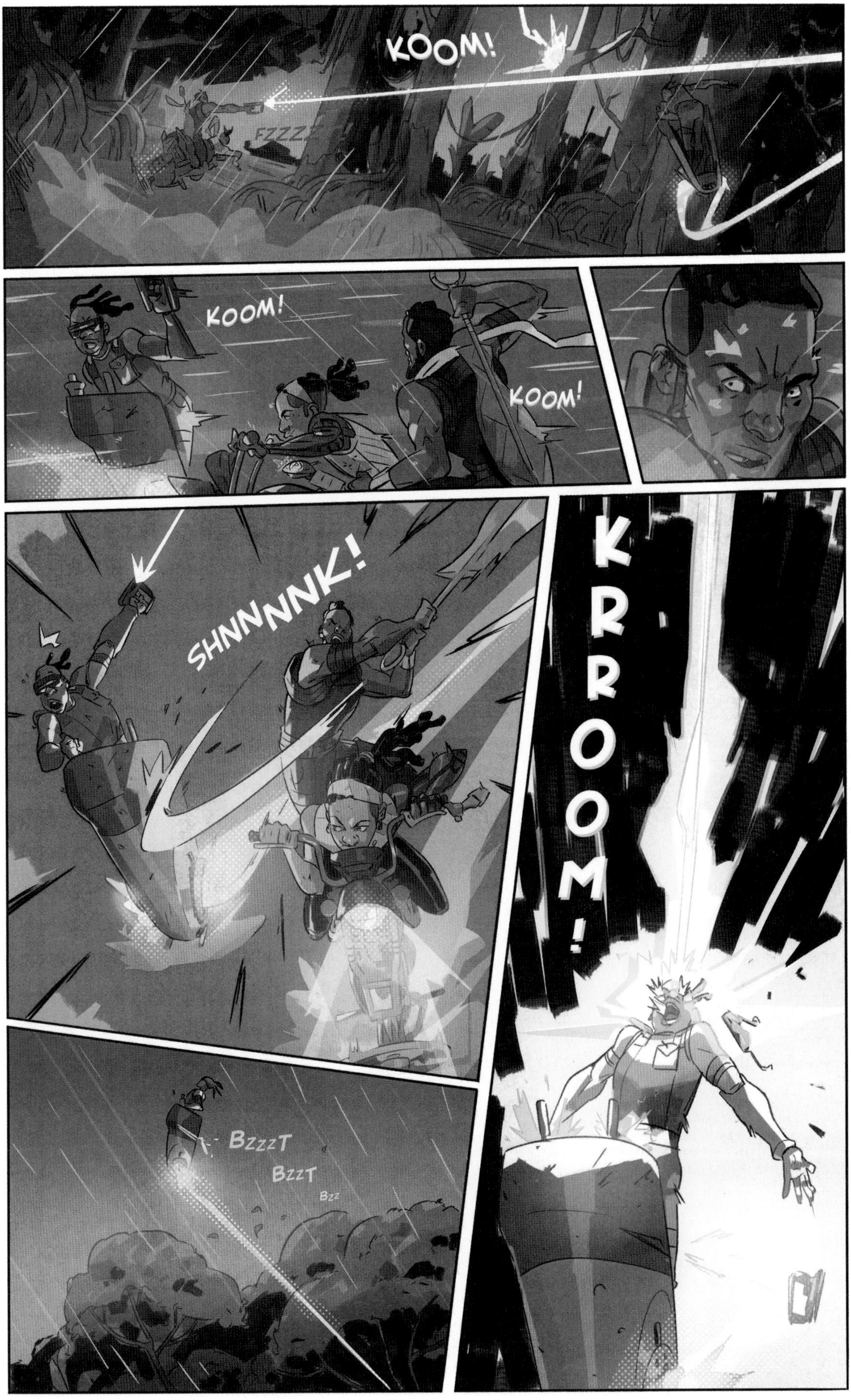
KOOM!
FZZZZ
KOOM!
KOOM!
SHNNNNK!
KRROOM!
BzzzT
BzzT
Bzz

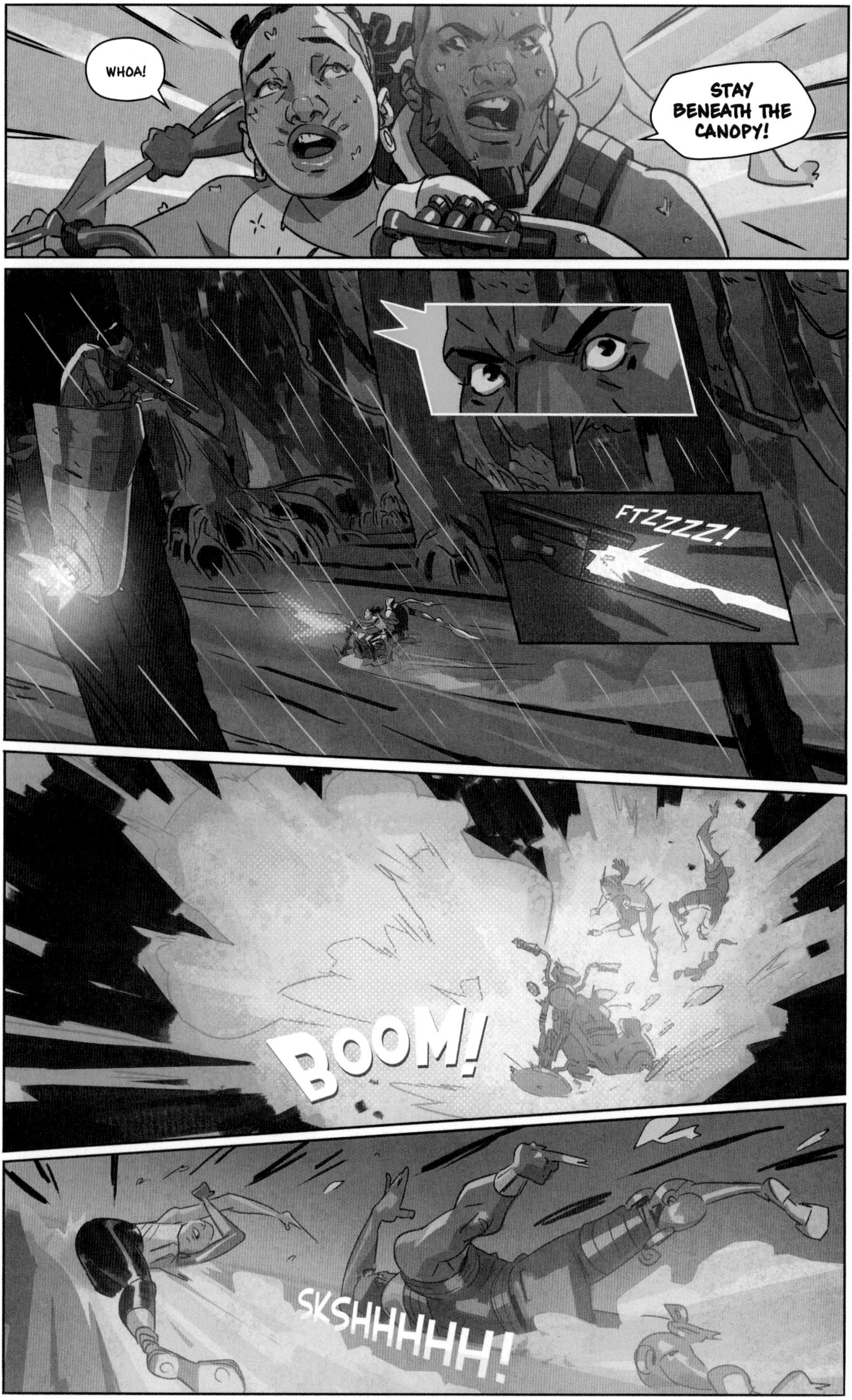
WHOA!
STAY BENEATH THE CANOPY!
FTZZZZ!
BOOM!
SKSHHHHH!

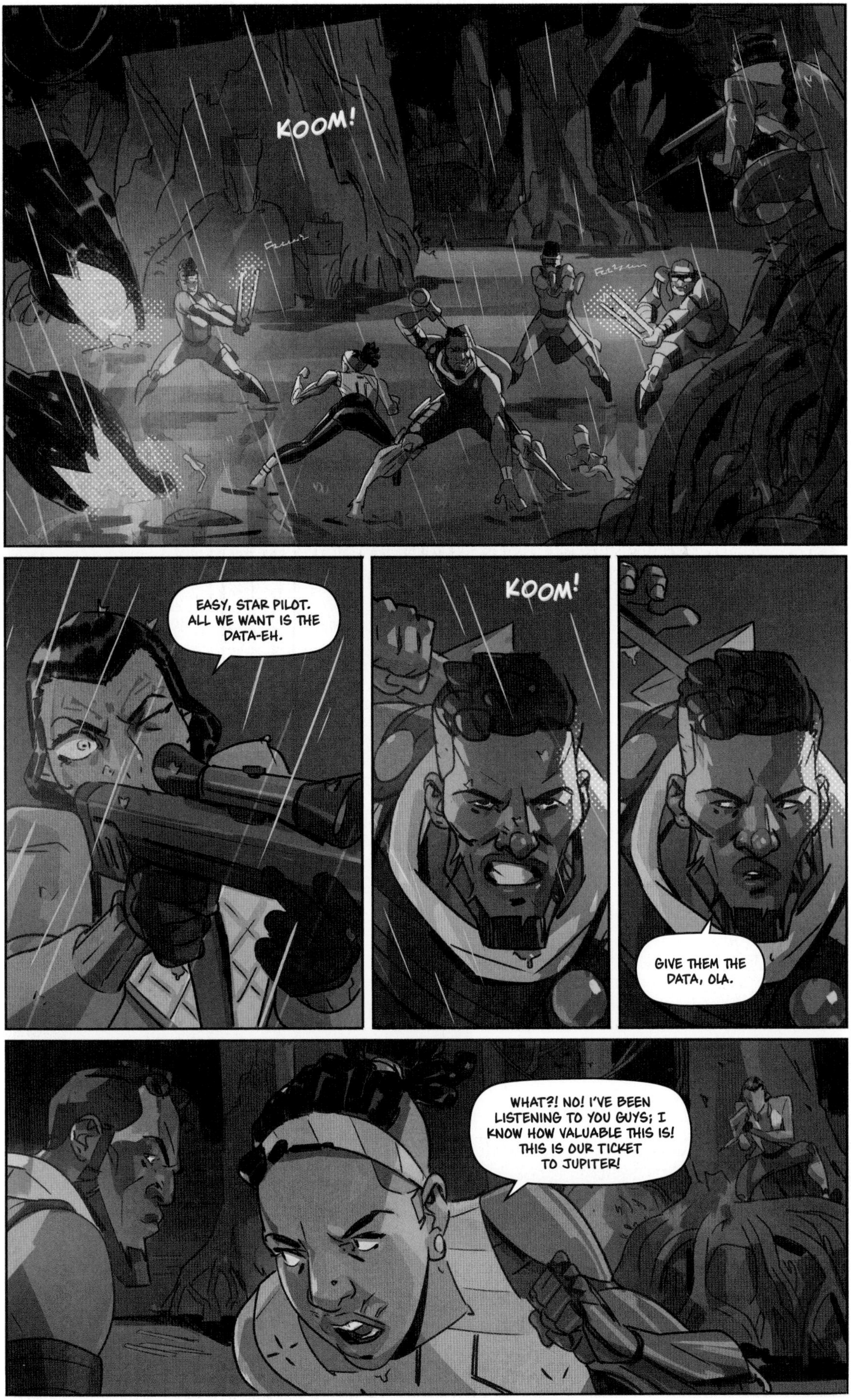
KOOM!
EASY, STAR PILOT. ALL WE WANT IS THE DATA-EH.
KOOM!
GIVE THEM THE DATA, OLA.
WHAT?! NO! I'VE BEEN LISTENING TO YOU GUYS; I KNOW HOW VALUABLE THIS IS! THIS IS OUR TICKET TO JUPITER!

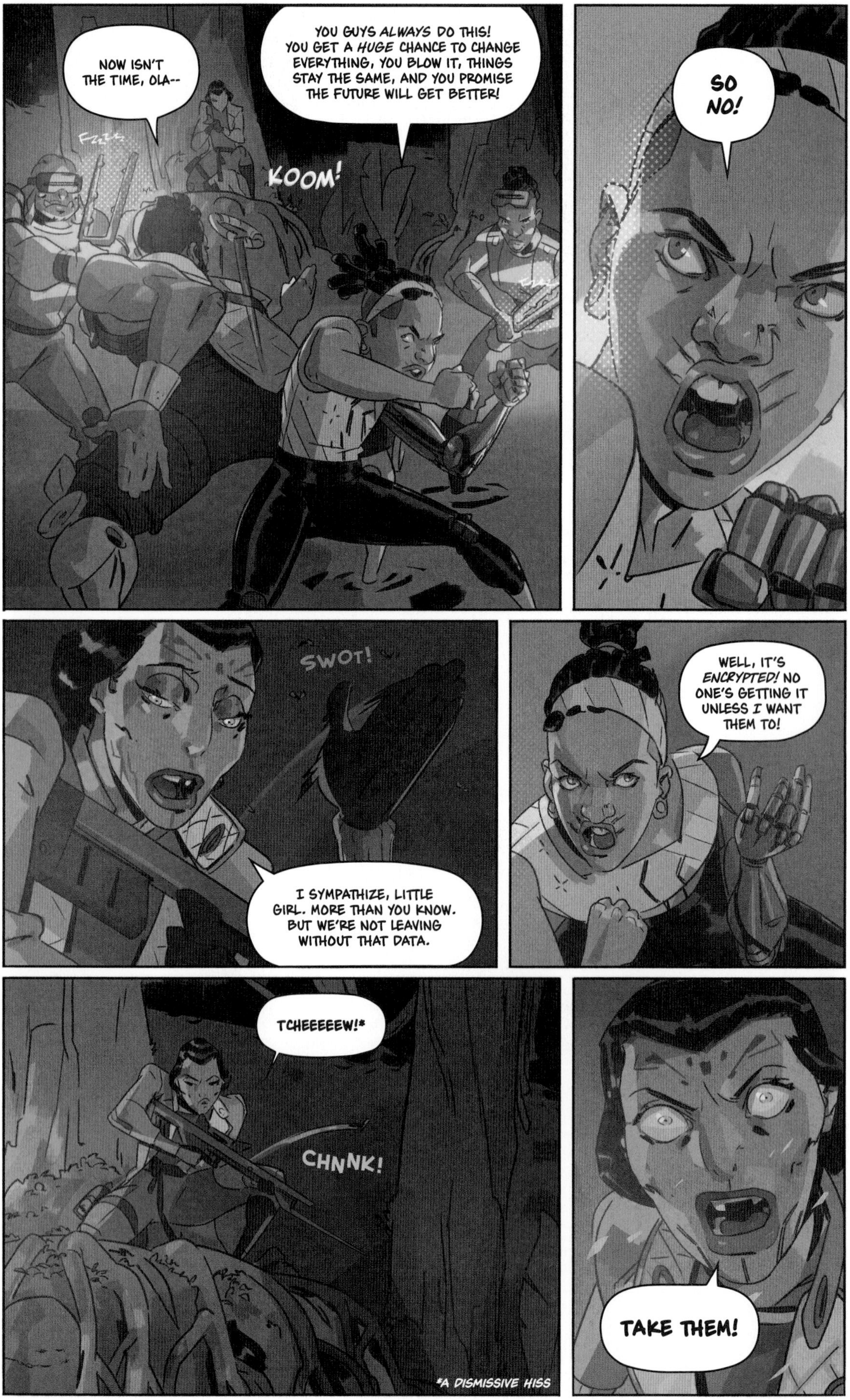
NOW ISN'T THE TIME, OLA--
YOU GUYS ALWAYS DO THIS! YOU GET A HUGE CHANCE TO CHANGE EVERYTHING, YOU BLOW IT, THINGS STAY THE SAME, AND YOU PROMISE THE FUTURE WILL GET BETTER!
KOOM!
SO NO!
SWOT!
I SYMPATHIZE, LITTLE GIRL. MORE THAN YOU KNOW. BUT WE'RE NOT LEAVING WITHOUT THAT DATA.
WELL, IT'S ENCRYPTED! NO ONE'S GETTING IT UNLESS I WANT THEM TO!
TCHEEEEEW!*
CHNNK!
*A DISMISSIVE HISS
TAKE THEM!

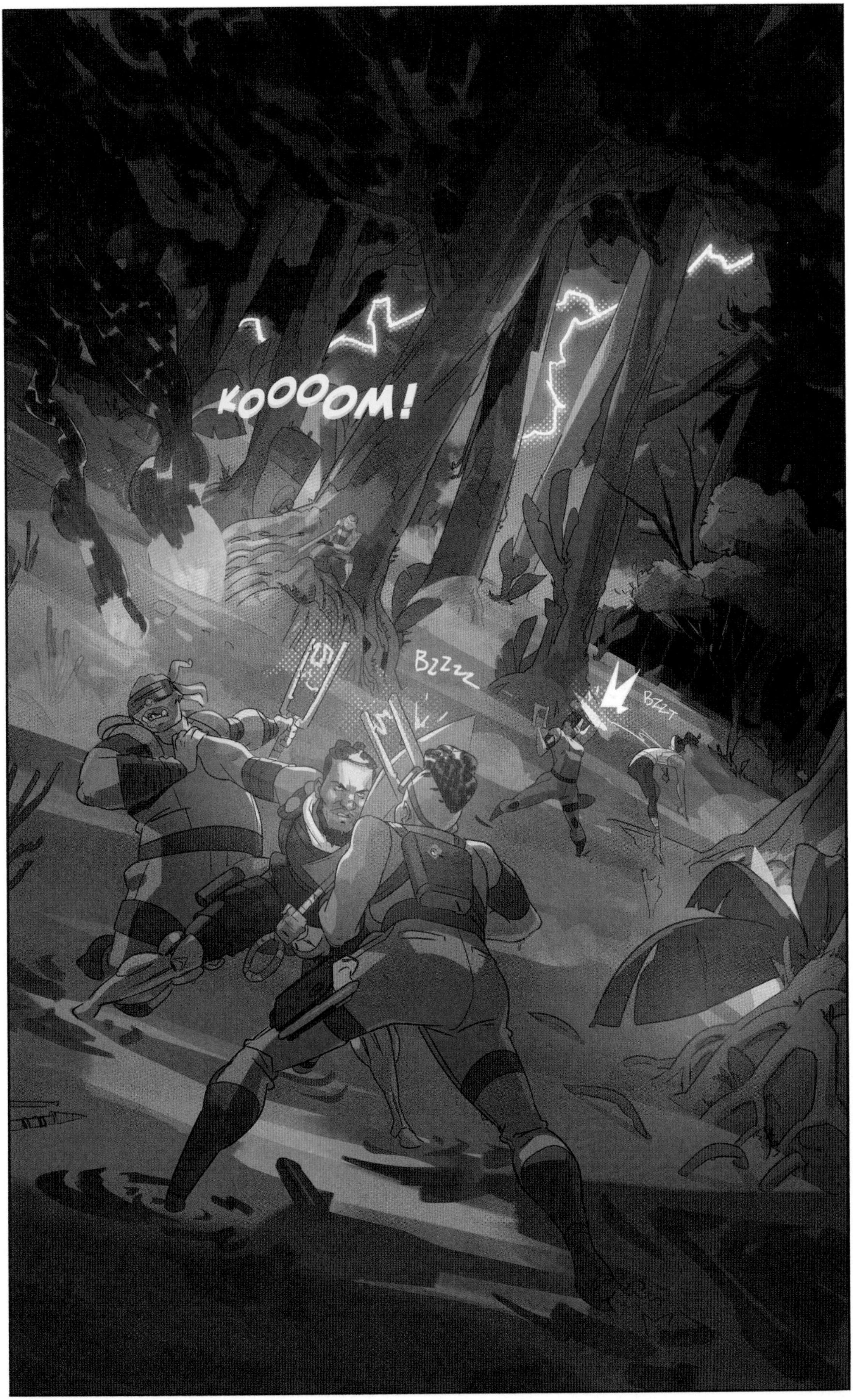
KOOOOM!
BZZZZ
BZZT

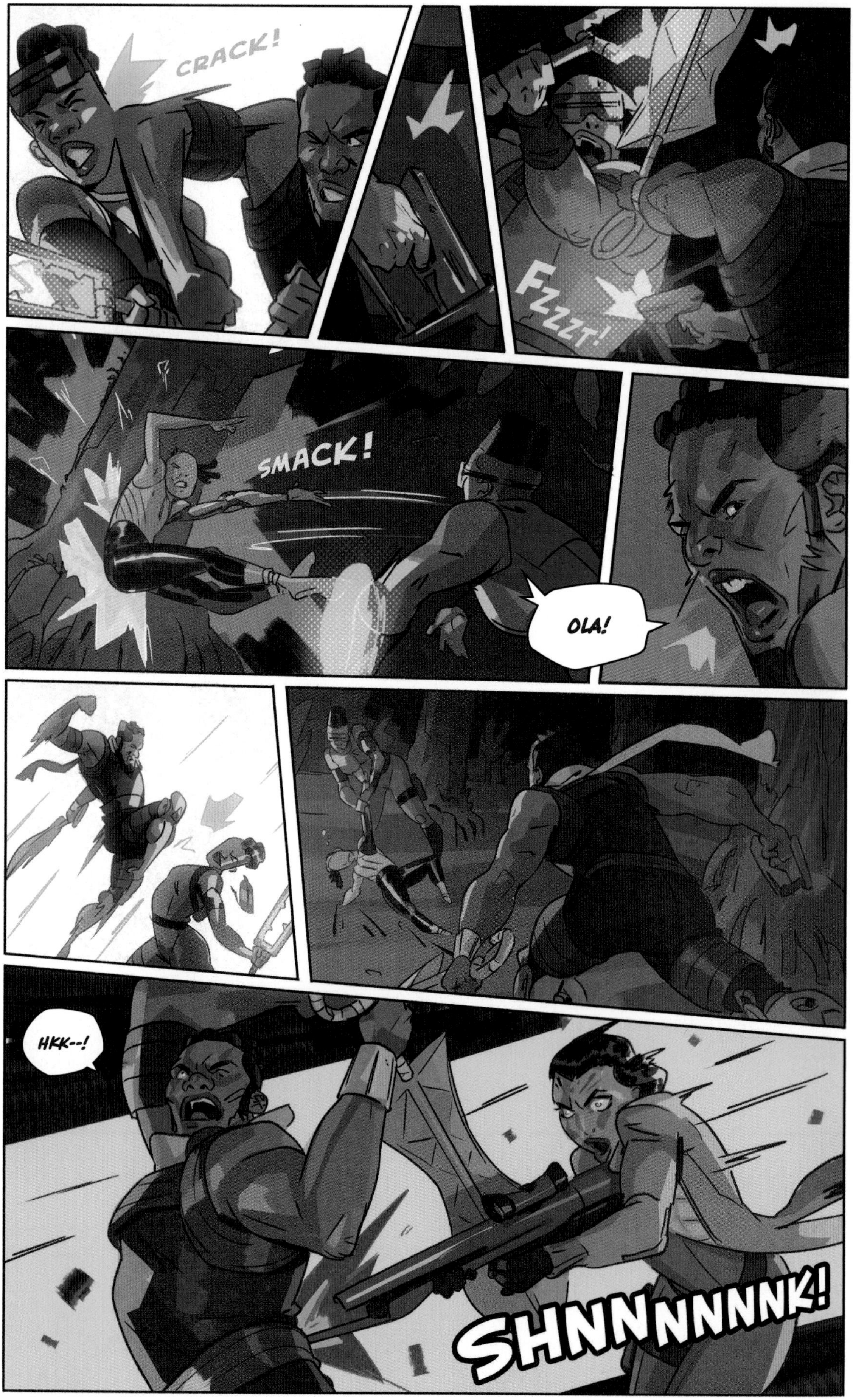
CRACK!
FZZZT!
SMACK!
OLA!
HKK--!
SHNNNNNNK!

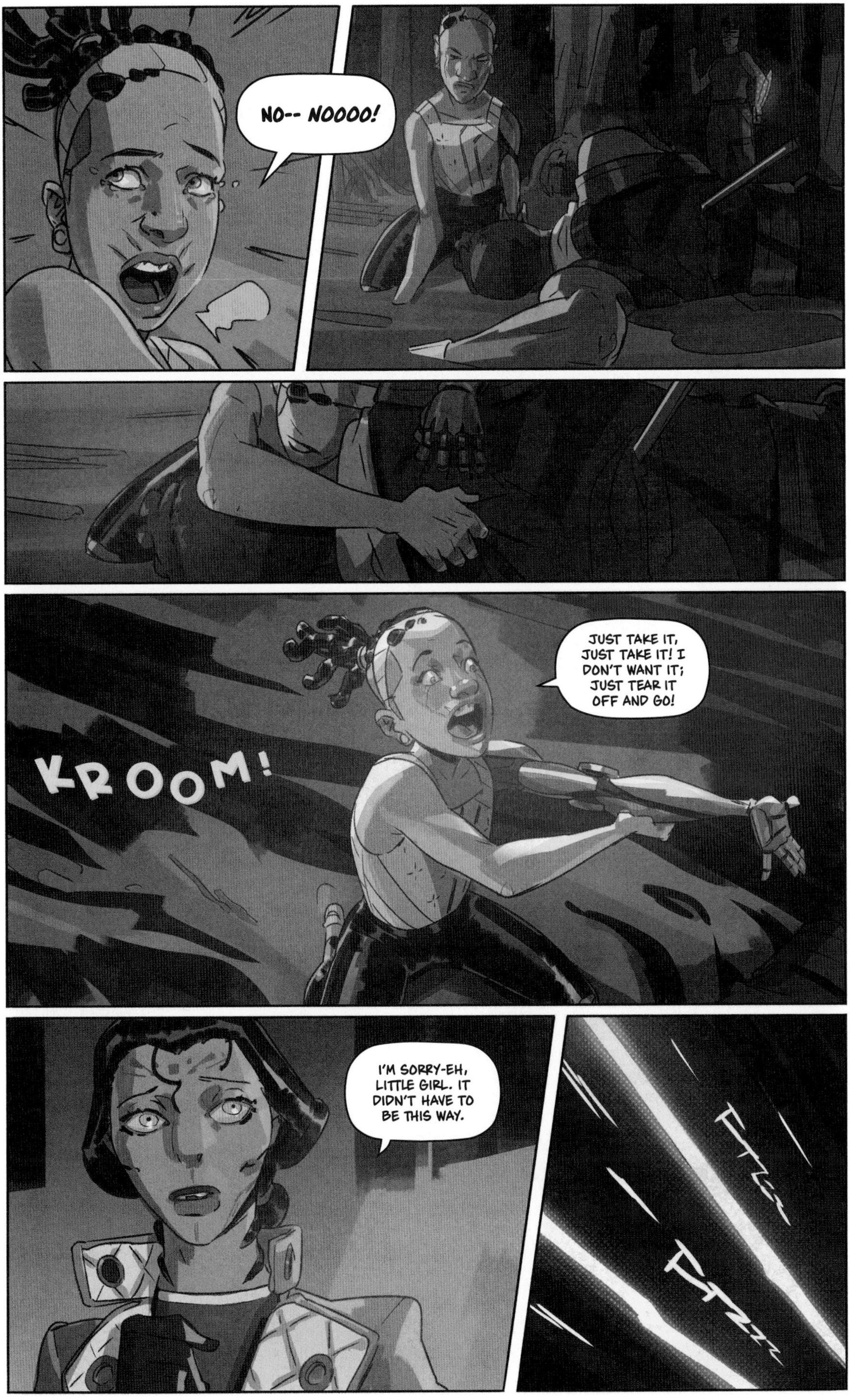
NO-- NOOOO!
JUST TAKE IT, JUST TAKE IT! I DON'T WANT IT; JUST TEAR IT OFF AND GO!
KROOM!
I'M SORRY-EH, LITTLE GIRL. IT DIDN'T HAVE TO BE THIS WAY.

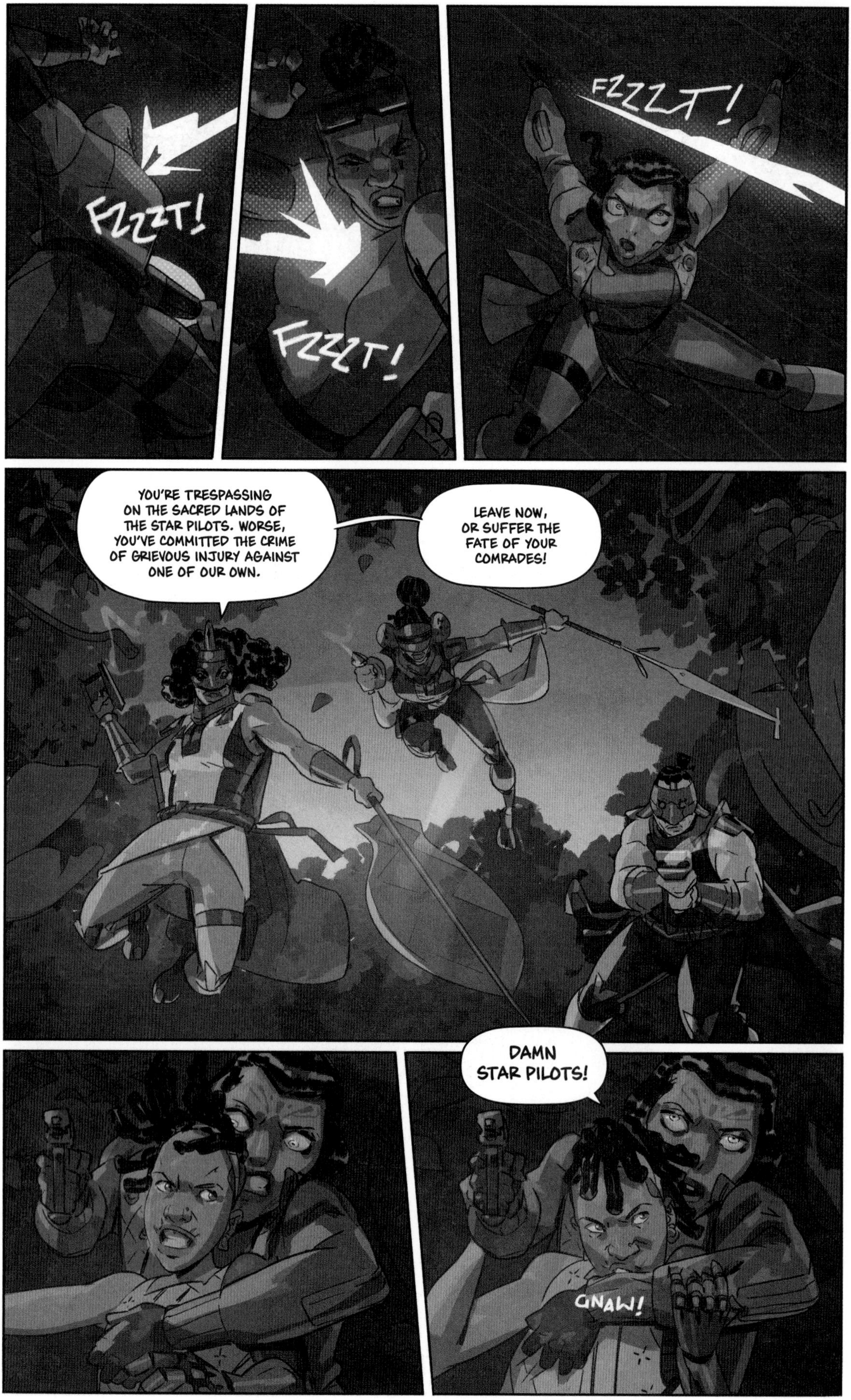
FZZZT!
FZZZT!
FZZZT!
YOU'RE TRESPASSING ON THE SACRED LANDS OF THE STAR PILOTS. WORSE, YOU'VE COMMITTED THE CRIME OF GRIEVOUS INJURY AGAINST ONE OF OUR OWN.
LEAVE NOW, OR SUFFER THE FATE OF YOUR COMRADES!
DAMN STAR PILOTS!
GNAW!

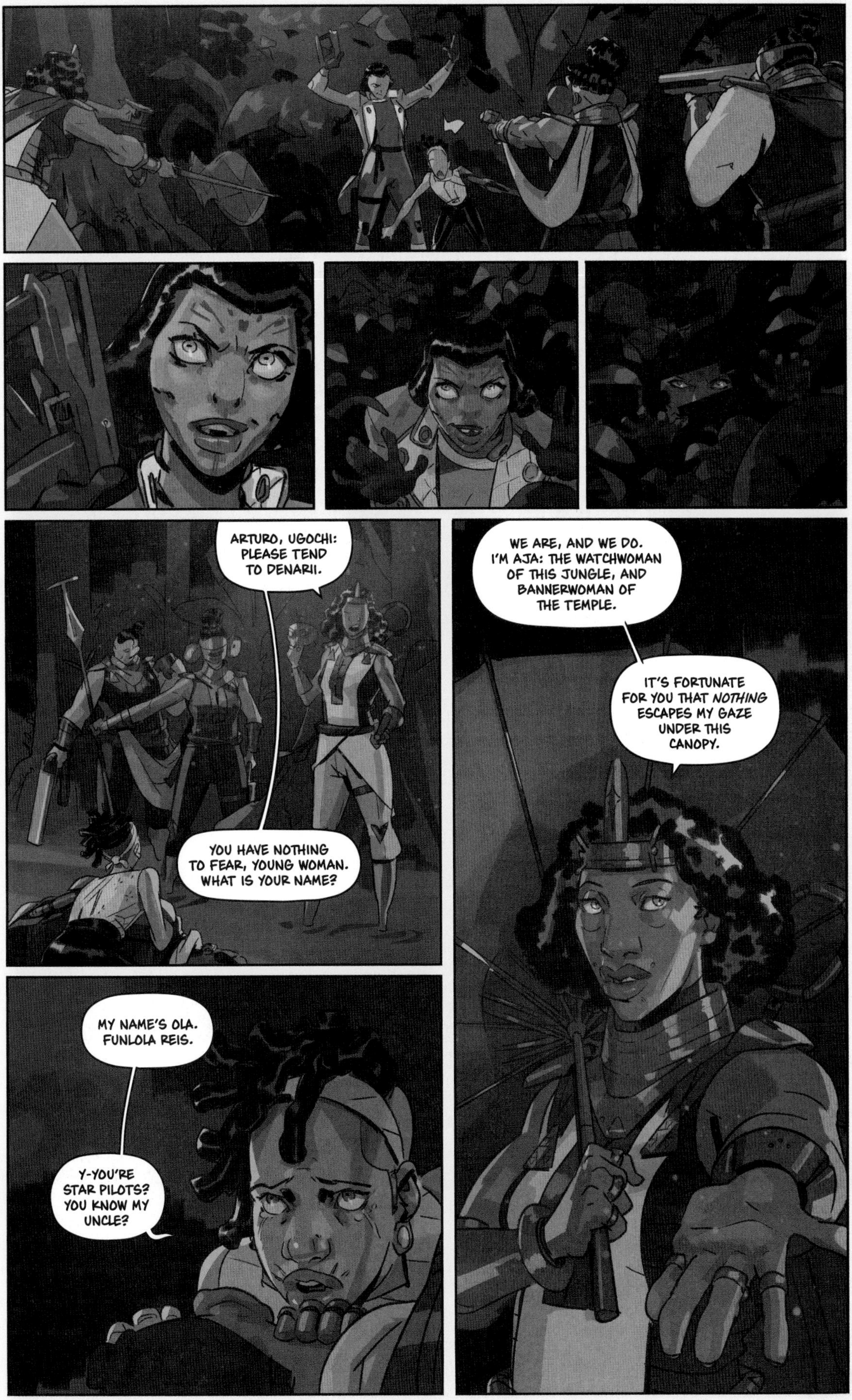
ARTURO, UGOCHI: PLEASE TEND TO DENARII.
YOU HAVE NOTHING TO FEAR, YOUNG WOMAN. WHAT IS YOUR NAME?
MY NAME'S OLA. FUNLOLA REIS.
Y-YOU'RE STAR PILOTS? YOU KNOW MY UNCLE?
WE ARE, AND WE DO. I'M AJA: THE WATCHWOMAN OF THIS JUNGLE, AND BANNERWOMAN OF THE TEMPLE.
IT'S FORTUNATE FOR YOU THAT *NOTHING* ESCAPES MY GAZE UNDER THIS CANOPY.

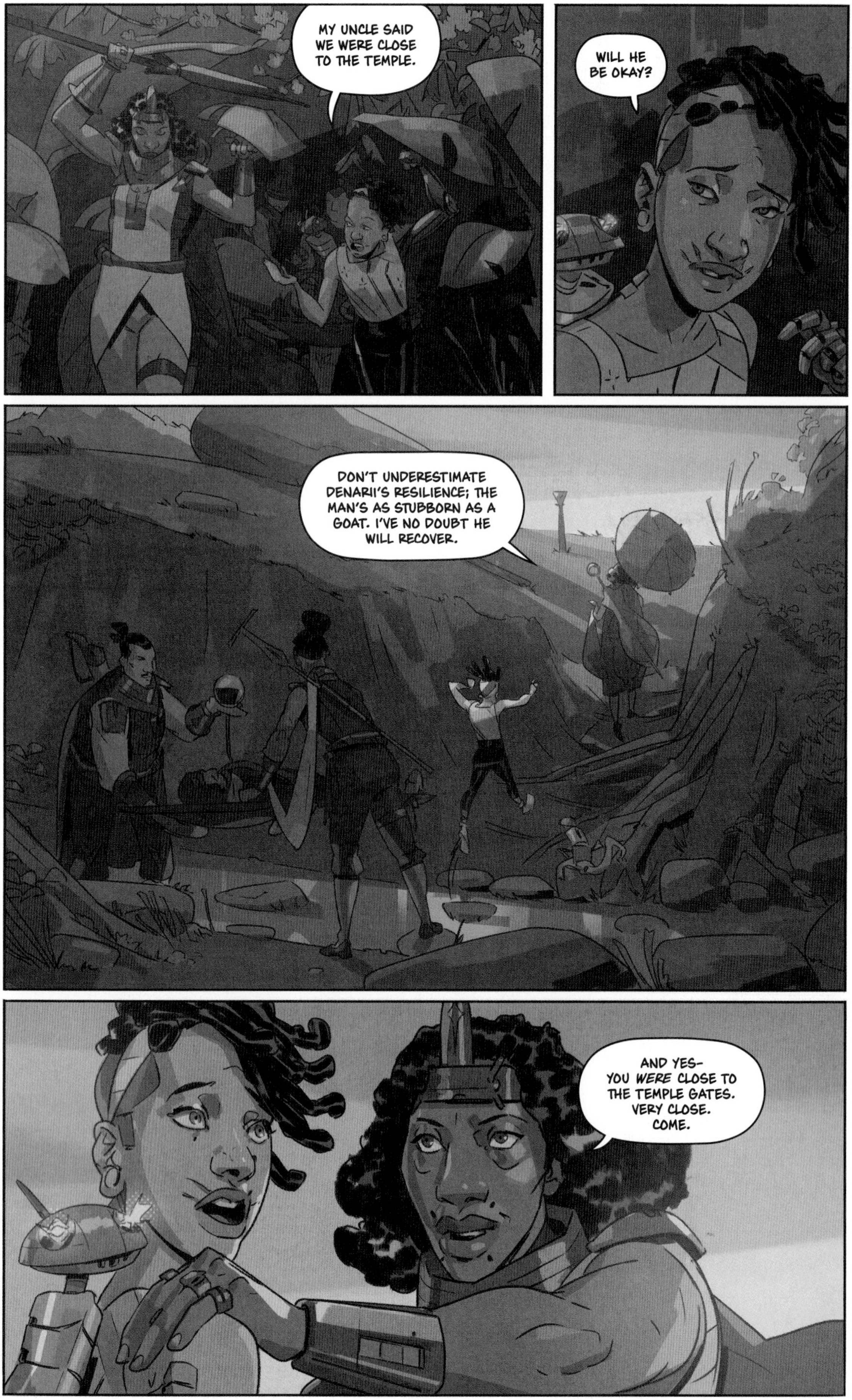
MY UNCLE SAID WE WERE CLOSE TO THE TEMPLE.
WILL HE BE OKAY?
DON'T UNDERESTIMATE DENARII'S RESILIENCE; THE MAN'S AS STUBBORN AS A GOAT. I'VE NO DOUBT HE WILL RECOVER.
AND YES- YOU *WERE* CLOSE TO THE TEMPLE GATES. VERY CLOSE. COME.

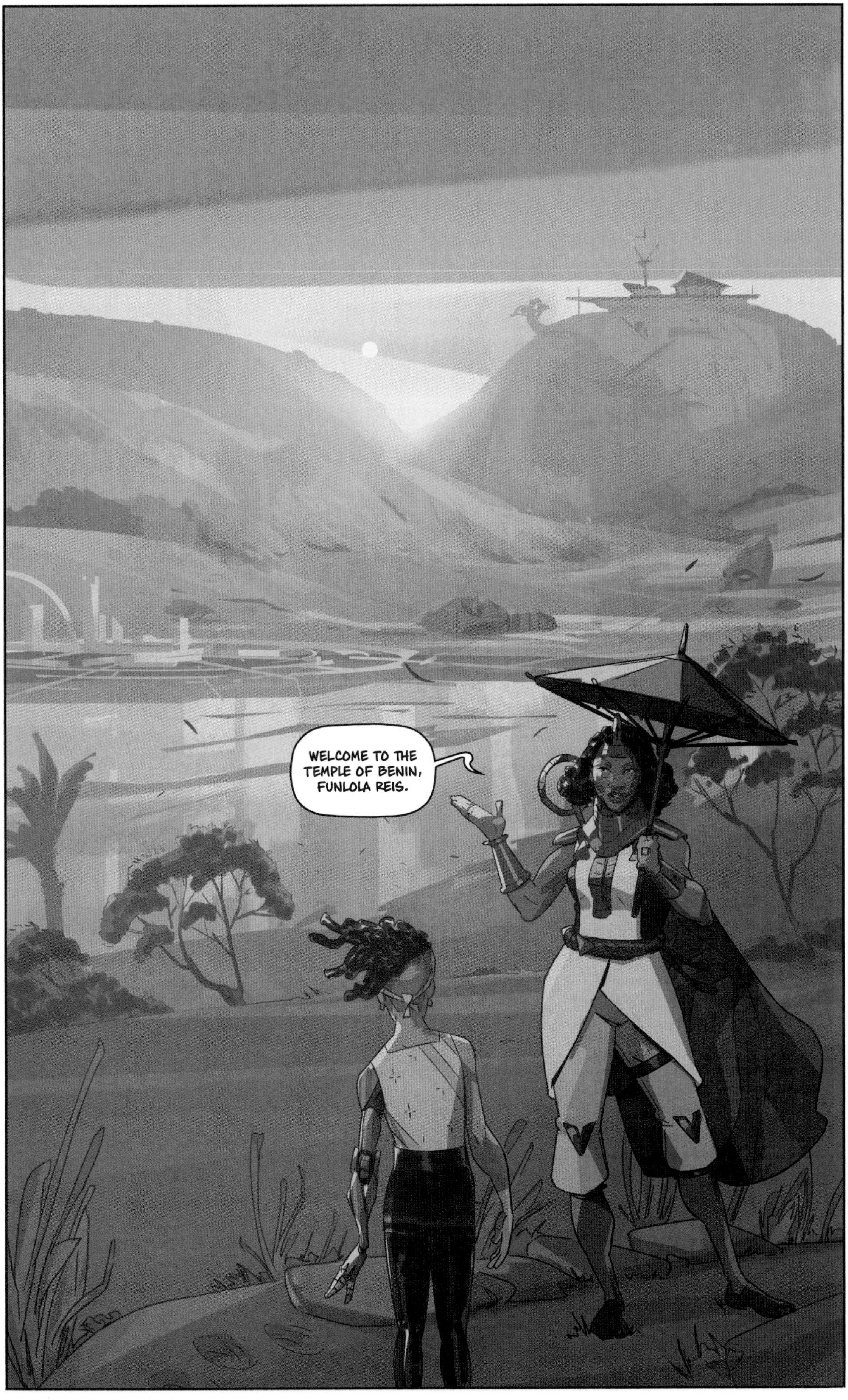
WELCOME TO THE TEMPLE OF BENIN, FUNLOLA REIS.

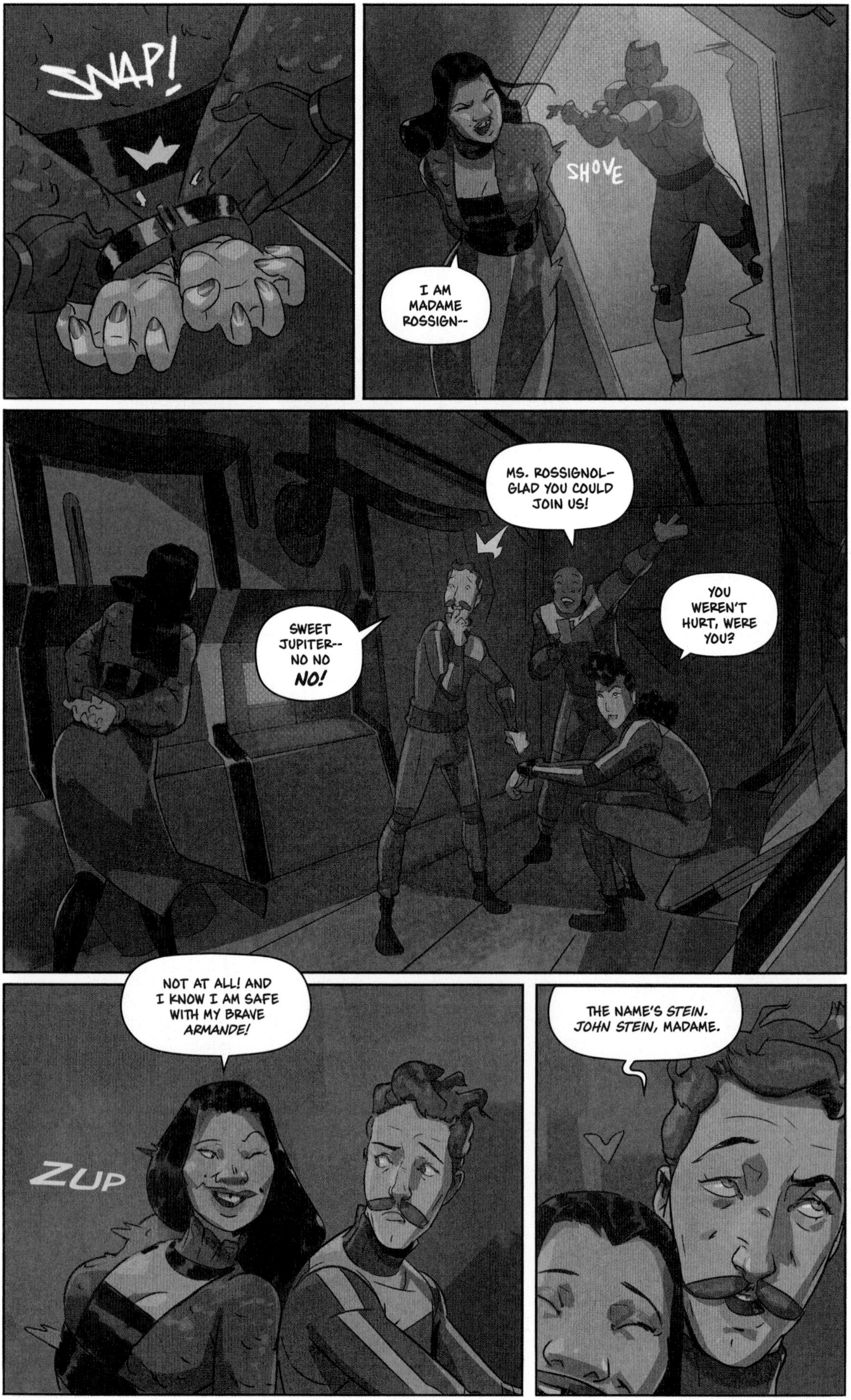
SNAP!
I AM MADAME ROSSIGN--
SHOVE
MS. ROSSIGNOL-GLAD YOU COULD JOIN US!
SWEET JUPITER-- NO NO *NO!*
YOU WEREN'T HURT, WERE YOU?
NOT AT ALL! AND I KNOW I AM SAFE WITH MY BRAVE *ARMANDE!*
ZUP
THE NAME'S *STEIN.* *JOHN STEIN,* MADAME.

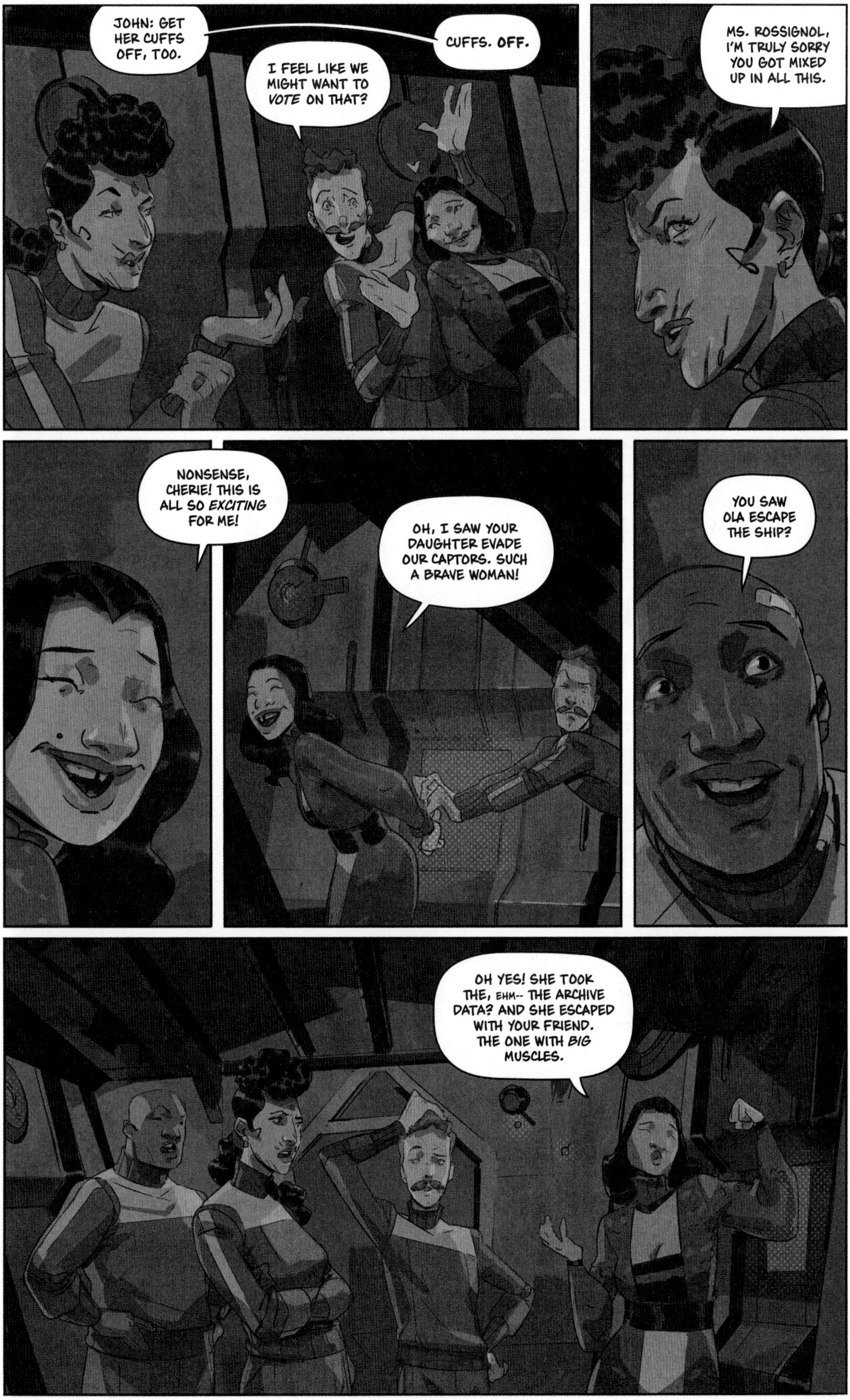
JOHN: GET HER CUFFS OFF, TOO.
CUFFS. OFF.
I FEEL LIKE WE MIGHT WANT TO *VOTE* ON THAT?
MS. ROSSIGNOL, I'M TRULY SORRY YOU GOT MIXED UP IN ALL THIS.
NONSENSE, CHERIE! THIS IS ALL SO *EXCITING* FOR ME!
OH, I SAW YOUR DAUGHTER EVADE OUR CAPTORS. SUCH A BRAVE WOMAN!
YOU SAW OLA ESCAPE THE SHIP?
OH YES! SHE TOOK THE, EHM-- THE ARCHIVE DATA? AND SHE ESCAPED WITH YOUR FRIEND. THE ONE WITH *BIG* MUSCLES.

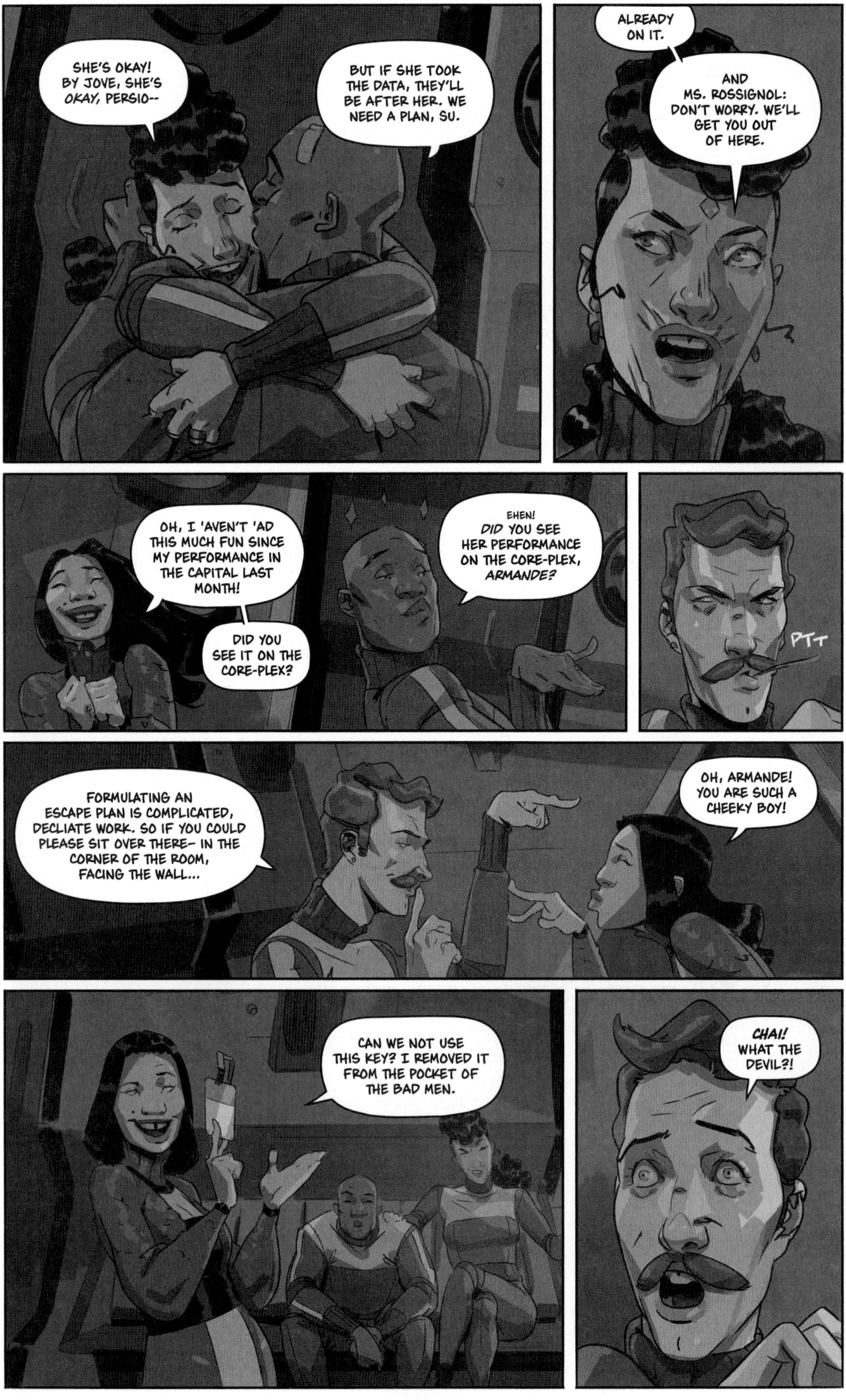
SHE'S OKAY! BY JOVE, SHE'S OKAY, PERSIO--
BUT IF SHE TOOK THE DATA, THEY'LL BE AFTER HER. WE NEED A PLAN, SU.
ALREADY ON IT.
AND MS. ROSSIGNOL: DON'T WORRY. WE'LL GET YOU OUT OF HERE.
OH, I 'AVEN'T 'AD THIS MUCH FUN SINCE MY PERFORMANCE IN THE CAPITAL LAST MONTH!
DID YOU SEE IT ON THE CORE-PLEX?
EHEN! *DID* YOU SEE HER PERFORMANCE ON THE CORE-PLEX, *ARMANDE?*
PTT
FORMULATING AN ESCAPE PLAN IS COMPLICATED, DECLIATE WORK. SO IF YOU COULD PLEASE SIT OVER THERE– IN THE CORNER OF THE ROOM, FACING THE WALL...
OH, ARMANDE! YOU ARE SUCH A CHEEKY BOY!
CAN WE NOT USE THIS KEY? I REMOVED IT FROM THE POCKET OF THE BAD MEN.
CHAI! WHAT THE DEVIL?!

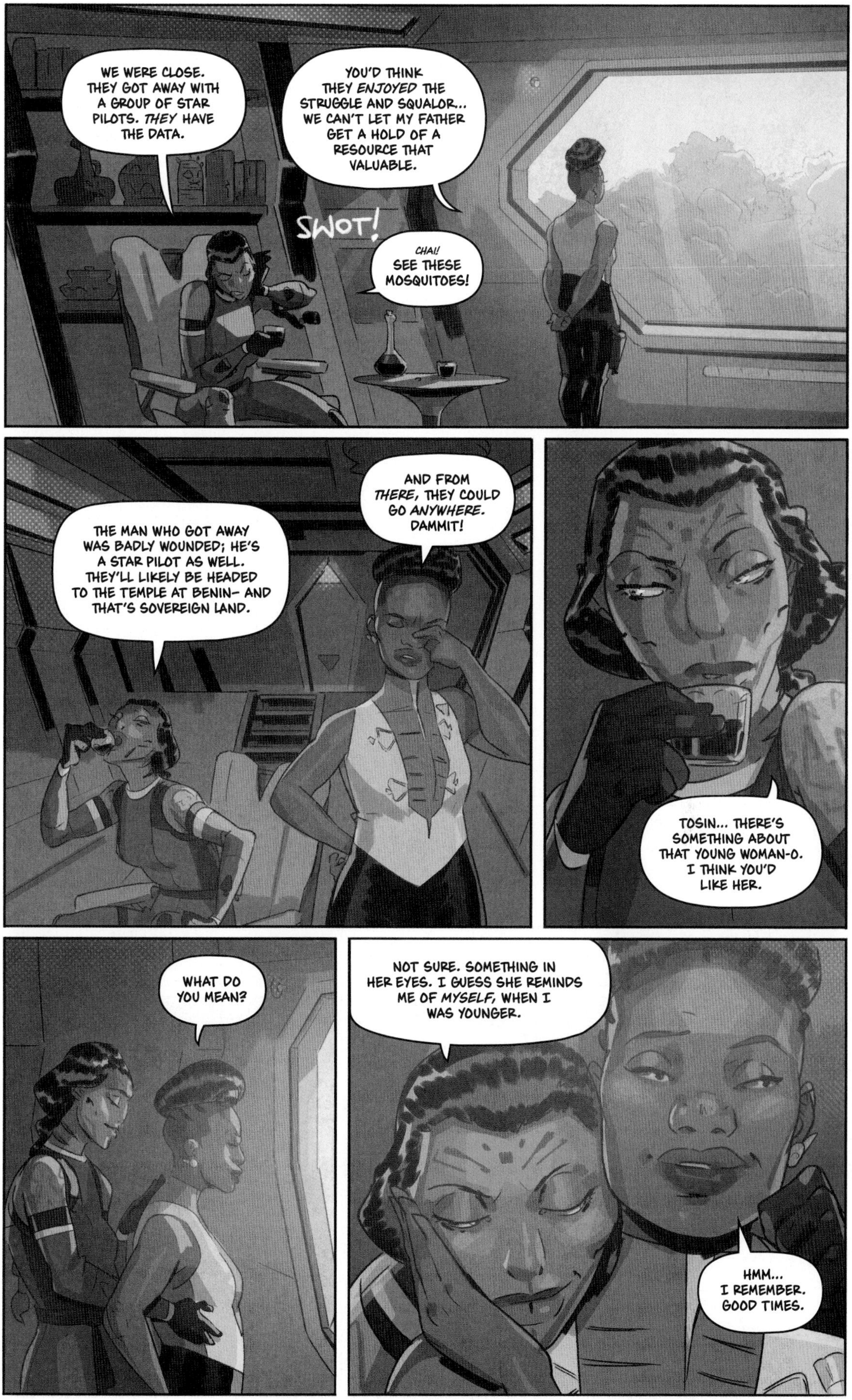
WE WERE CLOSE. THEY GOT AWAY WITH A GROUP OF STAR PILOTS. *THEY* HAVE THE DATA.
YOU'D THINK THEY *ENJOYED* THE STRUGGLE AND SQUALOR... WE CAN'T LET MY FATHER GET A HOLD OF A RESOURCE THAT VALUABLE.
SWOT!
CHAI! SEE THESE MOSQUITOES!
THE MAN WHO GOT AWAY WAS BADLY WOUNDED; HE'S A STAR PILOT AS WELL. THEY'LL LIKELY BE HEADED TO THE TEMPLE AT BENIN– AND THAT'S SOVEREIGN LAND.
AND FROM *THERE*, THEY COULD GO *ANYWHERE*. DAMMIT!
TOSIN... THERE'S SOMETHING ABOUT THAT YOUNG WOMAN-O. I THINK YOU'D LIKE HER.
WHAT DO YOU MEAN?
NOT SURE. SOMETHING IN HER EYES. I GUESS SHE REMINDS ME OF *MYSELF*, WHEN I WAS YOUNGER.
HMM... I REMEMBER. GOOD TIMES.

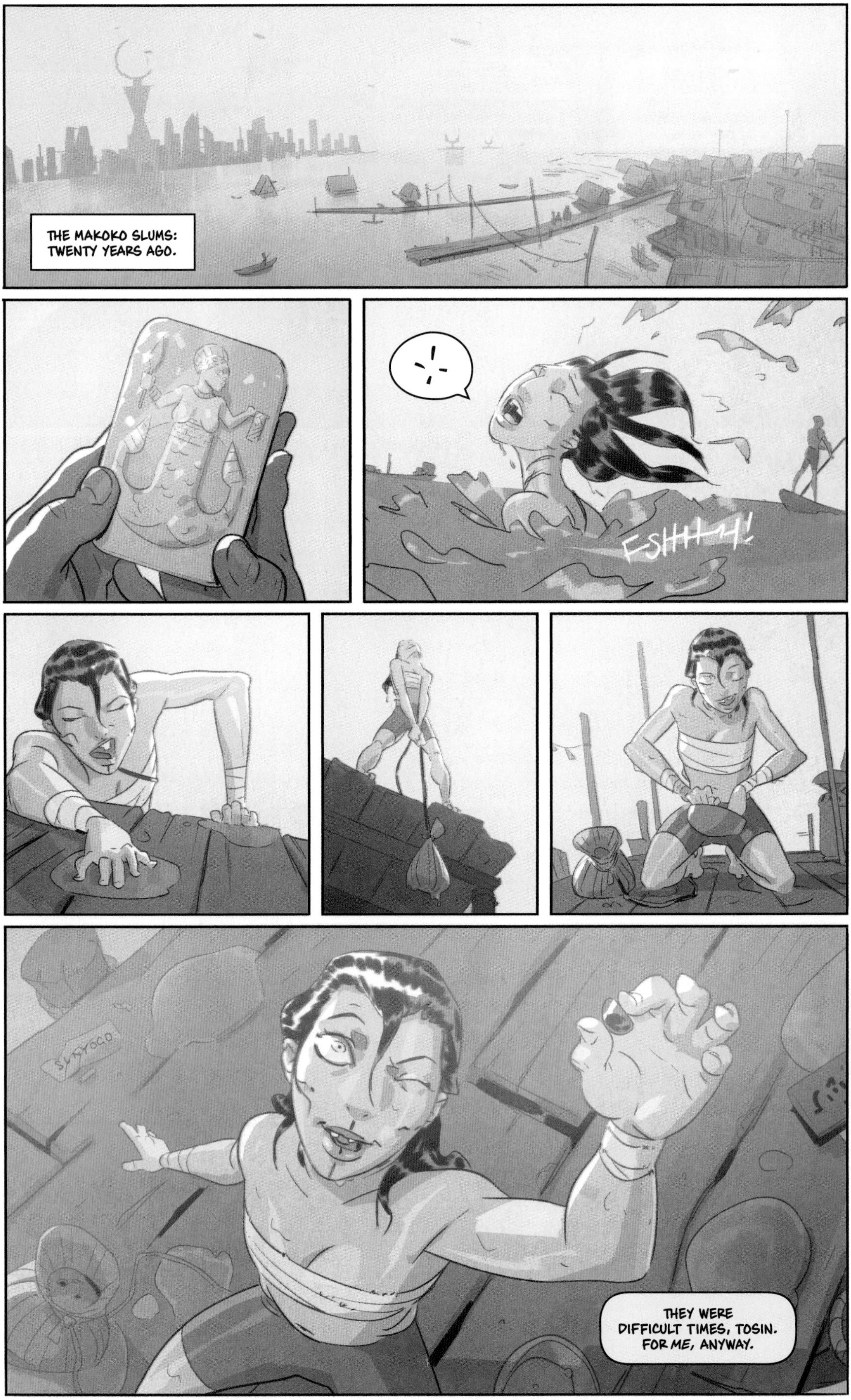
THE MAKOKO SLUMS: TWENTY YEARS AGO.
!
FSHHHH!
THEY WERE DIFFICULT TIMES, TOSIN. FOR ME, ANYWAY.

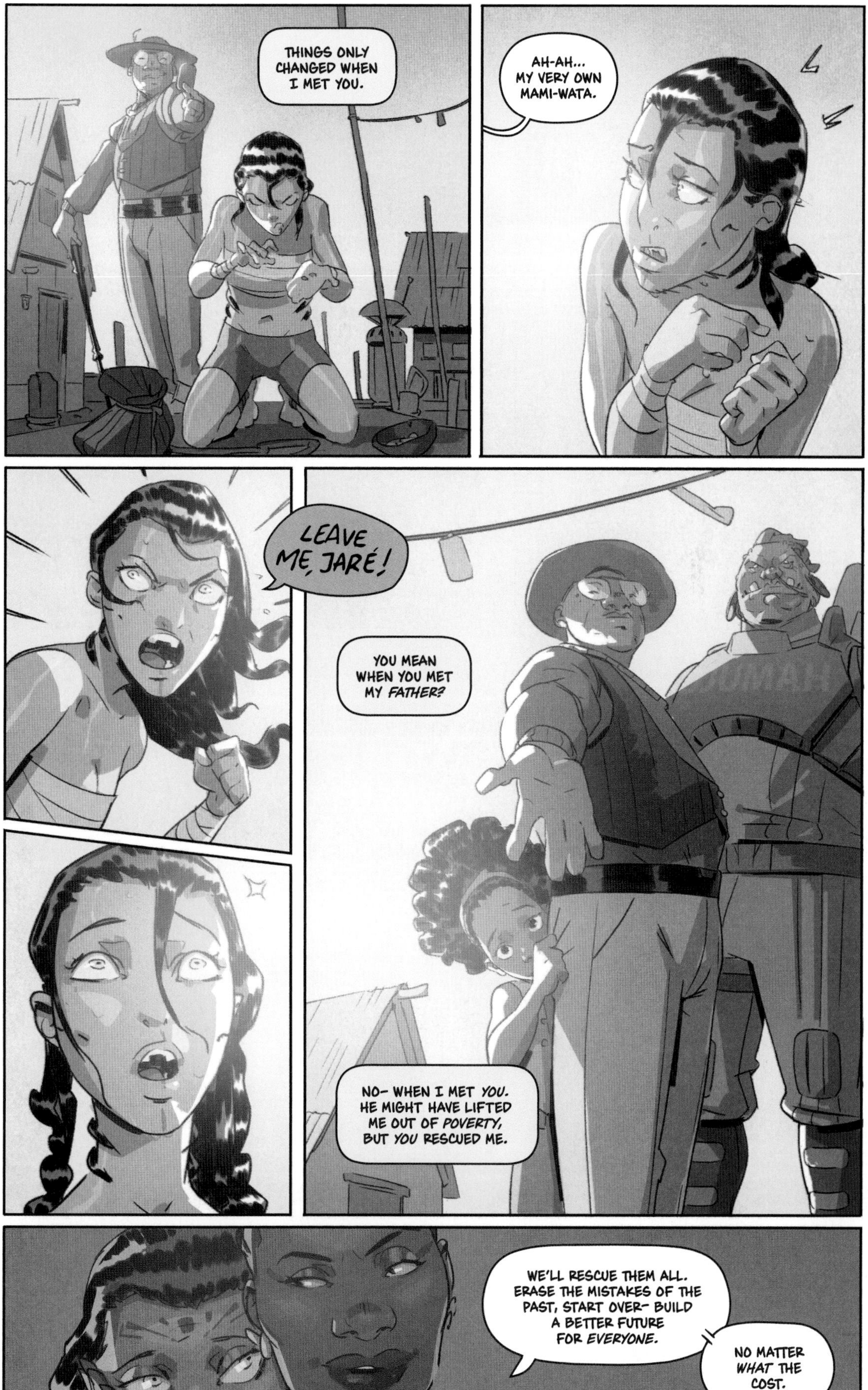
THINGS ONLY CHANGED WHEN I MET YOU.
AH-AH... MY VERY OWN MAMI-WATA.
LEAVE ME, JARÉ!
YOU MEAN WHEN YOU MET MY *FATHER?*
NO- WHEN I MET *YOU.* HE MIGHT HAVE LIFTED ME OUT OF *POVERTY,* BUT *YOU* RESCUED ME.
WE'LL RESCUE THEM ALL. ERASE THE MISTAKES OF THE PAST, START OVER- BUILD A BETTER FUTURE FOR *EVERYONE.*
NO MATTER *WHAT* THE COST.

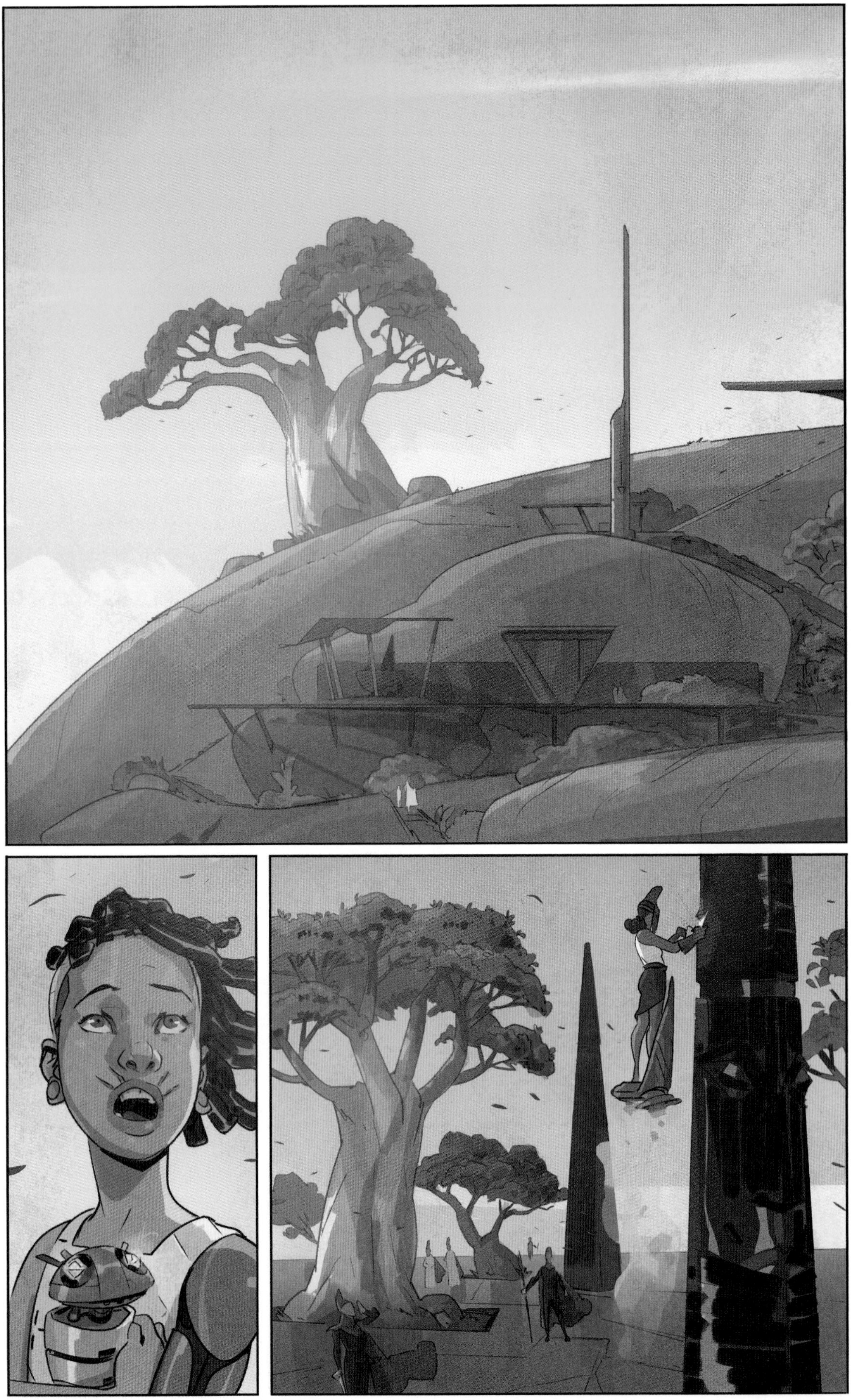

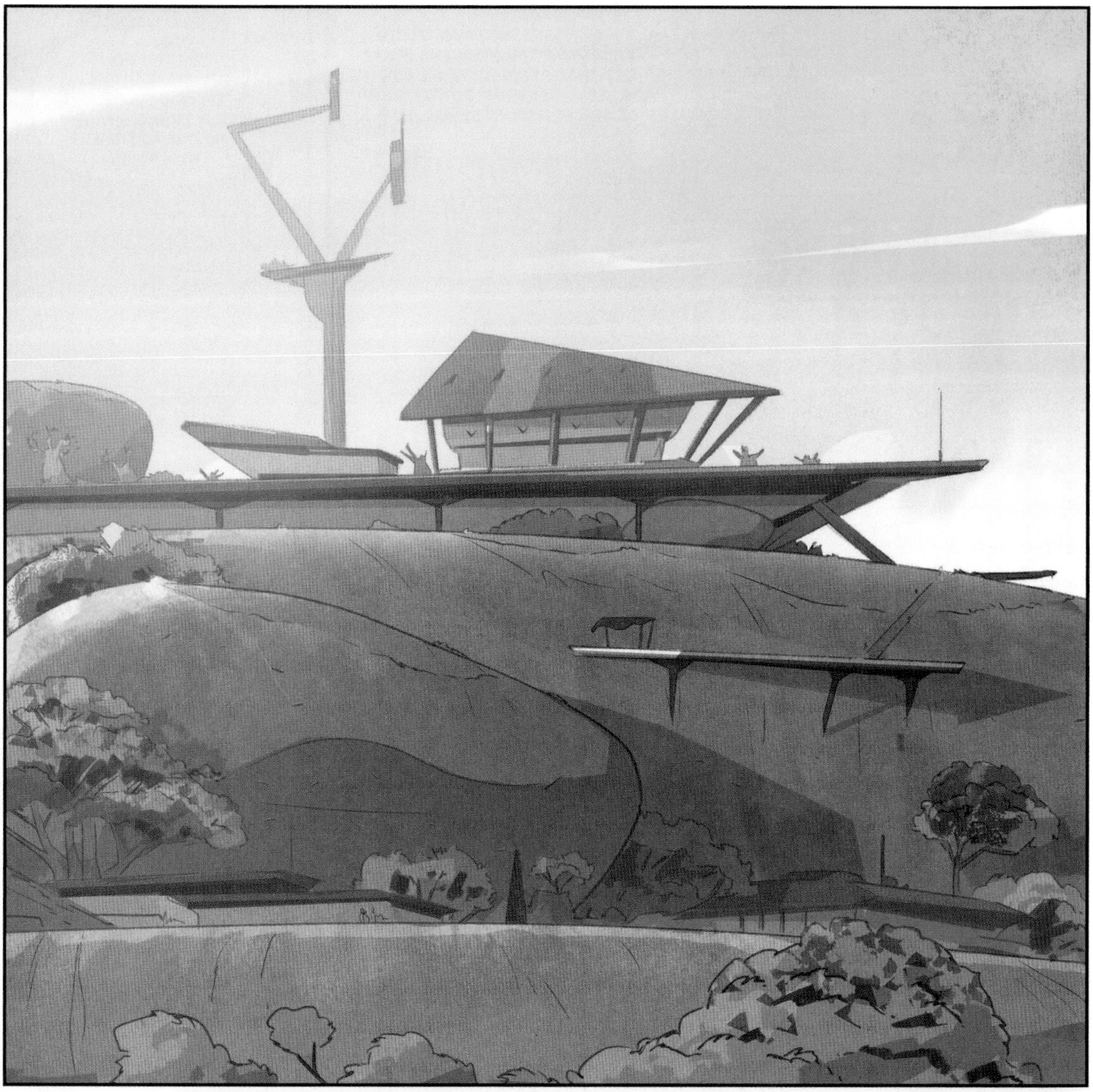

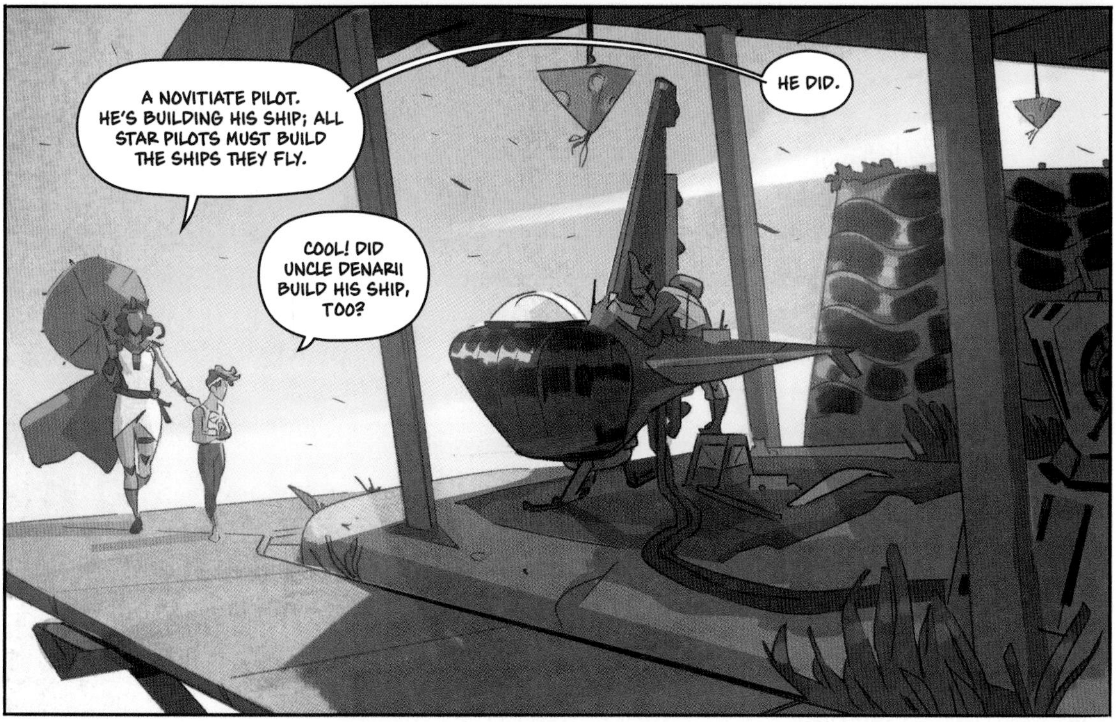

A NOVITIATE PILOT. HE'S BUILDING HIS SHIP; ALL STAR PILOTS MUST BUILD THE SHIPS THEY FLY.
COOL! DID UNCLE DENARII BUILD HIS SHIP, TOO?
HE DID.

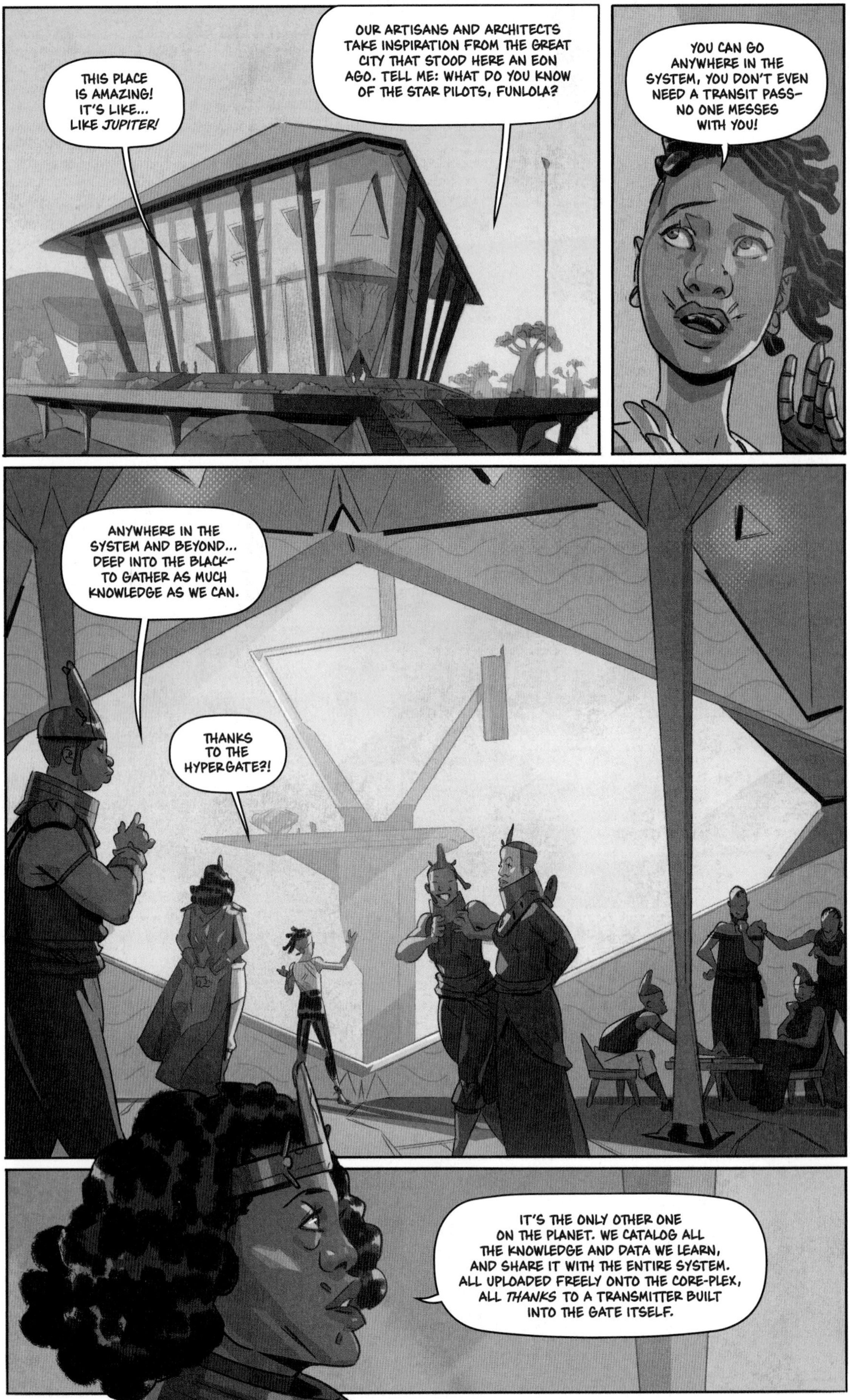
THIS PLACE IS AMAZING! IT'S LIKE... LIKE *JUPITER!*
OUR ARTISANS AND ARCHITECTS TAKE INSPIRATION FROM THE GREAT CITY THAT STOOD HERE AN EON AGO. TELL ME: WHAT DO YOU KNOW OF THE STAR PILOTS, FUNLOLA?
YOU CAN GO ANYWHERE IN THE SYSTEM, YOU DON'T EVEN NEED A TRANSIT PASS– NO ONE MESSES WITH YOU!
ANYWHERE IN THE SYSTEM AND BEYOND... DEEP INTO THE BLACK– TO GATHER AS MUCH KNOWLEDGE AS WE CAN.
THANKS TO THE HYPERGATE?!
IT'S THE ONLY OTHER ONE ON THE PLANET. WE CATALOG ALL THE KNOWLEDGE AND DATA WE LEARN, AND SHARE IT WITH THE ENTIRE SYSTEM. ALL UPLOADED FREELY ONTO THE CORE-PLEX, ALL *THANKS* TO A TRANSMITTER BUILT INTO THE GATE ITSELF.

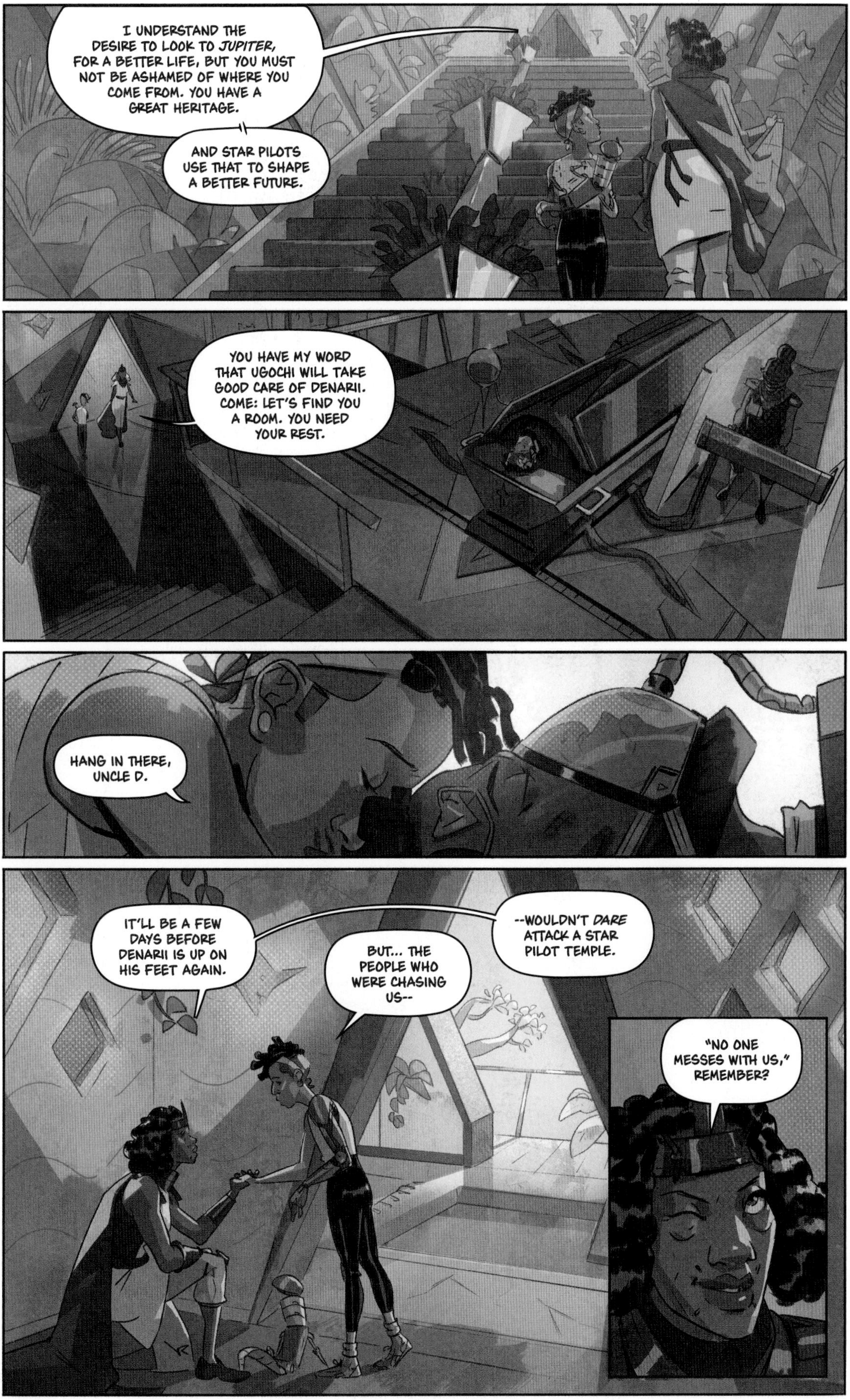
I UNDERSTAND THE DESIRE TO LOOK TO *JUPITER*, FOR A BETTER LIFE, BUT YOU MUST NOT BE ASHAMED OF WHERE YOU COME FROM. YOU HAVE A GREAT HERITAGE.
AND STAR PILOTS USE THAT TO SHAPE A BETTER FUTURE.
YOU HAVE MY WORD THAT UGOCHI WILL TAKE GOOD CARE OF DENARII. COME: LET'S FIND YOU A ROOM. YOU NEED YOUR REST.
HANG IN THERE, UNCLE D.
IT'LL BE A FEW DAYS BEFORE DENARII IS UP ON HIS FEET AGAIN.
BUT... THE PEOPLE WHO WERE CHASING US--
--WOULDN'T *DARE* ATTACK A STAR PILOT TEMPLE.
"NO ONE MESSES WITH US," REMEMBER?

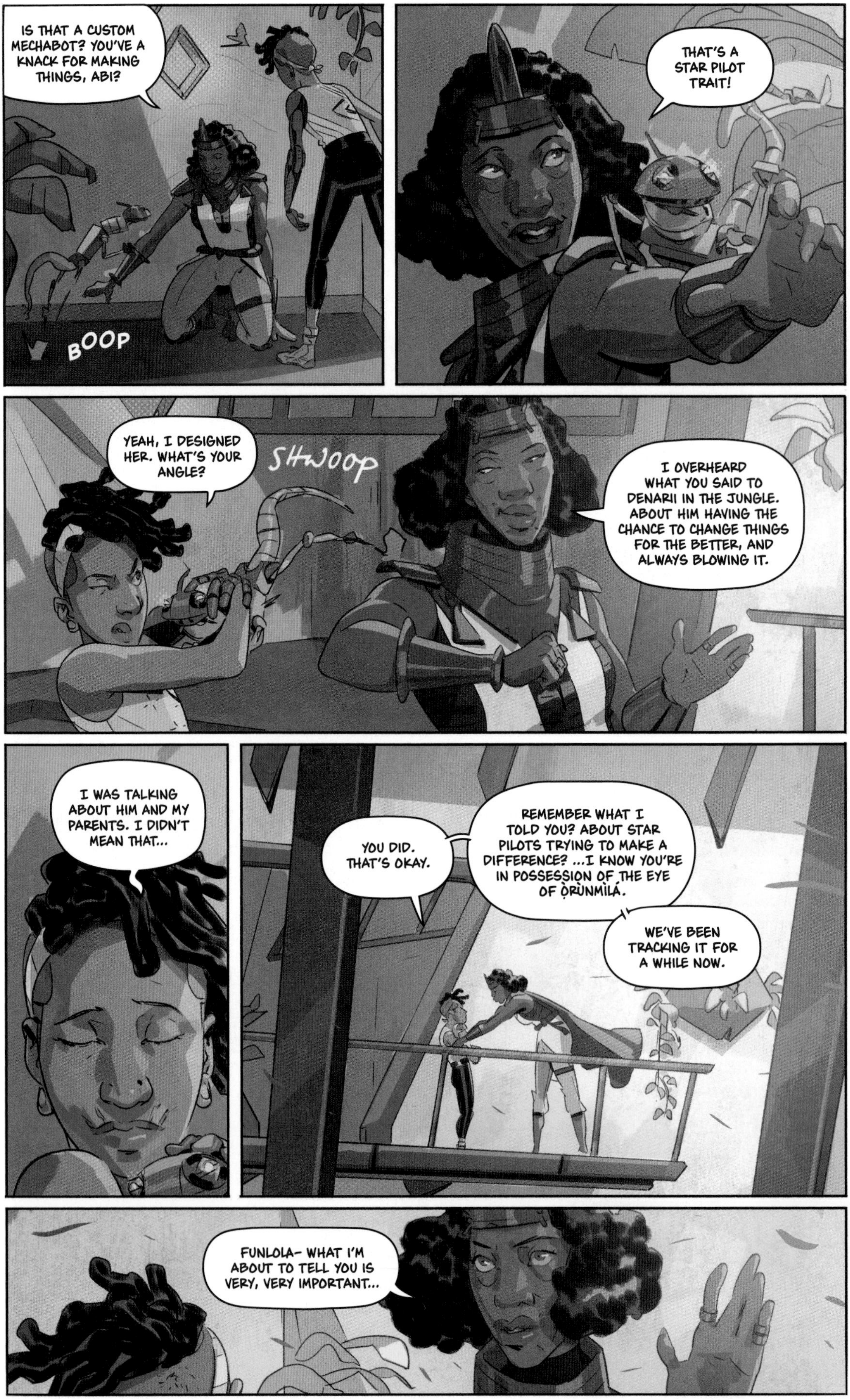
IS THAT A CUSTOM MECHABOT? YOU'VE A KNACK FOR MAKING THINGS, ABI?
BOOP
THAT'S A STAR PILOT TRAIT!
YEAH, I DESIGNED HER. WHAT'S YOUR ANGLE?
SHWOOP
I OVERHEARD WHAT YOU SAID TO DENARII IN THE JUNGLE. ABOUT HIM HAVING THE CHANCE TO CHANGE THINGS FOR THE BETTER, AND ALWAYS BLOWING IT.
I WAS TALKING ABOUT HIM AND MY PARENTS. I DIDN'T MEAN THAT...
YOU DID. THAT'S OKAY.
REMEMBER WHAT I TOLD YOU? ABOUT STAR PILOTS TRYING TO MAKE A DIFFERENCE? ...I KNOW YOU'RE IN POSSESSION OF THE EYE OF Ọ̀RÙNMÌLÁ.
WE'VE BEEN TRACKING IT FOR A WHILE NOW.
FUNLOLA- WHAT I'M ABOUT TO TELL YOU IS VERY, VERY IMPORTANT...

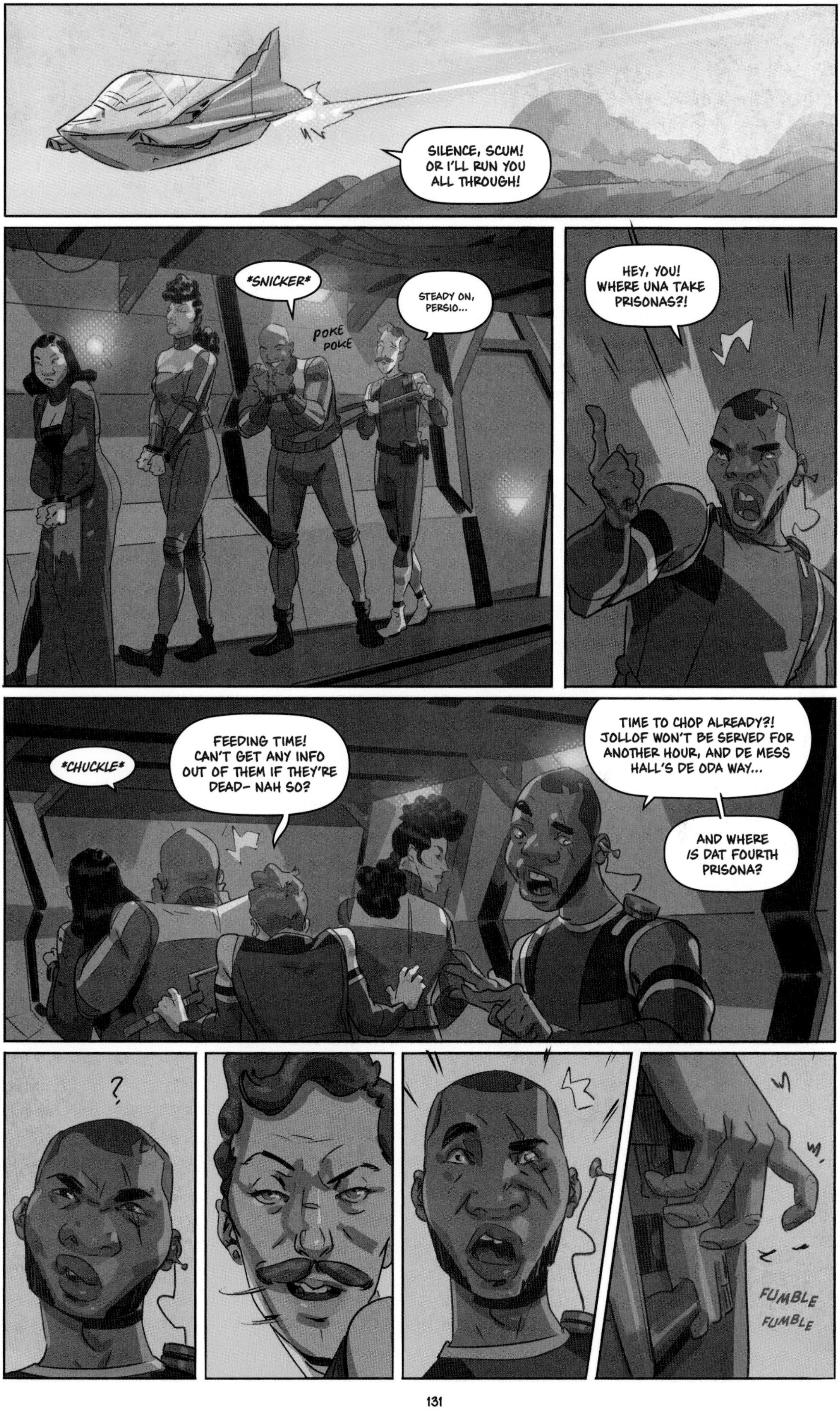
SILENCE, SCUM! OR I'LL RUN YOU ALL THROUGH!
SNICKER
STEADY ON, PERSIO...
POKE POKE
HEY, YOU! WHERE UNA TAKE PRISONAS?!
CHUCKLE
FEEDING TIME! CAN'T GET ANY INFO OUT OF THEM IF THEY'RE DEAD- NAH SO?
TIME TO CHOP ALREADY?! JOLLOF WON'T BE SERVED FOR ANOTHER HOUR, AND DE MESS HALL'S DE ODA WAY...
AND WHERE IS DAT FOURTH PRISONA?
?
FUMBLE FUMBLE

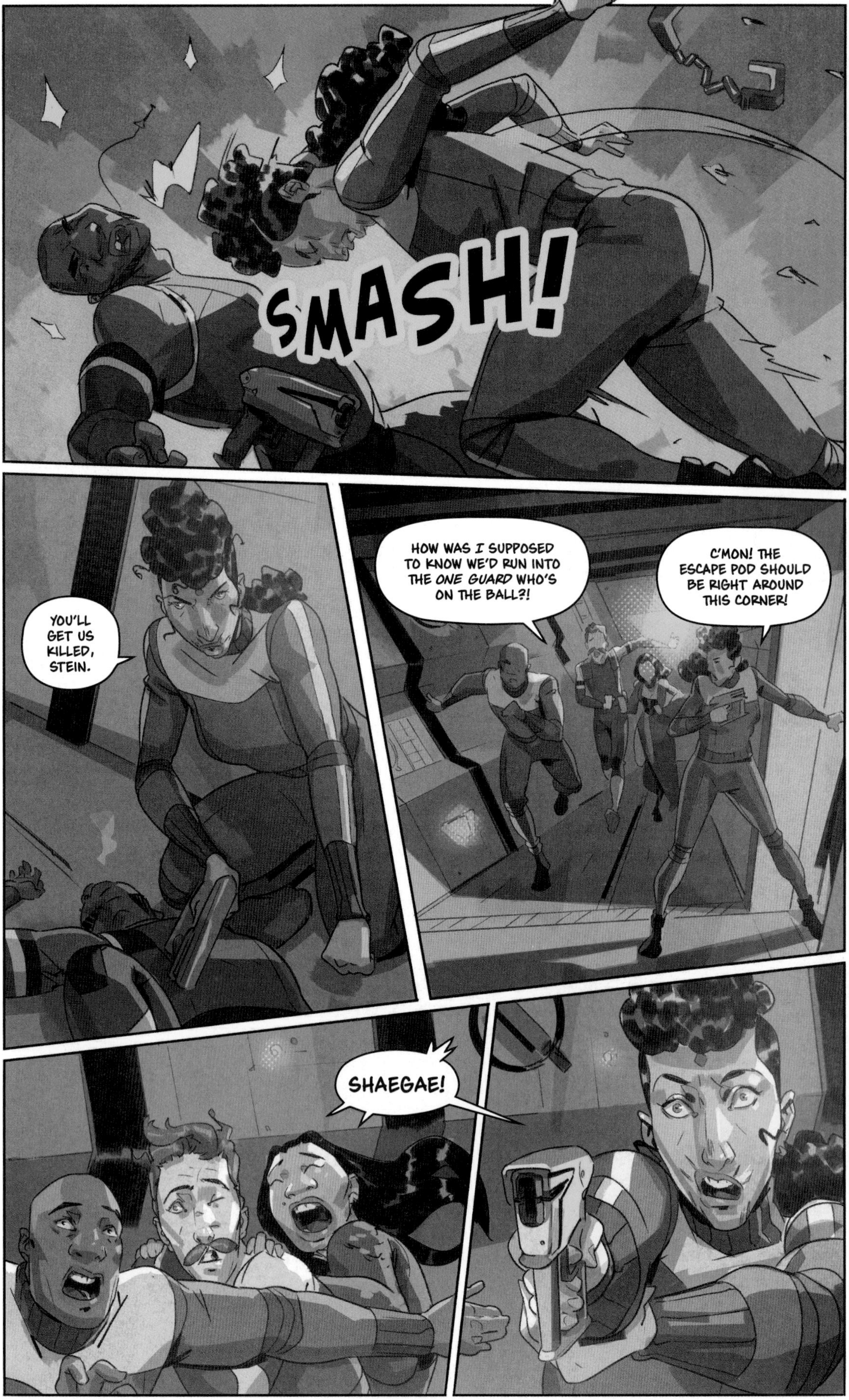
SMASH!
YOU'LL GET US KILLED, STEIN.
HOW WAS I SUPPOSED TO KNOW WE'D RUN INTO THE *ONE GUARD* WHO'S ON THE BALL?!
C'MON! THE ESCAPE POD SHOULD BE RIGHT AROUND THIS CORNER!
SHAEGAE!

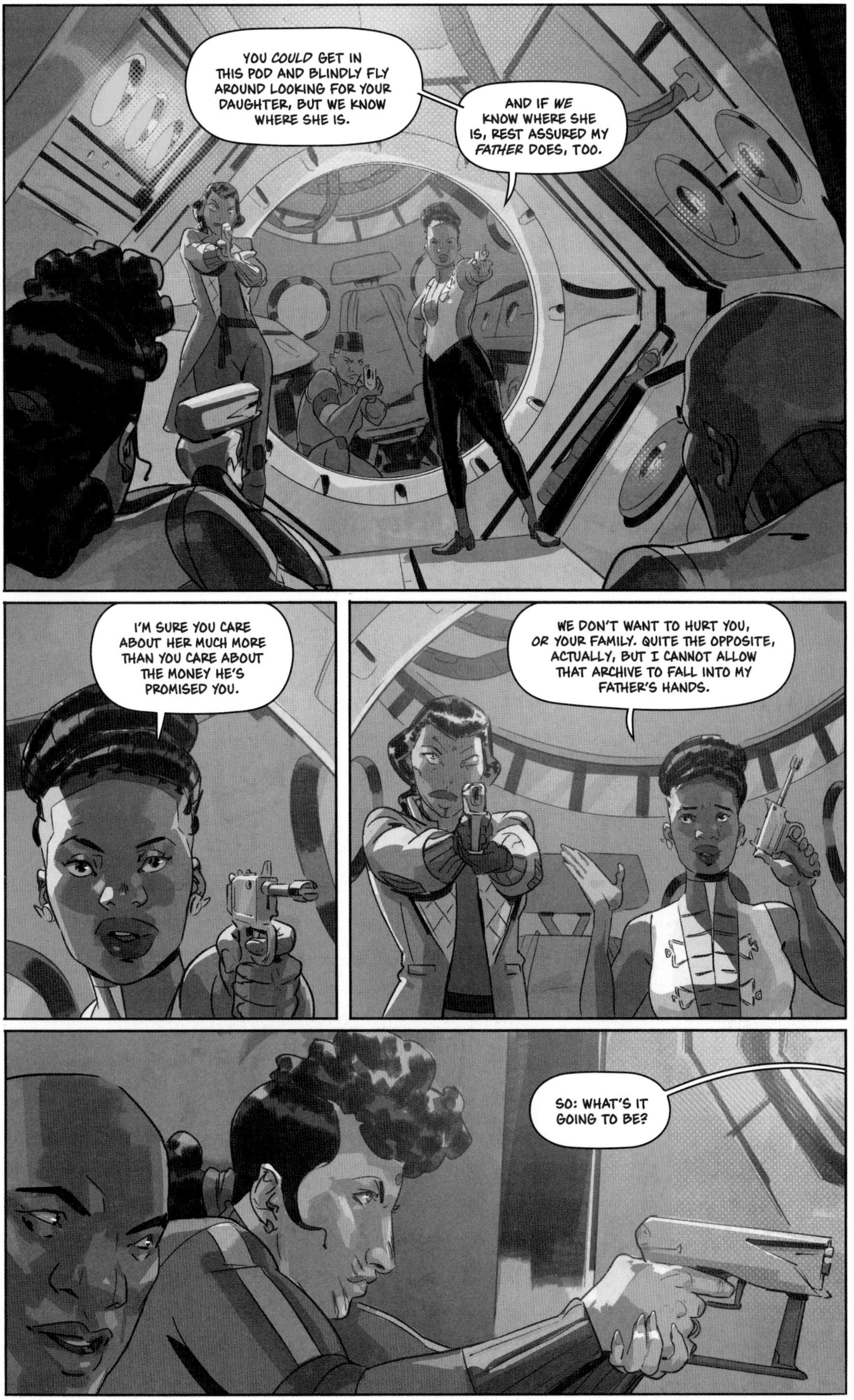
YOU *COULD* GET IN THIS POD AND BLINDLY FLY AROUND LOOKING FOR YOUR DAUGHTER, BUT WE KNOW WHERE SHE IS.
AND IF *WE* KNOW WHERE SHE IS, REST ASSURED MY *FATHER* DOES, TOO.
I'M SURE YOU CARE ABOUT HER MUCH MORE THAN YOU CARE ABOUT THE MONEY HE'S PROMISED YOU.
WE DON'T WANT TO HURT YOU, OR YOUR FAMILY. QUITE THE OPPOSITE, ACTUALLY, BUT I CANNOT ALLOW THAT ARCHIVE TO FALL INTO MY FATHER'S HANDS.
SO: WHAT'S IT GOING TO BE?

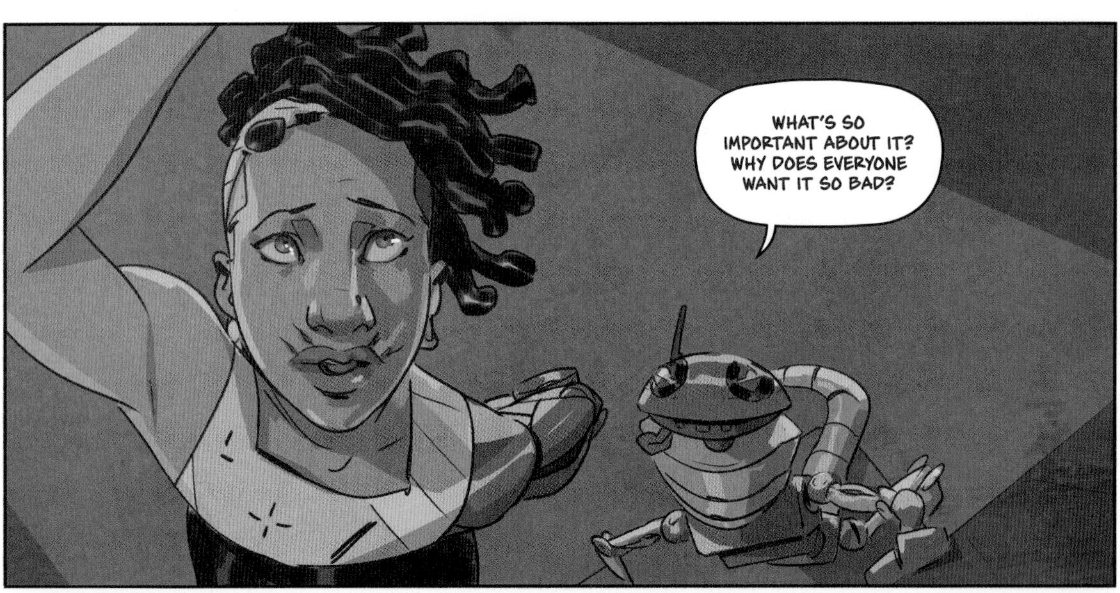
WHAT'S SO IMPORTANT ABOUT IT? WHY DOES EVERYONE WANT IT SO BAD?

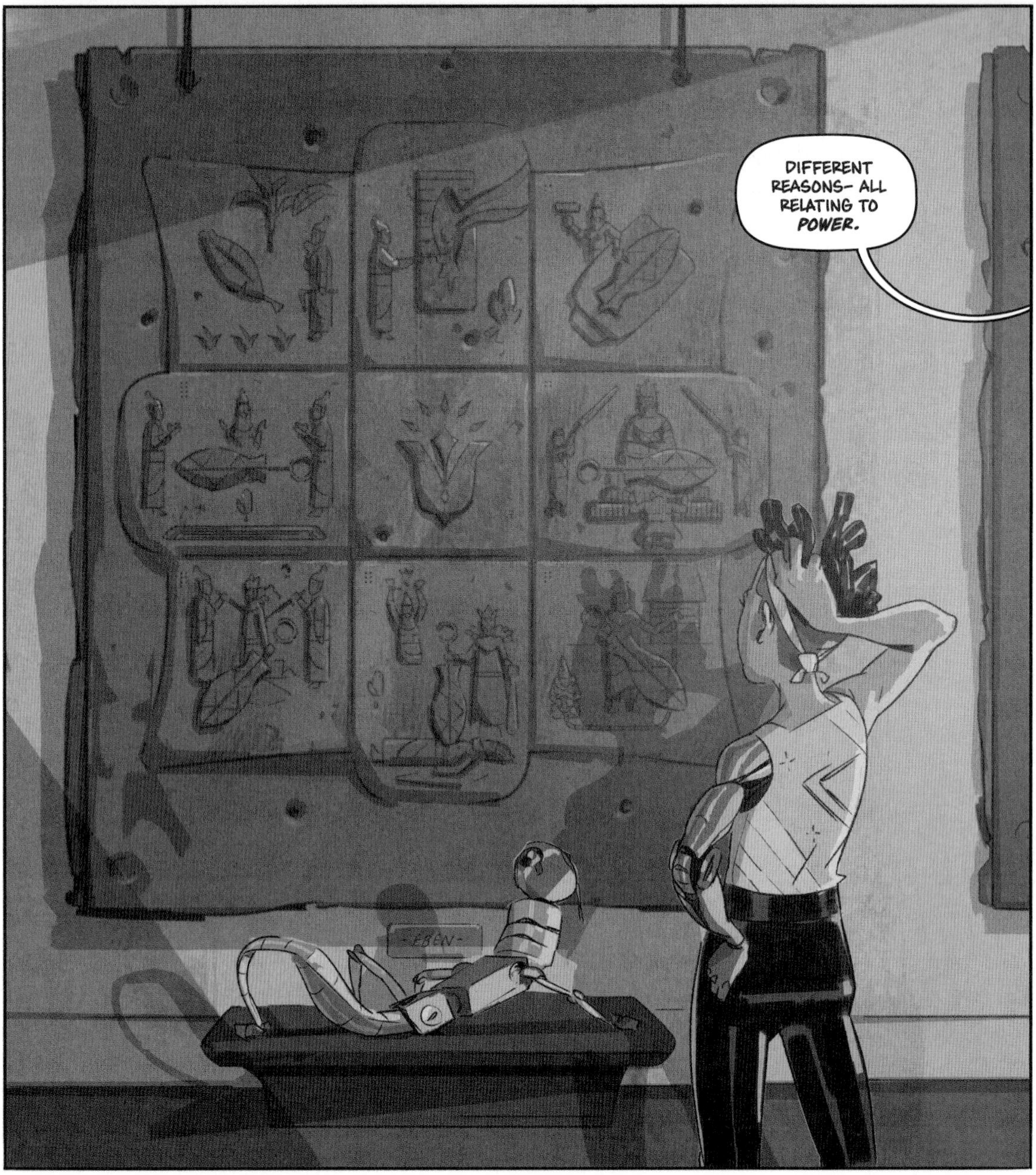
DIFFERENT REASONS- ALL RELATING TO *POWER.*

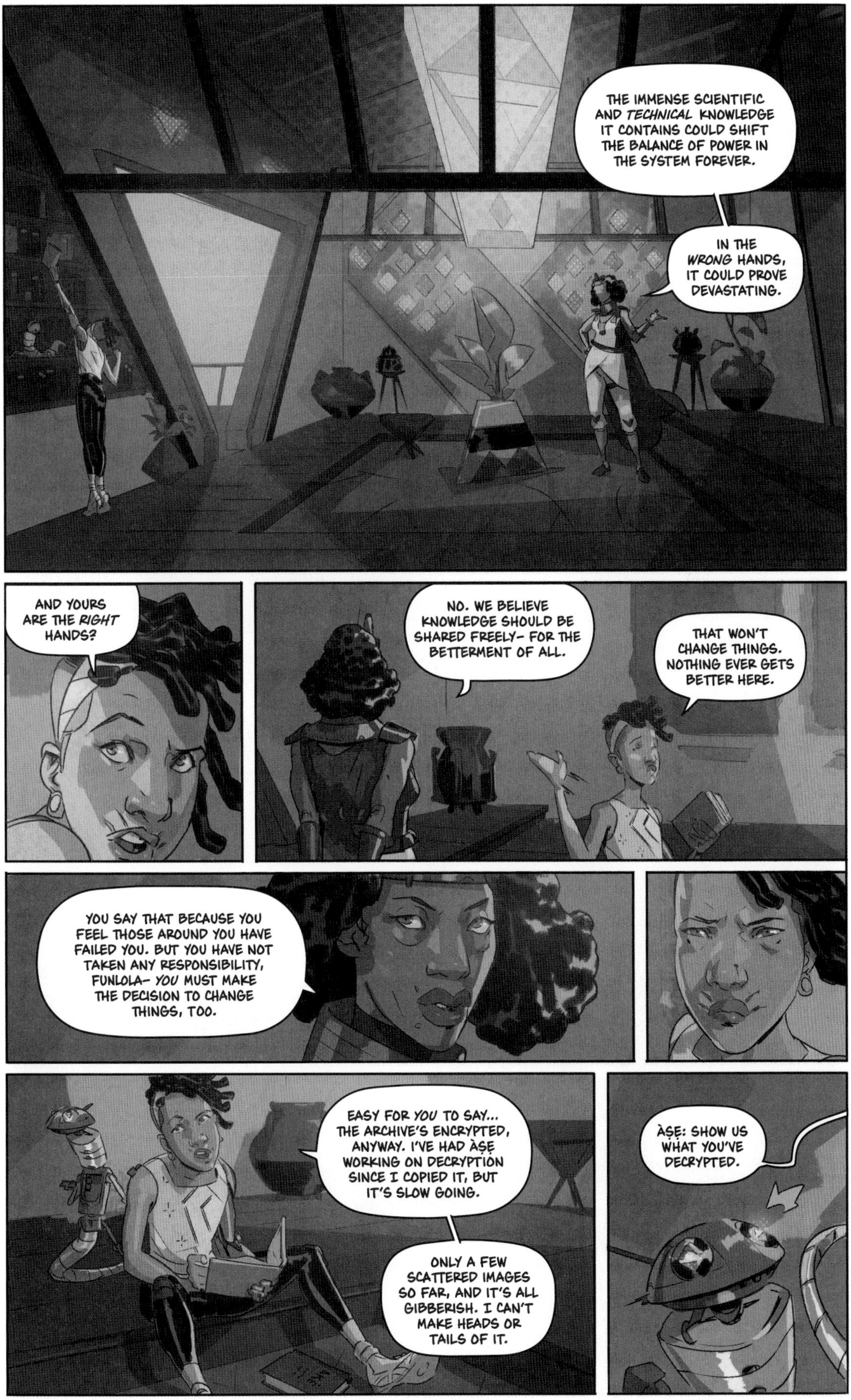
THE IMMENSE SCIENTIFIC AND *TECHNICAL* KNOWLEDGE IT CONTAINS COULD SHIFT THE BALANCE OF POWER IN THE SYSTEM FOREVER.
IN THE *WRONG* HANDS, IT COULD PROVE DEVASTATING.
AND YOURS ARE THE *RIGHT* HANDS?
NO. WE BELIEVE KNOWLEDGE SHOULD BE SHARED FREELY- FOR THE BETTERMENT OF ALL.
THAT WON'T CHANGE THINGS. NOTHING EVER GETS BETTER HERE.
YOU SAY THAT BECAUSE YOU FEEL THOSE AROUND YOU HAVE FAILED YOU. BUT YOU HAVE NOT TAKEN ANY RESPONSIBILITY, FUNLOLA- *YOU* MUST MAKE THE DECISION TO CHANGE THINGS, TOO.
EASY FOR *YOU* TO SAY... THE ARCHIVE'S ENCRYPTED, ANYWAY. I'VE HAD ÀṢẸ WORKING ON DECRYPTION SINCE I COPIED IT, BUT IT'S SLOW GOING.
ONLY A FEW SCATTERED IMAGES SO FAR, AND IT'S ALL GIBBERISH. I CAN'T MAKE HEADS OR TAILS OF IT.
ÀṢẸ: SHOW US WHAT YOU'VE DECRYPTED.

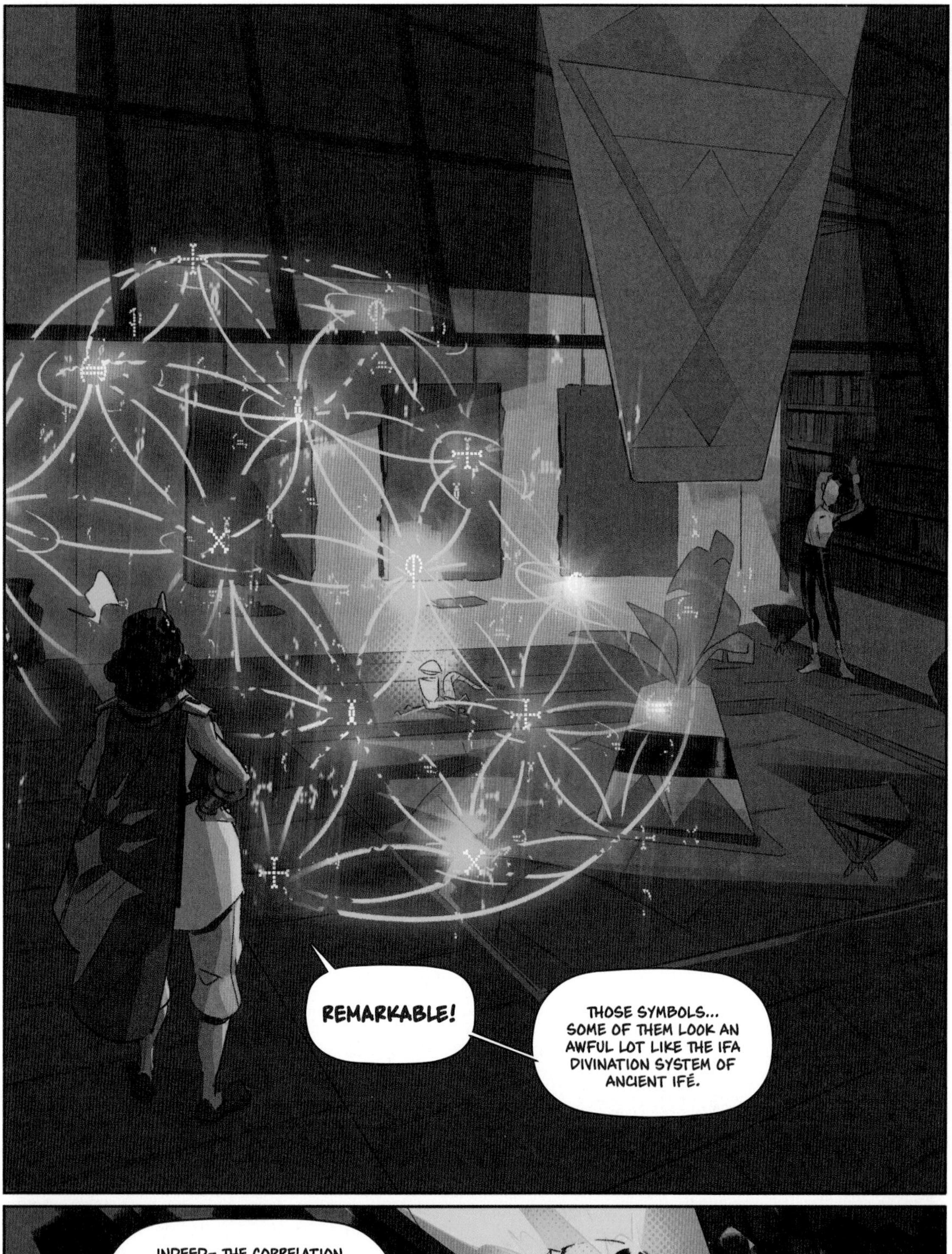
REMARKABLE!
THOSE SYMBOLS... SOME OF THEM LOOK AN AWFUL LOT LIKE THE IFA DIVINATION SYSTEM OF ANCIENT IFÉ.

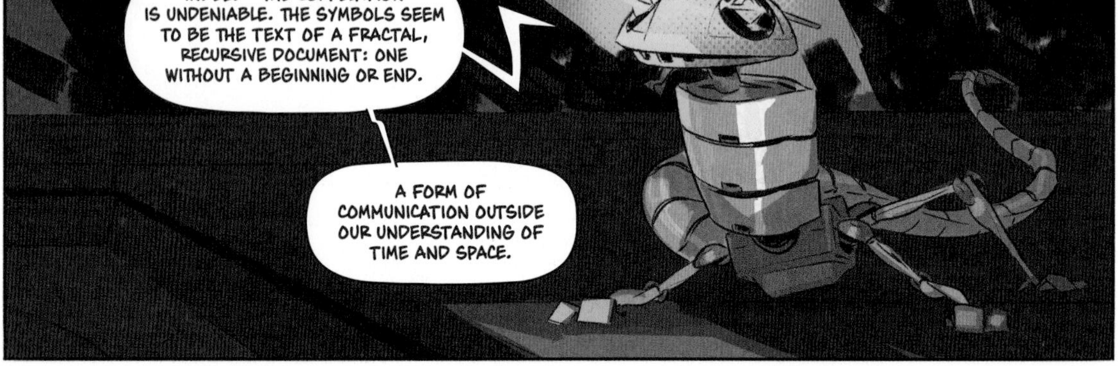
INDEED– THE CORRELATION IS UNDENIABLE. THE SYMBOLS SEEM TO BE THE TEXT OF A FRACTAL, RECURSIVE DOCUMENT: ONE WITHOUT A BEGINNING OR END.
A FORM OF COMMUNICATION OUTSIDE OUR UNDERSTANDING OF TIME AND SPACE.

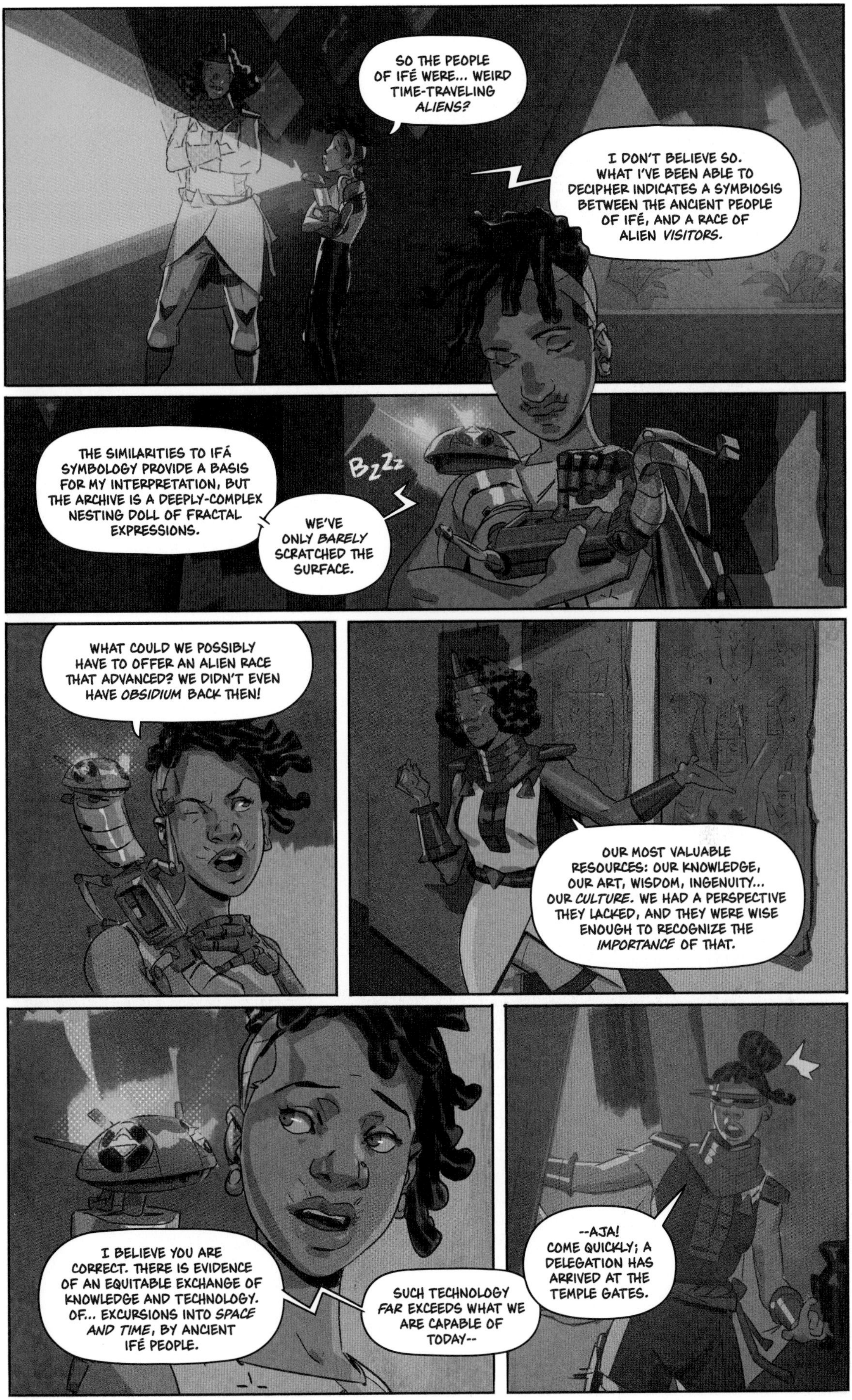
SO THE PEOPLE OF IFÉ WERE... WEIRD TIME-TRAVELING ALIENS?
I DON'T BELIEVE SO. WHAT I'VE BEEN ABLE TO DECIPHER INDICATES A SYMBIOSIS BETWEEN THE ANCIENT PEOPLE OF IFÉ, AND A RACE OF ALIEN VISITORS.
BZZZ
THE SIMILARITIES TO IFÁ SYMBOLOGY PROVIDE A BASIS FOR MY INTERPRETATION, BUT THE ARCHIVE IS A DEEPLY-COMPLEX NESTING DOLL OF FRACTAL EXPRESSIONS.
WE'VE ONLY BARELY SCRATCHED THE SURFACE.
WHAT COULD WE POSSIBLY HAVE TO OFFER AN ALIEN RACE THAT ADVANCED? WE DIDN'T EVEN HAVE OBSIDIUM BACK THEN!
OUR MOST VALUABLE RESOURCES: OUR KNOWLEDGE, OUR ART, WISDOM, INGENUITY... OUR CULTURE. WE HAD A PERSPECTIVE THEY LACKED, AND THEY WERE WISE ENOUGH TO RECOGNIZE THE IMPORTANCE OF THAT.
I BELIEVE YOU ARE CORRECT. THERE IS EVIDENCE OF AN EQUITABLE EXCHANGE OF KNOWLEDGE AND TECHNOLOGY. OF... EXCURSIONS INTO SPACE AND TIME, BY ANCIENT IFÉ PEOPLE.
SUCH TECHNOLOGY FAR EXCEEDS WHAT WE ARE CAPABLE OF TODAY--
--AJA! COME QUICKLY; A DELEGATION HAS ARRIVED AT THE TEMPLE GATES.

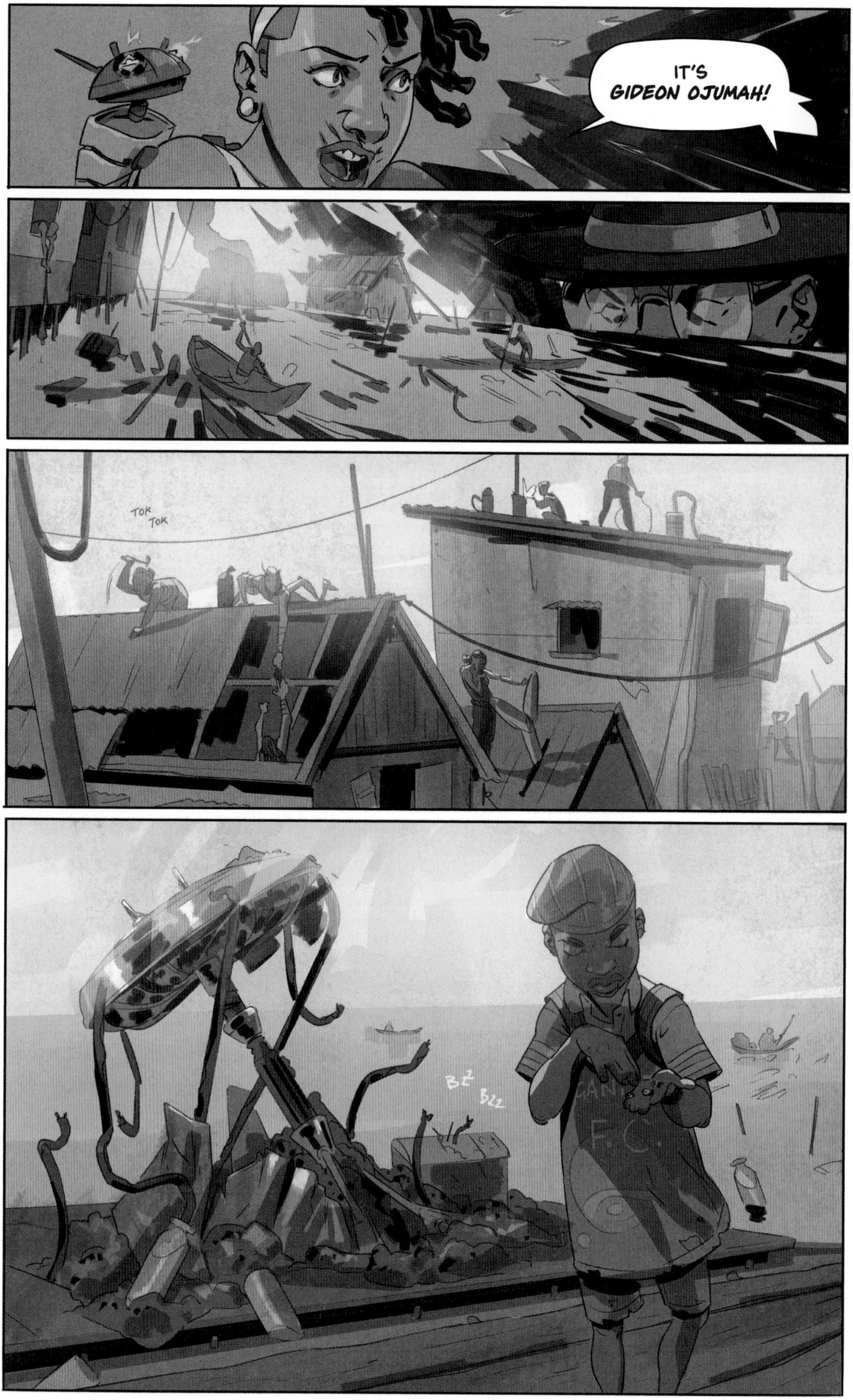
IT'S GIDEON OJUMAH!
TOK TOK
BZZ BZZ

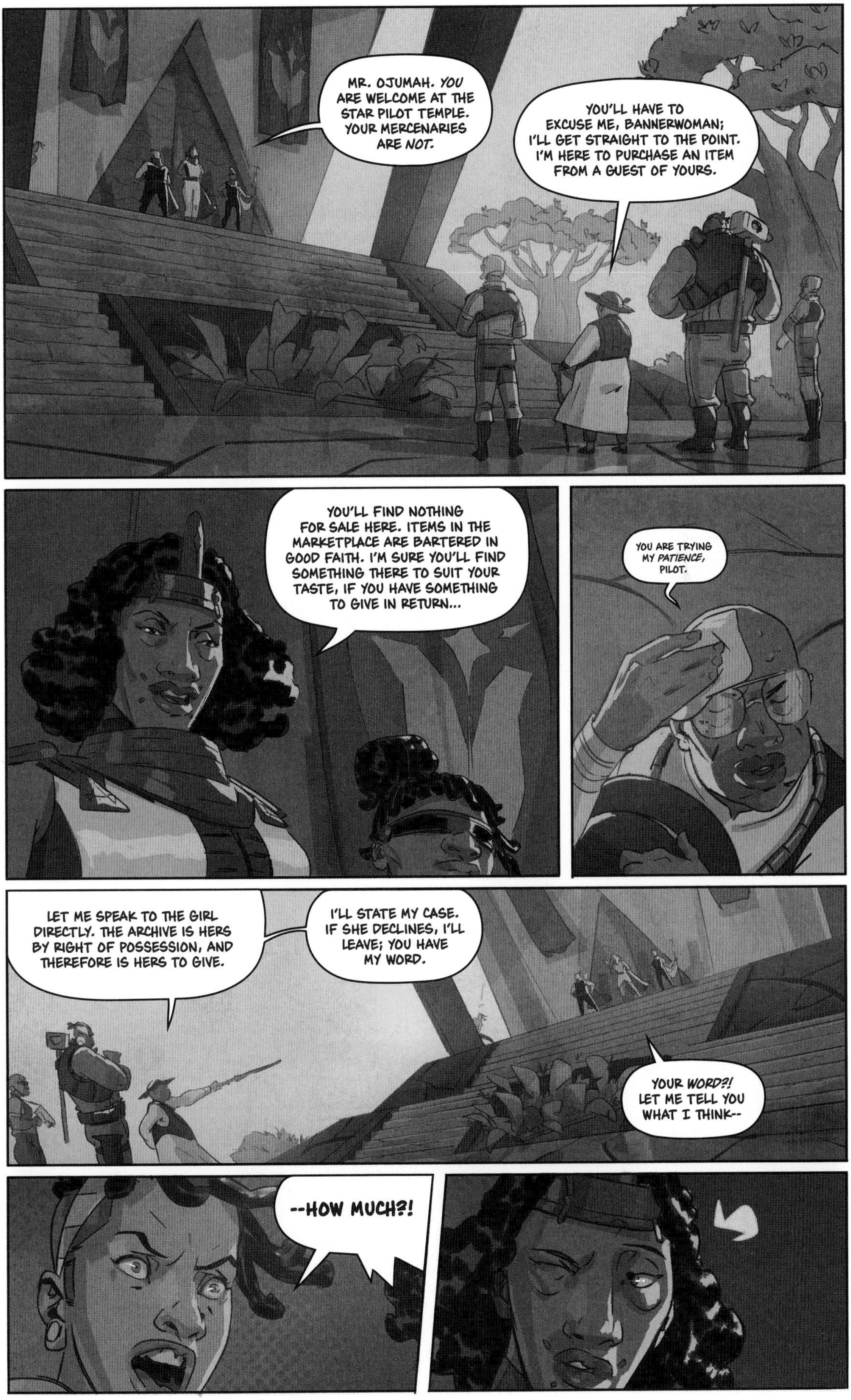
MR. OJUMAH. YOU ARE WELCOME AT THE STAR PILOT TEMPLE. YOUR MERCENARIES ARE NOT.
YOU'LL HAVE TO EXCUSE ME, BANNERWOMAN; I'LL GET STRAIGHT TO THE POINT. I'M HERE TO PURCHASE AN ITEM FROM A GUEST OF YOURS.
YOU'LL FIND NOTHING FOR SALE HERE. ITEMS IN THE MARKETPLACE ARE BARTERED IN GOOD FAITH. I'M SURE YOU'LL FIND SOMETHING THERE TO SUIT YOUR TASTE, IF YOU HAVE SOMETHING TO GIVE IN RETURN...
YOU ARE TRYING MY PATIENCE, PILOT.
LET ME SPEAK TO THE GIRL DIRECTLY. THE ARCHIVE IS HERS BY RIGHT OF POSSESSION, AND THEREFORE IS HERS TO GIVE.
I'LL STATE MY CASE. IF SHE DECLINES, I'LL LEAVE; YOU HAVE MY WORD.
YOUR WORD?! LET ME TELL YOU WHAT I THINK--
--HOW MUCH?!

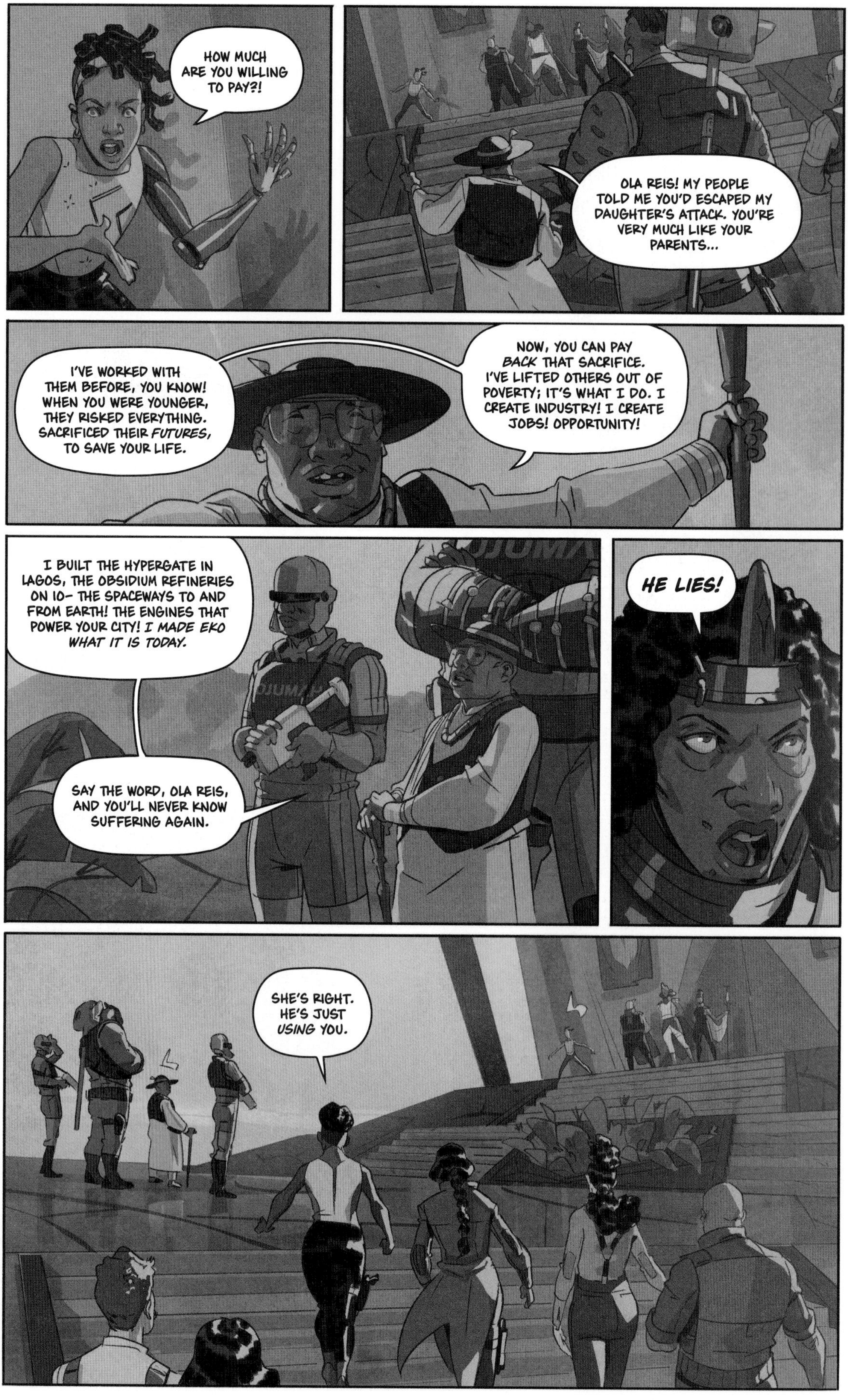
HOW MUCH ARE YOU WILLING TO PAY?!
OLA REIS! MY PEOPLE TOLD ME YOU'D ESCAPED MY DAUGHTER'S ATTACK. YOU'RE VERY MUCH LIKE YOUR PARENTS...
I'VE WORKED WITH THEM BEFORE, YOU KNOW! WHEN YOU WERE YOUNGER, THEY RISKED EVERYTHING. SACRIFICED THEIR *FUTURES*, TO SAVE YOUR LIFE.
NOW, YOU CAN PAY *BACK* THAT SACRIFICE. I'VE LIFTED OTHERS OUT OF POVERTY; IT'S WHAT I DO. I CREATE INDUSTRY! I CREATE JOBS! OPPORTUNITY!
I BUILT THE HYPERGATE IN LAGOS, THE OBSIDIUM REFINERIES ON IO- THE SPACEWAYS TO AND FROM EARTH! THE ENGINES THAT POWER YOUR CITY! *I MADE EKO WHAT IT IS TODAY.*
SAY THE WORD, OLA REIS, AND YOU'LL NEVER KNOW SUFFERING AGAIN.
HE LIES!
SHE'S RIGHT. HE'S JUST *USING* YOU.

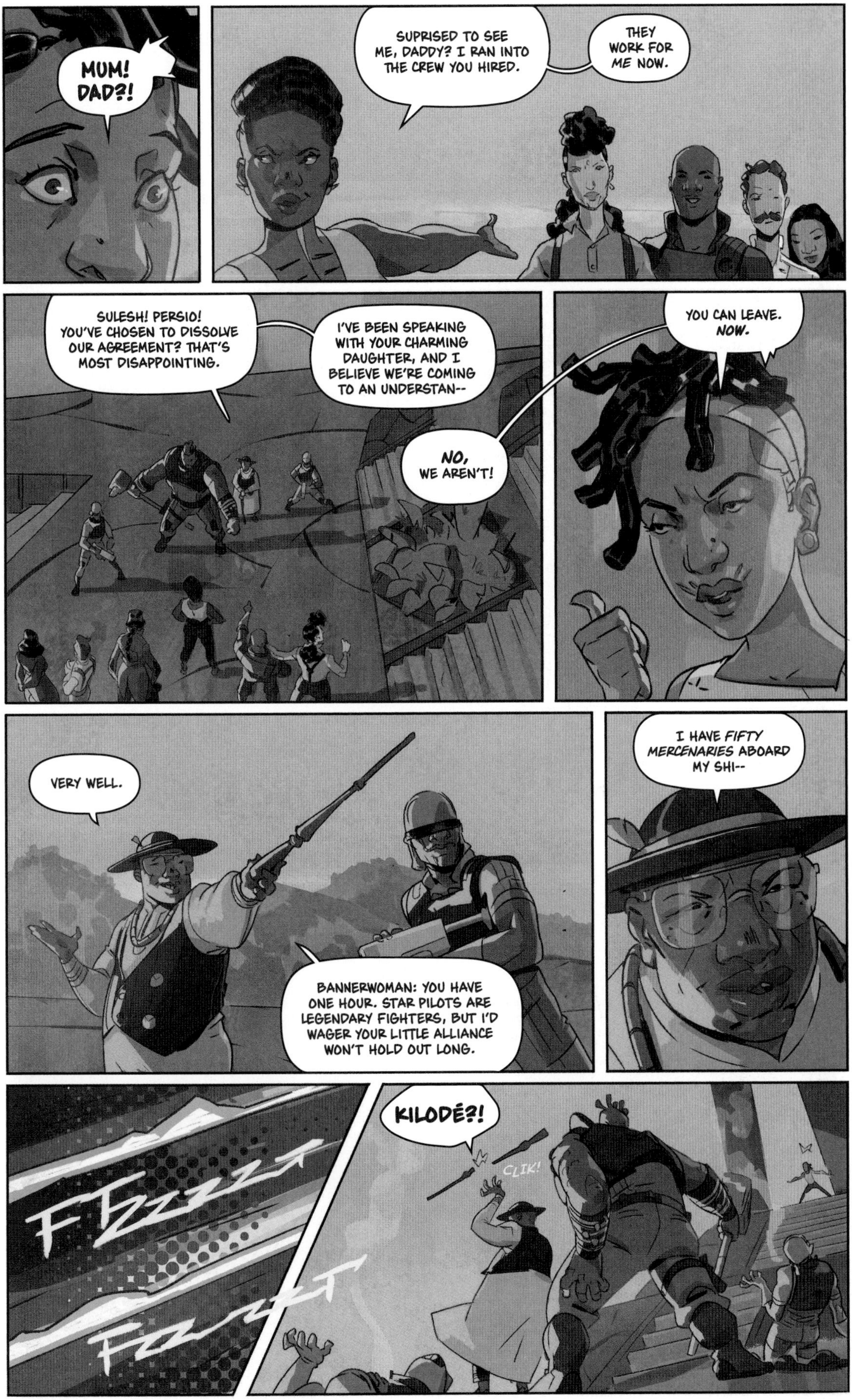
MUM! DAD?!
SUPRISED TO SEE ME, DADDY? I RAN INTO THE CREW YOU HIRED.
THEY WORK FOR ME NOW.
SULESH! PERSIO! YOU'VE CHOSEN TO DISSOLVE OUR AGREEMENT? THAT'S MOST DISAPPOINTING.
I'VE BEEN SPEAKING WITH YOUR CHARMING DAUGHTER, AND I BELIEVE WE'RE COMING TO AN UNDERSTAN--
NO, WE AREN'T!
YOU CAN LEAVE. NOW.
VERY WELL.
BANNERWOMAN: YOU HAVE ONE HOUR. STAR PILOTS ARE LEGENDARY FIGHTERS, BUT I'D WAGER YOUR LITTLE ALLIANCE WON'T HOLD OUT LONG.
I HAVE FIFTY MERCENARIES ABOARD MY SHI--
FTZZZZ
FZZZT
KILODÉ?!
CLIK!

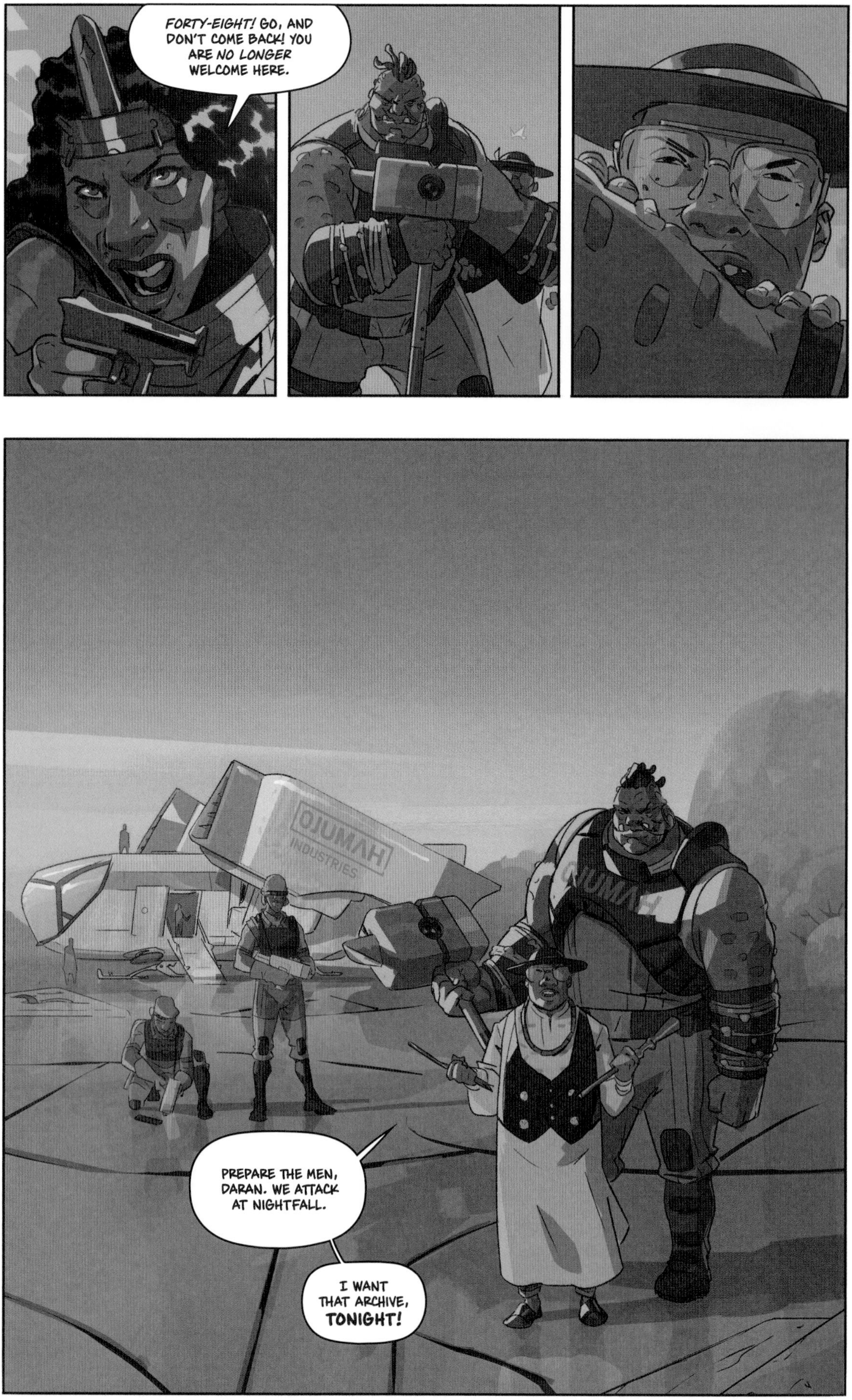
FORTY-EIGHT! GO, AND DON'T COME BACK! YOU ARE NO LONGER WELCOME HERE.
OJUMAH INDUSTRIES
OJUMAH
PREPARE THE MEN, DARAN. WE ATTACK AT NIGHTFALL.
I WANT THAT ARCHIVE, **TONIGHT!**

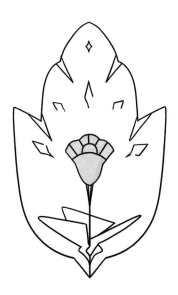

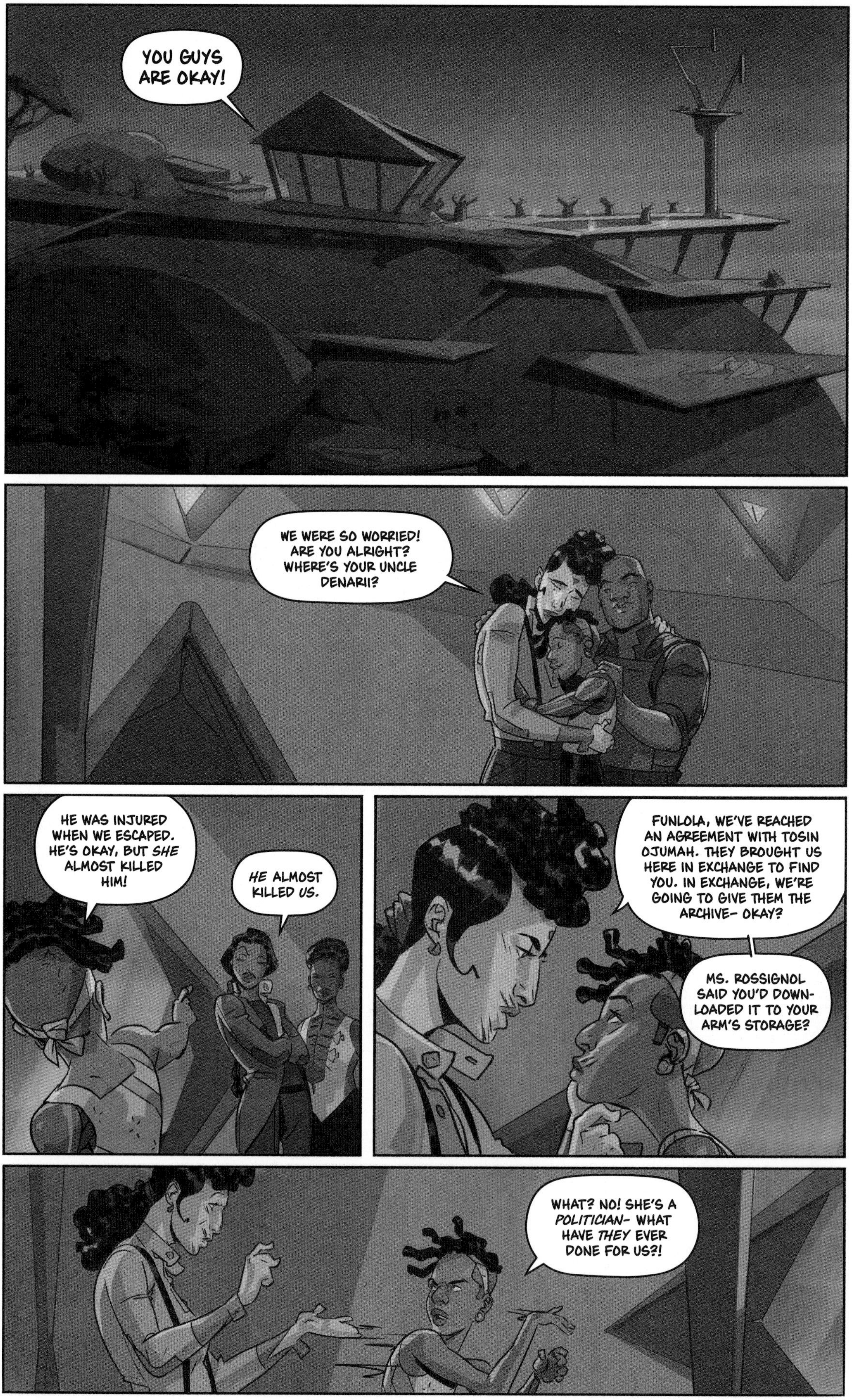
YOU GUYS ARE OKAY!
WE WERE SO WORRIED! ARE YOU ALRIGHT? WHERE'S YOUR UNCLE DENARII?
HE WAS INJURED WHEN WE ESCAPED. HE'S OKAY, BUT SHE ALMOST KILLED HIM!
HE ALMOST KILLED US.
FUNLOLA, WE'VE REACHED AN AGREEMENT WITH TOSIN OJUMAH. THEY BROUGHT US HERE IN EXCHANGE TO FIND YOU. IN EXCHANGE, WE'RE GOING TO GIVE THEM THE ARCHIVE- OKAY?
MS. ROSSIGNOL SAID YOU'D DOWN-LOADED IT TO YOUR ARM'S STORAGE?
WHAT? NO! SHE'S A POLITICIAN- WHAT HAVE THEY EVER DONE FOR US?!

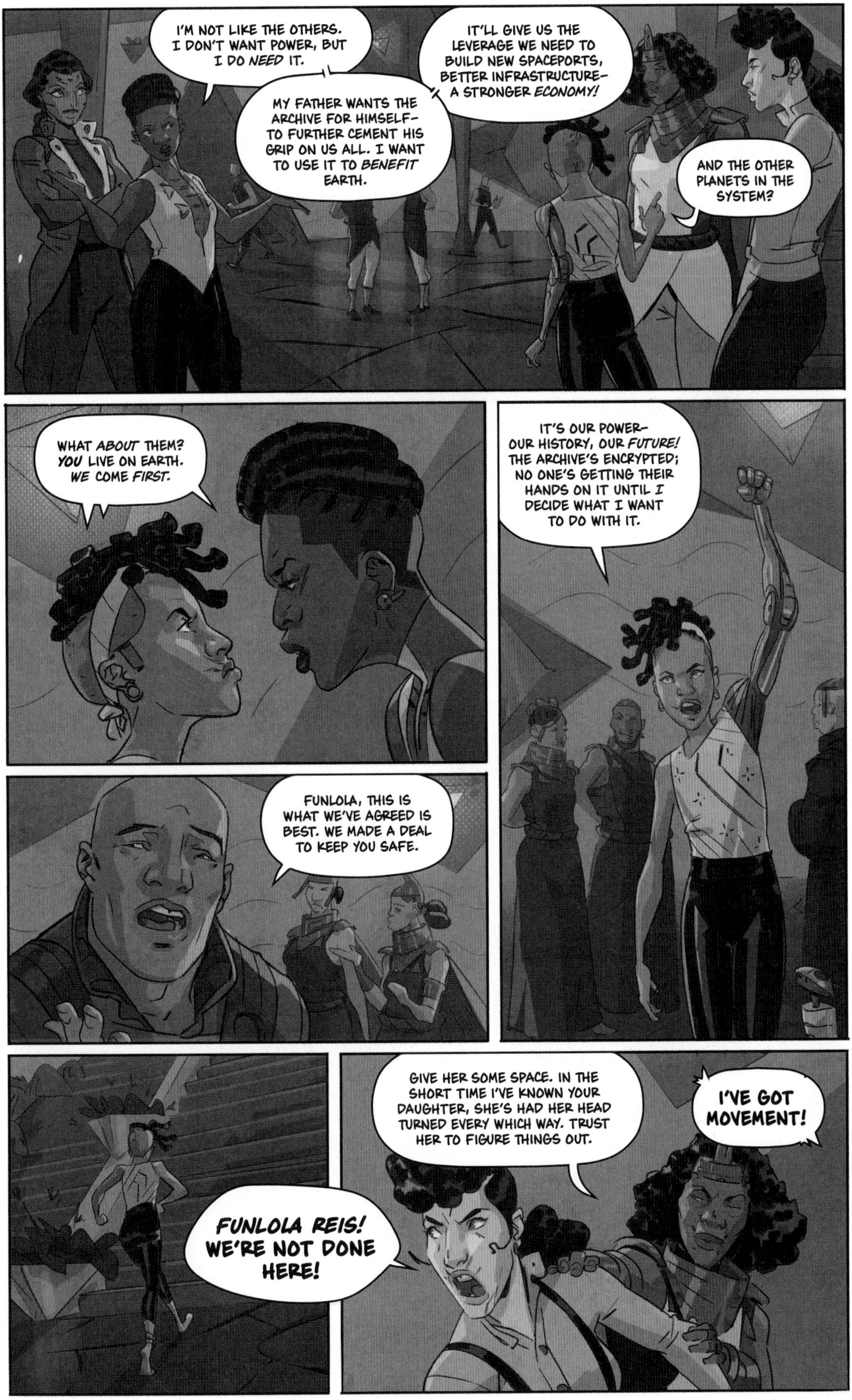
I'M NOT LIKE THE OTHERS. I DON'T WANT POWER, BUT I DO *NEED* IT.
MY FATHER WANTS THE ARCHIVE FOR HIMSELF– TO FURTHER CEMENT HIS GRIP ON US ALL. I WANT TO USE IT TO *BENEFIT* EARTH.
IT'LL GIVE US THE LEVERAGE WE NEED TO BUILD NEW SPACEPORTS, BETTER INFRASTRUCTURE– A STRONGER *ECONOMY!*
AND THE OTHER PLANETS IN THE SYSTEM?
WHAT *ABOUT* THEM? *YOU* LIVE ON EARTH. *WE* COME *FIRST.*
IT'S OUR POWER– OUR HISTORY, OUR *FUTURE!* THE ARCHIVE'S ENCRYPTED; NO ONE'S GETTING THEIR HANDS ON IT UNTIL *I* DECIDE WHAT I WANT TO DO WITH IT.
FUNLOLA, THIS IS WHAT WE'VE AGREED IS BEST. WE MADE A DEAL TO KEEP YOU SAFE.
FUNLOLA REIS! WE'RE NOT DONE HERE!
GIVE HER SOME SPACE. IN THE SHORT TIME I'VE KNOWN YOUR DAUGHTER, SHE'S HAD HER HEAD TURNED EVERY WHICH WAY. TRUST HER TO FIGURE THINGS OUT.
I'VE GOT MOVEMENT!

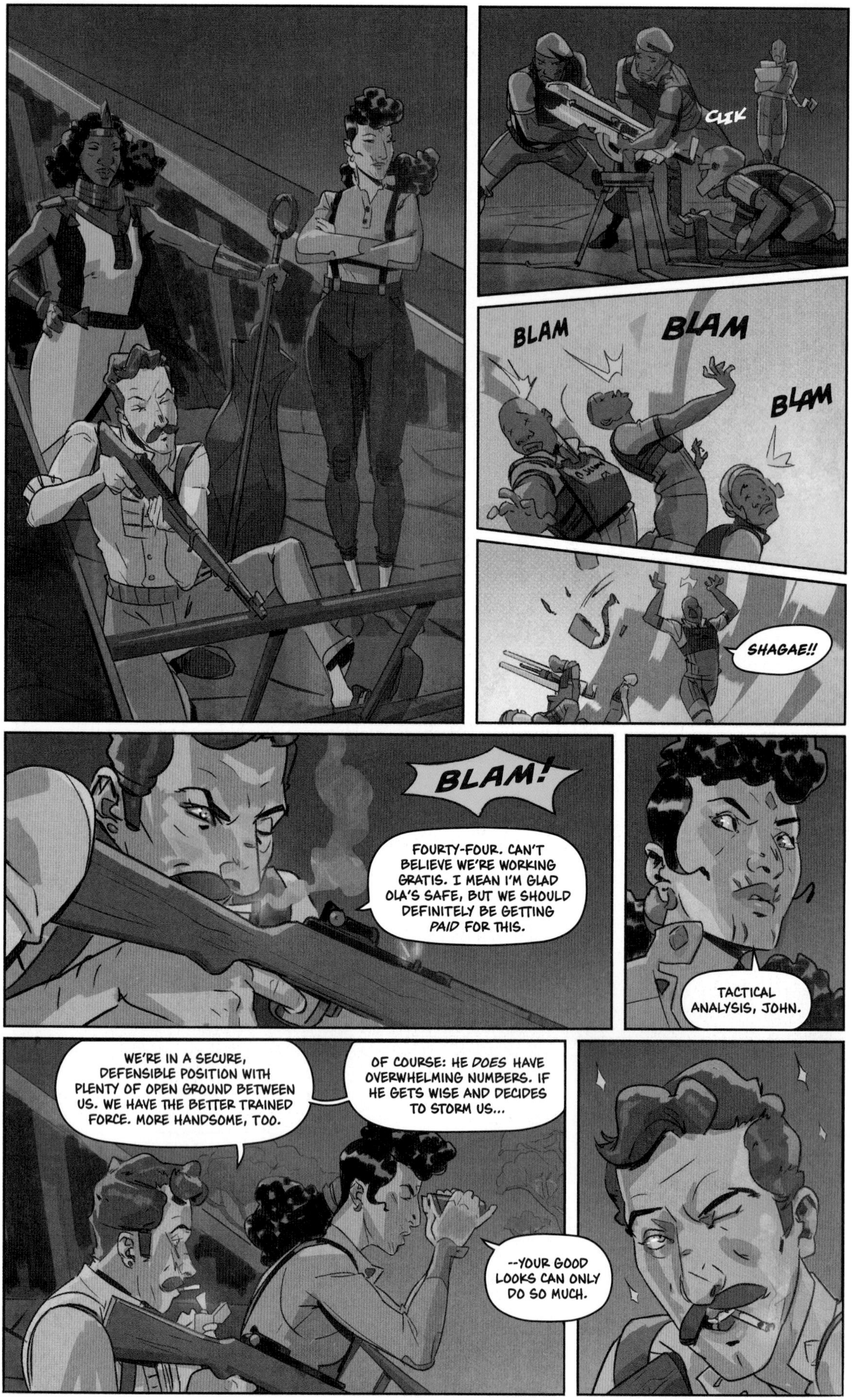
CLIK
BLAM
BLAM
BLAM
SHAGAE!!
BLAM!
FOURTY-FOUR. CAN'T BELIEVE WE'RE WORKING GRATIS. I MEAN I'M GLAD OLA'S SAFE, BUT WE SHOULD DEFINITELY BE GETTING *PAID* FOR THIS.
TACTICAL ANALYSIS, JOHN.
WE'RE IN A SECURE, DEFENSIBLE POSITION WITH PLENTY OF OPEN GROUND BETWEEN US. WE HAVE THE BETTER TRAINED FORCE. MORE HANDSOME, TOO.
OF COURSE: HE *DOES* HAVE OVERWHELMING NUMBERS. IF HE GETS WISE AND DECIDES TO STORM US...
--YOUR GOOD LOOKS CAN ONLY DO SO MUCH.

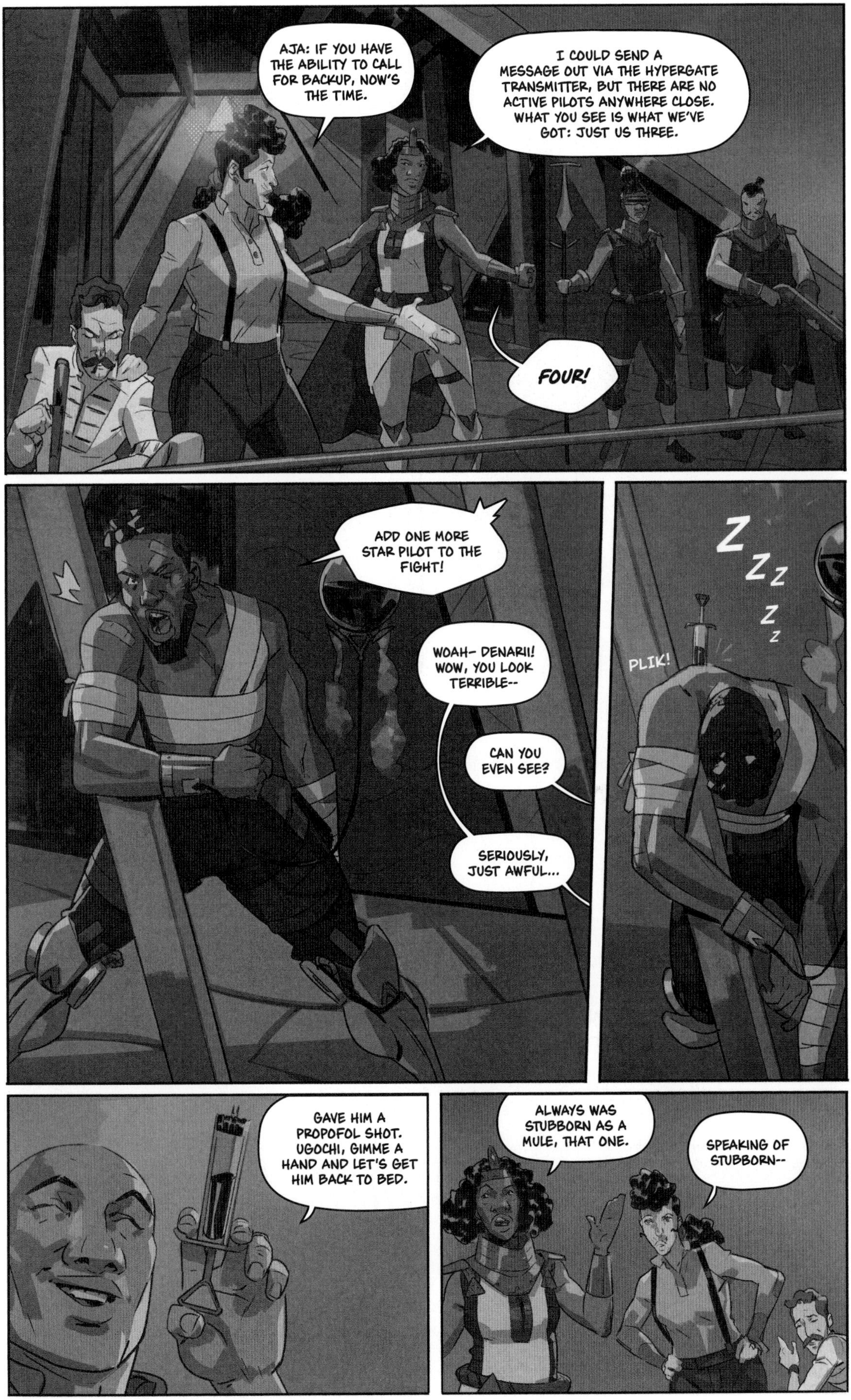
AJA: IF YOU HAVE THE ABILITY TO CALL FOR BACKUP, NOW'S THE TIME.
I COULD SEND A MESSAGE OUT VIA THE HYPERGATE TRANSMITTER, BUT THERE ARE NO ACTIVE PILOTS ANYWHERE CLOSE. WHAT YOU SEE IS WHAT WE'VE GOT: JUST US THREE.
FOUR!
ADD ONE MORE STAR PILOT TO THE FIGHT!
WOAH- DENARII! WOW, YOU LOOK TERRIBLE--
CAN YOU EVEN SEE?
SERIOUSLY, JUST AWFUL...
Z Z Z Z Z
PLIK!
GAVE HIM A PROPOFOL SHOT. UGOCHI, GIMME A HAND AND LET'S GET HIM BACK TO BED.
ALWAYS WAS STUBBORN AS A MULE, THAT ONE.
SPEAKING OF STUBBORN--

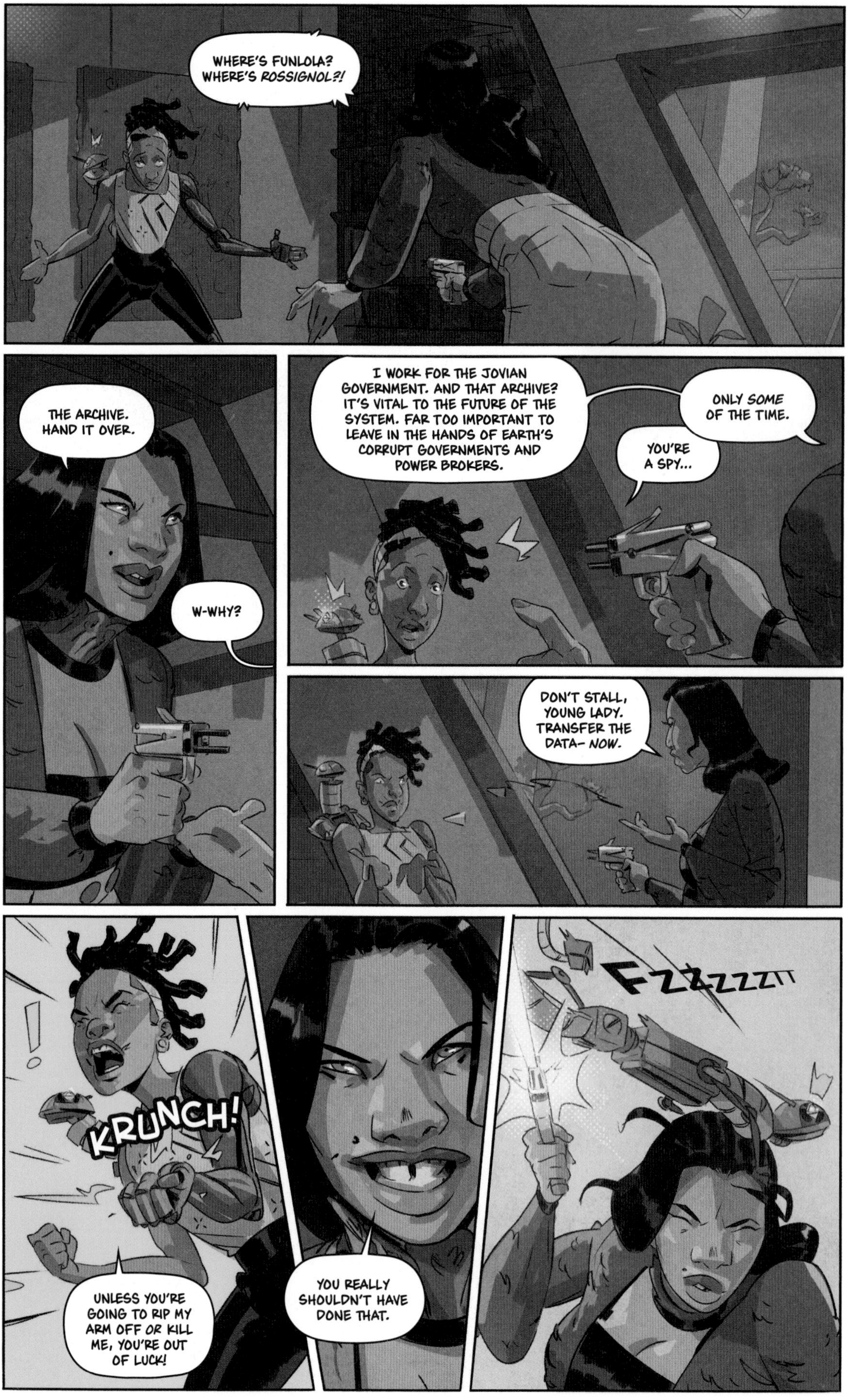

WHERE'S FUNLOLA? WHERE'S ROSSIGNOL?!
THE ARCHIVE. HAND IT OVER.
W-WHY?
I WORK FOR THE JOVIAN GOVERNMENT. AND THAT ARCHIVE? IT'S VITAL TO THE FUTURE OF THE SYSTEM. FAR TOO IMPORTANT TO LEAVE IN THE HANDS OF EARTH'S CORRUPT GOVERNMENTS AND POWER BROKERS.
YOU'RE A SPY...
ONLY SOME OF THE TIME.
DON'T STALL, YOUNG LADY. TRANSFER THE DATA- NOW.
!
KRUNCH!
UNLESS YOU'RE GOING TO RIP MY ARM OFF OR KILL ME, YOU'RE OUT OF LUCK!
YOU REALLY SHOULDN'T HAVE DONE THAT.
FZZZZZZTT

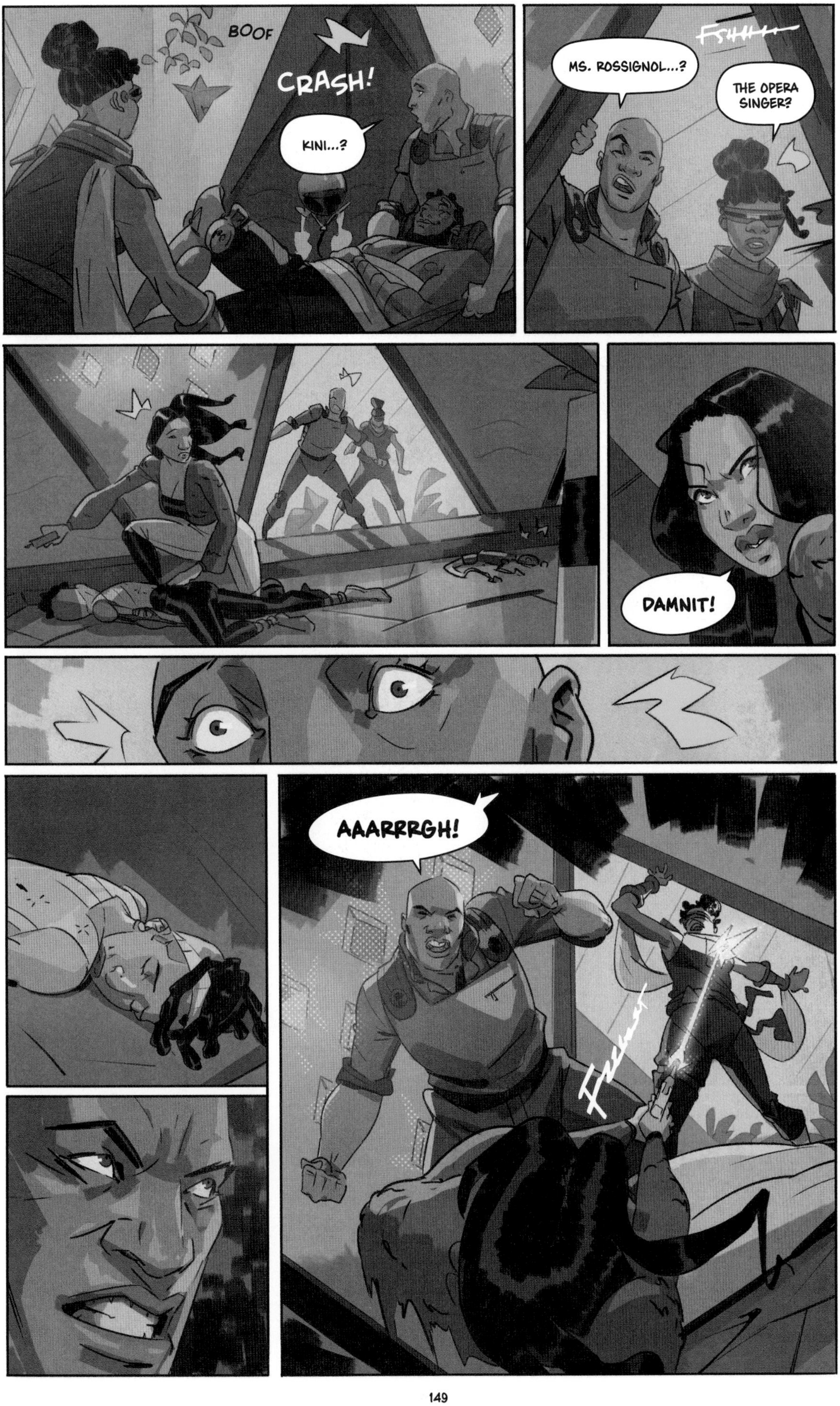
BOOF
CRASH!
KINI...?
FSHHH
MS. ROSSIGNOL...?
THE OPERA SINGER?
DAMNIT!
AAARRRGH!

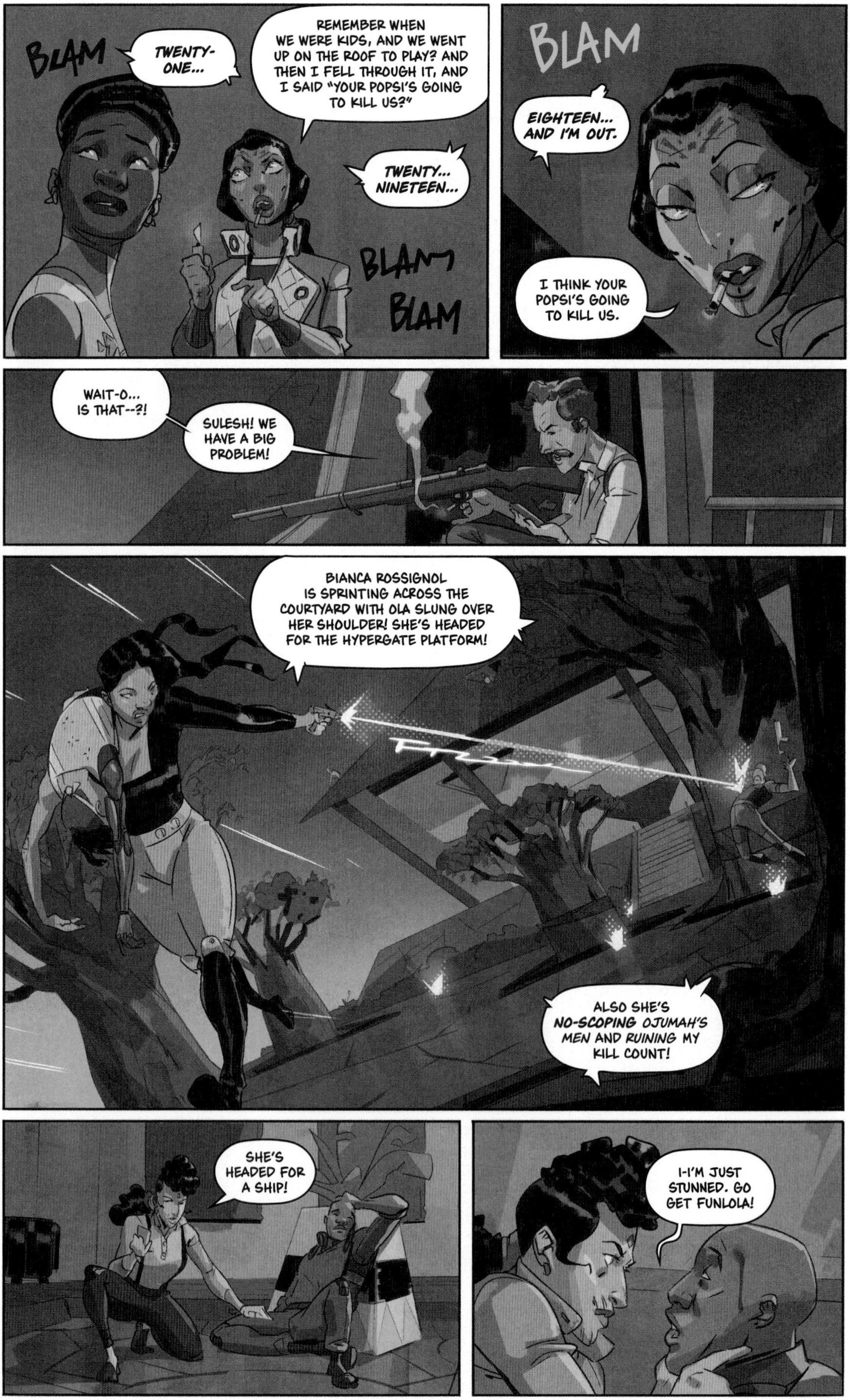
BLAM
TWENTY-ONE...
REMEMBER WHEN WE WERE KIDS, AND WE WENT UP ON THE ROOF TO PLAY? AND THEN I FELL THROUGH IT, AND I SAID "YOUR POPSI'S GOING TO KILL US?"
TWENTY... NINETEEN...
BLAM
BLAM
BLAM
EIGHTEEN... AND I'M OUT.
I THINK YOUR POPSI'S GOING TO KILL US.
WAIT-O... IS THAT--?!
SULESH! WE HAVE A BIG PROBLEM!
BIANCA ROSSIGNOL IS SPRINTING ACROSS THE COURTYARD WITH OLA SLUNG OVER HER SHOULDER! SHE'S HEADED FOR THE HYPERGATE PLATFORM!
ALSO SHE'S NO-SCOPING OJUMAH'S MEN AND RUINING MY KILL COUNT!
SHE'S HEADED FOR A SHIP!
I-I'M JUST STUNNED. GO GET FUNLOLA!

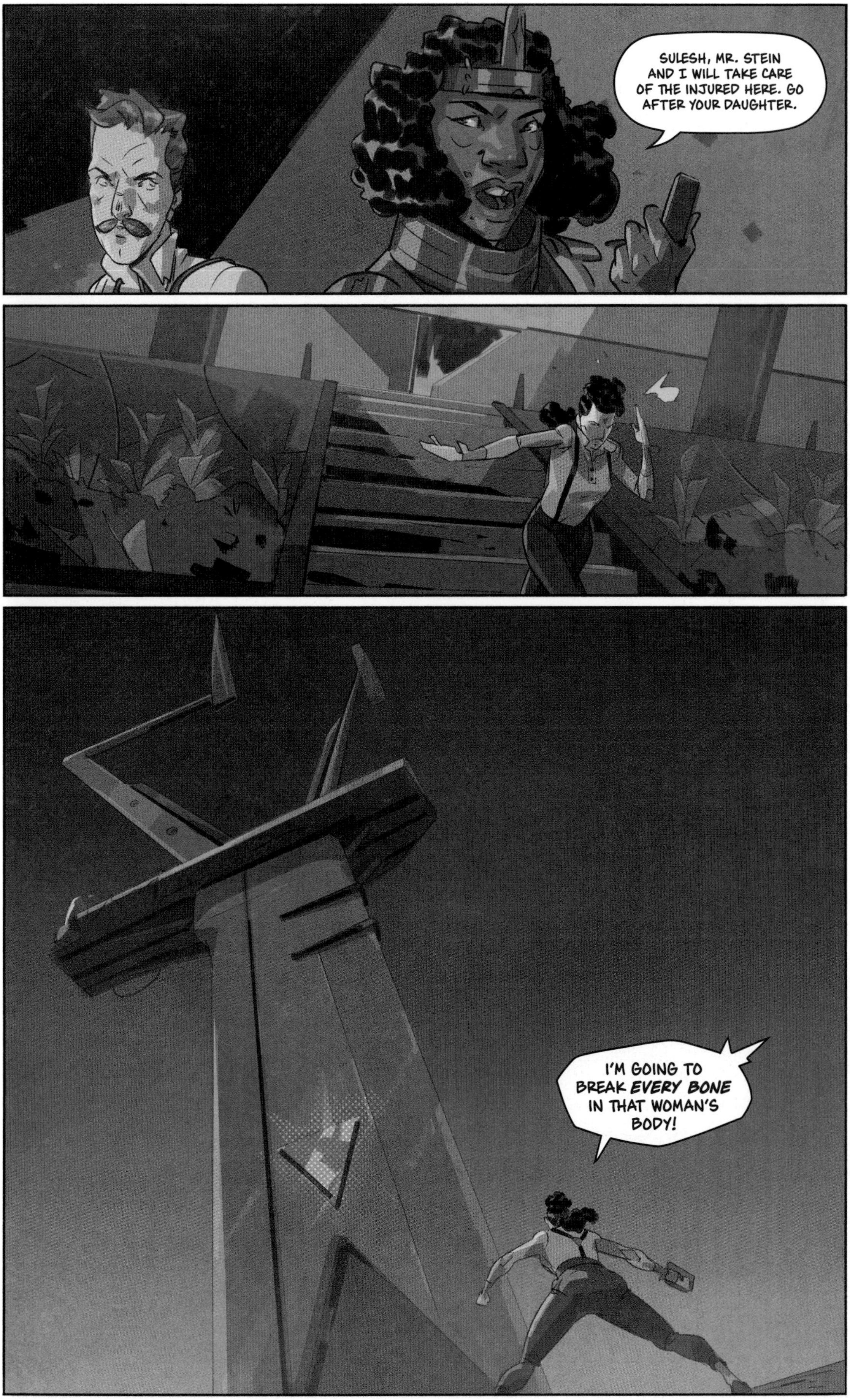
SULESH, MR. STEIN AND I WILL TAKE CARE OF THE INJURED HERE. GO AFTER YOUR DAUGHTER.
I'M GOING TO BREAK EVERY BONE IN THAT WOMAN'S BODY!

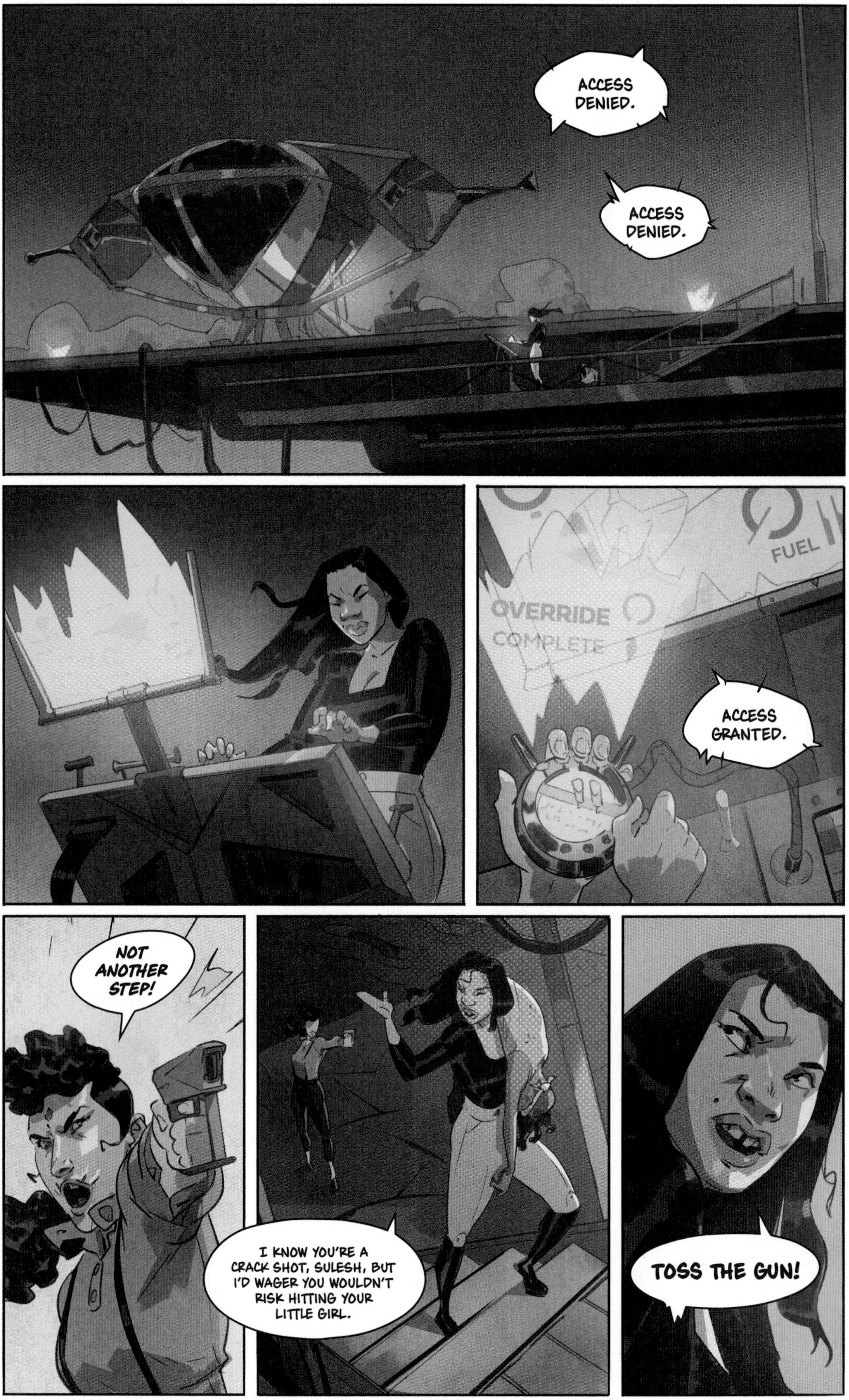
ACCESS DENIED.
ACCESS DENIED.
OVERRIDE
COMPLETE
FUEL
ACCESS GRANTED.
NOT ANOTHER STEP!
I KNOW YOU'RE A CRACK SHOT, SULESH, BUT I'D WAGER YOU WOULDN'T RISK HITTING YOUR LITTLE GIRL.
TOSS THE GUN!

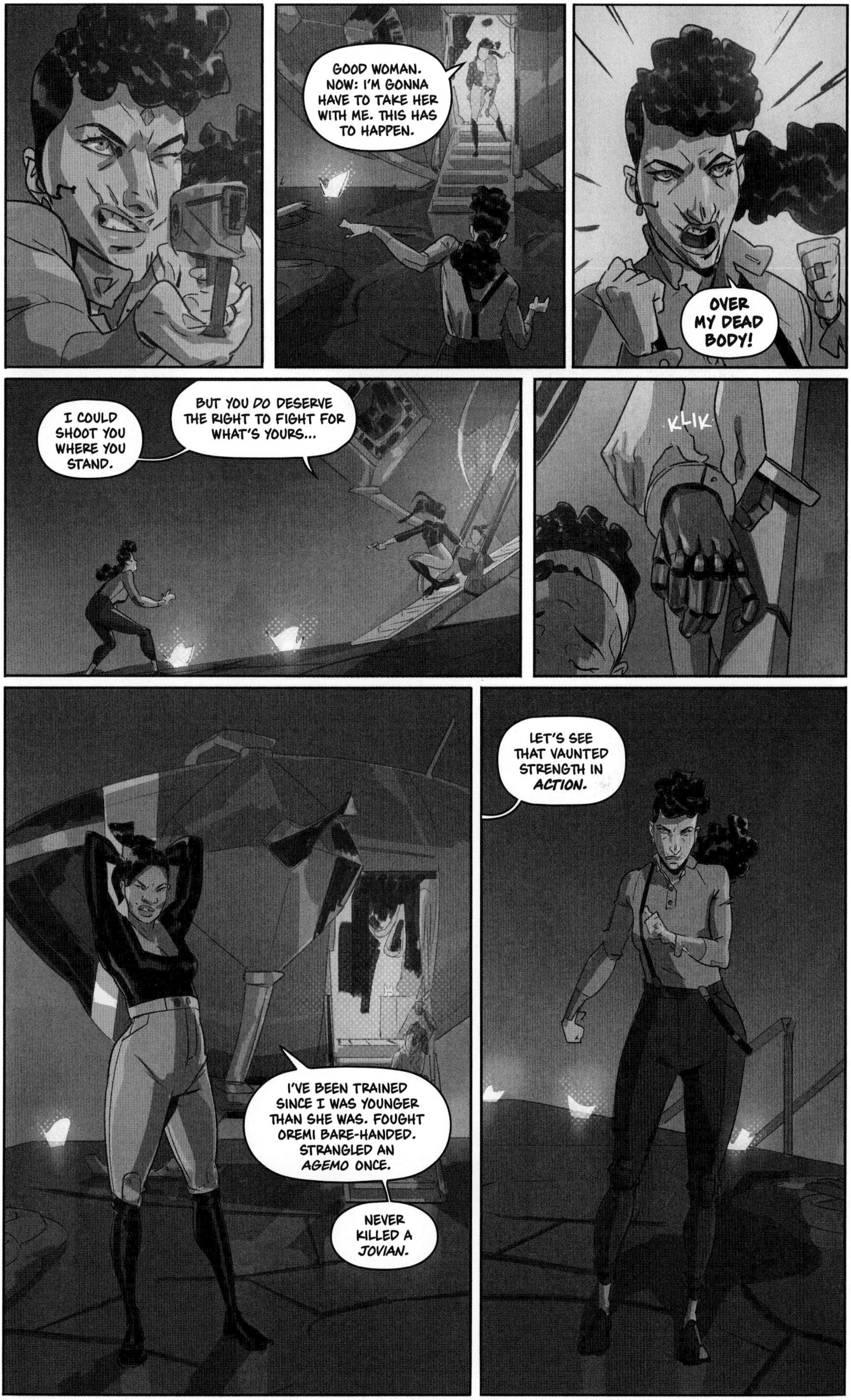
GOOD WOMAN. NOW: I'M GONNA HAVE TO TAKE HER WITH ME. THIS HAS TO HAPPEN.
OVER MY DEAD BODY!
I COULD SHOOT YOU WHERE YOU STAND.
BUT YOU DO DESERVE THE RIGHT TO FIGHT FOR WHAT'S YOURS...
KLIK
I'VE BEEN TRAINED SINCE I WAS YOUNGER THAN SHE WAS. FOUGHT OREMI BARE-HANDED. STRANGLED AN AGEMO ONCE.
NEVER KILLED A JOVIAN.
LET'S SEE THAT VAUNTED STRENGTH IN ACTION.

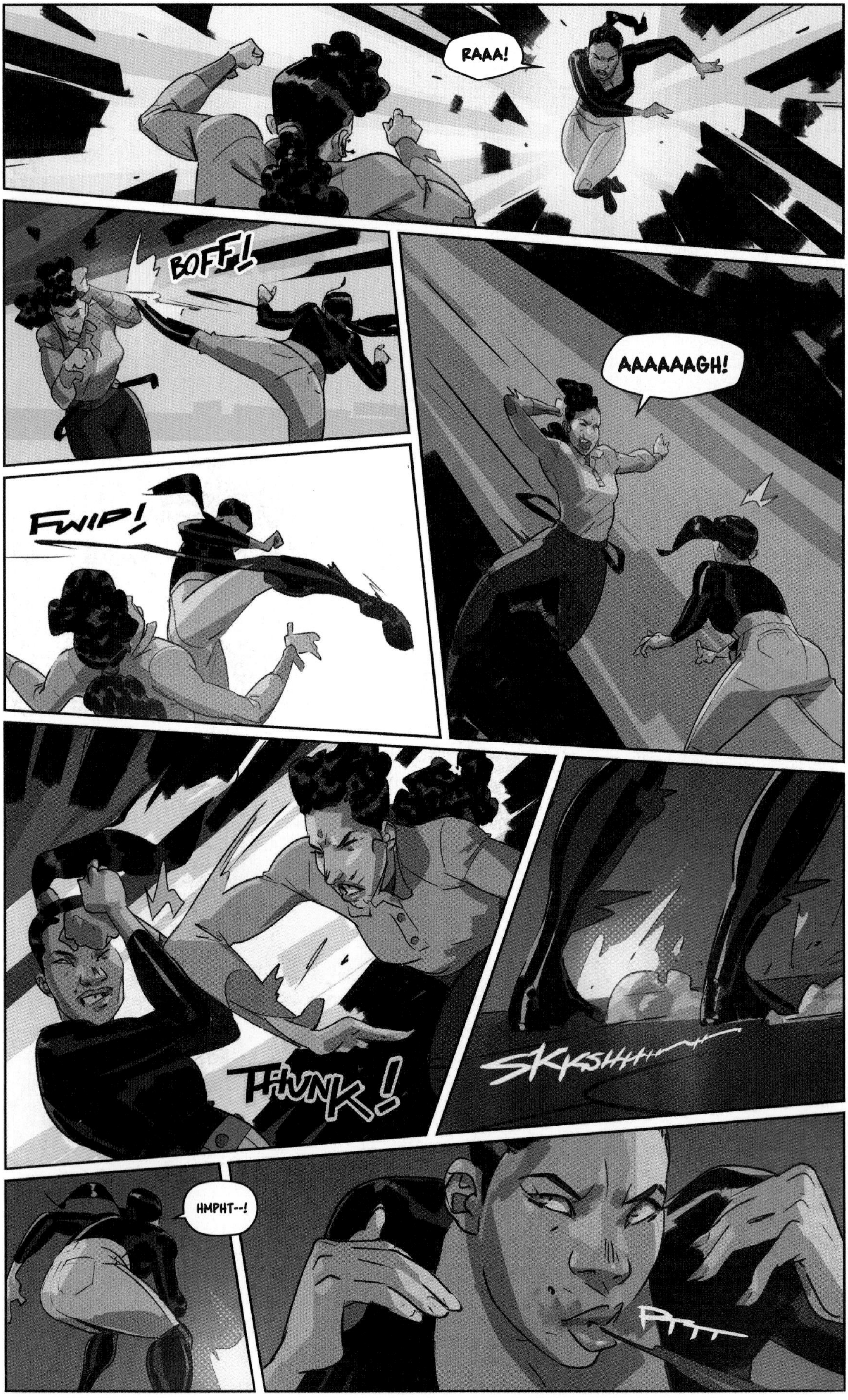
RAAA!
BOFF!
AAAAAAGH!
FWIP!
THUNK!
SKKSHHH
HMPHT--!
PTTT

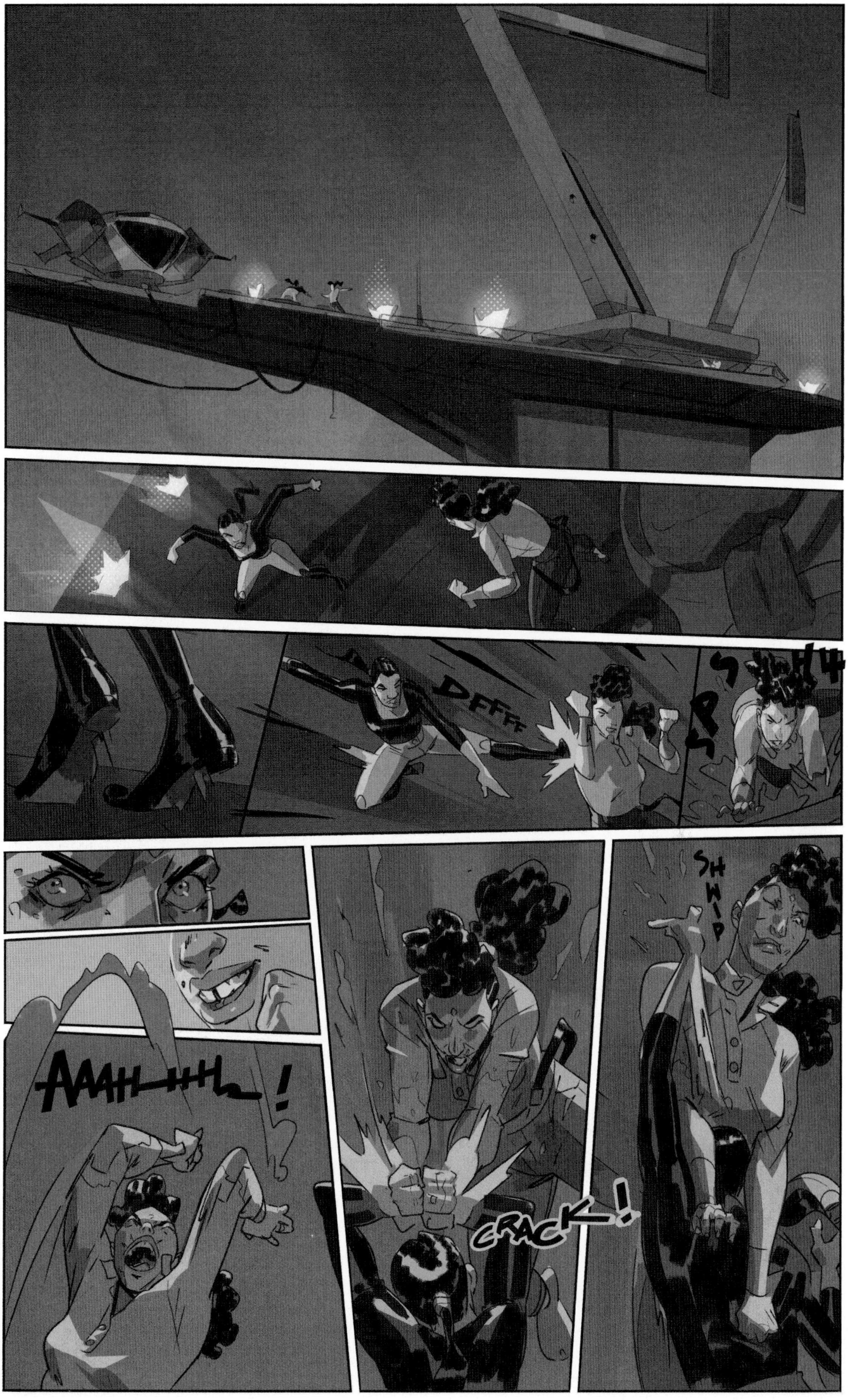
DFFFF
SHWIP
AAAHHHH!
CRACK!

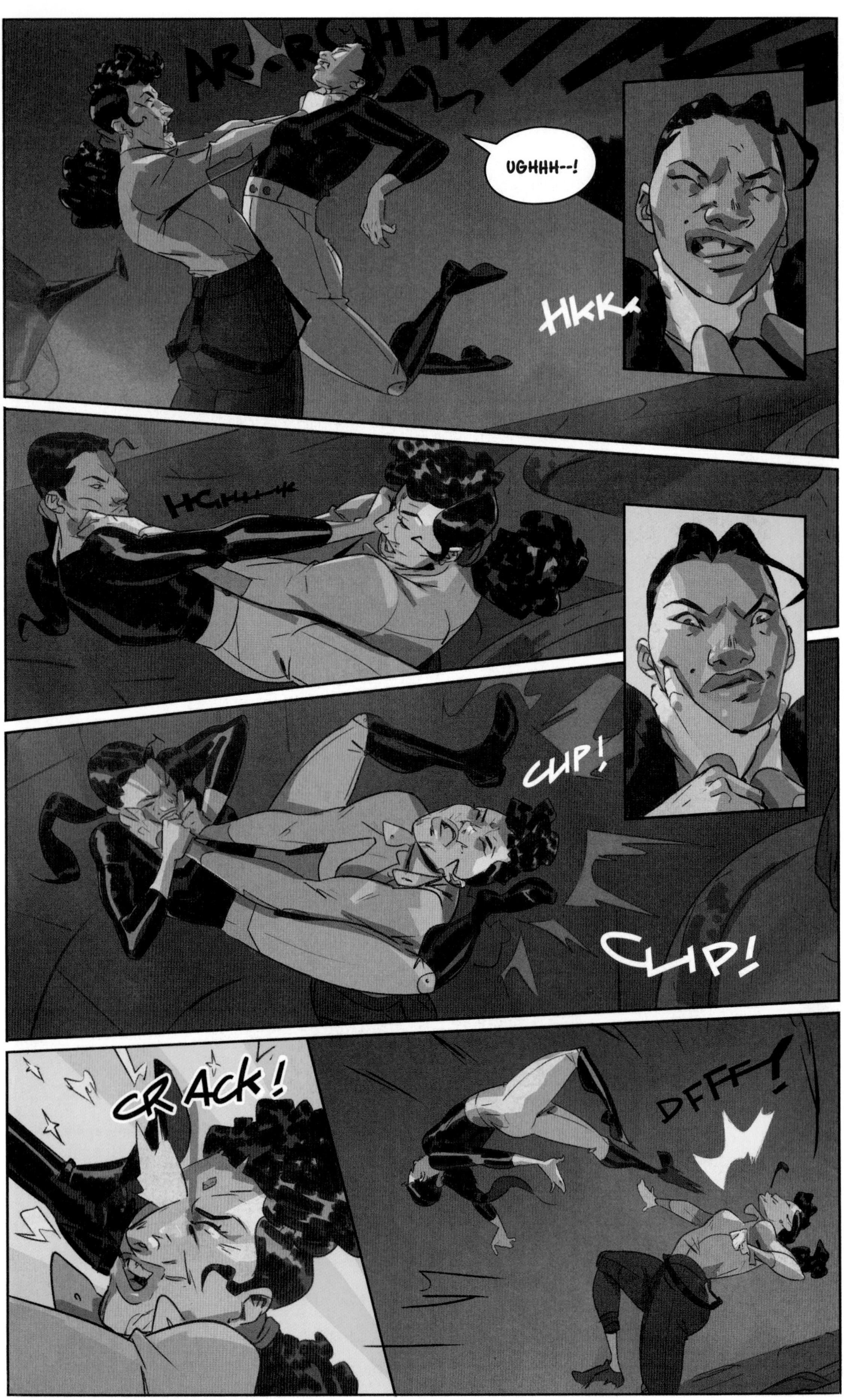
ARRRGHH
UGHHH--!
HKK
HGHHHK
CLIP!
CLIP!
CRACK!
DFFF!

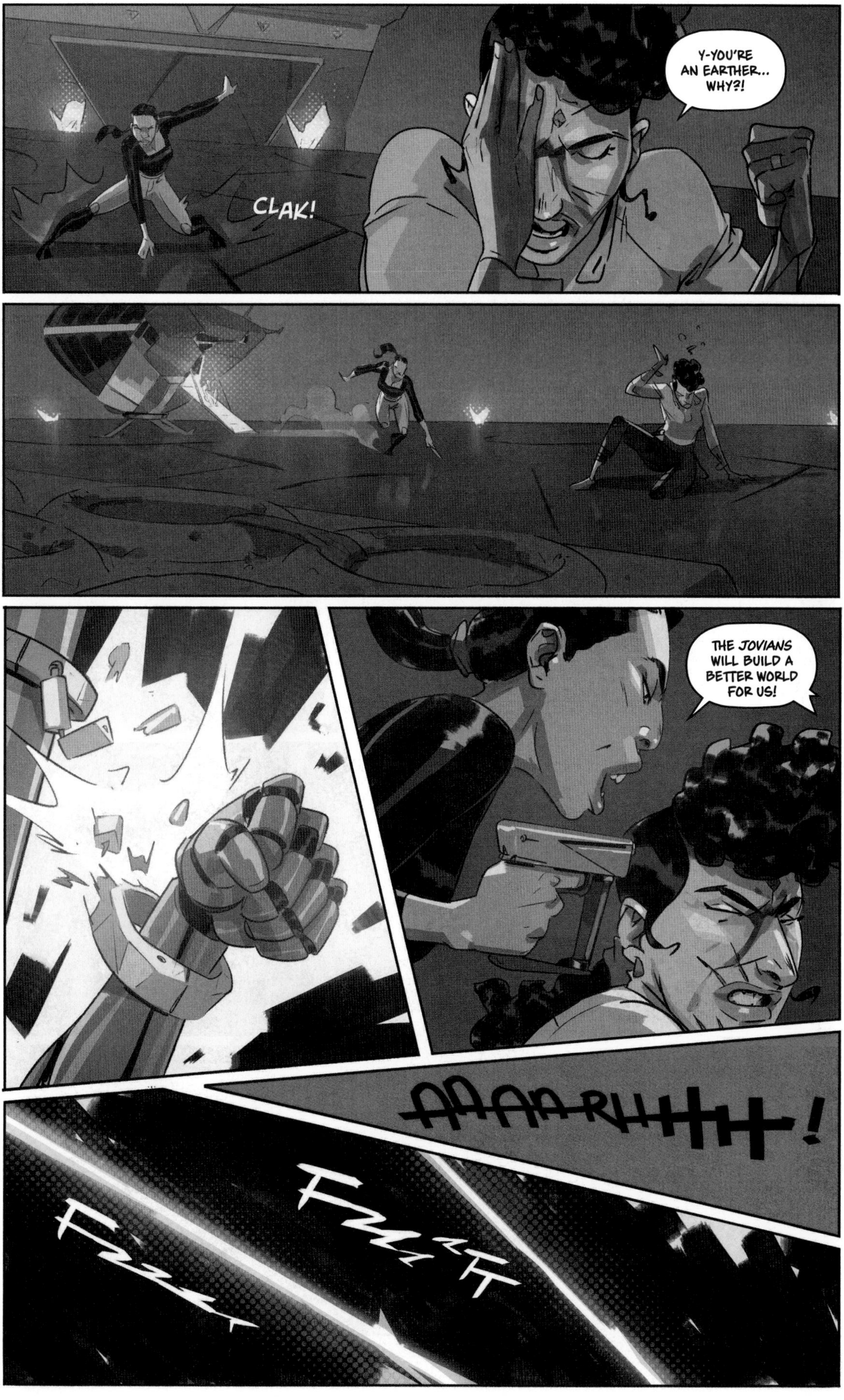
Y-YOU'RE AN EARTHER... WHY?!
CLAK!
THE JOVIANS WILL BUILD A BETTER WORLD FOR US!
AAAARHHHHH!
FZZZT
FZZZT

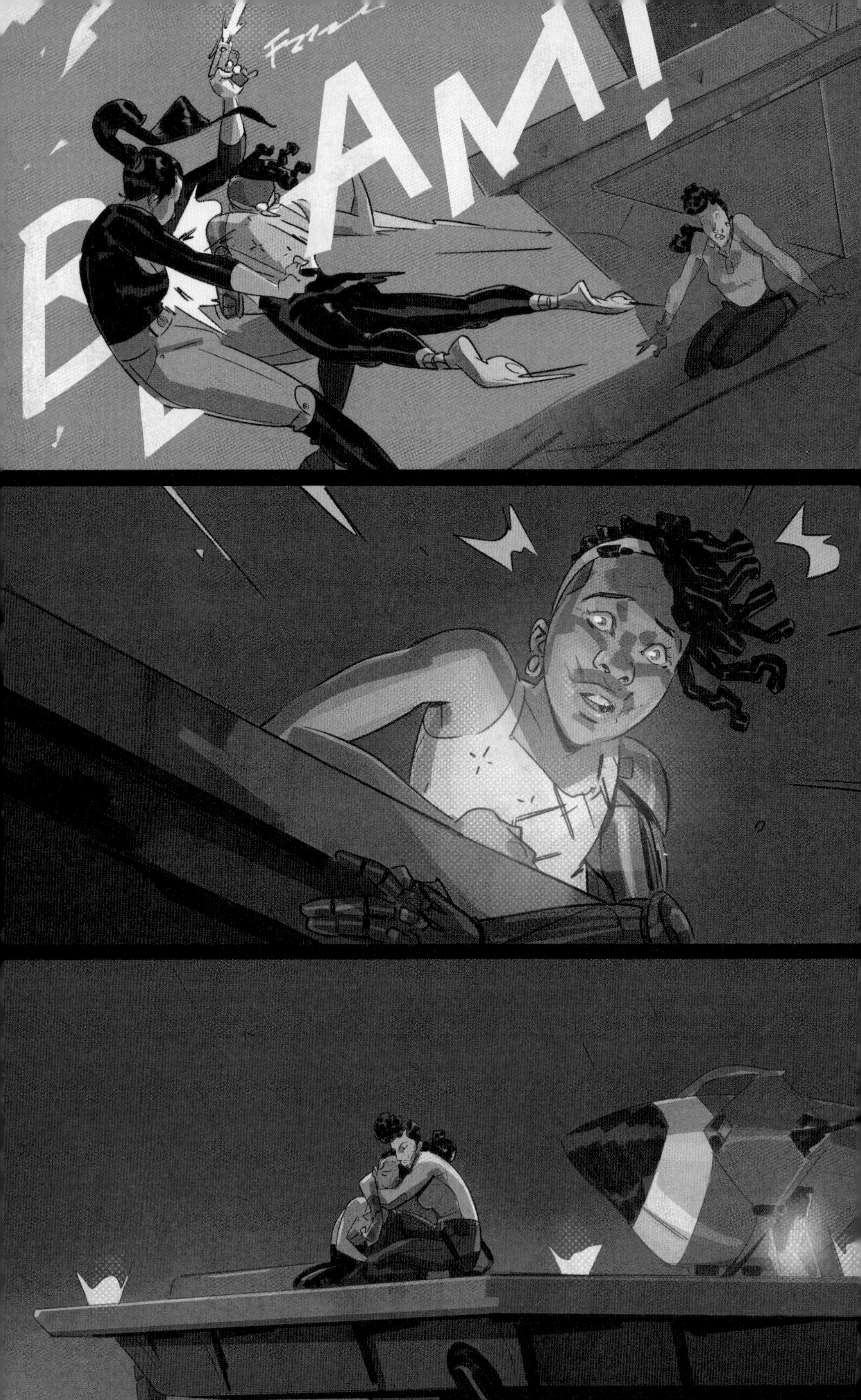
BLAM!

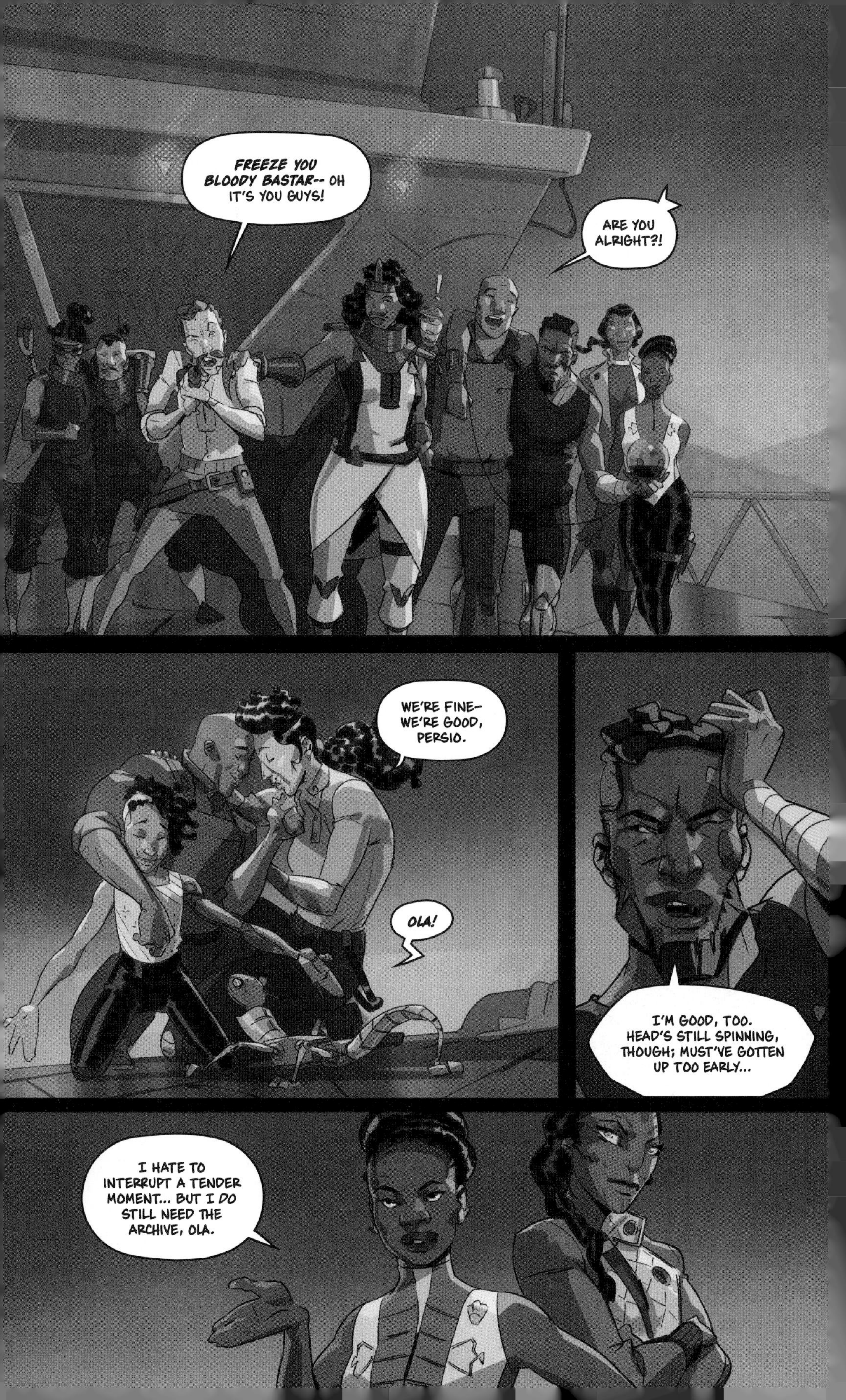
FREEZE YOU BLOODY BASTAR-- OH IT'S YOU GUYS!
!
ARE YOU ALRIGHT?!
WE'RE FINE- WE'RE GOOD, PERSIO.
OLA!
I'M GOOD, TOO. HEAD'S STILL SPINNING, THOUGH; MUST'VE GOTTEN UP TOO EARLY...
I HATE TO INTERRUPT A TENDER MOMENT... BUT I DO STILL NEED THE ARCHIVE, OLA.

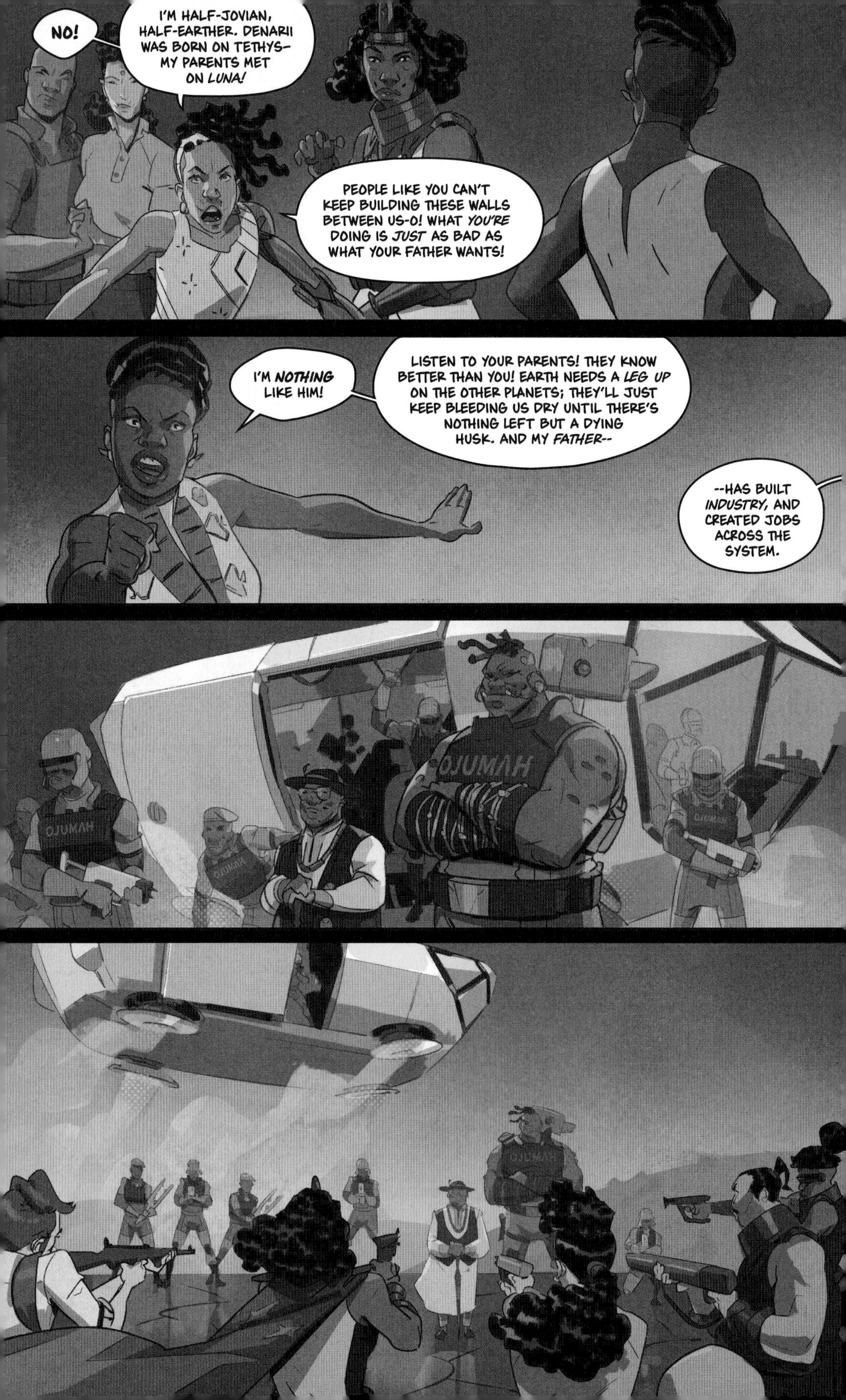
NO!
I'M HALF-JOVIAN, HALF-EARTHER. DENARII WAS BORN ON TETHYS-MY PARENTS MET ON *LUNA!*
PEOPLE LIKE YOU CAN'T KEEP BUILDING THESE WALLS BETWEEN US-O! WHAT *YOU'RE* DOING IS *JUST* AS BAD AS WHAT YOUR FATHER WANTS!
I'M ***NOTHING*** LIKE HIM!
LISTEN TO YOUR PARENTS! THEY KNOW BETTER THAN YOU! EARTH NEEDS A *LEG UP* ON THE OTHER PLANETS; THEY'LL JUST KEEP BLEEDING US DRY UNTIL THERE'S NOTHING LEFT BUT A DYING HUSK. AND MY *FATHER*--
--HAS BUILT *INDUSTRY,* AND CREATED JOBS ACROSS THE SYSTEM.
OJUMAH
OJUMAH
OJUMAH
OJUMAH
OJUMAH

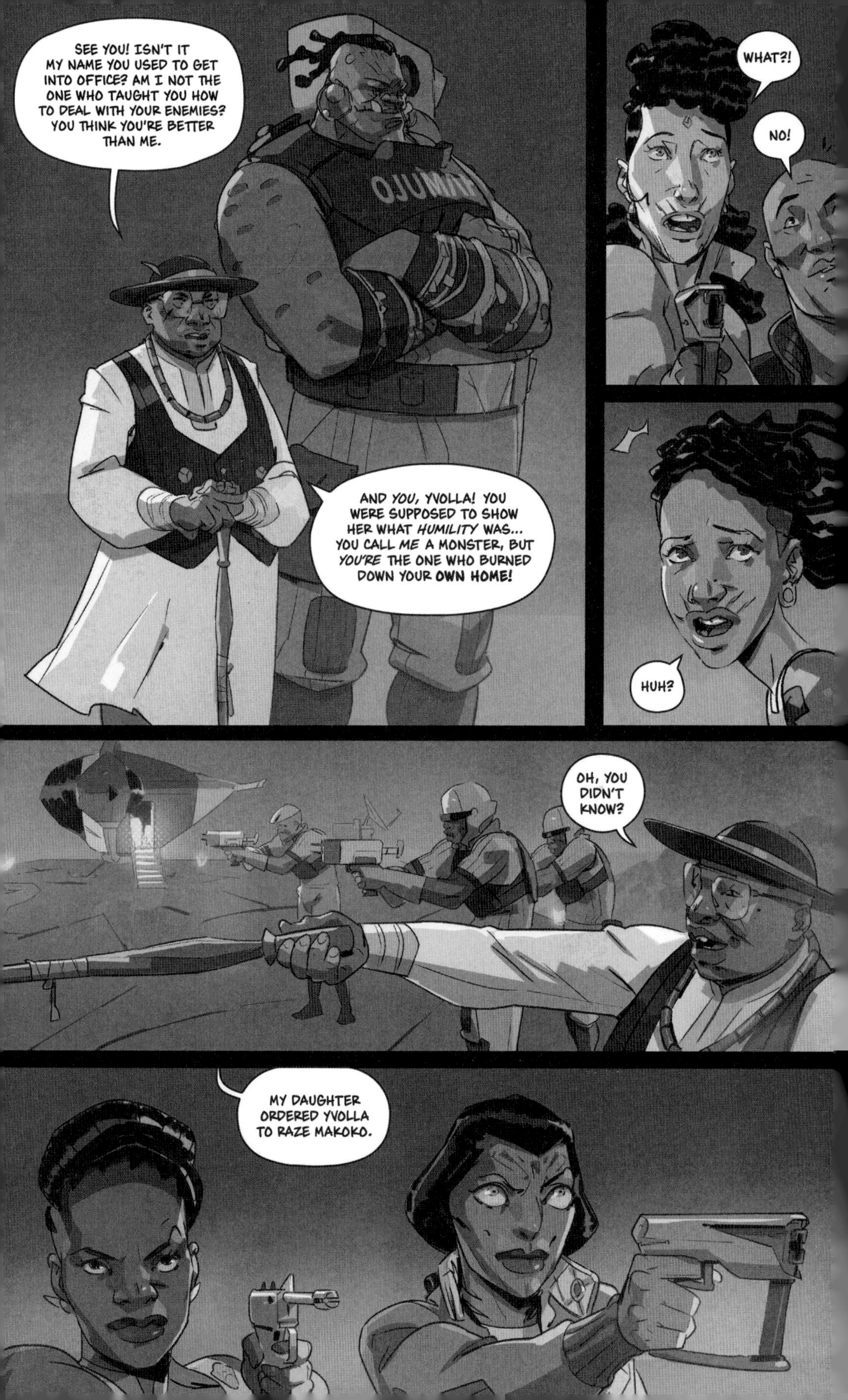
SEE YOU! ISN'T IT MY NAME YOU USED TO GET INTO OFFICE? AM I NOT THE ONE WHO TAUGHT YOU HOW TO DEAL WITH YOUR ENEMIES? YOU THINK YOU'RE BETTER THAN ME.
OJUMA
AND YOU, YVOLLA! YOU WERE SUPPOSED TO SHOW HER WHAT HUMILITY WAS... YOU CALL ME A MONSTER, BUT YOU'RE THE ONE WHO BURNED DOWN YOUR OWN HOME!
WHAT?!
NO!
HUH?
OH, YOU DIDN'T KNOW?
MY DAUGHTER ORDERED YVOLLA TO RAZE MAKOKO.

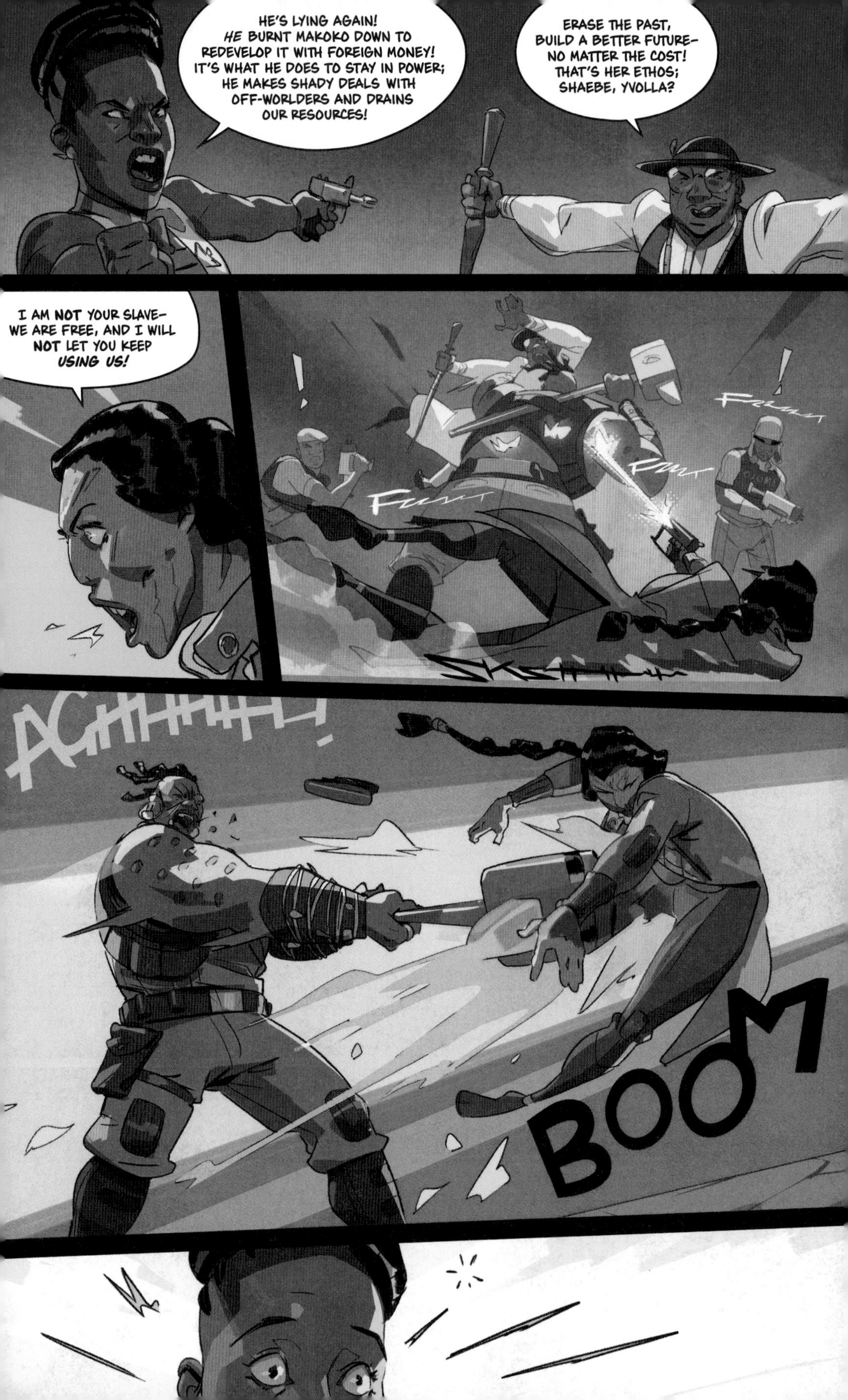

HE'S LYING AGAIN! *HE* BURNT MAKOKO DOWN TO REDEVELOP IT WITH FOREIGN MONEY! IT'S WHAT HE DOES TO STAY IN POWER; HE MAKES SHADY DEALS WITH OFF-WORLDERS AND DRAINS OUR RESOURCES!
ERASE THE PAST, BUILD A BETTER FUTURE- NO MATTER THE COST! THAT'S HER ETHOS; SHAEBE, YVOLLA?
I AM **NOT** YOUR SLAVE- WE ARE FREE, AND I WILL **NOT** LET YOU KEEP *USING US!*
!
!
FZZZZT
FZZZT
FZZZT
SKSHHHH
ACHHHH!
BOOM

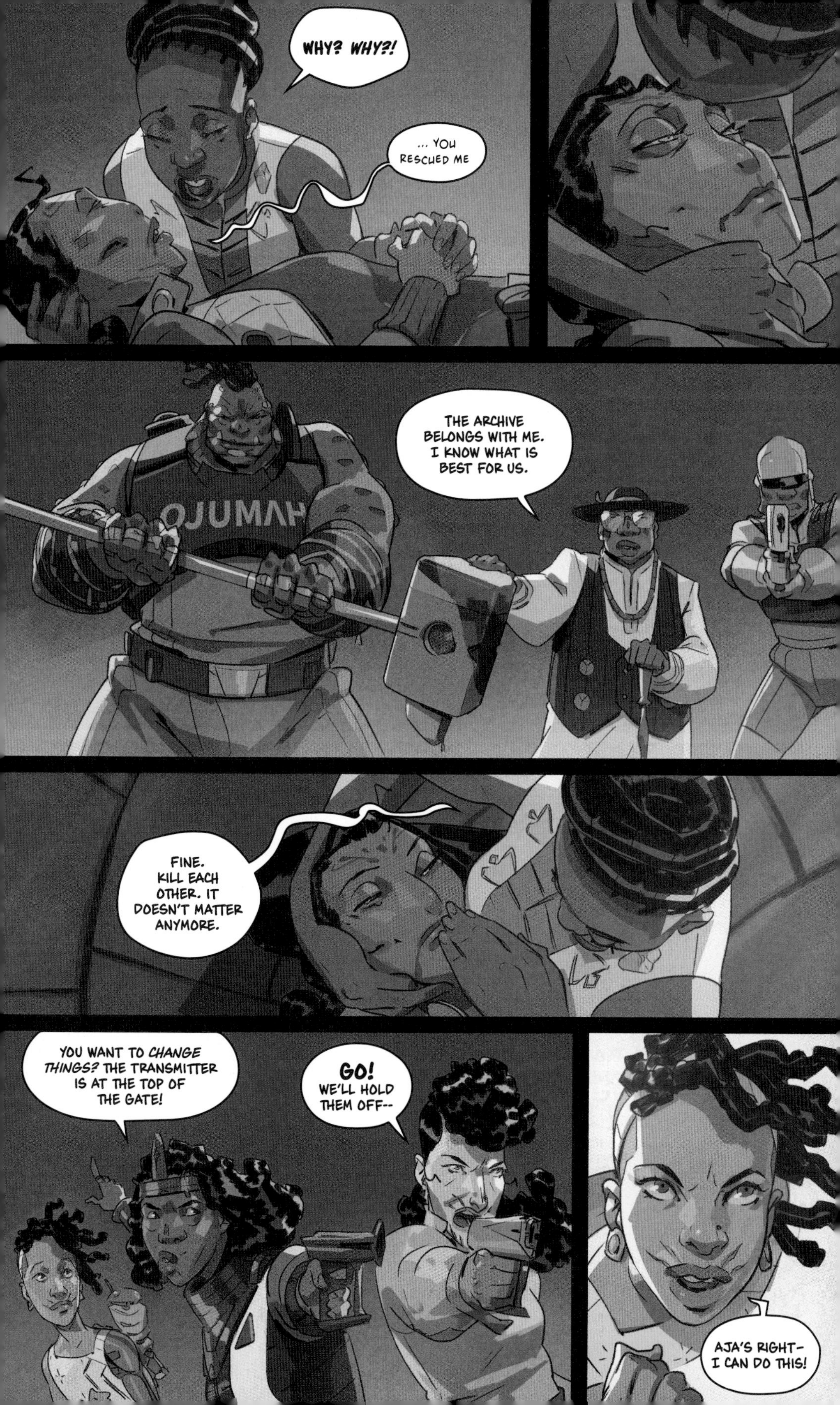
WHY? WHY?!
... YOU RESCUED ME
THE ARCHIVE BELONGS WITH ME. I KNOW WHAT IS BEST FOR US.
OJUMAH
FINE. KILL EACH OTHER. IT DOESN'T MATTER ANYMORE.
YOU WANT TO *CHANGE THINGS?* THE TRANSMITTER IS AT THE TOP OF THE GATE!
GO! WE'LL HOLD THEM OFF--
AJA'S RIGHT- I CAN DO THIS!

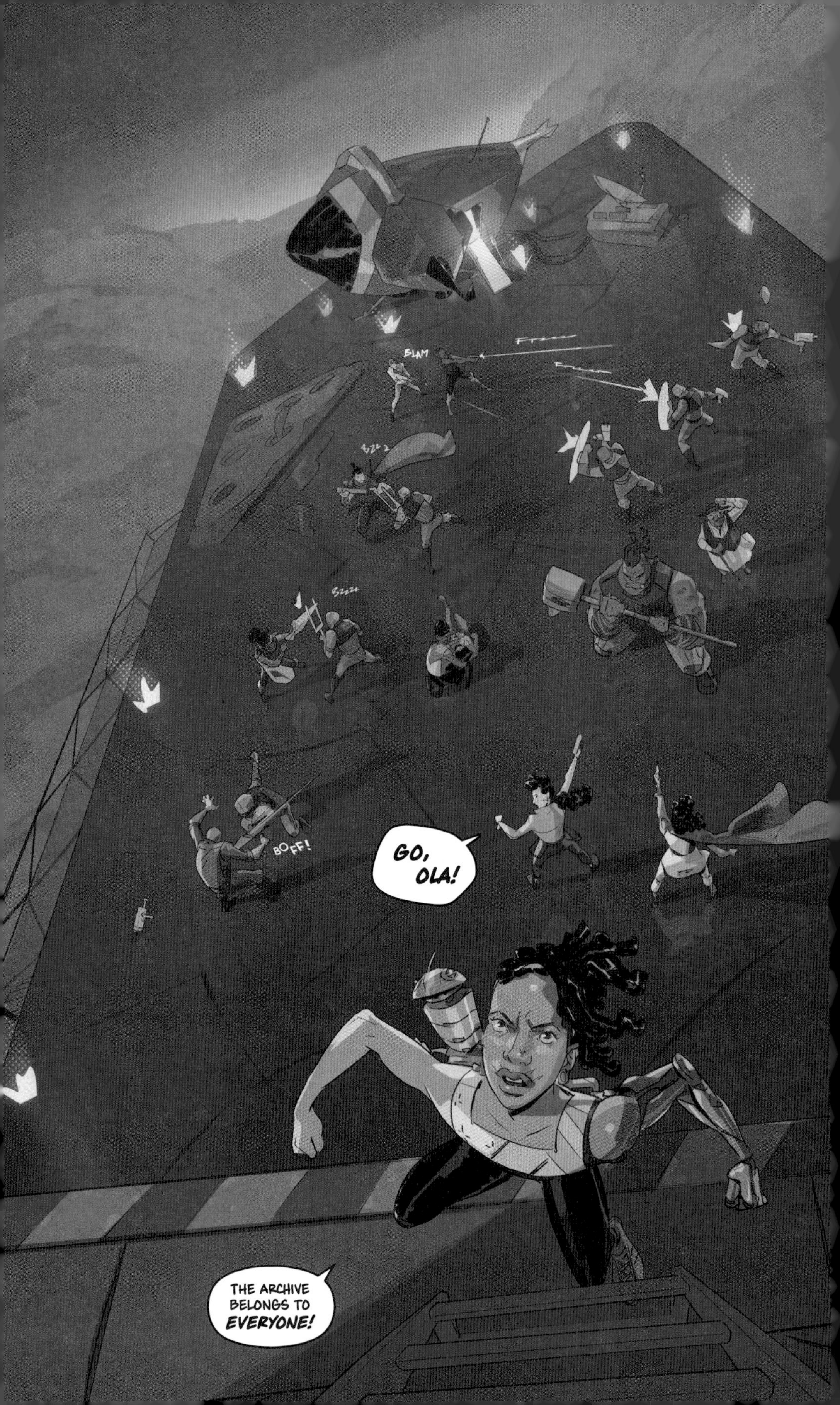
BLAM
BOFF!
GO, OLA!
THE ARCHIVE BELONGS TO EVERYONE!

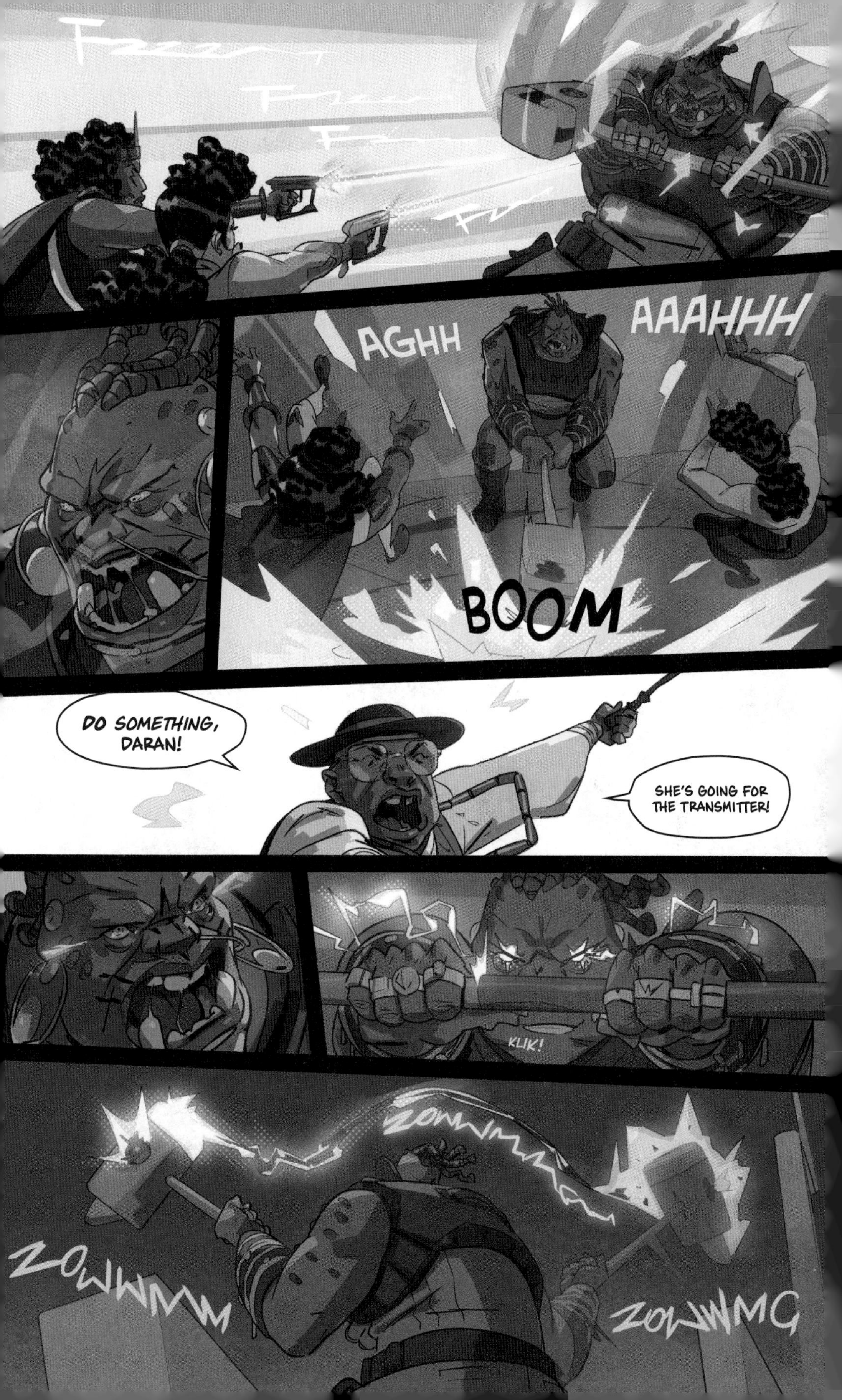
Fzzzrrr
AGHH
AAAHHH
BOOM
DO SOMETHING, DARAN!
SHE'S GOING FOR THE TRANSMITTER!
KLIK!
ZOWWMMMMG
ZOWWMMM
ZOWWMG

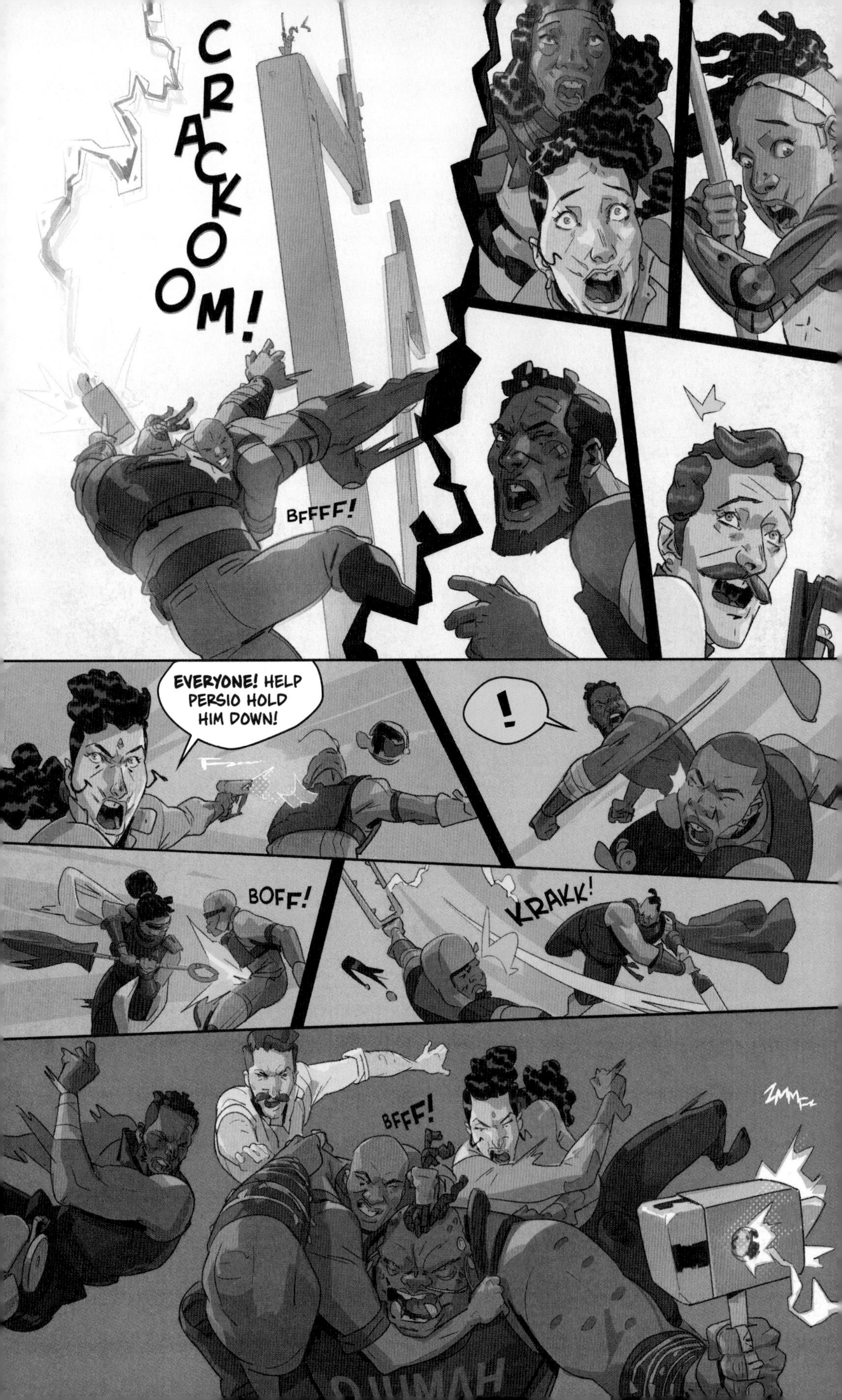
CRACKOOM!
BFFFF!
EVERYONE! HELP PERSIO HOLD HIM DOWN!
!
BOFF!
KRAKK!
BFFF!

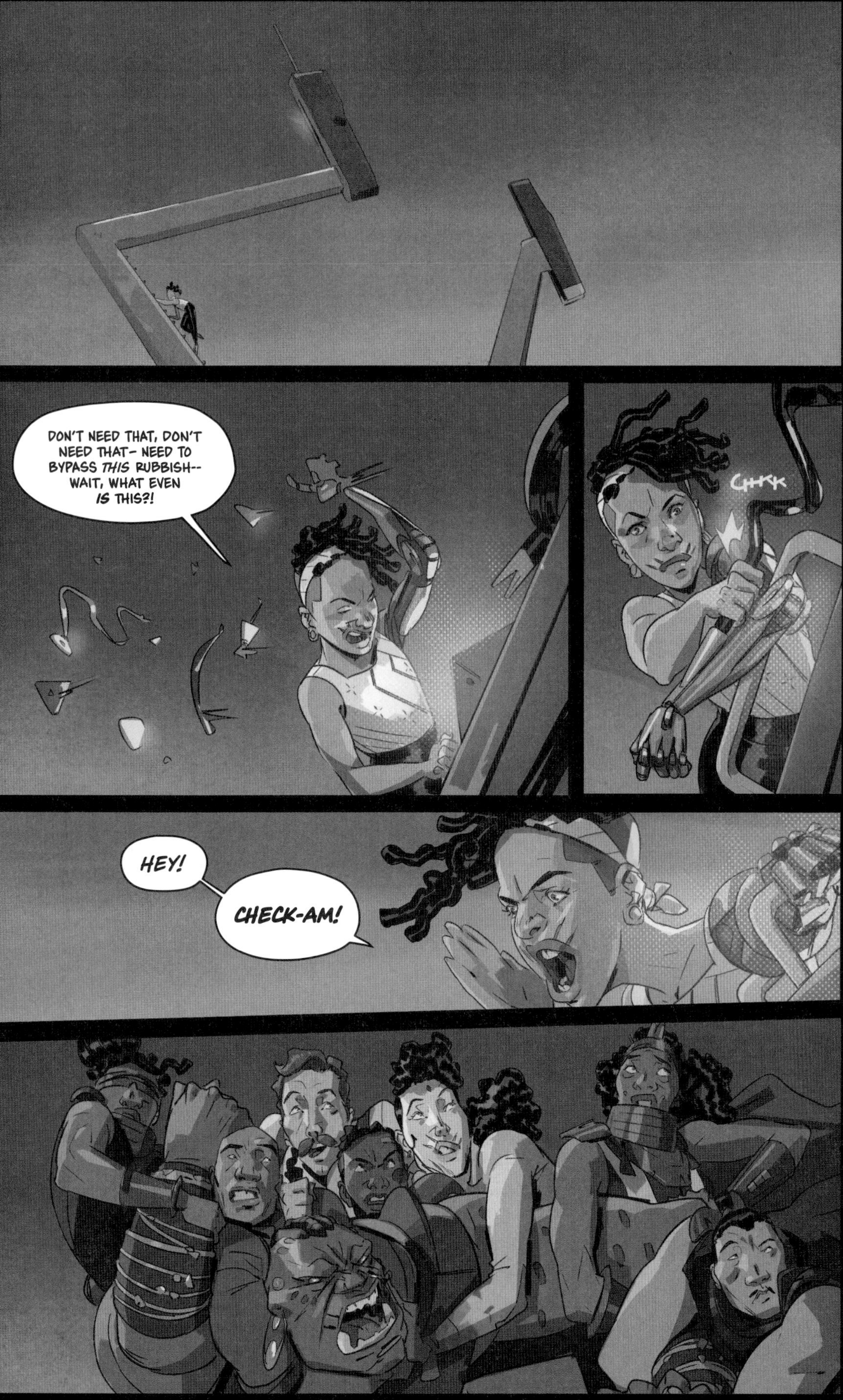
DON'T NEED THAT, DON'T NEED THAT- NEED TO BYPASS *THIS* RUBBISH-- WAIT, WHAT EVEN *IS* THIS?!
CHKK
HEY!
CHECK-AM!

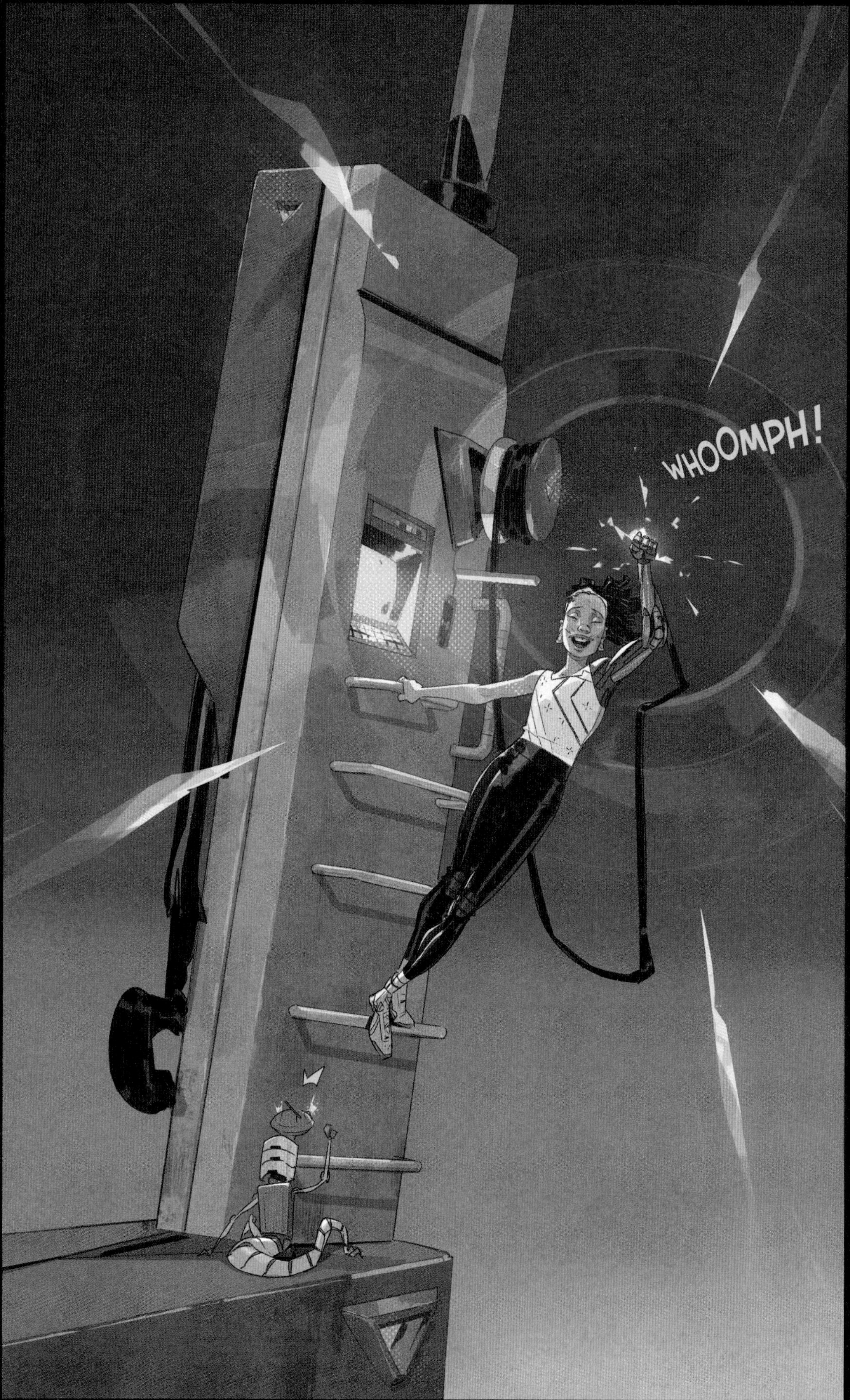
WHOOMPH!

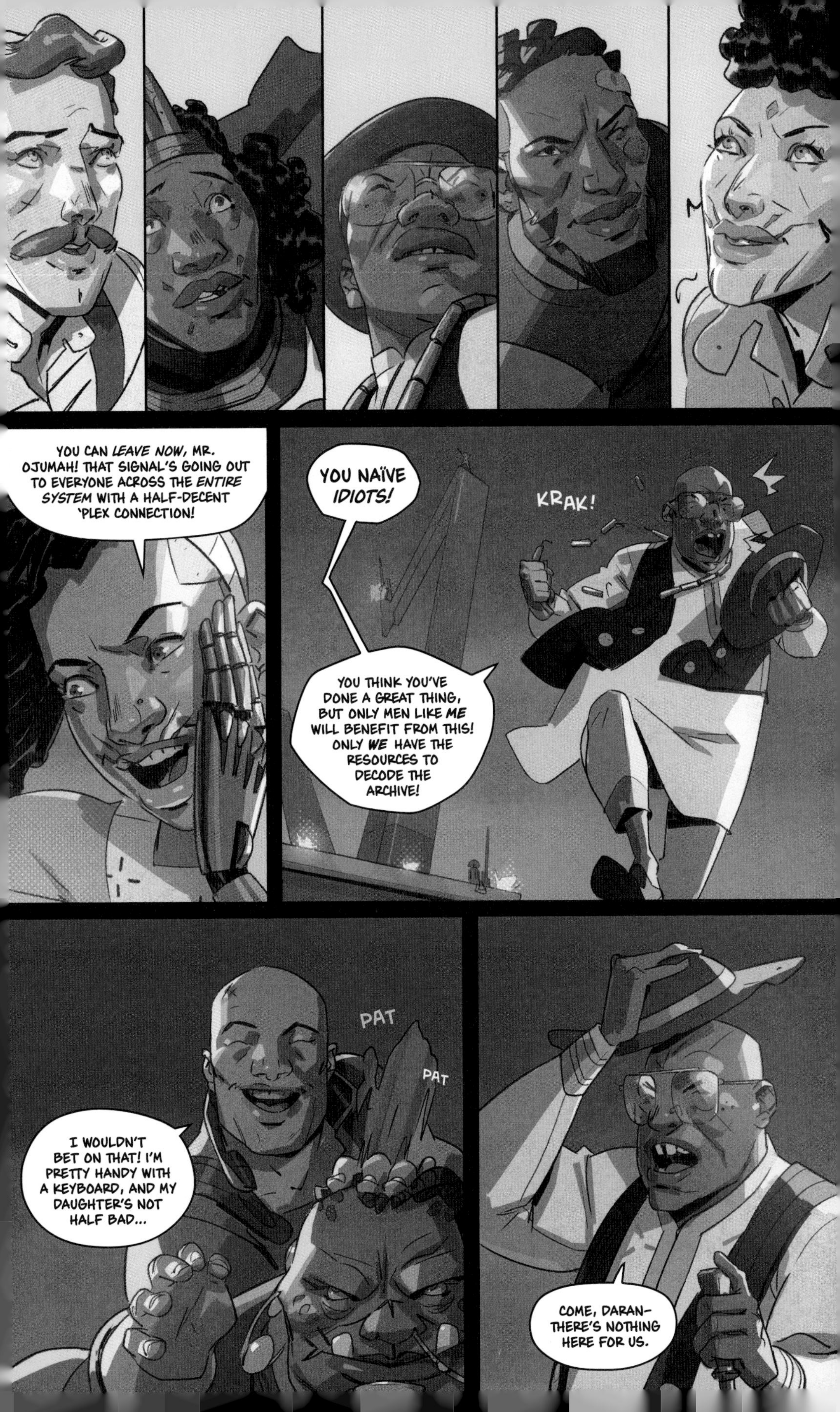
YOU CAN LEAVE NOW, MR. OJUMAH! THAT SIGNAL'S GOING OUT TO EVERYONE ACROSS THE ENTIRE SYSTEM WITH A HALF-DECENT 'PLEX CONNECTION!
YOU NAÏVE IDIOTS!
YOU THINK YOU'VE DONE A GREAT THING, BUT ONLY MEN LIKE ME WILL BENEFIT FROM THIS! ONLY WE HAVE THE RESOURCES TO DECODE THE ARCHIVE!
KRAK!
PAT
PAT
I WOULDN'T BET ON THAT! I'M PRETTY HANDY WITH A KEYBOARD, AND MY DAUGHTER'S NOT HALF BAD...
COME, DARAN- THERE'S NOTHING HERE FOR US.

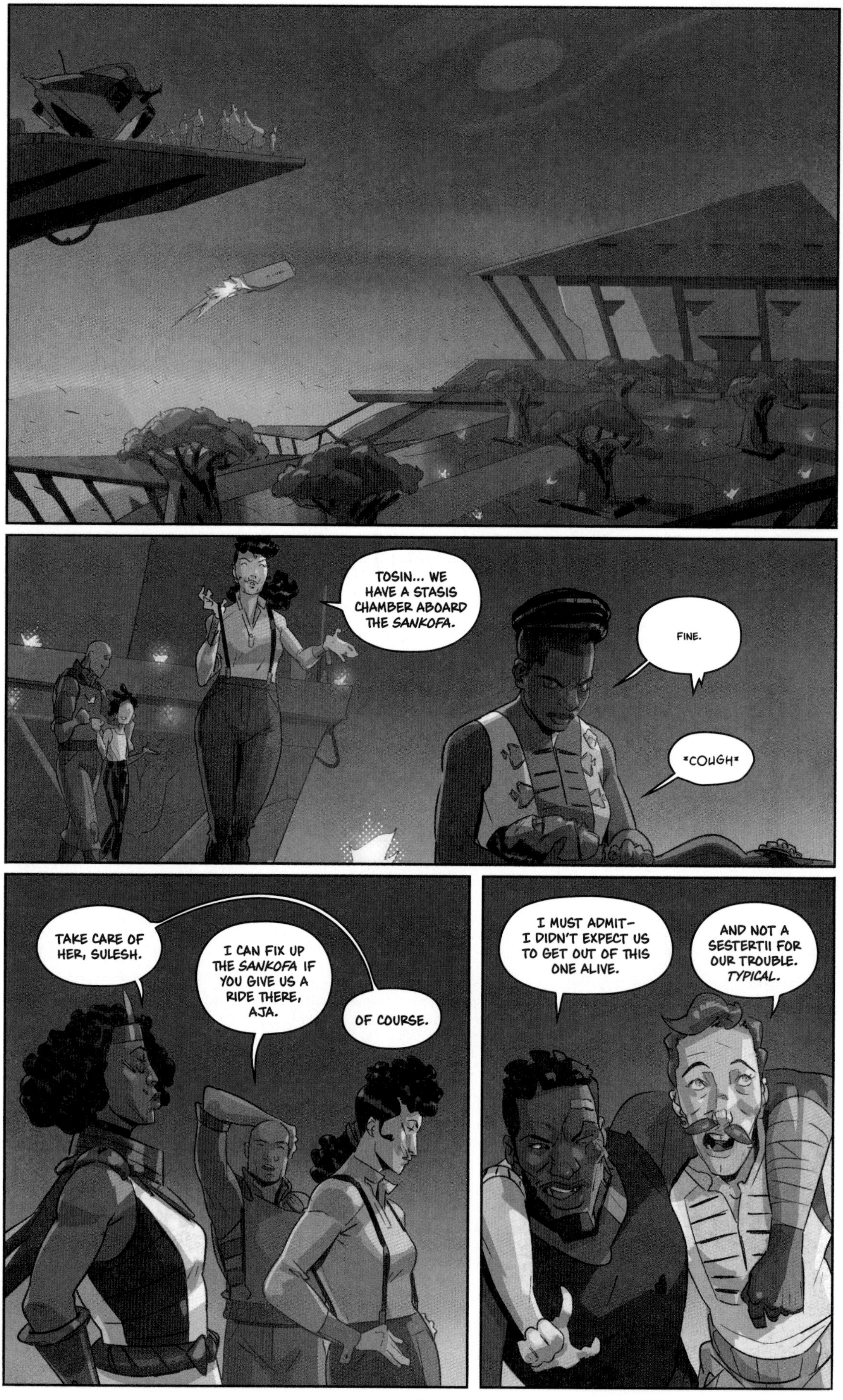
TOSIN... WE HAVE A STASIS CHAMBER ABOARD THE *SANKOFA*.
FINE.
COUGH
TAKE CARE OF HER, SULESH.
I CAN FIX UP THE *SANKOFA* IF YOU GIVE US A RIDE THERE, AJA.
OF COURSE.
I MUST ADMIT– I DIDN'T EXPECT US TO GET OUT OF THIS ONE ALIVE.
AND NOT A SESTERTII FOR OUR TROUBLE. *TYPICAL*.

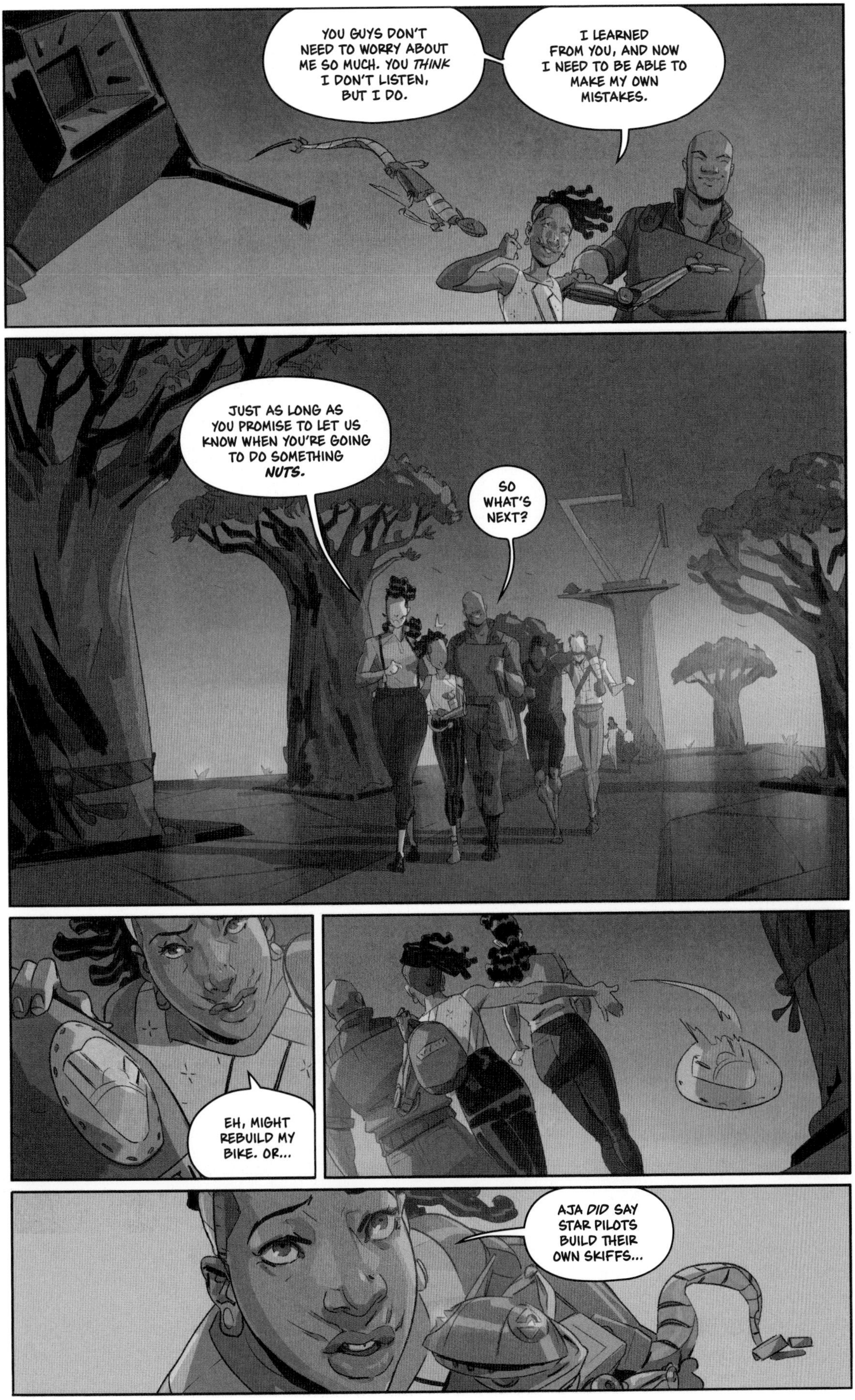
YOU GUYS DON'T NEED TO WORRY ABOUT ME SO MUCH. YOU *THINK* I DON'T LISTEN, BUT I DO.
I LEARNED FROM YOU, AND NOW I NEED TO BE ABLE TO MAKE MY OWN MISTAKES.
JUST AS LONG AS YOU PROMISE TO LET US KNOW WHEN YOU'RE GOING TO DO SOMETHING ***NUTS.***
SO WHAT'S NEXT?
EH, MIGHT REBUILD MY BIKE. OR...
AJA *DID* SAY STAR PILOTS BUILD THEIR OWN SKIFFS...

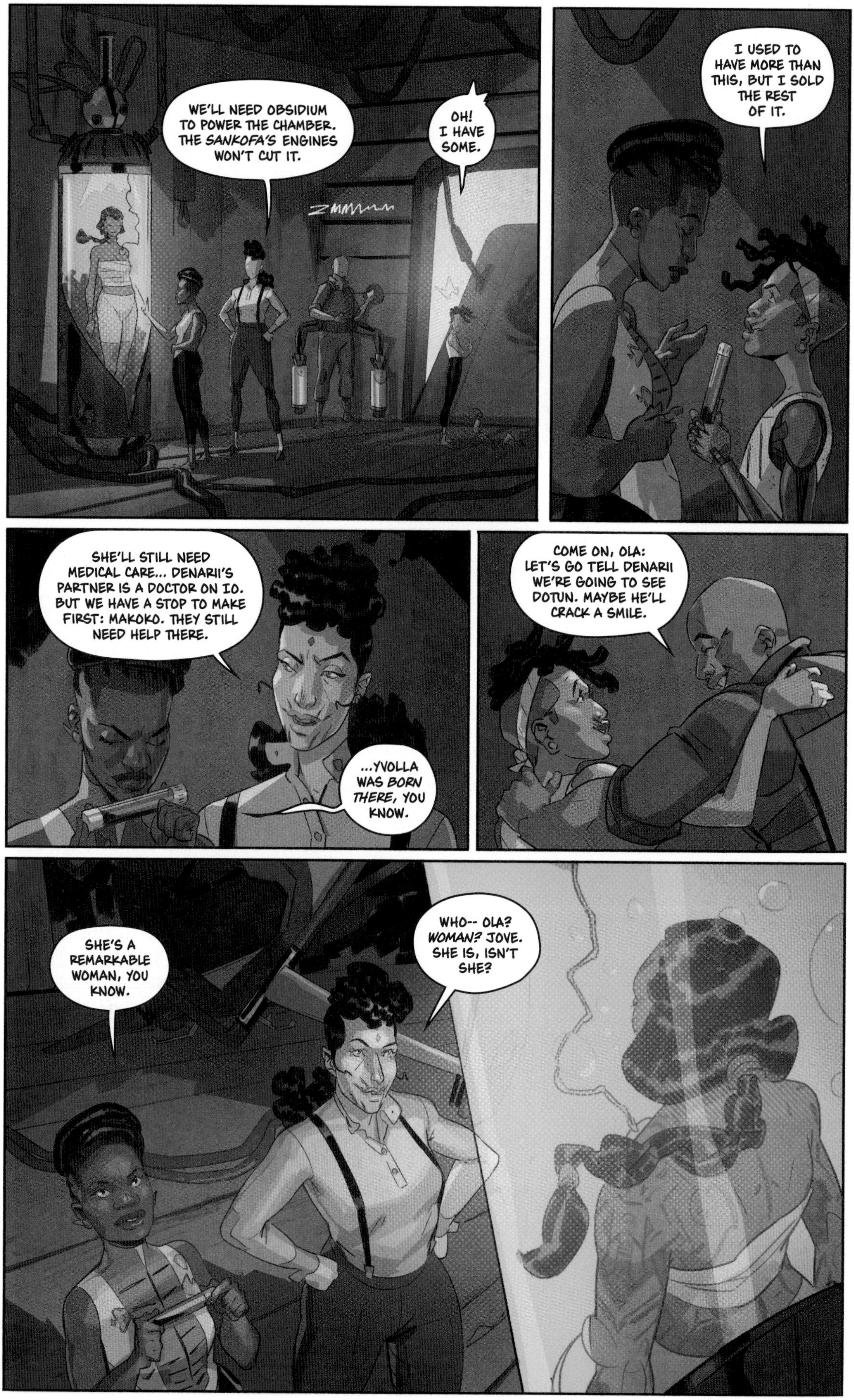
WE'LL NEED OBSIDIUM TO POWER THE CHAMBER. THE SANKOFA'S ENGINES WON'T CUT IT.
OH! I HAVE SOME.
ZMMMmm
I USED TO HAVE MORE THAN THIS, BUT I SOLD THE REST OF IT.
SHE'LL STILL NEED MEDICAL CARE... DENARII'S PARTNER IS A DOCTOR ON IO. BUT WE HAVE A STOP TO MAKE FIRST: MAKOKO. THEY STILL NEED HELP THERE.
...YVOLLA WAS BORN THERE, YOU KNOW.
COME ON, OLA: LET'S GO TELL DENARII WE'RE GOING TO SEE DOTUN. MAYBE HE'LL CRACK A SMILE.
SHE'S A REMARKABLE WOMAN, YOU KNOW.
WHO-- OLA? WOMAN? JOVE. SHE IS, ISN'T SHE?

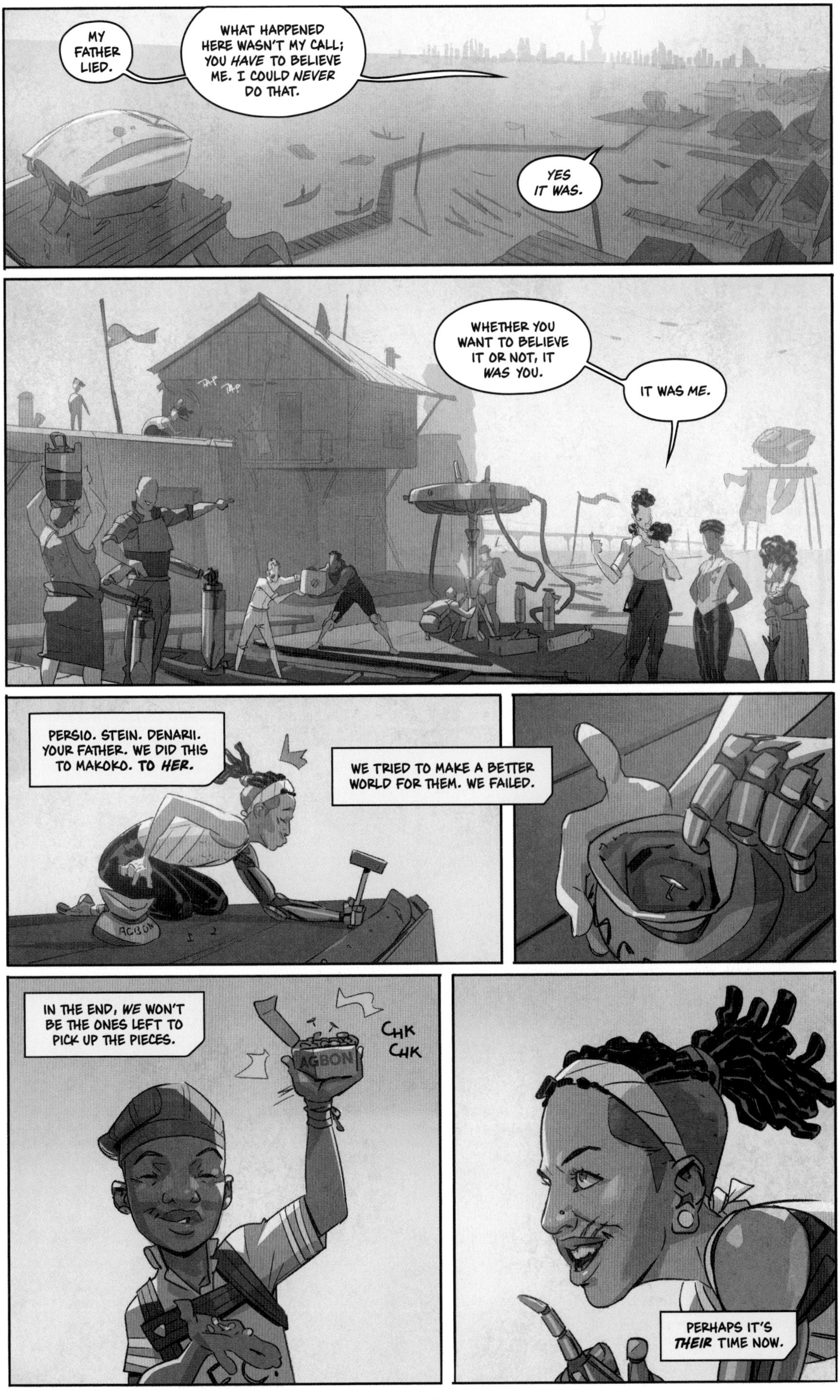
MY FATHER LIED.
WHAT HAPPENED HERE WASN'T MY CALL; YOU *HAVE* TO BELIEVE ME. I COULD *NEVER* DO THAT.
YES IT WAS.
WHETHER YOU WANT TO BELIEVE IT OR NOT, IT *WAS* YOU.
IT WAS *ME.*
PERSIO. STEIN. DENARII. YOUR FATHER. WE DID THIS TO MAKOKO. TO *HER.*
WE TRIED TO MAKE A BETTER WORLD FOR THEM. WE FAILED.
IN THE END, *WE* WON'T BE THE ONES LEFT TO PICK UP THE PIECES.
AGBON
CHK CHK
PERHAPS IT'S *THEIR* TIME NOW.

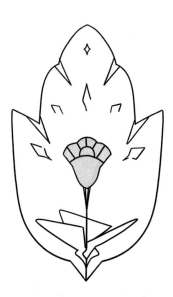

FUNLOLA REIS

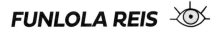

OLA wasn't initially intended to be the focus of ***New Masters.*** In our first drafts, she played a fairly passive role, and much of the story revolved around Persio, Sulesh, Stein, and Denarii trying desperately to find a cure for the terminal illness that eventually robbed her of her arm. In the end, we decided this first series needed to focus on Ola, because Africa's greatest hope—its greatest resource—is not oil, money, or gold: it's the youth. Writing from Ola's perspective allowed us to talk about the excitement, wonder, and frustration we often felt as kids.

Funlola's mechabot, Àṣẹ, is named after the Yoruba concept of self-determination. This concept refers to the special power in all of us— indeed, in every living thing—to manifest change by sheer force of will. In this adventure, Àṣẹ is still quite young, having only been designed and built by Ola a little over a year ago. In the coming years, I've no doubt we'll see Àṣẹ grow and evolve with Ola.

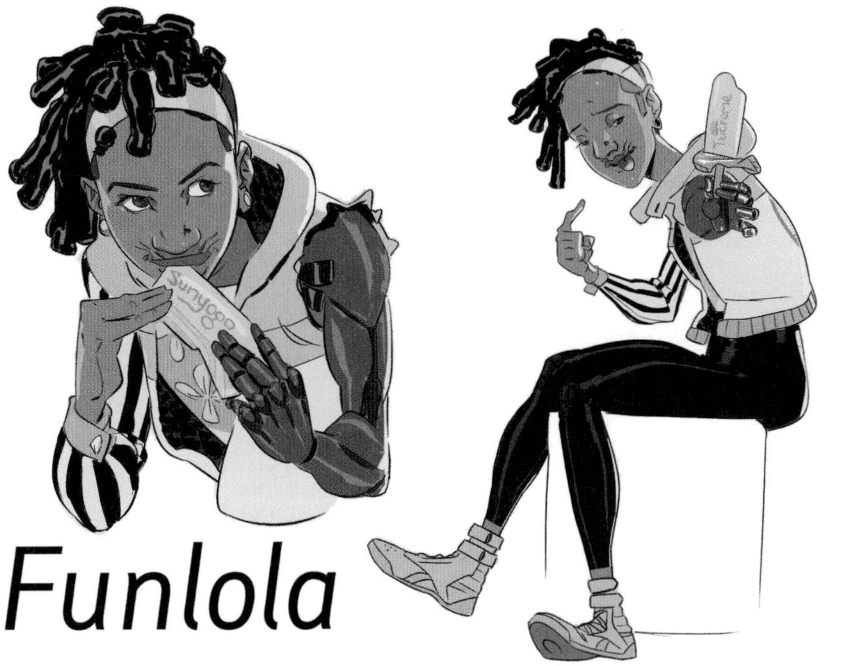
Funlola

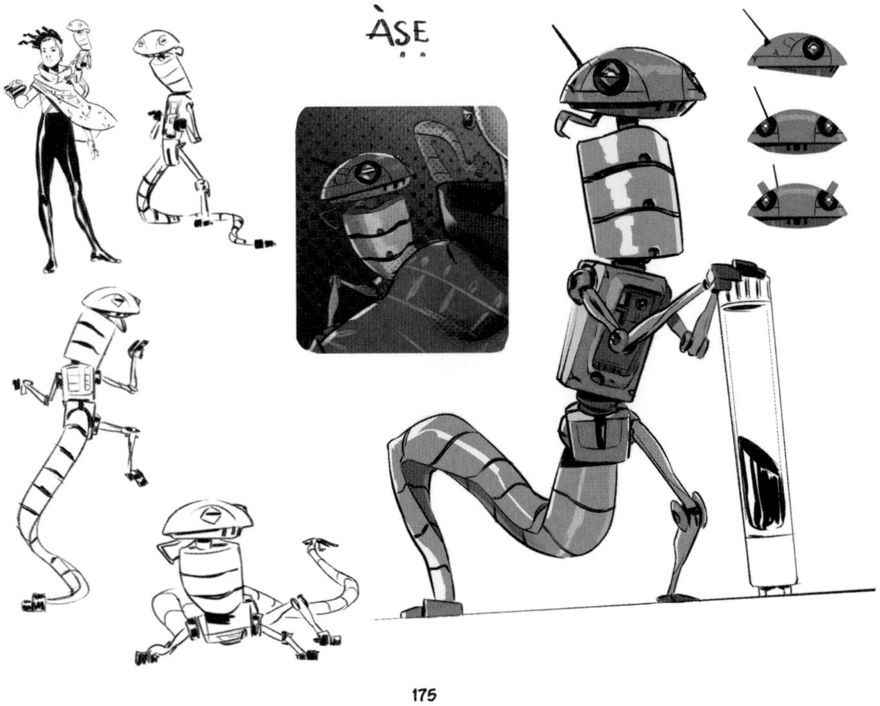
ÀṢE

The designs of most of the vehicles in Eko—particularly those in the poorer sections of the city—are based on age-old chassis refreshed with newer materials. The idea of use and re-use is ingrained in Nigerian culture.

Funlola's trusty flutter-bike design is based on the ubiquitous Nigerian **"OKADA,"** a much-derided method of public transportation and one of the best ways to experience the chaotic pulse of our city, Lagos.

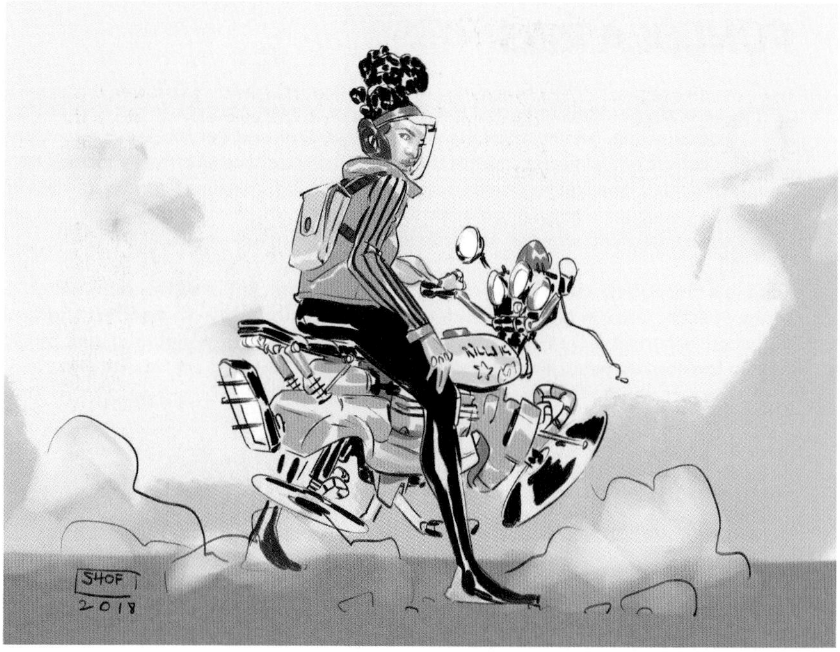

SHOF
2018

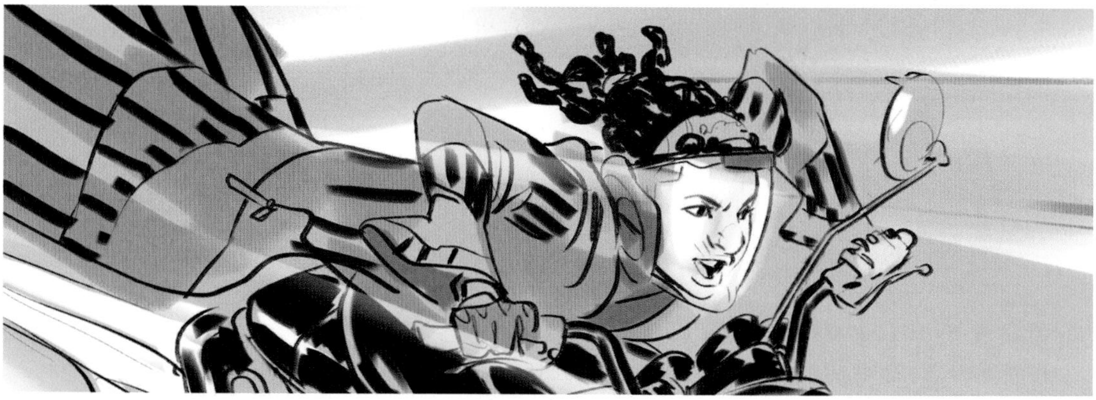

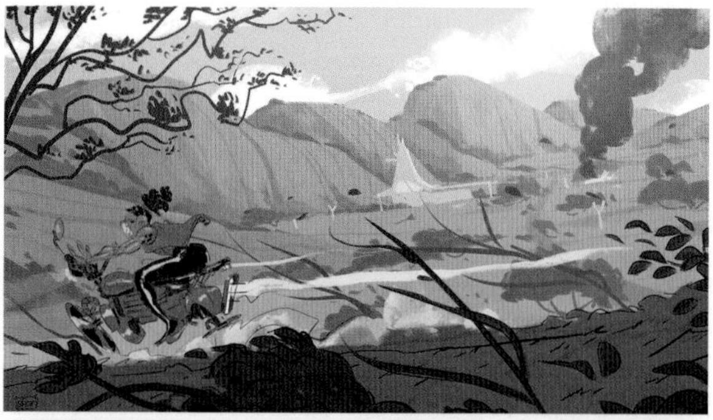

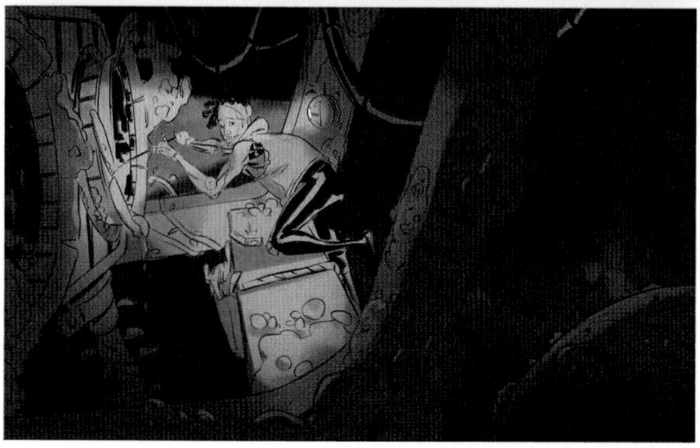

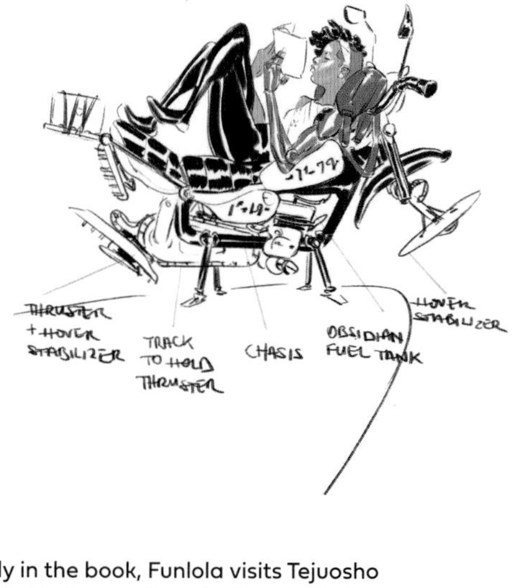

THRUSTER + HOVER STABILIZER
TRACK TO HOLD THRUSTER
CHASIS
OBSIDIAN FUEL TANK
HOVER STABILIZER

Early in the book, Funlola visits Tejuosho Market to buy replacement parts for her flutter-bike. Shof and I took inspiration from the real Tejuosho in Lagos—as it was in the 90's—and a famous electronics market outside Lagos, known as Alaba Market.

COVER ARTWORK

The **COSTUS SPECTABILIS,** or "yellow trumpet," is Nigeria's national flower. It is found all over the landscape and on the country's national coat of arms. In our story, the Costus Spectabilis represents hope and heralds change. We felt it made sense to tie all the covers together with this strong symbol.

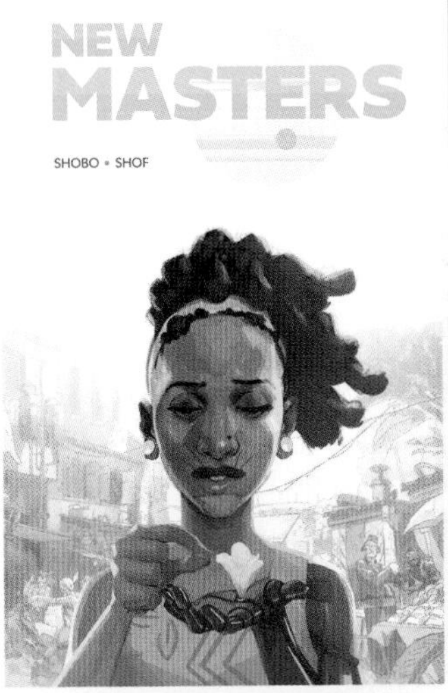
NEW
MASTERS
SHOBO • SHOF

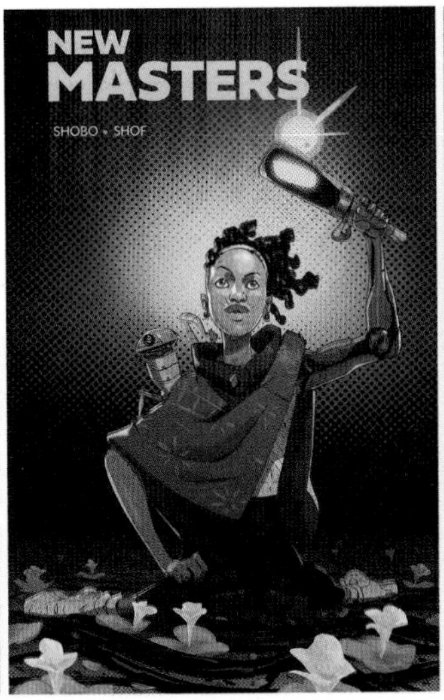
NEW
MASTERS
SHOBO • SHOF

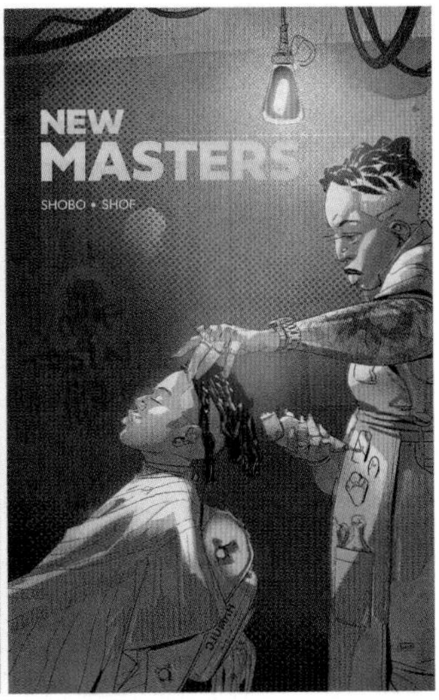
NEW
MASTERS
SHOBO • SHOF

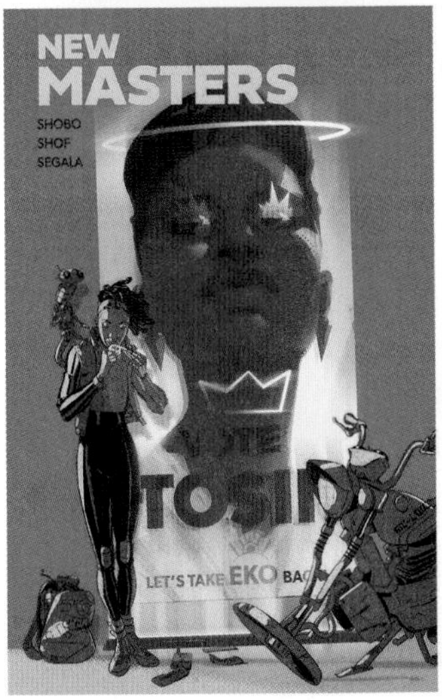
NEW
MASTERS
SHOBO
SHOF
SEGALA

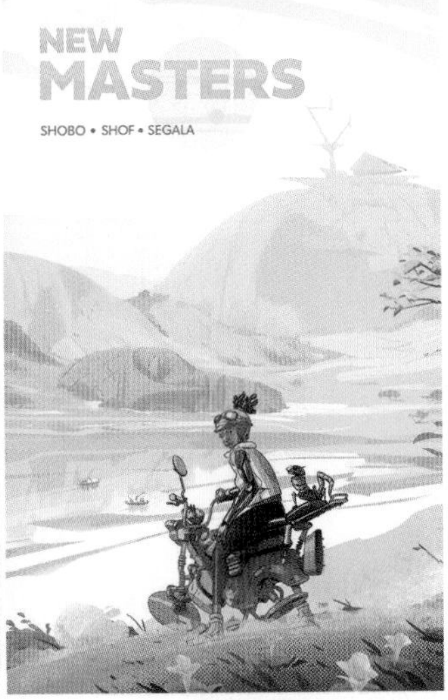
NEW
MASTERS
SHOBO • SHOF • SEGALA

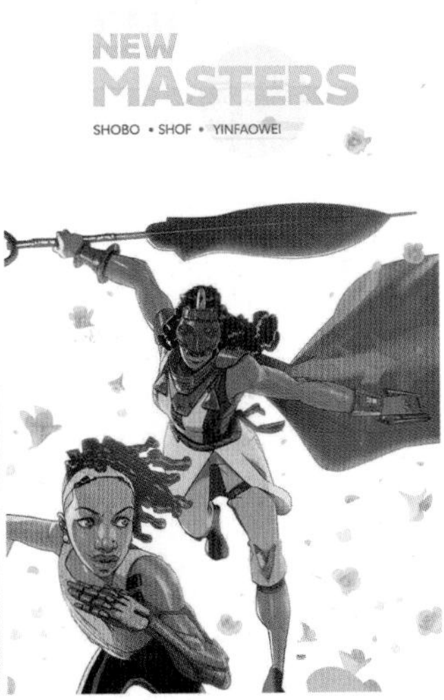
NEW
MASTERS
SHOBO • SHOF • YINFAOWEI

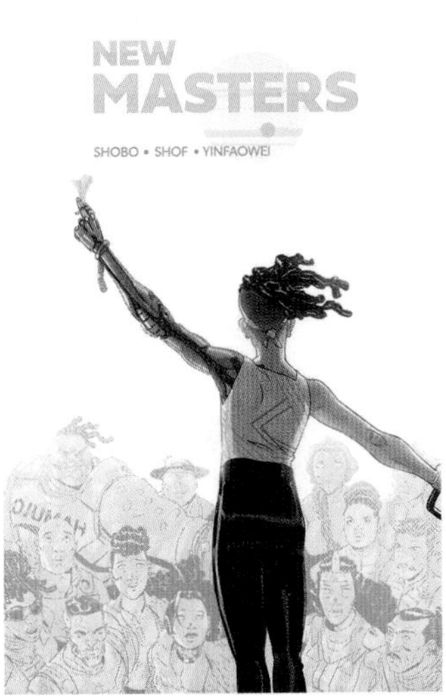
NEW
MASTERS
SHOBO • SHOF • YINFAOWEI

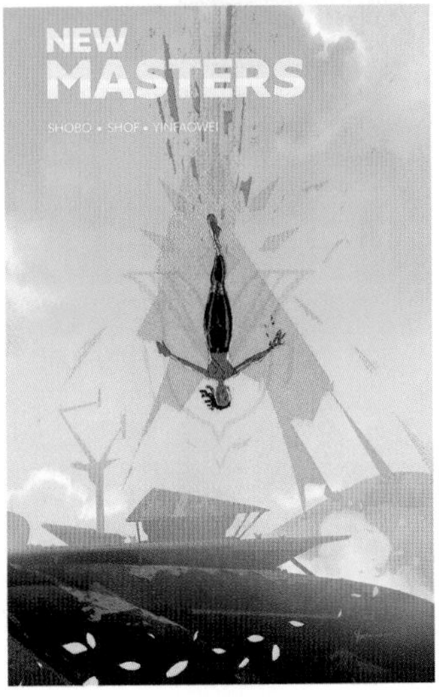
NEW
MASTERS
SHOBO • SHOF • YINFAOWEI

ISSUES 1-6 COVER ART BY SHOF

Issue 6 Variant was a wonderful collaboration with Harrison Yinfaowei (BG Paint) and Shof (Inks and Design).

The world of **NEW MASTERS**

IN THE EARLY PART OF THE 21ST CENTURY, the Jovian fleet burst into our solar system, bringing with it the Ark of Species. When the fleet slammed into Earth, it scattered debris across the planet's surface and leaked exotic fuels into the soil. This cataclysmic event swallowed great cities like New York, London, Paris, and Berlin. However, it also fueled the rise of new interplanetary ports of call such as Lagos, Morocco, Mumbai, and Hong Kong. As memories of the old world faded into myth and legend, the import and influence of a new society grew.

New Masters is our sci-fi love letter to the African continent, a letter that's taken the better part of a decade for us to pen. We invite you to immerse yourself in a universe that weaves African experience, philosophy, and culture indelibly into its fabric.

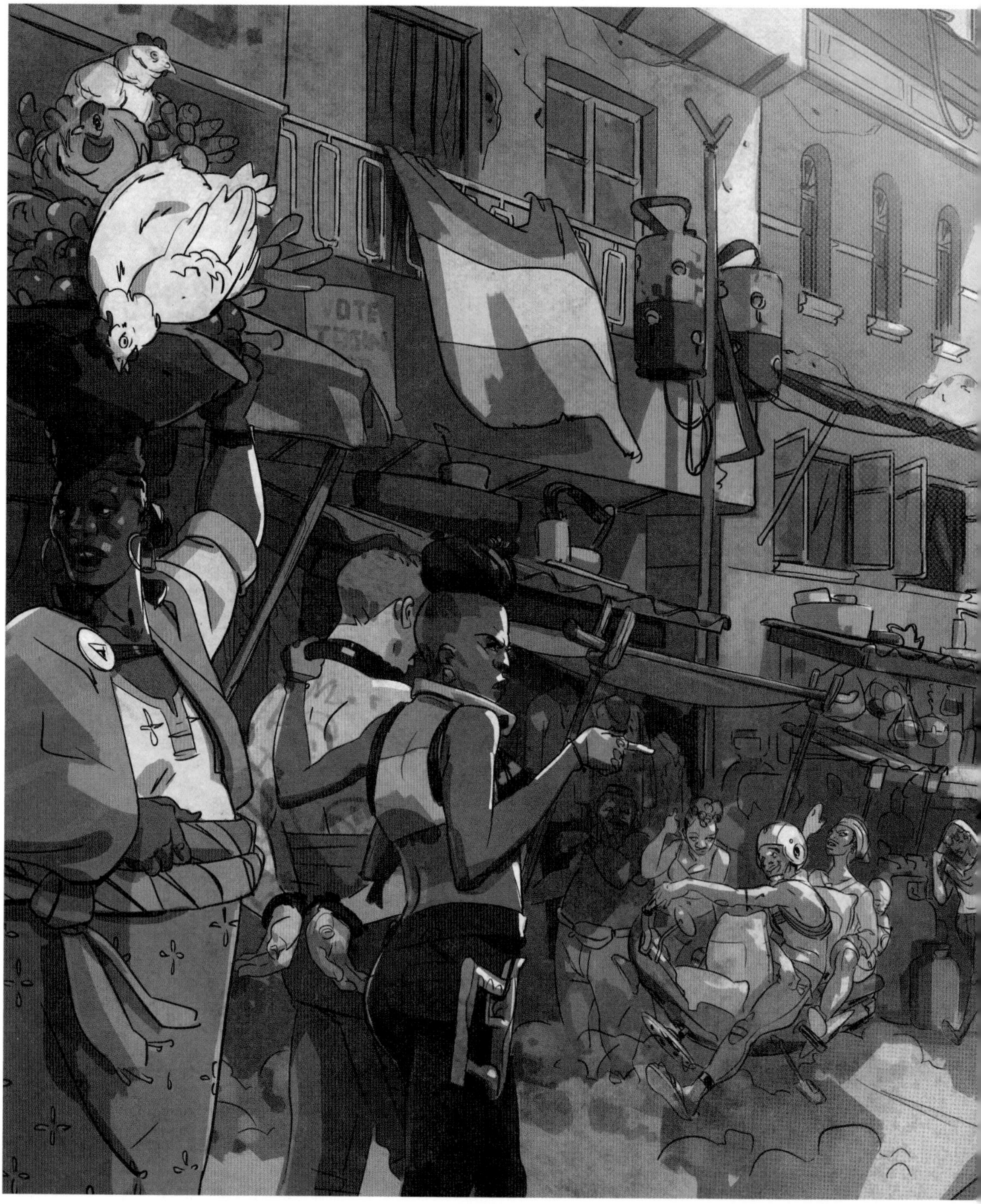

We began work on what would become ***New Masters*** in 2014, when we got funding to create a Kickstarter comic called ***Outcasts of Jupiter.*** This "missing chapter" in New Masters' history took place in Morocco, in a coastal kingdom known as the City of Seven Faces It saw Denarii, Stein, and Sulesh launch a desperate rescue attempt to save Persio. You see, Persio had gotten himself captured while searching for a cure to a disease that was slowly poisoning Ola, who was then quite young. Also, Denarii fights a panther in the book.

We consider the events of ***Outcasts of Jupiter*** a sort of vague prehistory. The events that unfolded in the City of Seven Faces definitely happened, but maybe not exactly as they were recorded in the book.

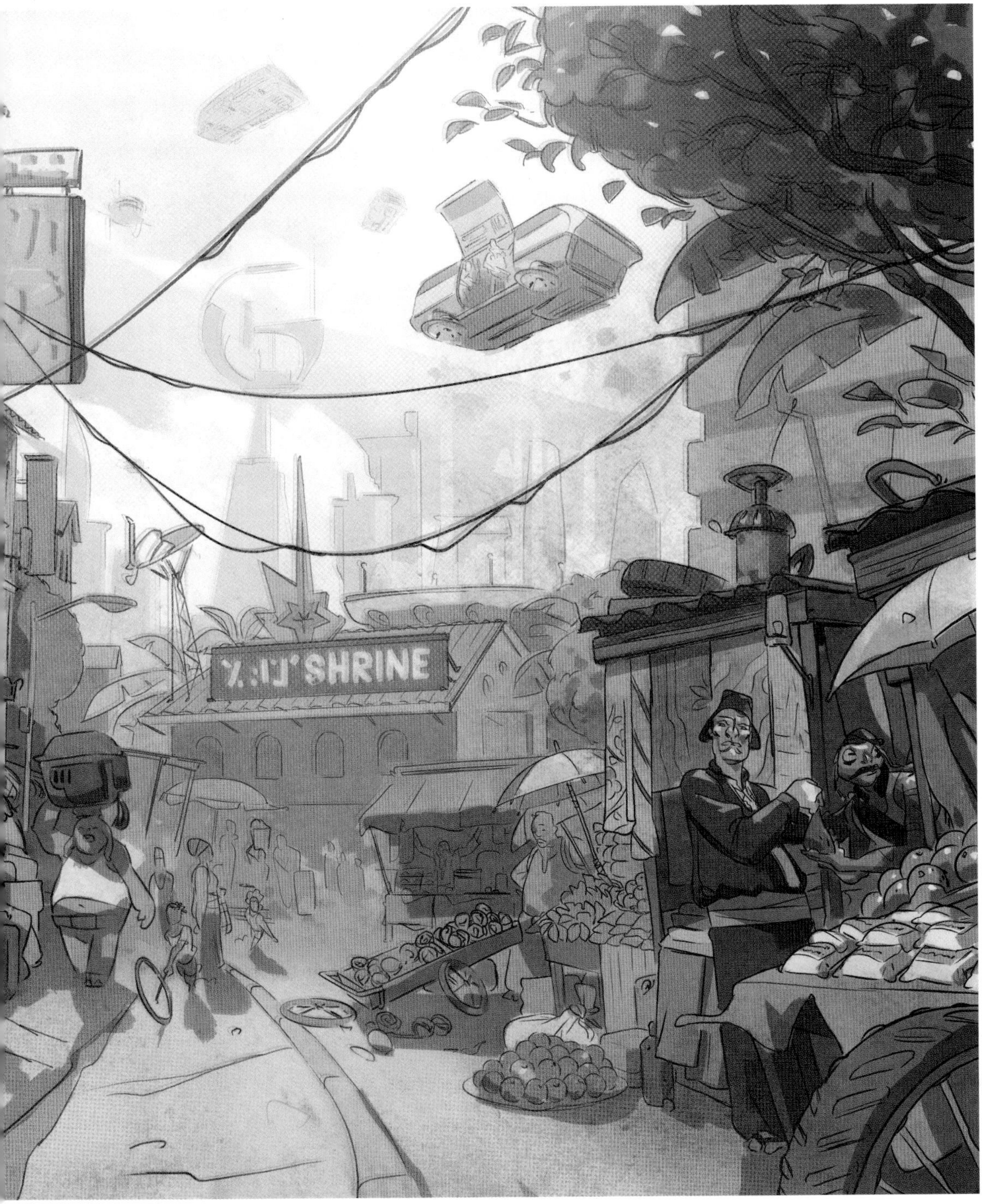
SHRINE

DEVELOPMENT

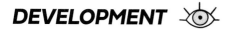

Clear communication is the ultimate goal in developing a page. I think of color and light very early in the rough stages; this helps me with ideas for staging and compositional flow through the panels. When you have a page like the one below (which mostly features talking heads), acting and body language are key— so we have to define a consistent style and color language that avoids visual fatigue. When I use Zbrush models for mechanical construction, I try to infuse energy in my drawings by omitting details or abstracting line work. Environmental storytelling is also quite important to me; whenever time permits, I try to sneak in elements that hint at the larger ***New Masters*** universe, or add in-jokes between Shobo and I. The book Ola reads here is a comic Shobo wrote years ago that helped spark the world of ***New Masters*** you see today.

— SHOF

ANYTHING TO DRINK?
I HAVE SMOKED FISH?
CHAI! I'M GOOD.
HEY OLA!
KNOCK
KNOCK
I KNOW YOU'RE MAD, BUT I'VE GOT SOME SMOKED FISH FROM HAKOKO...
AND HOT AKARA!
COME IN!
HEY POPSI, CHECK OUT WHAT I FOUND IN THE E-ZONE.
AH-AH, THIS PLACE IS A MESS, OLA, YOU NEED TO--
WAIT! YOU WENT TO THE E-ZONE?! JOVE. JUST... DON'T TELL YOUR MOTHER.
HEY THOSE MICRO SERVOS ARE PRETTY COOL. DID THEY COME FROM A JOVIAN NAVICULA?
YUP! I ALMOST LOST MY ARM FOR IT.
"NOTHING SPOIL". I BUILT THAT ARM TO OUTLIVE THE HEAT DEATH.

ANYTHING TO DRINK?
I HAVE SMOKED FISH?
CHAI! I'M GOOD.
HEY OLA!
KNOCK
KNOCK
I KNOW YOU'RE MAD, BUT I'VE GOT SOME SMOKED FISH FROM HAKOKO...
AND HOT AKARA!
COME IN!
HEY POPSI, CHECK OUT WHAT I FOUND IN THE E-ZONE.
AH-AH, THIS PLACE IS A MESS, OLA, YOU NEED TO--
WAIT! YOU WENT TO THE E-ZONE?! JOVE. JUST... DON'T TELL YOUR MOTHER.
HEY THOSE MICRO SERVOS ARE PRETTY COOL. DID THEY COME FROM A JOVIAN NAVICULA?
YUP! I ALMOST LOST MY ARM FOR IT.
"NOTHING SPOIL". I BUILT THAT ARM TO OUTLIVE THE HEAT DEATH.

ANYTHING TO DRINK?
I HAVE SMOKED FISH?
CHAI! I'M GOOD.
HEY OLA!
KNOCK
KNOCK
I KNOW YOU'RE MAD, BUT I'VE GOT SOME SMOKED FISH FROM HAKOKO...
AND HOT AKARA!
COME IN!
HEY POPSI, CHECK OUT WHAT I FOUND IN THE E-ZONE.
AH-AH, THIS PLACE IS A MESS, OLA, YOU NEED TO--
WAIT! YOU WENT TO THE E-ZONE?! JOVE. JUST... DON'T TELL YOUR MOTHER.
HEY THOSE MICRO SERVOS ARE PRETTY COOL. DID THEY COME FROM A JOVIAN NAVICULA?
YUP! I ALMOST LOST MY ARM FOR IT.
"NOTHING SPOIL". I BUILT THAT ARM TO OUTLIVE THE HEAT DEATH.

ANYTHING TO DRINK?
I HAVE SMOKED FISH?
CHAI! I'M GOOD.
HEY OLA!
KNOCK
KNOCK
I KNOW YOU'RE MAD, BUT I'VE GOT SOME SMOKED FISH FROM MAKOKO...
AND HOT AKARA!
COME IN!
HEY, POPSI! CHECK OUT WHAT I FOUND IN THE E-ZONE!
AH-AH, THIS PLACE IS A MESS, OLA, YOU NEED TO--
WAIT! YOU WENT TO THE E-ZONE?! JOVE. JUST... DON'T TELL YOUR MOTHER.
LAKUNLE JALILO! DID YOU GET THAT FLOW REGULATOR FROM A JOVIAN NAVICULA?
SKSHHHH
YUP! I ALMOST LOST MY ARM FOR IT.
"NOTHING SPOIL." I BUILT THAT ARM TO OUTLIVE THE HEAT DEATH.

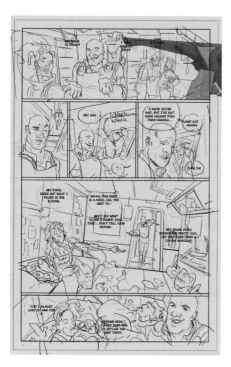

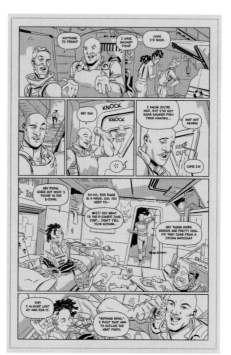

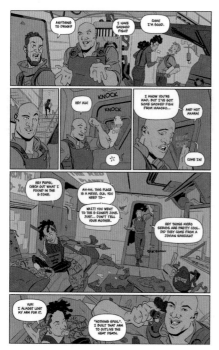

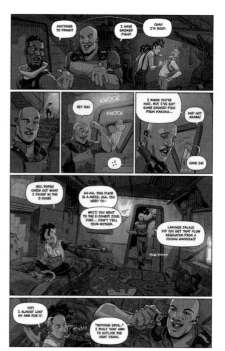

*The **OJUMAHS.** In Nigeria (as in many other countries), families in power tend to stay in power... for generations.*

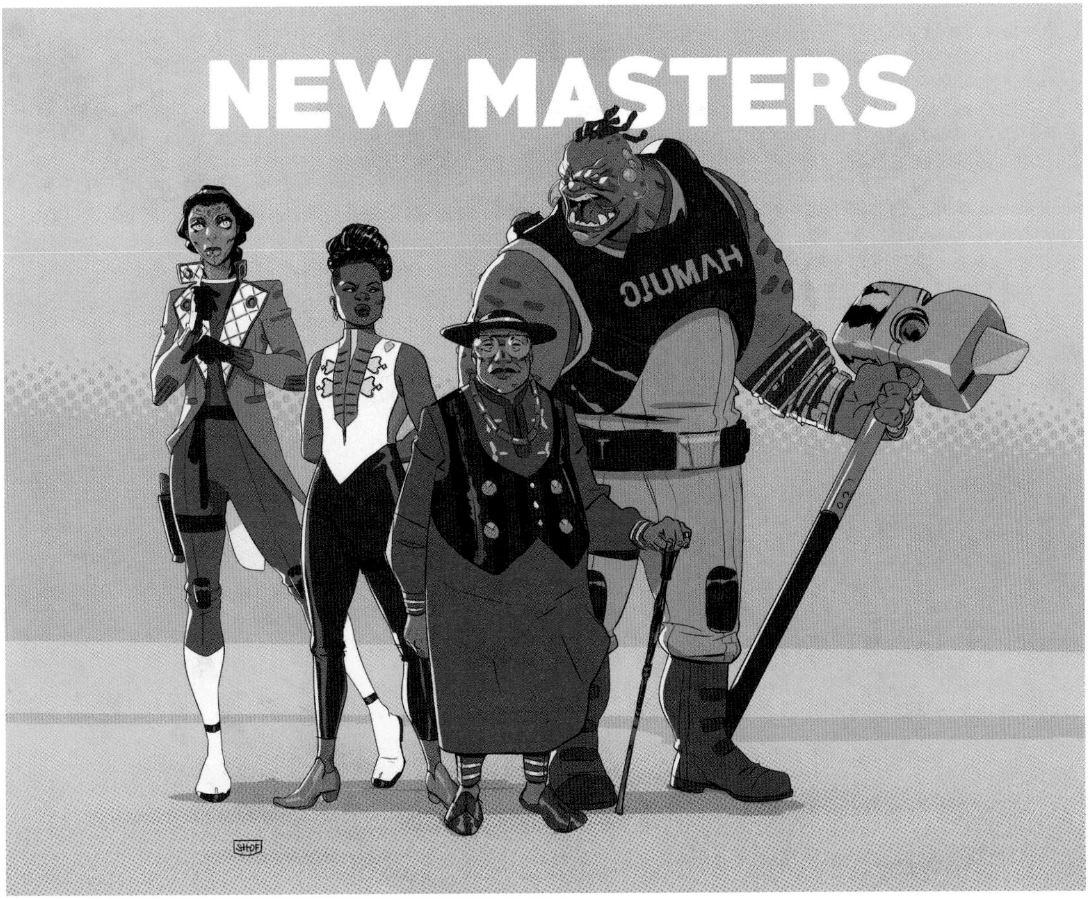
NEW MASTERS
OJUMAH

The area boys — "agbèrò" in Yoruba — that accost Ola in Tejuosho are based on the gangs of street toughs and hustlers often found prowling the streets of Lagos.

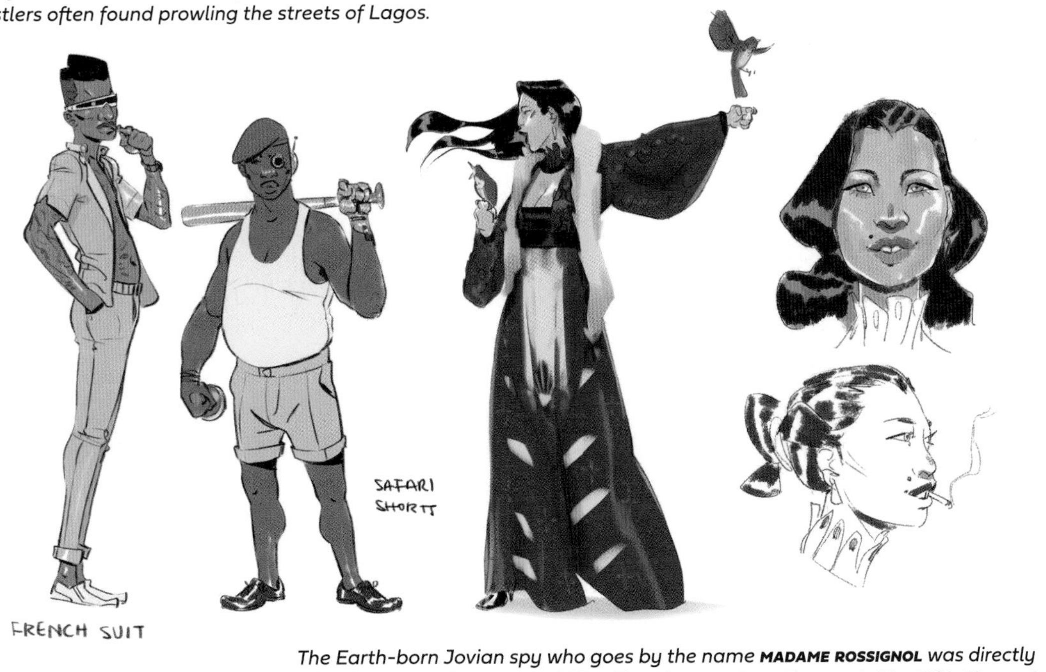
SAFARI
SHORTS
FRENCH SUIT

*The Earth-born Jovian spy who goes by the name **MADAME ROSSIGNOL** was directly inspired by the characters of Diva Plavalaguna from the movie The Fifth Element, and Bianca Castafiore from The Adventures of Tintin comic series.*

The JOVIANS

THERE HAVE BEEN FOUR SYSTEM-WIDE WARS fought over the hyper-fuel known as obsidium. The First Obsidium War was sparked only a few decades after the Jovian Ark of Species slammed into Earth, depositing its cargo of refugees from dozens of worlds. The war saw the formation of the Jovian Alliance, a group of races led by the Jovians and backed by Earth. The Alliance engaged in conflict with the Independent Powers (led by the Agemo), who pushed for secession from what they believed to be an autocracy.

By the end of the Fourth War, Earth had been granted independence from the Jovian Empire, and the rest of the system soon followed. The Jovian Empire might be no more, but its roots run deep, and its influence lingers across the system.

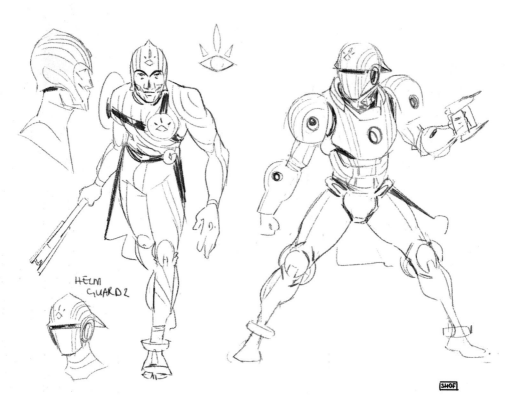

*Jovian soldiers, armor types,
and their various weaponry.*

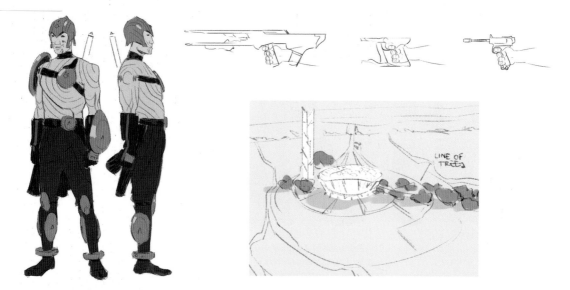

While largely benevolent today, the dominance of the Jovian Empire was built on the backs of the races it once called its subjects. This legacy can be felt in the difficult and often complicated relationships the empire maintains with the other races in the Sol system. Jovians have historically had a fascination with Earth; to this day, Jovian fashion, culture, names, and even language are derived from Earthen origins. They want to be like us— the irony, of course, being that *we* want to be like *them*.

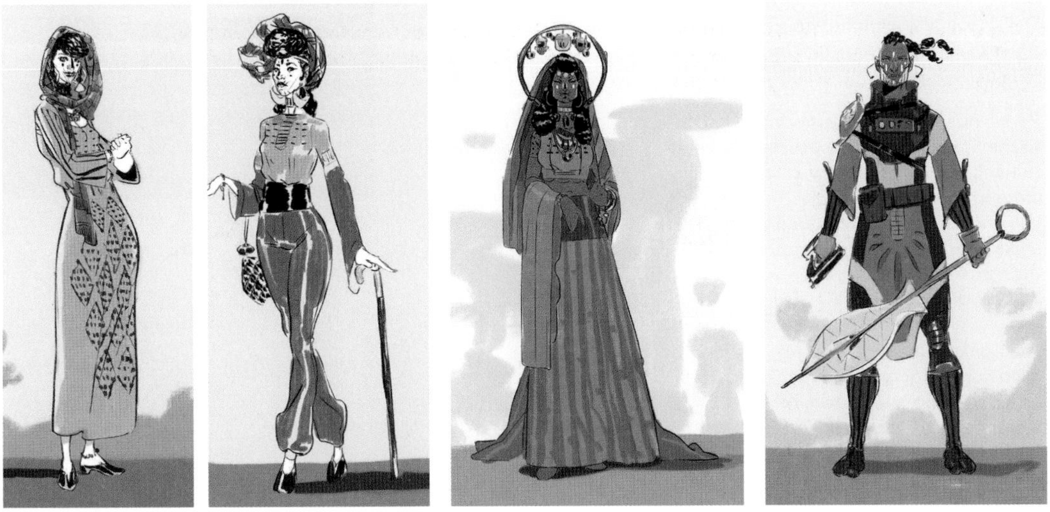

The Jovians were forced to flee their home system when a terrible calamity befell it. Unfortunately, much of their history was lost in the exodus. They spent generations drifting through space in hypersleep, until a navigational malfunction threw them off-course and into the Sol system.

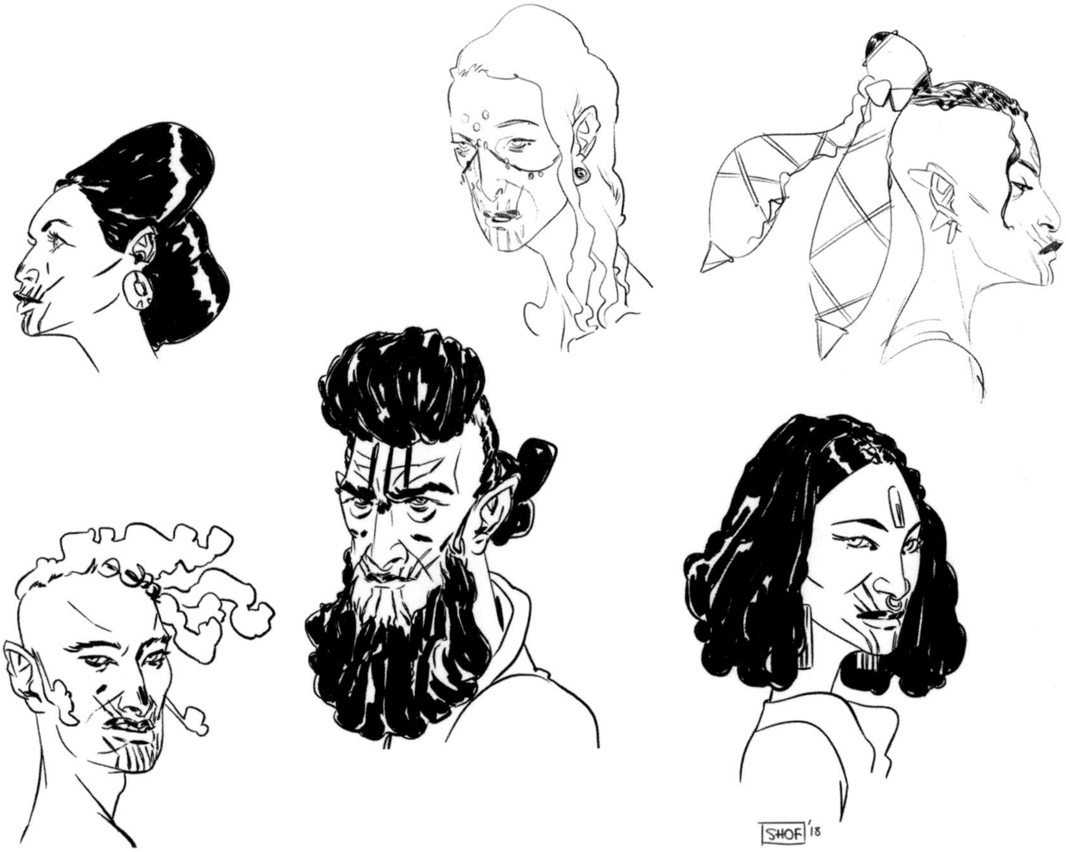
SHOF '18

SANKOFA* and *STARGLIDER

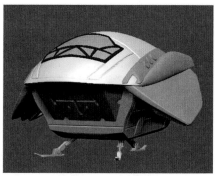

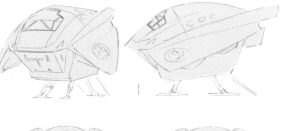

THE *SANKOFA* is a modified long-haul, light cargo transport vehicle. The *Bedford*-Class was designed by Persio's father Obafemi Reis to assist transport of humanitarian aid within the Sol system at the end of the Fourth Obsidium War. Obafemi created this specific ship as a wedding present for his son and daughter-in-law, though he never lived to see it built.

MED BAY
COCK PIT LADDER
ARMORY
VACCUUM
ENGINE ROOM
COCKPIT
MESSHALL
SCIENCE LAB
PORTHOLE
SPACE GEAR
HATCH EXTERIOR
LADDER INTERIOR

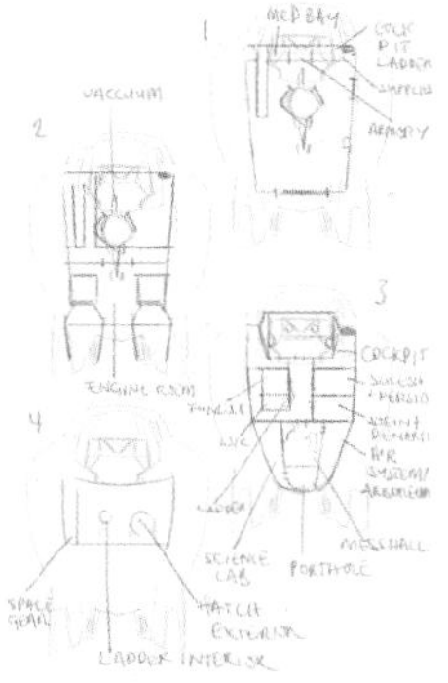

Persio has made many modifications to the *Sankofa* over the years— refining the engines for durability, and upgrading avionics according to Sulesh's unique specifications. What the *Bedford*-Class lacks in speed and mobility, it more than makes up for in dependability and hardiness.

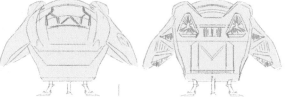

The *Sankofa* is more than just a ship; it's a home. For over twenty years, Persio and Sulesh have tinkered, modified, and expanded its innards to create a sanctuary for the outcasts— a refuge.

When it came time to design the *Sankofa,* Shof needed to make sure the ship's geography worked logically because it played a pivotal role in the story. So what did he do? He worked out the layout of the entire ship, plotting out all four decks to figure out where everyone's quarters were located, including the medbay, arboretum, armory, cargo area, engine room, atmospherics... and of course, the cockpit.

STAR PILOT SHIPS do not have names; they are merely referred to by their class designation: **STARGLIDER.** Swift, agile and robust beyond their initial appearance, Stargliders are constructed by the Pilots who own them, using the raw materials available at the Benin Temple. As a result, the pilot knows every screw, bolt, rivet, and avionic quirk of their craft. These tiny ships are intended to carry Star Pilots deep into the cold black of space and bring them back safely upon completion of their pilgrimage. Because of the inherent danger of the Star Pilot journey, Stargliders are among the only civilian ships authorized to carry weapons.

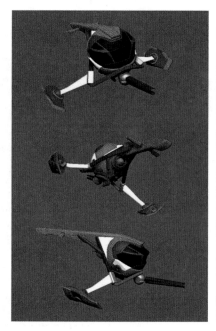

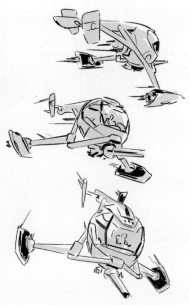

OUTCASTS of JUPITER

THE PERIOD FOLLOWING THE FIRST OBSIDIUM WAR was a period of prosperity for Earth. It saw the rise of our greatest civilization, centered around what is now known as *the Dead City of Ife.* The people of Ife built the Obsidium mines at Kainji, constructed to harness the obsidium deposits hidden deep within the bowels of crashed Jovian Naviculae. In addition, the Ifelites built statues to venerate their ancestors. These giant stone protectors watched over the vast countryside of West Africa, as well as the Star Pilot temple at Benin. But of course, the peace did not last; many of these accomplishments were wiped away during the Second Obsidium War.

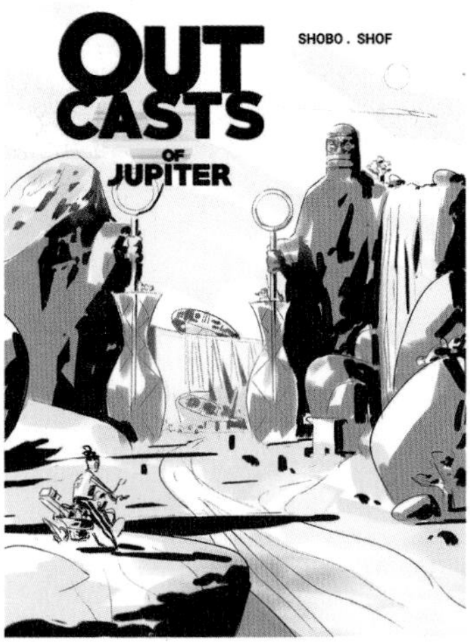

OUT
CASTS
OF
JUPITER
SHOBO . SHOF

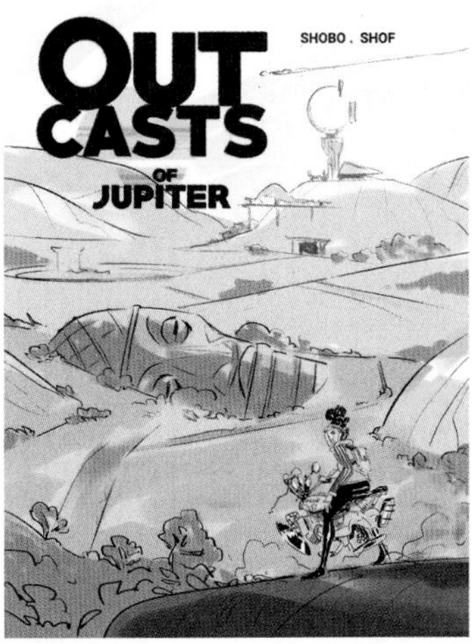

OUT
CASTS
OF
JUPITER
SHOBO . SHOF

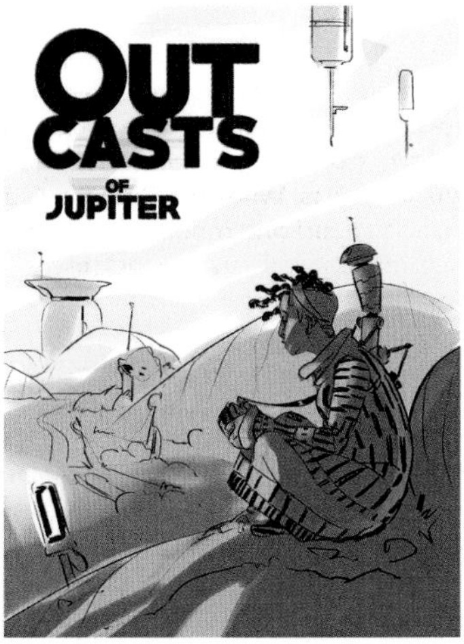

OUT
CASTS
OF
JUPITER

New Masters began life in 2014 as a Kickstarter pitch called ***OUTCASTS OF JUPITER.*** Shof and I will forever be grateful to the 471 backers who helped bring that original story to life. Since then, the story has evolved as I've expanded histories, created characters, conflicts, and lore, while Shof has developed new alien races, technology, and places.

— SHOBO

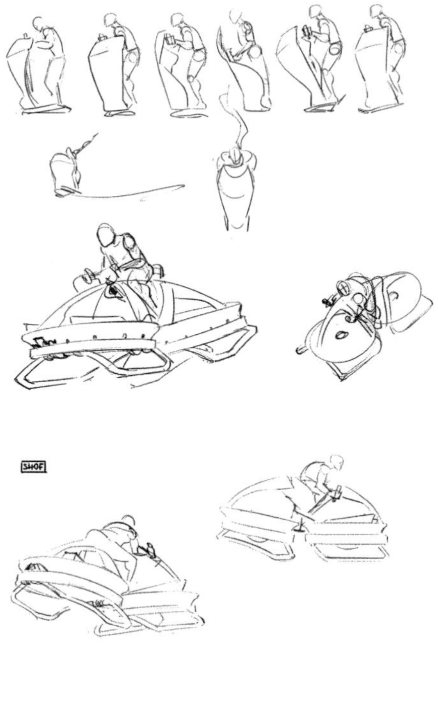

SHOF

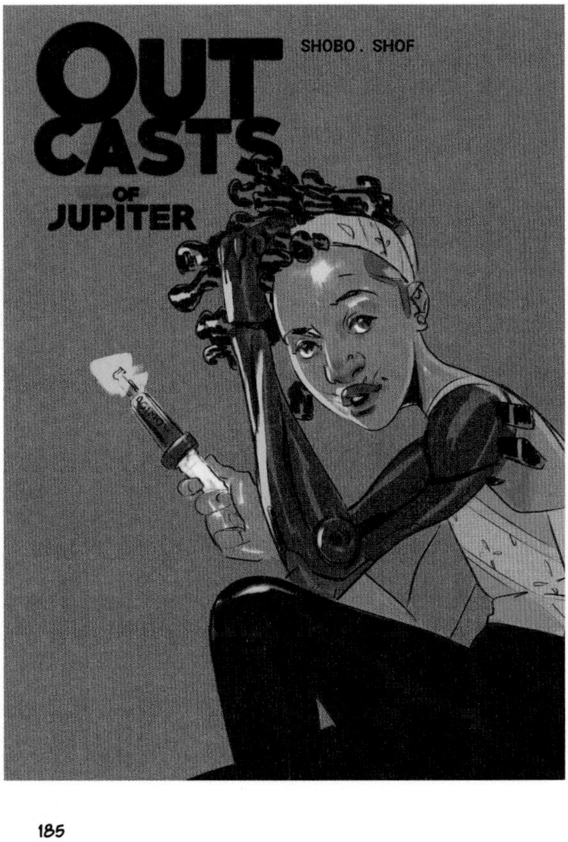

OUT
CASTS
OF
JUPITER
SHOBO . SHOF

The *BENIN TEMPLE*

THE BENIN TEMPLE is both the ceremonial home of the legendary Star Pilots, and the location of one of only two HyperGates on Earth.

 The first gate—built by the Jovians and sponsored by the Ojumah family—is located at the Independence House in Eko. The gate at Benin Temple, however, was reverse-engineered, and constructed entirely by Star Pilots after the First Obsidium War. While those that run the Eko HyperGate charge exorbitant fees, the gate at Benin is free for all to use, with only a transit pass required. This fact speaks to the Star Pilots' core value of providing free access to information and opportunity for all Earthers.

When the great cities of Ifé, Eko, and Abeokuta either fell or were occupied by the Coalition Powers during the Second Obsidium War, humans retreated to the safety of the Benin Temple. It stood as the last bastion of human sovereignty, culture, and accomplishment, and its remote location and defensible vantage point allowed it to remain unconquered through the end of the war. By the time the Ekiti Accords were signed and the fighting had come to an end, the temple was considered hallowed ground.

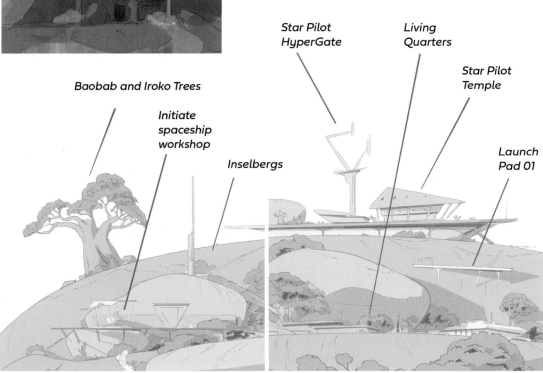

Baobab and Iroko Trees

Initiate spaceship workshop

Inselbergs

Star Pilot HyperGate

Living Quarters

Star Pilot Temple

Launch Pad 01

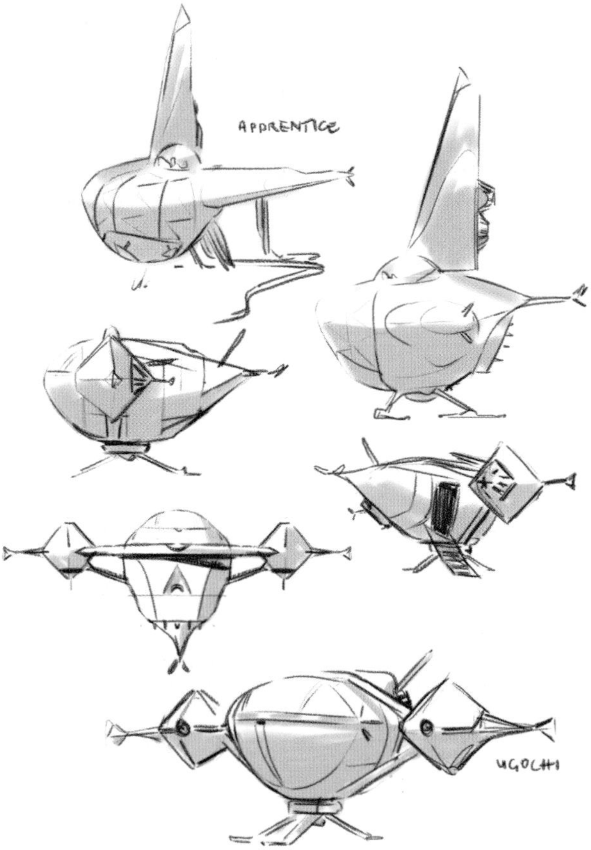
APPRENTICE
UGOCHI

The beginnings of the Star Pilot movement date back to the earliest days of the **POST-ADVENTU** era: made possible by the availability of relatively cheap spacecraft capable of sustained deep space flight. Handfuls of adventurous thrill-seekers and explorers from all walks of life, embarked on journeys to the outer edges of known space.

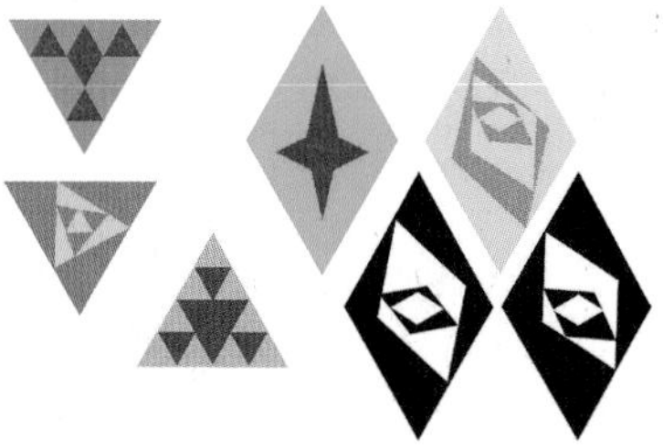

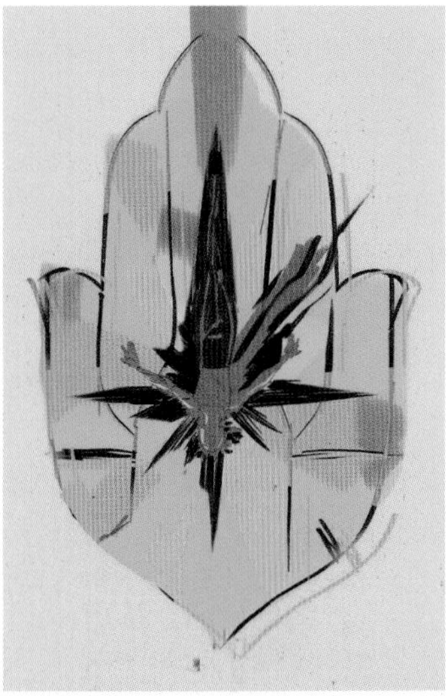

Akimitsu: the first ever recorded Star Pilot. They left earth in 2102, depositing beacons far into deep space. They never returned.

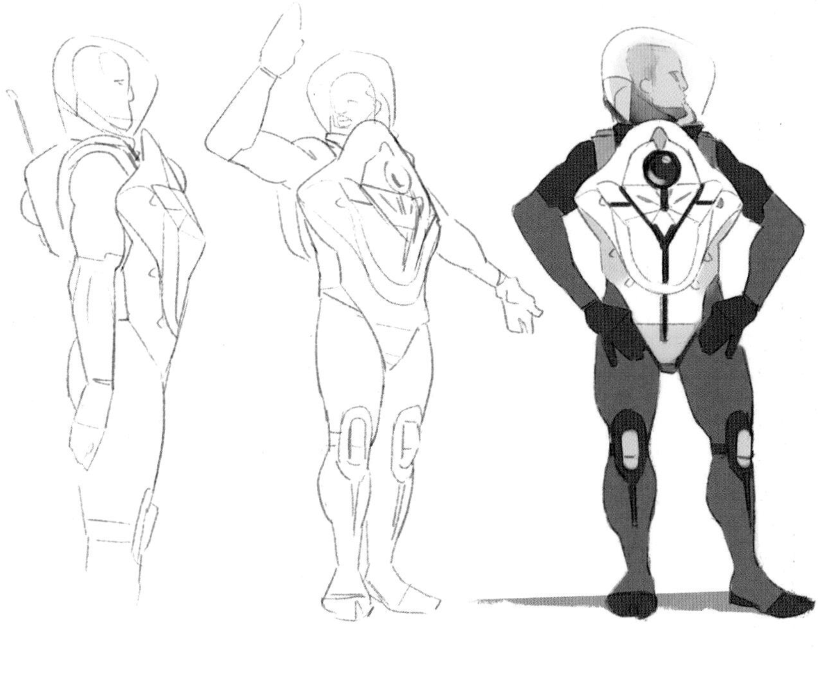

STAR PILOTS

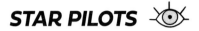

MOST PEOPLE WILL NEVER MEET A STAR PILOT, though they are likely to hear tales of their daring and exotic adventures on far-flung worlds.

To become a Star Pilot is to answer a deeply personal calling. You must be willing to confront the darkest elements of yourself, and only a few complete the rigorous training required. Every Pilot must go on a pilgrimage into uncharted space on a voyage of self-discovery. The goal is to give to the self, and to bring back knowledge for the benefit of all.

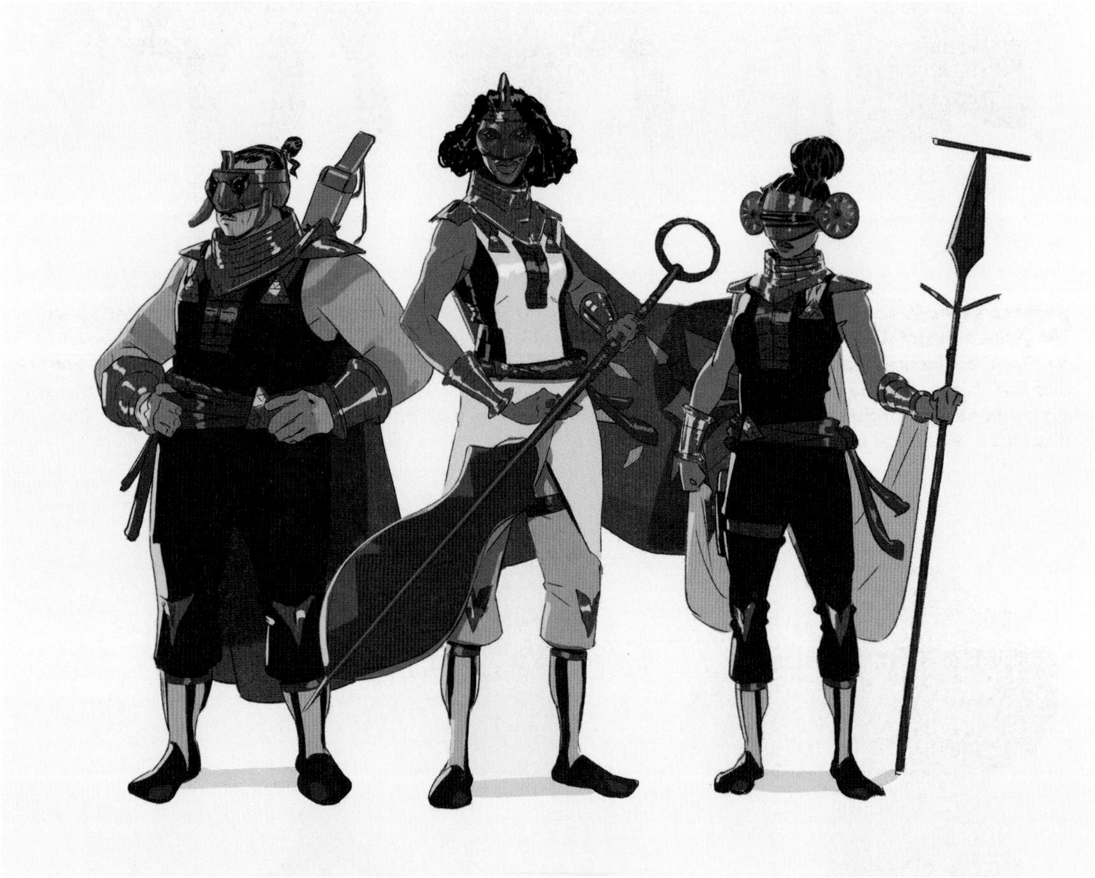

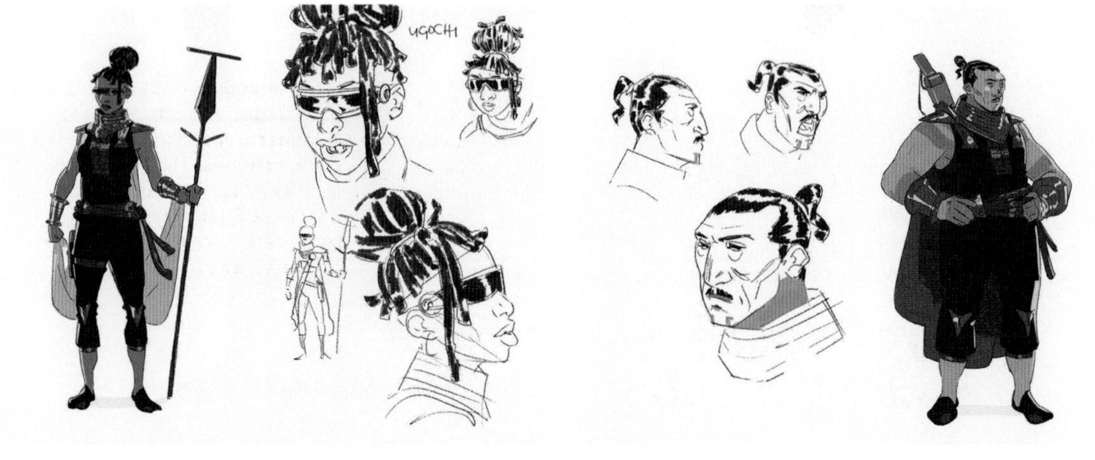
UGOCHI

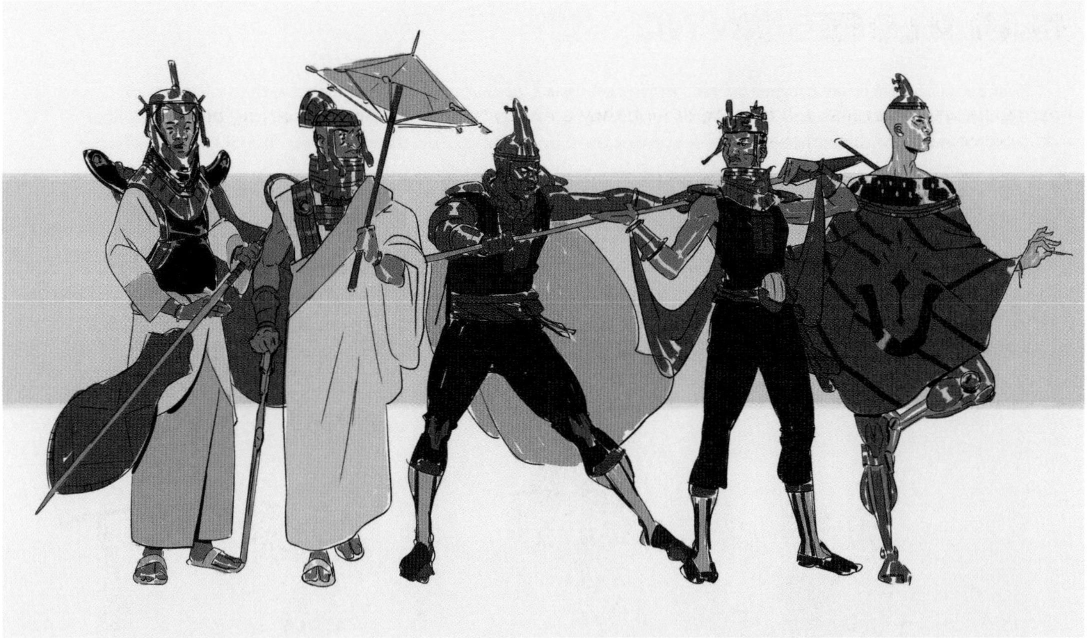

Star Pilots literally map the darkness by depositing nav points in the farthest reaches of uncharted space. In the course of their journey, a Star Pilot will make stops at dozens of space-ports, asteroid-based waystations, and backwater moons to refuel and replenish supplies. They will learn new languages, explore alien cultures and their traditions, map new planets, and gather nav data to take back to the temple at Benin. Star Pilots also act as wandering arbiters and law-keepers on the Edgeworlds— delivering justice to the unjust and settling disputes in exchange for room and board.

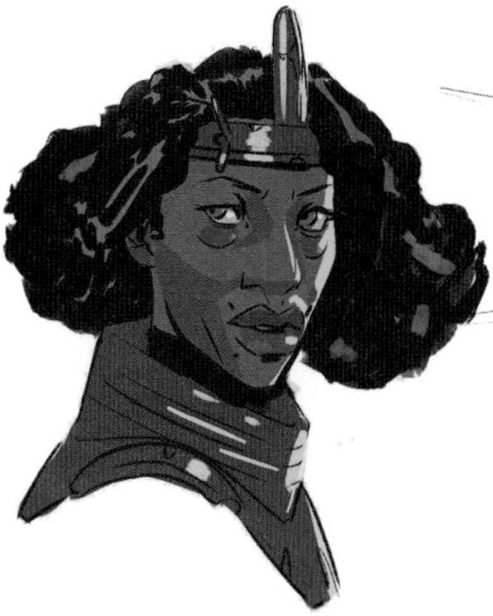

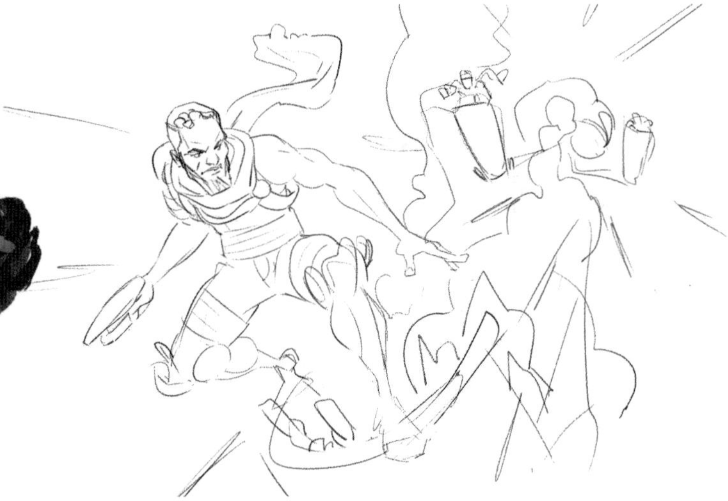

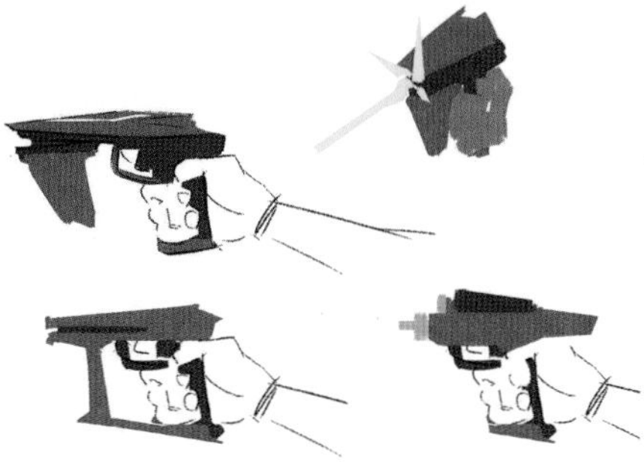

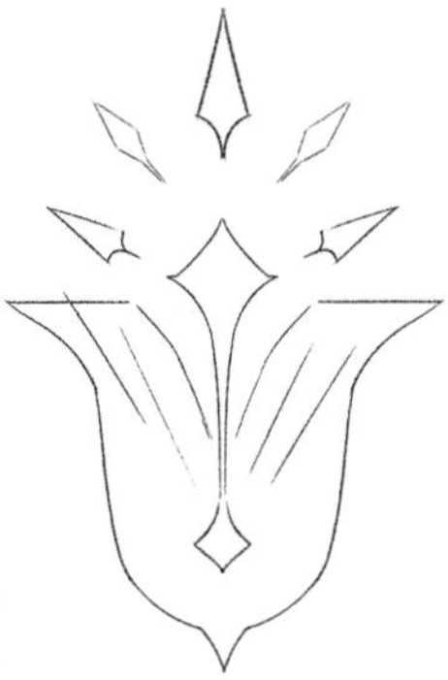

Over the centuries, Star Pilots have forged a reputation built on honesty, martial prowess, and resourcefulness. Though with a mortality rate around 99%, the vast majority of Star Pilots are never heard from again once they leave known space.

The end is the BEGINNING

THERE ARE DOZENS MORE STORIES TO TELL IN THIS UNIVERSE, and we can't wait to share them. Stories of the Obsidium Wars, Stein's exploits as a part-time actor,* Denarii's journey of self-discovery as a Star Pilot, and the innumerable times the crew of the *Sankofa* cheated death by the skin of its teeth. Those stories will have to wait; for now, we come to the end of this first chapter.

**see: "Jupiter Jonah and the Mami-Watas of Mercury," and "Jupiter Jonah and the Seven Sons of Callisto."*

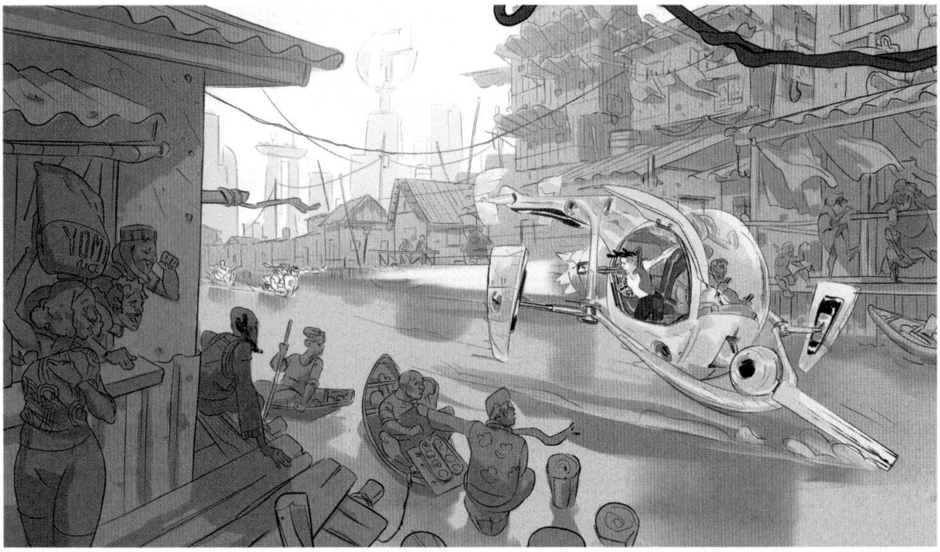

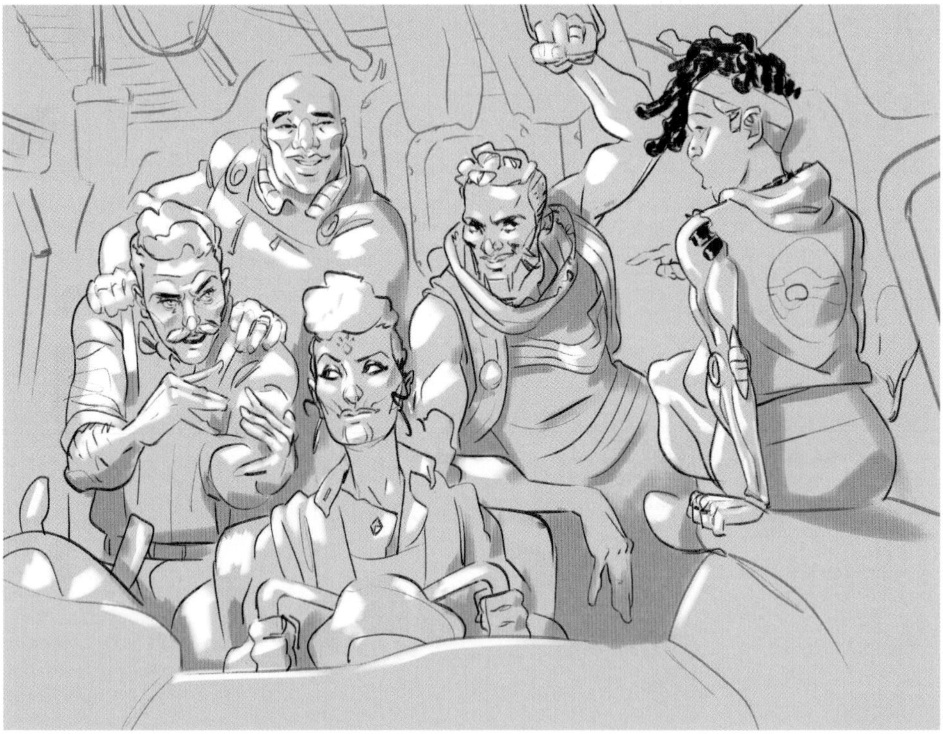

If you picked this book up not knowing what you were getting into, thank you for stepping outside your comfort zone— for trying something different. If you picked the book up because you wanted to immerse yourself in a new science fiction universe rooted in African mythology and tradition, we hope we lived up to the billing. If you're African, *we hope we made you proud.*

We'll be back. We'll go incredible places, we'll meet amazing people, and we'll do extraordinary things.

'TILL THE NEXT ADVENTURE,
— Shobo & Shof

ABOUT *the* ***AUTHORS***

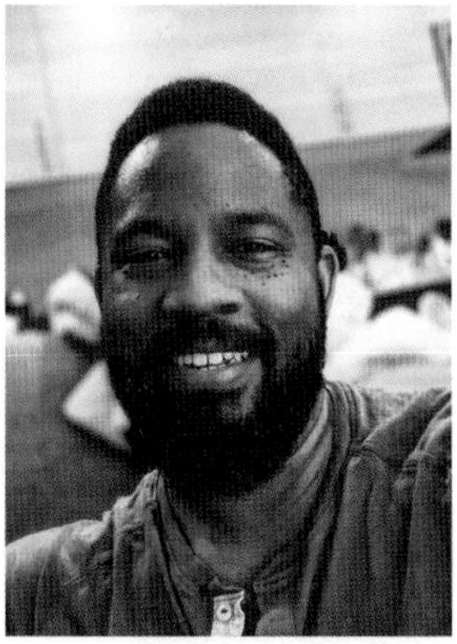

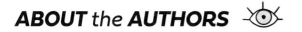

SHOBO COKER is a Nigerian videogame developer and writer of African science fiction and fantasy from Lagos, Nigeria. He co-created and Kickstarted the African futurist science fiction comic, *OUTCASTS OF JUPITER,* and the all-ages adventure comic *BUCKHEAD.* He is a recipient of the 2019 Creators for Creators Grant and spends much of his time writing comics and video games and researching the mythology, religious concepts, and history of the Yoruba people.

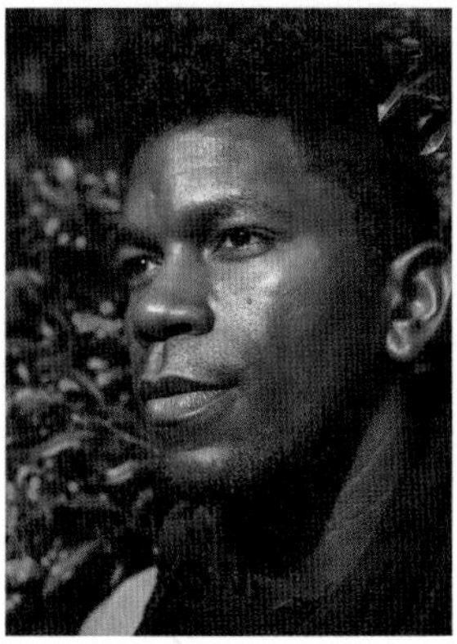

SHOFELA COKER is an Illustrator/Art Director born and raised in Lagos, Nigeria. He has worked in videogames and animation as a character designer and art director for over a decade. *OUTCASTS OF JUPITER* was his first official foray into comics. He then worked on the 2017 animated documentary, *LIYANA,* which has won several awards including Best Documentary at the LA Film Festival and Grand Prize at the New York Children's Film Festival. He is currently directing an animated short with Triggerfish and Disney titled *MOREMI.*

He still has dreams to one day play for the Nigerian national football (soccer) team.

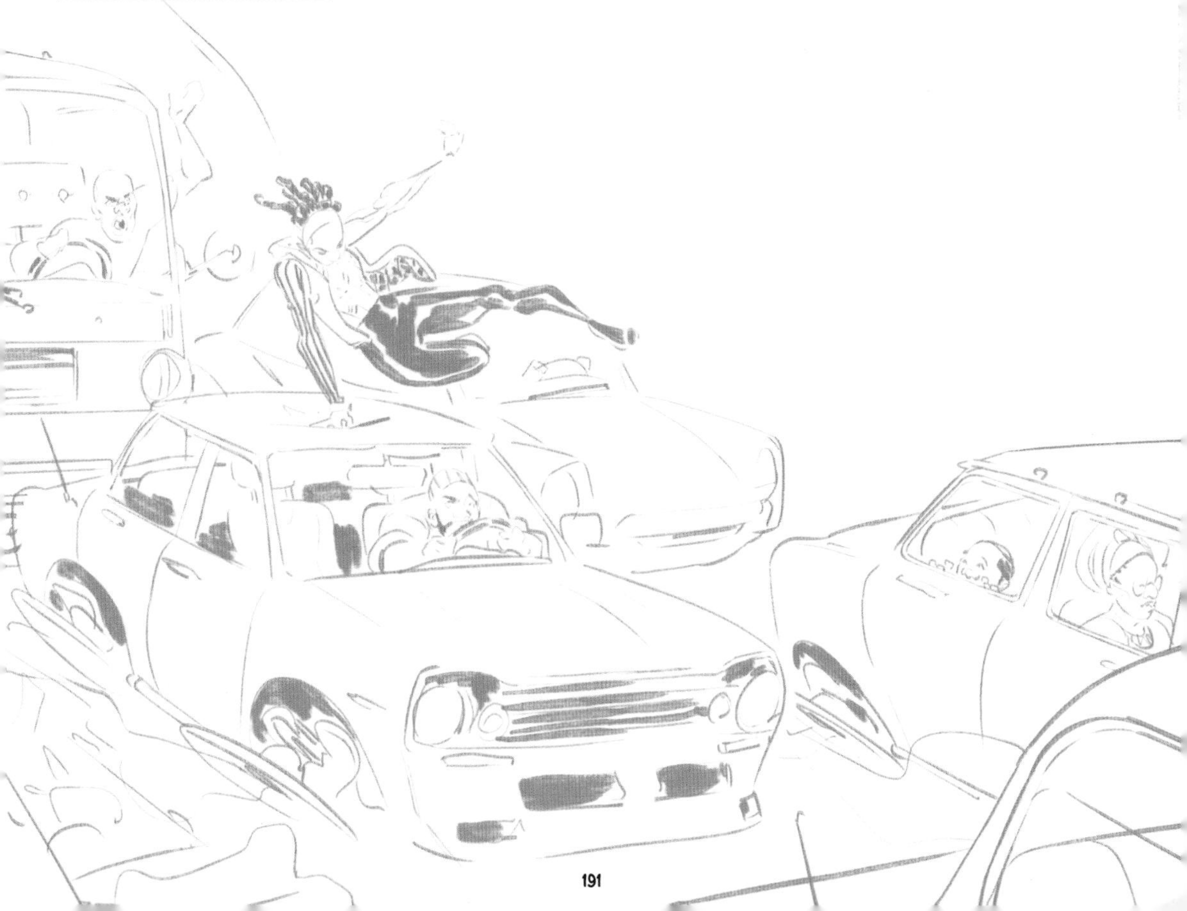

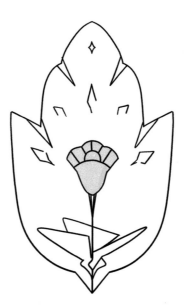